A disturbing, darkly funny fictionalization of the life of Fred A. Leuchter, the garage tinkerer turned execution authority who became a darling of the neo-Nazi movement, and subject of the Errol Morris documentary, *Mr. Death*.

He comes to fix your photocopier, but really, Fred's an inventor. At night, he goes to work. He has goals, ambitions, and when offered the task of building a better electric chair, he jumps at the chance. People have to die—he believes in the occasional necessity of evil—but what if we could kill them more humanely?

A death specialist, first in his field but forever under-appreciated, he's charmed when a new generation of fascists come calling for his expertise. A Holocaust denier is on trial in Toronto—could Fred prove the gas chambers never existed?

Newspapers descend. Talking heads have their say. A documentarist makes a film. Everyone will know his name, though some things society will simply not abide. Dishonoured, discredited, disgraced. But Fred's work does not stop, and the world may yet be reminded of the dangerous truth that some men are driven by forces far more powerful than shame.

First published in 2013, this is the updated and definitive edition of Eugene Marten's chilling masterwork of transformational historical fiction.

Praise for *Layman's Report*

"I am so, so grateful that Eugene Marten's writing exists. Nobody else writes like he does. What a shame! *Layman's Report* is full of the most strange, beautiful sentences. Marten is unafraid to look directly at the brutal things people do, but there is so much empathy lurking underneath this, too. He is a truly exceptional, one of a kind, talent."

—Rachel Connolly, author of *Lazy City*

"However Eugene Marten does what he does with language is from another world. You think about the end of things, of all life, at every turn of phrase. It's not just what he renders in his characters, but how well he constructs the bleakness of the consequences the narrator faces. Like a chiaroscuro painting, Marten gently reveals what the light touches, but barely. What remains is the darkness of the story, and that is what draws the reader in."

—Elle Nash, author of *Deliver Me*

"*Layman's Report* is a propulsive and dazzling novel—Eugene Marten's sculpted sentences captivate with their cadence and striking imagery. Fred Junior, an eccentric inventor of death devices turned Holocaust denier and victim of his own vanity, is one of the most enigmatic characters I have encountered in contemporary fiction."

—Babak Lakghomi, author of *South*

LAYMAN'S REPORT

LAYMAN'S REPORT

A Novel

Eugene Marten

STRANGE
LIGHT

Library and Archives Canada Cataloguing in Publication Data is available upon request.

ISBN: 978-0-7710-5186-9
ebook ISBN: 978-0-7710-5187-6

Cover and book design: Kate Sinclair
Cover art: mikroman6 / Getty Images, ZU_09 / DigitalVision Vectors / Getty Images DigitalVision Images
Typeset in Sabon by Sean Tai
Printed in Canada

Published by Strange Light,
an imprint of Penguin Random House Canada Limited,
a Penguin Random House Company
www.penguinrandomhouse.ca

10 9 8 7 6 5 4 3 2 1

Penguin
Random House
Canada

For Kelly

And to Robert Cole, teacher

Though it has taken me some time
I have come to know
That I am a part of everybody
And everybody is a part of me
And that no matter where I go
Or how I go
Everyone goes with me

*Final statement of Richard Tucker Jr., electrocuted
May 29, 1987, for the kidnapping, rape, and murder
of Edna Sandefur, retired nurse.*

*Final statement of Lum You, Chinese laborer
convicted of shooting Oscar Bloom in retaliation for
robbery, hung by the neck on January 31, 1902:*

Kill me good.

These are the Objects of Interest: the first,
free-standing crematory, now removed; Bath &
Disinfection Bldg. #2, whose function can be
confirmed by a glance through the windows; and
Bath & Disinfection #1. The rebuilt crematory
and its adjacent structure (an undressing room,
according to museum literature), though
discussed at length in the previous section,
will be considered, briefly, again.

There were two men. Half brothers. Shared a father but not a mother. The younger one had ideas. The older one listened (all he wanted was drinking money). He was two years older and named for his father, who was half his size. The younger brother was also small in stature. He couldn't read but he had ideas. His name was invented just for him.

He spent time in the mirror. "This a robbery, let's not make it murder," he told his bloodshot reflection.

His other self looked nonplussed. It held something small and snub-nosed. "There's two kinda people," it said, and the gun jumped at the glass. The mirror cracked. The little brother took this for a good sign.

———

They waited out in the cold till the A-rab was alone with a tabloid. He sat smoking, drinking out of a Styrofoam cup. Reading with one eye. They crossed the street. There was a plan of sorts and the older one was to stay outside in the capacity of lookout.

"But next time," he said.

"We'll see how you do," his half brother said, like some cautious employer observing a probationary period. There was a wreath on the door, a lone concession to the season. It jingled coming and going. The A-rab looked up from behind the counter, one eye colorless and always half closed as if it had seen more than it could bear. A radio played.

"Cold as what out there," the little brother said sincerely.

"I'm close five minute," the A-rab said.

The little brother came up the aisle, its dirty warped floor. Off-brands, smell of freezer burn. The deli case empty, trays covered with white cloth. When he got to the counter he laid the gun on its side like merchandise. He was going to say, "There's two kinda people" (as rehearsed) but the A-rab tossed the contents of the cup in his face and reached behind the counter. The coffee was by now lukewarm but the little brother screamed anyway, fired blindly three times. When he opened his eyes the A-rab was sitting back down on his stool next to the register, his hand on his chest like he was taking an oath. A wooden club rolled on the floor.

The radio was silent. There was no trace of the other bullet.

The wreath on the door rang and the big brother came in. He looked cautiously down the aisle and said, "The hell you done did?" as if gunfire had no place here.

The little brother was breathing like he'd run a mile. His voice shook and he looked ready to hand over the gun. It had jumped in his hand, seemed to fire by itself. "Sumbitch tried to be strong on me. I told him we wasn't playin."

The older one got behind the counter. "Drawer ain't even open. You drippin."

"He made a move," the younger one said irritably and sleeved coffee off his face. He could taste it.

The A-rab sat with his hand still at his chest. Something dark, not coffee, pulsed out between his fingers. The cigarette was still in his lips.

"The drawer," the big brother said.

"I need emergency," the A-rab said.

"This your goddamn emergency," the little brother said and shoved it in the A-rab's face. "You don't need but one hand."

The A-rab showed no interest in the gun. He started to raise his arm, then froze with a sound half stuck in his throat, good eye shut tight. He dropped his arm and said, "No sale."

"The fuck?" the little brother said, outraged.

"You simple . . ." His half brother hit the key. The drawer slid open and the little brother, who couldn't read but could tell one bill from the other, said, "Bout time you pull your weight."

They emptied it into a small brown bag from behind the counter, then got two bigger bags and couldn't help helping themselves: beer, wine, Kools, bags of skins, batteries for no reason, a shrink-wrapped *Penthouse*, Little Debbie. The big brother sipped a Miller's. A car door slammed somewhere close and they ducked behind the magazine display.

"We good?" the little brother said.

3

"You tell me."

"You ain't lock the door?"

"Wasn't no keys in it."

The little brother stepped out into the aisle then but he could already hear the little bells. She stood near the door and the empty gumball machine in a bulky parka, he in the middle of the aisle with the gun behind his groceries. Twenty-four, twenty-five, and seven or eight months in her belly.

"Hello?" she said.

"We closed," he said.

She tried to look over his shoulder and called the A-rab by his name, which means One Who Distinguishes Truth from Falsehood.

"This a robbery," the little brother began, faltering, but she turned to leave before he could finish and he shot her through the back as if to complete his sentence.

"We got to go now," the big brother said.

"We gone," the little brother said.

They looked behind the counter. The A-rab sat as before, his good eye shut, and now he was softly mumbling.

"He prayin?"

"Wouldn't you?"

"They Muslim, right?"

"Puerto Rican Jew for all I care."

"We got to go."

"All right then," the little brother said and raised his arm. The cigarette went out.

She was still breathing when they pried the keys from her hand. Brand-new Camaro—St. Francis standing on the dashboard, Tupperware in the trunk. In the morning they found out she wasn't breathing anymore but her baby had survived and been delivered. The little brother felt his holiday spirit returning.

The pawnbroker had a safe in the back of his shop. He had Smith and Wesson, Springfield, a daughter just turned fourteen. Then he had nothing. At the state liquor store the little brother indulged tastes that were not his own—Rémy Martin, Courvoisier. A bottle of twelve-year-old scotch. Then he indulged other tastes, though later neither could always remember who had done exactly whom, or if they'd even done the pharmacist at all. Sometimes killing was an afterthought, like turning out the lights when you leave.

They pushed their luck and it held. They were wanted men now, at large, though not as large as the little brother would have preferred and in the car he shuffled through stations, desperate for top stories of which they were the subject, like a performer attending reviews.

"We some cold motherfuckers," he said.

"It's on," the big brother said, pulling onto the freeway. The little brother still had all the ideas but couldn't operate a car, and though the older privately doubted the younger's leadership, their roles had been cast and he preferred not to make too many decisions. He stayed behind the wheel, let the other do the driving.

South, into the country—there'd be small towns, jewelry stores, small-town security. After twenty miles of it they pulled into a rest stop and traded the Dodge for a Buick Riviera. Left the owner sitting in a stall with his pants down, the water beneath him reddening, ghastly surprise for some future motorist or maintenance worker. When they pulled out the radio was playing "Jingle Bell Rock" and it had just begun to snow, a light dusting on branches and embankments. "Turn that shit up," the younger brother said and watched the tree trunks swing by, slender and brown or white as bone. Within ten minutes it was a blizzard so fierce you could hear it pelting the windshield and nothing was visible beyond the headlights. The back of the car kept swinging out from behind them and they had trouble with the defrost; the little brother had to use his hand. The big brother said "Here?" at each exit they passed, and the little brother kept saying "No," for reasons known only to him if he had any. By now the road was so covered with ice and snow its boundaries were indiscernible and they'd drifted onto a ramp before they realized it. The town whose half-covered sign welcomed them was known mainly for its high school football teams but would soon add another distinction to its name. They had chosen each other.

It seemed deserted. A town square strung with lights of every color, thirty-foot tree swaying in the middle, the gazebo transformed into the birthplace of the King of Kings. They were creeping around it through the barrage of snow when the younger brother bid the older one stop. He got out of the car and trudged through knee-high drifts and the scouring wind to the manger, where the cradle had tipped and the infant lay on the floor, and under the watch of its parents, the magi, the shepherds and attendant livestock, he righted the rough wooden box, restored the messiah to his place and headed back to the passenger side of the Buick, a savior of saviors.

Down the main drag and back onto Route 3. Past a strip mall, high school, soccer field, getting back into the country. The homes still houses, but the yards becoming spreads, acreage.

"Maybe next time we'll trade off for a dog sled," the big brother said.

"There." The little brother pointed and they pulled off into a construction site. Wooden frames and tar paper; townhouses, condos maybe. They parked behind it so they were hidden from the road, lights off, engine running, as close as they would ever get to taking up residence there. They drank wine and malt liquor and the older brother smoked his first cigar, and they swallowed things taken from the pharmacy, shapes and colors that made them invisible but unbounded, filled with motion and beyond boredom, and then they drank more and played the radio and talked. The little brother recounted the last few days with great sentiment as if recalling the distant past, their humble origins, savoring what he decided were the highlights, even suggesting the names history might remember them by. It had stopped being about just money. The big brother wanted to play cards. He opened the twelve-year-old scotch and declared, "I don't like this shit too tough but it ain't gettin any older," and when they tried the brandy the little brother gargled it like mouthwash and spat it out the window. It had seemed the preference of every woman he'd ever come at in every club and hole he'd haunted, and his older brother observed he couldn't even pronounce it let alone afford it, and laughed, and the little brother took exception to this and they argued over it, then reconciled, then lapsed into thoughtful silence, which the younger one broke by singing along to songs he barely knew, improvising his own lyrics. The big brother grew so annoyed he turned off the radio, but the other seemed not to notice and continued singing along as with the wind.

A state trooper drove by, neither seeing nor seen.

It was still light when the storm let up. Unbearable brightness. There was a field next to the site and across that a house that had just become visible. Buried shapes of a car and van in the driveway. A picture window like an outsize postcard through which you could see a tree and an elderly woman holding a mug. A teenaged boy came out in the fresh calm and cleared the driveway with a snow blower. A man poked his head out the side door, shouted at the boy, went back inside. Stiff with resentment, the boy shoveled off the car and scraped the windows, and later another woman and a girl about the boy's age drove off in the newly cleared sedan. In the big window the elderly woman and the man fussed with the tree, and the half brothers watched without comment. Considerable time passed before the woman and the girl came back with shopping bags, groceries, laughing, perhaps smuggling gifts. Despite the distance and the shapeless bundling of winter attire, the little brother looked at the girl as if he already knew the color of her hair, as if she were the embodiment of every gift ever denied him, and after which none other need be given. He rubbed himself without knowing it.

"You thinking what I'm thinking?" he asked the big brother.

"Ain't nobody thinkin that but you," the big brother said. He was reading *The Star*. "My stomach thinkin I'm hungry."

"You always hungry."

"This Riv run on air?"

"Well guess who comin to dinner then," the little brother said and the big brother, face in the tabloid, mumbled about an invitation.

"Right here," the little brother said and felt around on the seat next to him, then kept feeling around saying, "The hell is it?" and the big brother just shook his head and showed him where the gun was and stepped out of the car to relieve himself.

They drank some more and smoked, swallowed something that offset what they'd swallowed earlier and fell asleep, and as they slept the snow turned the color of the evening and lights came on all over town. The tank ran empty and they woke in the night shivering and wreathed in their own breath, the house radiant with figurations of tiny white lights. It was time. Without speaking they took what they would need and got out and emptied themselves again, opened the trunk and left it open as they trudged across the field toward the house, into the postcard, each step crashing through a layer of ice like a skin of glass.

In the morning they woke in the same bed in a motel room, naked, the shotgun between them like a child in the parental fold. The younger one first. He did not remember how they'd gotten there. His mouth felt like a pothole and his brain seemed to swell against the inside of his skull, but what woke him was the sound of knocking.

9

The older one stirred. The little brother rolled out of bed, took the Cobra off the nightstand and made for the door at an angle, dragging up his pants with one hand. He heard the knock again and realized it was next door. Voices. The window above the heater, day flaring at the edge of the curtain. His back against the wall next to it, he moved the curtain with his finger and in that inch of light saw everything.

"Get dressed," he whispered at the bed and grabbed his shirt up off the floor, keeping low like he was already in the line of fire.

The big brother stayed in bed, sitting up now with the Springfield. "Who it is?" he asked, and as if to reverse the order of things there was a loud knock. His shoulders jumped then and the shotgun went off and the little brother thought he would jump back out of his pants.

A ray of light crossed the room.

"Picklehead fool!" he hissed in their father's voice.

The big brother sat in a cloud of blue smoke. "I barely touched it," and he shrugged like he'd just spilled something.

"Get dressed," the little brother said again in the acrid aftermath, ears ringing, and his head seemed to have been cleared of all other thought by the blast. He put his shirt on. The big brother got out of bed with the shotgun and headed naked and at his leisure for the door, the brilliant hole in it like a jagged cold sun.

"Where is you going?" the little brother said, and the big brother said, "Tell you where I ain't goin," something decided in his voice. He put his face to the opening. After the shotgun the sound that followed was almost a cough, but the back of his head flowered red and the light from the door shone through it like a revelation uncontained.

They were only half brothers and the one left behind was already into the bathroom shoving up the sash of the window that was small but not as small as he was, tumbling through it free of thought because he was already caught, already dead. Bright white doom scoured his brain. Shirt, gun, pants. He bounced up on the frozen paving and the first two steps tore the skin off the bottoms of his feet. Where were they? Across the back parking lot, behind a maintenance shed where they should have been but weren't, into a field, weaving like they'd taught him in Basic. A line of trees ahead. Running and waiting for a shout, a shot, or just a thump in his back and the beginning of that last fall into what lies beyond last things. Then he heard it and realized he only had because they'd missed and he was in the woods.

Bare trunks like the ones they'd seen from the freeway; strange to be among them, the ground partially clear so he could see what was doing the damage he couldn't feel. He jumped a frozen stream, fell, ran. There was a clearing and railroad tracks and he considered jumping a train—bend down and listen to the iron like a goddamn Indian—but instead he stumbled over them and went back into the woods. Saw one bird sitting on a branch as if frozen to it. It called. He answered: "Fuck you." Another field then, snow-covered, his breathing so labored he couldn't hear the thud of his feet. Frigid air burning his throat and lungs, morning light pink like blood in water. In the evergreens now. They opened and he saw a roof and slowed. A fence, a backyard. His toes seemed to have fused into a dull edge and could not negotiate the links, so he threw himself at it and tumbled over as if thrown, somehow holding on to the gun. He lay on his back on the other side listening for dogs, maybe a helicopter, and when he heard neither was both relieved and dimly affronted. A scraping somewhere instead— a shovel. He grabbed the links and hauled himself back up, the fence making a sort of music. There was a garage, a modest wreath fastened to the back of the house like good tidings even for trespassers. He made for the sound while he still could.

A woman shoveled snow in her driveway. So heavily dressed she had to pivot her whole body to get a look at him. Knock-kneed, his footprints a trail of dead roses. He felt nothing between his legs and the ground, as if he were floating, a pound and a half of cold metal in his hand.

"I need a car," he said, and when he spoke he remembered he couldn't drive, and how thirsty he was, that he was only at the beginning of his needs.

"The keys are in the house," she said at last. "We may have to dig it out though."

"Water too," he said and realized the metal was stuck to his skin. "Who inside?"

"Nobody." She looked at his feet. "I live alone."

"Somebody put up them lights."

"Somebody did," but she didn't explain. She looked old enough to have kids with lights of their own.

"All right then," he said and waved the gun toward the house. Helped himself along the siding to the door. The warmth hit him with a pure feeling he did not recognize as gratitude.

A short flight of stairs up to the kitchen; he practically had to go up on his knees. He kept the gun on her but hadn't yet noticed he didn't need it, only how heavy it had become.

"Anybody here?" he yelled. His voice had not far to travel: dining room, living room, hallway, bedroom. No basement, no upstairs he would have to take her word for. She waited patiently. Dark wood paneling, shag carpet he could barely feel. A fireplace with no fire, and the biggest picture on the mantel of a bride and groom.

"He put them lights up?"

"Some years ago," the woman said. "He's gone now. I haven't taken them down since."

"Ain't that a bitch."

"I guess that's one way to put it."

"I just lost my big brother."

"I'm sorry."

"You wouldn't be if you knew."

She looked at him. "The family in the field."

"More like half brothers, we was."

"Well it's all or none, isn't it?" She spoke rapidly, as if to forestall something.

"I need to sit down," the little brother said and fairly collapsed onto the couch. Striped wooden armrests. He gestured her into the other end of it, a gun-wielding host. She asked him if he wanted a pair of socks but now it felt like someone was nailing his feet to the floor and he couldn't speak through it. She asked him if she could take off her coat and when he could he gasped "Go ahead" and she took it off without standing up.

"Did you see the wreath on the back of the house?" she asked. "He said you should always put some Christmas where no one knows it's there. Someone will find it, he used to say."

"I need to tie you up," he blurted like a child confessing. He thought he could stand now.

She took it better than he expected. "I'll have to see what I have."

"I ain't made no promises," he said.

"It's probably better that way," she said, and something in her made something in him not pistol-whip her or shut her the fuck up. He just said, "All right."

There was duct tape and twine in a drawer in the kitchen and he took her into the bathroom and crouched her in the tub while he lashed her hands and wrists to the faucet fixture. Something in her made his hands shake. He apologized without knowing it. He knew nothing about tying knots.

"For I can sleep," he said, not normally given to explanation, and she told him where he could find something for his feet just before he taped her mouth shut. He told her to close her eyes and took a leak. His head was pounding so hard he couldn't think and before he left he went into the medicine cabinet. There were no ideas in the mirror.

Out in the hall was a trapdoor in the ceiling he hadn't noticed before. Attic or crawlspace; he thought about it but doubted he could climb a ladder. He found a closet where she said it would be. Plastic bags with what was probably someone's name scrawled on them and he limped into the bedroom wearing a dead man's woolen socks. He lay down. When the factory in his head quieted a little he half slept, but instead of dreams there came to him a sense of forces outside the house, movement and rumbling, something audible in spite of itself like a giant trying to be stealthy. Then a phone rang and he sat up.

It stopped ringing. A furry pink slipper in the likeness of a rabbit next to the bed, its counterpart beneath it. He put them on and walked down the hall, something wrong with his left foot. He looked into the bathroom. The rope in the tub like a snake's shed skin. He was neither angry nor surprised she was gone but the sound of pots and pans somewhere was not expected. He smelled coffee, breakfast. Went to the kitchen with his feet in furred pink slippers and the blood of ten on his hands, peered in the doorway gun first. Watercolor wallpaper. It smelled like a home.

"Hope you like French toast," she said. Even from behind you could tell she enjoyed what she was doing. In her back and shoulders.

"I am so hungry," he said like he'd just realized it. He listened. "Listen," he said. "They out there."

"They just called," she said. "I told them not yet. I said you weren't ready." She looked at his feet.

They sat at the kitchen table, the gun next to his plate, silver like another utensil. Wood grain on the grips. French toast, sausage, coffee, orange juice. She lowered her head with her hands in her lap and recited grace in the Lutheran fashion, asked that the family in the field be blessed as well, and that the little brother find forgiveness, amen.

"Amen," he said, and the food tasted as food does when joy has gone into its making.

"I am tired," he said, his plate clean.

15

"Go back and lie down. There's all the time in the world."

"I don't think I can sleep," he said. "I'll get plenty a rest where I'm goin."

"Would you like me to read to you?" she said. "That always worked for us." He stared at her and she said he could bring it with him. She understood.

It was the first time. They went into the bedroom and he lay down again and she read to him from what she'd been reading to herself. She started over: a white bird, a seabird, more concerned with perfecting the art of flying than the gathering of food. He is mocked and ridiculed and soon becomes an outcast, a loner dedicated to flying higher, faster, farther. Eventually he reaches a height where like-minded creatures reside, communicating telepathically. He wonders if this is heaven, and one of the elders tells him there is no such thing, only a state of perfection that cannot be attained but must be striven for.

The little brother slept. Through the sound of the helicopter, the dogs, the amplified voice, she kept turning pages, and his dreams consumed the story and became indistinguishable from it.

The daughter of the family in the field testified from a wheelchair. Her legs and spine had been crushed; she'd lost an arm and her nose to frostbite; there were still bullet fragments in her brain and she had obvious difficulty speaking. She suffered from severe headaches, tinnitus, was assailed by strange colors and flashing lights, tastes on her tongue, uncontrolled spasms and inappropriate emotional responses. But she was able to recount that night in great detail and the little brother, in his oversized suit and tie and minus the toes of his left foot, listened as raptly as the jury and equally dumbfounded, as at the actions of someone else entirely, some stranger who had invaded her home and, with his accomplice, sexually assaulted not just her but every member of the household, male and female, exploiting every bodily ingress and position to the limits of imagination, and after this reconfiguring the family at gunpoint, coupling father and daughter, mother and son, brother and sister and father and grandmother, and devising other combinations she recalled relentlessly and in spite of herself, including even the reek of this strange new chemistry mingled with the smell of evergreen and the pork roast she remembered having for dinner.

The defendant, against all advice serving as his own counsel, was shrewd enough to object that a brain-damaged witness could hardly be considered reliable, but her testimony was more than corroborated by the forensic evidence and continued on to robbery for robbery's sake: cash, jewelry, credit cards, both television sets, a Super 8 camera, the living room stereo, even the presents under the tree ferried out to the family van by the hostages themselves who, still naked, shoeless, shivering, sobbing, were crowded into the backseat with the exception of the witness, who rode up front between the intruders en route to the soccer field, where all were ordered out onto a tract of undisturbed white, harried, lined up, made to kneel in the headlights like novitiates to an ultimate order. Only the father, an algebra teacher and assistant football coach, had refused, and his end was no better nor worse than the others'; only the daughter, the last remaining, had asked for mercy, and so on her knees too but facing the little brother, the metal barrel pressed to her head, the small warmth of her mouth as much as he'd ever felt of affection, but he had nothing left to spend and in place of his own release had pulled the trigger, and as she dropped back in the snow with her legs folded beneath her, the assailants returned to the vehicle, rolling over the bodies of their victims on their way back to the state highway, unaware she would somehow survive and drag herself over a hundred yards to the shoulder of the road . . . And at the conclusion of this portion of her statement, when the state's attorney asked if she felt her miraculous deliverance at the height of this holy season might not be evidence of higher purpose, she was racked by yet another convulsion, laughed painfully and said, "It don't mean a thing if it ain't got that swing."

The little brother chose not to cross-examine. He called no witnesses and remained in his seat until the summations, during which he stood before a nervous jury box, evoking his debased childhood, mental and physical abuse at the hands of parents and foster parents, juvenile delinquency, the horrors of Vietnam (where he had never served, having been dishonorably discharged during boot camp), drug and alcohol addictions, a series of petty crimes escalating into increasingly ruthless felonies, reducing himself to tears and such foul language the judge ordered him restrained and set about instructing the jury.

No one had ever read to him, he sobbed in his seat.

His mother sat in the back of the courtroom, behind sunglasses, befurred, bewigged, bejeweled. She had habitually sold her children to both men and women for money, drugs, and other favors, the little brother had explained, and when sentence was pronounced she cried out and fainted as if it had been passed upon her, which in a sense it had.

The judge asked her son if he had anything left to say. The little brother turned to the young woman he'd sentenced to life in a wheelchair, looked at her as if he'd been her victim all along, and said, "If you sucked a proper dick I might remember just what it is they fixin to fry me for."

The woman who'd read to him was his only visitor. She'd witnessed for the prosecution but taught him the alphabet as if in redress. She taught him how to put two letters together to make other sounds and simple words . . . three letters, four. She gave him money for a radio that became a nest to the cockroaches that invaded his cell from the chow cart. When it shorted out he told her what had happened and she gave him a children's Bible.

He did his laundry in the sink, hung it to dry on a line that ran from the vent in the back of his cell to the bars. Once he went two weeks without toilet paper. When it rained his cell would flood and archipelagos of black mold infested the walls. In winter he'd wear the wool socks she'd bought him to bed, two pairs, and one stretched over his head. Saw his own breath. Summers he'd lie naked on the concrete floor for hours on end, so still the mice sometimes crawled over him. He'd listen to the other inmates getting on the bars—Payday, Frosty, talking themselves hoarse; there were fifteen of them in the wing but they sounded like fifty. He spoke little but said too much. Learned to listen. He'd hear splashing in the toilet.

The cat sat on the mat. The hen is in a pen. A previous occupant had set the cell on fire and the smell never went away.

Breakfast on the chow cart at six in the morning. Sometimes, after the tray had passed through the food slot, there would appear in the opening a full-lipped mouth, or an ass like a pair of tires on a rack, spreading to show him another way out. Or it was the little brother's turn to kneel or turn the other way. He barely saw the trusty's face and couldn't remember his name, but he wondered if this was what love felt like.

"You'll know it when it hurts," Payday shouted on the bars. The oldest man on DR. "Welcome to the U.S.A."

At night they would come and shine a light in your face on the hour. They'd wake you and strip you and put you in a portable cage while they tossed your cell—random spot check or because they thought they had a reason. The little brother left his cell twice a week to take a shower and twice a week for yard, another hard rectangle—never again would he stand on soil or grass—basketball hoop, chin-up bar, two card tables, a sixty-by-forty sky. The yard was not a safe place for him; even among the condemned there is a hierarchy of honor and a self-confessed rapist-murderer is not in the top tier. Only once did he drop his guard: the ball had rolled near his feet and, instead of returning it to the players, he'd set himself and leaned back to take a shot from twelve feet out. Woke up in the infirmary with a line of stitches like a great dead centipede running from the middle of his chest to the top of his groin, and three-quarters of his blood a gift from strangers.

After he got back to D-Pod he didn't see the trusty again, nor the woman who'd taught him to read. Never found out if she'd moved away, fallen ill, forgotten him. But apparently most of his self-pity had bled out as well, and after the stitches were pulled he began a daily regimen of calisthenics. (The only way to do fifty pushups is to do fifty-one.) He kept his cell clean. He practiced writing with a pencil stub and ten sheets of paper from the canteen. Practiced killing flies with his hands. He had no TV or radio but the book cart rolled by once a week. He'd finished his children's Bible, got the one meant for adults, and when he could write well enough he joined the pen pal program. He read history books, Malcolm, Du Bois, the Koran, rejected Christianity and appended an X to his name. The cart rolled by. The title *Man and Superman* tilted on its end caught his eye and he grabbed the spine but it was not a comic, it said God was dead. He'd begun to suspect as much himself but he wasn't sure why, and laboriously worked his way back to the beginning to find out. What wasn't on the cart he could request from the library or enjoin his correspondents to send: the Dialogues, the Poetics, the Republic, *cogito ergo sum*, the phenomenology of the spirit. A dictionary. It was slow going, like digging a tunnel with a spoon. He moved his lips but made no sound and the words slipped through his skull like ghosts through a wall. He crawled through the Realm of Objects, the Realm of Desire—where the trouble starts—the fear and trembling and the sickness unto death. He had no use for fiction. He read instead the critiques of judgment and of pure and practical reason, studied the categorical imperative, the transvaluation of all values, the Will to Power and the Eternal

Return. He somehow avoided Marx but not the Upanishads, the Books of the Dead both Egyptian and Tibetan. He began to meditate and for a month he was a Buddhist. He stopped jerking off, stopped killing flies—just caught them in midair and let them go. Then walking the perimeter of the yard for the first time since he'd been gutted there, on the very spot, he stopped and looked up at the blue rectangle of the universe, its faded gray bricks, and renounced all religion as superstition and all philosophy as gibberish, and never opened another book except for those from the legal section and those he would attempt to write.

He was his own lawyer, and his appeals churned in the imperceptible machinery of due process. Writs of habeas corpus, petitions, motions to vacate, to Recall the Mandate and Reconsider, issued to local courts of appeal, the circuit court, the Eastern District, to the State Supreme Court, and the Supreme Court of the United States. Three hundred and fifty-six pages on twenty-seven grounds, pending.

Stays issued and lifted, one at a time, like gifts given and revoked, unopened.

A committee re-evaluated his behavior every six months, and after seven years he was upgraded to Condemned A. They were still going to kill you but moved you to a cell that smelled better and you got your toilet paper on time. He'd taught himself chess and played with other inmates on the wing, shouting the King's Indian Attack down the run to opponents he never saw. He competed in international tournaments by mail, fifty days to make ten moves. Stopped speaking for weeks at a time. He exchanged letters with a woman from Indiana. She sent him money, bought him a radio, sent pictures of herself in a pantsuit; a pale, demure, middle-aged virgin who lived in Plainfield with her mother. Wore glasses. A mouth like a paper cut. In his fifth letter he proposed. She accepted and they were married by the chaplain in the visitors' room, the warden as witness. The groom wore shackles and waist-chains and the state did not permit touching during the ceremony, nor during the visitations that followed. These came twice a month, and sometimes the allotted hour would pass painfully and awkwardly with hardly a word being exchanged; she was much more voluble on the page than in person, and who is to say this isn't love?

Sometimes nights were bad. He dreamt of the daughter of the family in the field, the one he'd left for dead. She crawled to him, convulsed and contorted, across lunar landscapes of ice and time, and they met and coupled with great difficulty, but in their joining his ejaculations were curative, restoring her limbs and straightening her spine so that she walked away whole again, without leaving footprints, without looking back, and he woke not remembering what he'd dreamt nor that he had at all, but shaken and sobbing as with irrevocable loss.

"You all just keep my dominoes," Payday shouted on the bars. "Just tell em it was natural causes," and he hung himself with his bedsheets.

The little brother wrote it down. He wrote a children's book about a rat with no name who crawls up out of a toilet into a housing project and tries to join the human family. Started work on a less disguised autobiography and wondered if he would finish in time. Others had done it before him, had achieved publication and critical acclaim, had attracted the intercession of celebrities and celebrity attorneys, earned reprieves, even commutation, another chance, but he had no illusions about being forgiven. Innocence was never an option; he wanted only to live.

His wife stopped visiting. The next word he received from her was through a lawyer, just before his petition for clemency was denied. The grounds were mental cruelty and sexual neglect. His feelings for her didn't change.

Five days after the warrant was issued, five days before one minute past midnight, they came to his cell and had him throw all his possessions into a laundry cart. Then he pushed the cart to the holding cell in the death house.

Deathwatch was a considerable improvement over the wing. The cell was bigger and cleaner, there was a TV and VCR (the little brother hadn't seen one before), and you enjoyed free canteen privileges. The only downside, other than the fact that they were going to kill you, was the guard who sat right outside the bars looking in twenty-four hours a day. The guard kept a log and in it he wrote down everything the little brother did and said in the holding cell, including when he used the toilet and what he babbled in his sleep.

"You want to count the corn in that turd?" the little brother asked, and the guard wrote down that he'd said this.

The warden visited several times a day. The little brother didn't find him particularly objectionable, nor did he take it personally that the warden would supervise his execution—

someone had to do it, he supposed—but the chaplain came only once before the appointed hour. He'd been a hay farmer in the eastern end of the state and late in his life when he felt the call, though apparently with some reluctance.

"I was just talking to the Father and he instructed me to drop by and say hello." As if he had no choice in the matter, but he seemed to know better than to call the little brother *son*. "Is there anything you need?"

"Can't say in fronta mixed company," the little brother said. The guard scribbled.

The chaplain stared through the bars. "Aren't you beyond lust at this point?"

"I wish I was," the little brother said. "Come on in and I'll show you what I'm beyond." In truth, sex was the furthest thought from his mind, affianced as he was to the most jealous of suitors; he just wanted to burn the old boy's butter.

"I'm referring to the needs of your immortal soul," the chaplain said, and the little brother cited the Gita, which says that worn-out garments are shed by the body, and worn-out bodies are shed by the dweller within the body. (The dweller within dons new bodies like said garments.)

The guard asked how *Gita* is spelled.

"With all due respect," the chaplain said, "those people should stick to cooking curry."

"Now you're making me hungry," the little brother said and asked the guard about the fare in the dining hall.

"What about forgiveness?" the chaplain said. "Is that on the menu?"

"Mashed, boiled, baked, whipped," the little brother said.

"'Except ye eat of the flesh of the Son of Man,'" the chaplain said, "'ye have no life in you.'"

"You left out the blood," the little brother said. "How I'm supposed to wash it down?"

"'Give me to drink; thou wouldest have asked of him, and he would have given thee living water,'" the chaplain said. "John, chapter six."

"I think you mean chapter four."

"The Word is the Word."

"Well maybe you should get your ass up off the block and come back when you got your thing down."

The guard looked at the chaplain. The chaplain looked as if he'd felt the call to regroup. "I'll continue to pray for you," he said like a threat, backing away.

"Just pray they don't burn my pork chop," the little brother said; he'd remembered that today was Tuesday.

Nights were no longer a problem. He watched movies all day and well into the evening and then slept so soundly even he wondered at it. They parked the set right outside the cell. The titles were to be entirely his choice but at night they seemed to watch only what the second shift preferred—gangsters machine-gunning each other, barbarians of the nuclear future, shape-shifting aliens. The little brother didn't mind but when out of curiosity he asked the night watch why he never selected a tamer genre—comedy, even melodrama, if only for variety's sake—the guard responded, "They don't know how to make people laugh no more," and said nothing else on the subject. He didn't write it down.

On the morning of his last day the Korean prison doctor came to his cell with two guards and had him remove his clothing. The doctor weighed him and took his temperature. Listened to his heart. Tapped his knee. Cupped his balls and told him to cough. The little brother obliged but for some reason had expected a more thorough examination. They told him to get dressed.

"So how long you give me?" he asked, and the doctor, whose English was poor and spoken only when necessary, gave him a thumbs-up. "You good to go."

On deathwatch the visitors were brought right to your cell, and that afternoon the little brother had two: his mother and a man wearing a suit that looked twenty years too small on him.

"My baby!" and she fell upon him like a child in the Lost and Found. His response, if he'd given one, would have been buried in the crush of reunion.

She backed up to get a good look. She wore a platinum wig and looked dressed for both funeral and wake. "My baby is gray," she said, amazed.

"Well it's been a while, ain't it?" her son said and reverted instantly to a self they would recognize. "Bet you is too up under that."

"Don't hold it against me," she said. "I just couldn't bear to see my child caged up like a dog. Are they feeding you?"

"He ain't missed too many meals."

The little brother turned to look at the speaker. A short round man with a thin hoarse voice. Mustache, hair waved and slicked back.

"I'd like you to meet my fiancé," the little brother's mother said and held up a ring.

"He work?"

"Sanitation department," her fiancé said without defensiveness. "Twenty-three years."

"Garbage man."

"I wouldn't trade it. You can learn more about folks by they trash than all the books ever wrote. And it kept me from runnin the streets—mighta done you some good too."

"But now," the mother said, "it ain't all his fault. I think that war messed with his head—they got a name for it."

"Only war I been in I never fired a shot."

"Too late to play that card," her fiancé said. "You got your affairs in order, boy?" and he looked in the wastebasket as if with professional interest.

"Only affairs I got left is what I'm having for supper," the little brother said. "Boy."

"That ain't what I'm talking about."

"Y'all wanna watch a movie?"

"Oh, you gonna see a movie all right. It's called This Was Your Life, now playing at Heaven's Gate, and there ain't but one Critic and His review is everlasting judgment. You know what I'm talking about now?"

"He used to be a preacher," the mother told the guard, who'd stopped writing momentarily and was listening as though it were his own past that would soon be up for assessment.

"The question is," the fiancé said, "when they call the roll up yonder, will your name be on that list?"

"I ain't got but a number," the little brother said, "and where I'm going I won't need that either."

"My baby's lost his way," his mother lamented.

"How would you know?"

"Take it easy, boy," the fiancé said. "She's a changed woman—I've seen to it."

"I'm sorry if you think I wasn't there for you," his mother said. "If there was anything I could do now . . ."

Her son looked at her. "You can go sit your fat ass up in that chair and we'll call it even."

"Say what?" her fiancé said.

"Well I rather do that than sit here and listen to you tear my heart out," she said, but her eyes were narrowed and dry.

"Take it back," her fiancé said. "Take it back or when I'm through with you you'll be hollerin for that chair."

"All right," the guard said, not quite looking up, having resumed his endless transcription.

"Why can't you just be happy for me?" the little brother's mother said. She held up the hand that wore the ring.

"You know what?" the little brother said to the fiancé, as if the thought had just occurred to him. "I kill a motherfucker now, I could probably do another year on the DR while they decide which one they gonna do me for," and the guard said, "This visit is terminated."

Dinner was fish, coleslaw, French fries, iced tea.

At seven they synchronized the clocks and tested the phones. Half an hour later they came to the holding cell with a new set of clothes. Shaved the top of his head like a monk, shaved his ankle, put a plug up his ass and inserted a catheter that drained into a bag taped to his thigh.

The Egyptians thought mummification transfigured the corpse into a new body filled with magic.

Black pants and a clean white shirt. He looked like a busboy.

"You like sedative for you?" the doctor asked.

"I'll take all you got," the little brother said. Though refusal is the first choice available to us, and sometimes the last, he knew if he said no they'd force it on him.

The chair was tested with a tub of saline solution in place of a human being and declared ready. The blinds were closed.

They checked the phones at regular intervals. At ten thirty the chaplain reported to the holding cell and the little brother was too full of liquid Valium to mind.

"Would you care to pray?" the chaplain asked.

"Go ahead start without me," the little brother said. He went back to whatever he'd been thinking about but it was no longer there, only the chaplain's voice reading the Bible, empty as a parrot's speech.

The tower guards were doubled. The state witnesses arrived and the hearse was parked at the sally port. The department director telephoned the governor's office to see if there was a stay. He looked at his watch. His watch looked back: 11:35.

The hall was narrow, twenty-seven steps long. They took it slow. The little brother wore handcuffs and leg irons and there was a guard on each side of him, two in front and two behind. The chaplain led the way with Job: "'But I am a worm, and no man; a reproach of men, and despised of the people.'"

A door. A room. Another door behind the chair. The room was bigger than he'd expected and the chair smaller. Heavy oak dark with age, and when they sat him down it was almost a perfect fit because he was a small man like his father. They took off the iron and strapped him in like a test pilot. Leather belts for his ankles and his wrists, and for his lap, arms, and chest, tightened and fastened with clamp buckles. Before him were two windows covered with blinds, and on the other side was a small amphitheater divided by a partition; state witnesses sat in one half, and the inmate witnesses in the other. The little brother did not know who his witnesses were, nor if he had any at all; he was allowed to submit a list but hadn't done so.

"'I was cast upon thee from the womb: thou art my God from my mother's belly.'"

The room filled: the warden, the director, the deputy director, the doctor, the plant maintenance chief, the chaplain, the assistant superintendent of programs. The telephones were tested. They listened for the ring. At midnight the department director called the superintendent to ask if there was a stay. The blinds were opened. The windows were smoked black and the little brother couldn't see through them, didn't know that the parents of the pregnant woman he'd shot in the A-rab's store—they'd raised the child as their own—sat among the state witnesses, couldn't know that his mother had chosen not to attend, that in her place on the other side of the partition there sat only one observer, a pale slumped figure installed in an electric wheelchair, unattended, often prone to spasms and emotional outbursts but now uncharacteristically still and silent.

The warden read the death warrant in his nasal voice. He asked the little brother if he had anything left to say.

The little brother opened his mouth and then closed it.

"God bless you, son," the warden said.

They put the mask on him then and the last thing he saw of the world was a roomful of men who weren't looking at him and the blackness in the window that was. He heard a gush of water like a sponge being squeezed, felt its wetness on top of his head, then the cold metal bowl of the helmet and the taut leather of the chinstrap. Something cold and greasy on his ankle. No countdown. (His heart would be weighed in the Field of Reeds. If it was so heavy with sin it tipped the scales, it would be) two knocks at a door and it was like they shot a blowtorch into his ear. His invisible audience felt the hum that filled the room, saw his body stiffen upright as with some great realization. A blue-white flame burst from one side of the mask. (Lights like a swarm of fireflies in his eyes, a taste in his mouth like) the hum ceased. The little brother was seen to take a deep breath and point his finger.

The director, the deputy director, the assistant superintendent of programs, the doctor, the chaplain, and the maintenance chief all looked at the warden. He nodded again. Two more knocks at the door and in response the hum resumed. Now the blue-white flames flared from both sides of the mask, and blood dripped from behind it onto his white shirt from his mouth and nose, and then from two new holes in his face as his eyeballs burst with the steam pressure in his skull.

Someone screamed through the darkened glass and the chaplain fainted away. The ankle electrode sparked and the little brother's trousers ignited. Another scream. The warden drew his finger across his throat and the plant maintenance chief removed the fire extinguisher from the wall. Three knocks this time. A sweet burnt smell. The warden picked up a microphone.

"At this time," he was heard to say in his nasal voice, "I would ask that the theater be cleared in a safe and orderly fashion. A guard will escort you back to the waiting area."

The plant maintenance chief sprayed the little brother's legs with foam. The doctor revived the chaplain, who immediately vomited and was escorted from the smoky room. The door to the hall was kept open. The doctor approached the chair with a handkerchief over his face. The little brother took another breath. His finger was still pointing, though they couldn't tell exactly where. The warden knocked on the door himself.

At the third jolt the ankle electrode sparked again. The little brother convulsed so violently his shoulder was heard to separate with a loud snap. The foam on his trousers kept them from reigniting but the mask was burning outright now, contracting to the contours of his face. A hole opened for his mouth and its only utterance was a strip of flesh blackened and shriveled as a piece of jerky. His shirt burst into flame. The plug in his rectum melted and the catheter shattered. His bodily waste streamed forth and cooked and reeked, but he was no longer moving nor pointing so the warden gave the final signal and the only sound was the maintenance chief emptying the fire extinguisher. All that remained now was to wait for the little brother's body to cool so that the doctor could pronounce him in as few words as possible and the remains then be removed.

But in all the smoke and commotion one witness had been forgotten, left behind, still sat unseen behind the dark glass. She'd watched from her wheelchair, had never taken her eyes away and regarded him now without judgment: a scorched and smoking monarch still enthroned and holding court. She took a deep breath of him then and gripped the armrests with both hands, one artificial, gathering all her strength and will, preparing to stand and walk again as if reborn. And all around her the prison strangely quiet, condemned men watching an X-rated film parked in front of their bars.

All of the ovens have multiple retorts. They are
of an older design. They are constructed of red
brick and mortar and lined with a refractory
brick. Some are blowered, though none utilize
direct combustion. None have afterburners, and
all are coke-fired except for one facility no
longer extant. (It should be noted that unless
specifically designed for a greater bone-to-
flesh-to-heat ratio, the retort may not consume
the material assigned to it. It should also be
noted that the odor issuing from a tannery or
ironworks has sometimes been compared to that of
burning flesh.)

After Okinawa, after the Divine Wind, after Fat Man and Little
Boy, Fred Sr. delivered the mail. Instead of raining napalm B
and hand grenades down on nips hiding in underground caves
and tunnels, he started his day sorting and casing and bundling,
then finished it delivering to some three hundred recipients out
of a leather satchel weighing more than his flamethrower. There
were dogs. Four months and a thousand miles and a rat terrier
kicked half to death later, he heard they were taking applications at OSP. Because he was a veteran and had already passed
his civil service exam, the assistant superintendent hired him
on the spot. The quartermaster gave him a shitstick. He also
issued Fred Sr. two pairs of black pants, three gray shirts, one
hat, and a black coat. The pants were short in the legs and wide
in the waist. You had to buy your own shoes.

The captain of the night shift was a middle-aged man who'd served under Pershing and wore the same mustache. His best friend had been gassed in the Argonne and spent six weeks choking to death, tied to a bed. He assigned Fred Sr. East Block—six tiers high, two ranges per tier, fifty cells per range. Twelve hundred men who showered once a week. Your sissies were on Three North, coloreds on Six South. Gangs and troublemakers were kept apart—the Settle brothers, the Latin Kings, the Short North Bandits. Fred Sr. checked the strap locks, listened for disturbances. If an inmate needed help he rang his tin against the bars. Five rings meant Range Five, and you could tell by listening if it was North or South. You would tell the lieutenant or the captain. To open a cell you had to unbolt them all, and you turned a crank in the wheelroom at the end of the block. In summer the upper tiers were hottest, the bottom ones coldest in winter. A service passage ran the length of each tier between ranges: pipe chases and conduits, no light, a narrow catwalk Fred Sr. walked every night, looking for signs of a digout. He could hear them through the vents in the backs of their cells: "Goodnight, Peaches, I love you." "I love you too, Georgia, goodnight." He heard the Settle brothers call to each other, and young men and old crying in their sleep.

Twelve days on, three days off. Then thirteen on and two off. Fred Sr. was also a relief officer and worked every job but death row. He worked every Christmas.

Archie worked West Block. Archie was not his name but he was called that because he had flat feet and hadn't been allowed to enlist. He was often late because he lived in the city and would visit the girls downtown on his way out. When he

LAYMAN'S REPORT

caught something they changed his nickname, but not to his face. He and Fred Sr. checked the Hole every hour. The cells in the Hole were under the bullpen and the temperature was always ninety degrees. No light, no bed, just an opening in the middle of the floor. You wore white coveralls and a pair of cloth slippers in the Hole. They kept track with cards: white for white inmates, blue cards for coloreds. Your sissy's card was red.

The cells in the Hole were made for one man at a time but sometimes they doubled them up. Once two men went in and one came out. The other was never found—so the story goes. If the Hole didn't straighten you out, you'd wish it had because beneath that was the Box, in which you couldn't stand erect, and there goes another story of another confinement in which conditions were so unspeakable it was not even given a name, but this is where the expression "under the jail" comes from.

When they put Fred Sr. on days they gave him another fifteen dollars a month and a uniform that fit. The shifts were longer but not as boring as nights. He got to use his shitstick. When an inmate spoke to you he was to stand no less than three feet away with his arms folded. Any closer you gave him a whitecap, and this was the most action Fred Sr. had seen since the war, since Cactus Ridge.

Rape of civilians. Schoolboy soldiers. Fourteen thousand troops withdrawn from the front line with nervous breakdowns. He hadn't told a soul back home.

On days they blew reveille at seven in the morning, and the inmates washed and shaved with cold water. West Block fed first. *Fives out and down! Fours out and down!* And they marched in lockstep to the dining room, right hand on the right shoulder of the man in front. Blue shirts, blue pants, red stripes down the side. No talking or smoking in line or in the dining room. If anyone spoke you could whitecap him. In the dining room hundreds of mouths shredding food, teeth clicking on metal, clattering utensils. The guard in the center aisle controlled the flow, and when they were done he cleared them out two rows at a time.

Across the yard, Zone Two. Inmates could smoke and talk on their way to work; everybody worked, and everybody made eight cents an hour. Half went into your commissary fund, and half you could take with you if you ever left. You worked in the laundry or the kitchen or in the shops: print shop, tailor shop, furniture factory, powerhouse. Setting type with hot lead. There was a garage in Zone Three and officers could bring their cars in for repairs—ten dollars not including parts. If you had a blue slip from the Parole Board, you went to the tailor shop for a fitting thirty days before getting out. Clack and drone of fifty electric sewing machines. They would cut the pattern from whole cloth and sew it right there on the floor. They made your shoes from plain hides, dyed, cut, and sewed them on a last. If no one came for you on the day of your release you sat in the bus station in your new suit and shoes, waiting, perhaps trembling, my God where is home now?

But for a while after Okinawa, after the caves and kamikazes, Fred Sr. was shop officer in the furniture factory. Boards from the sawmill were seasoned, cut, assembled with glue, sanded, stained, hand-rubbed with wax. A table for the warden's quarters, a chest of drawers for the governor's mansion. Fred Sr. sat on a pedestal and signed passes and filled out discipline sheets. A brass bell at the back of the shop he could ring if there was a fight or some other disturbance.

Fighting was sixty days lost time, sixty days grace. You rang the bell three times for a riot.

Inmates would sniff the paint thinner in the finishing area. 57635, who'd robbed a milkman and ran the belt sander, sniffed so much the lining of his skull was eaten away and he was paroled home to his family, legally blind, stumbling over furniture in childhood rooms. 55901 poured it all over himself, then went out into the yard and lit a match. (He'd gotten a letter.) When he charged another inmate, either for aid or accompaniment, the east tower guard cut him down with a single .30-caliber round. Because his family could not be contacted, or because he had none, his blackened husk was shoved into a dark suit of unfinished seams (hastily made in the tailor shop) and buried with a few words in the inmate cemetery at the north wall. Only a number was inscribed in the stone, as if even after death you remained property of the state.

On the grounds beyond the north wall where the institution quartered its dead, it raised its own crops and livestock. The inmates who worked the farm stayed in the honor dorms. There were apple and peach orchards along Route 13, a cannery, a hog and poultry farm, a horse barn, a dairy farm and pasture with a herd of Holstein cows. A slaughterhouse. There was a dirt road to the greenhouse and the warden's dog liked to sleep in the middle of it, covered in dust, so that you would have to drive around him. A small lake between the hog lot and J-Dorm and in the summer boys would swim in the lake and fish for bluegill and crappie, and feed apples to the big

Belgian horses in the barn. Girls could only swim on certain days. In the fall when corn was being canned, Archie would drive a truckload of husks to the dump off Route 13. Once when he got out of the truck to drop the tailgate, 61342 rose from beneath the pile of husks like some Halloween specter and stabbed him in the chest with a brass flush rod. (He'd honed it on the floor of his cell.) Archie drew his service revolver and shot 61342 in the neck, pulled the rod from his breastbone, and drove them both to the infirmary, the inmate squeezing his throat with both hands as if to choke himself for ineptitude. Both were treated and recovered, and 61342 was tried and sentenced in the prison court in West Diagonal.

Five years grace, five years lost time.

Supper was at four. At three forty-five Fred Sr. would ring the bell in the back of the shop and the inmates lined up for count. They marched back to the dining hall for another noisy, speechless meal. The music bell rang at eight and they could plug headphones into the walls of their cells (the institution had its own radio station), or they could play their guitars for the hour. Singing was forbidden. Guitars were the only instrument permitted at OSP, and though some players were more proficient than others, and rarely did they play in accompaniment, occasionally the stray sounds of scales and chords, crude attempts at a blues, even a fragment of the classical repertoire, would meet by some harmonic accident in the dead air of the tier and bring it to life. For that moment the range would grow quiet with listening, and perhaps those without hope of parole or pardon listened hardest, hearing a song that sang itself and belonged to no one, and whose last perfection could only be silence. Then the bell sounded to warn them that the lights would go out in five minutes, and five minutes later the lights went out.

They took showers on Saturday. The Car Wash was located at the end of West Block and the guards ran them through fifty at a time. They went to commissary on Saturday after showering, and after lunch they went to the yard or the gym where they played baseball, basketball, or put on gloves. Sunday morning you could go to chapel, Catholic or Protestant, and before dinner there was a movie in the high school. Not everyone attended church but almost everyone went to the movies, to *Forbidden Planet* or *The Ten Commandments*, and in addition to these entertainments the institution could provide its own. Once a year the inmates would mount a stage production in the high school—Shakespeare, O'Neill, Gilbert and Sullivan—filling every role and capacity themselves—director, conductor, lighting technician; Titus, Ophelia, Peter Pan. Or they would perform a work of their own creation, presented under the title *The Little Show in the Big House* and open to the public for a modest admission.

After the riots in the dining hall Fred Sr. made lieutenant. He received the largest increase of his tenure and bought a new blue Mercury station wagon with hardtop styling and a Super Marauder V8. He drove his family once a year to OSP to see *The Little Show* in the new blue Voyager, and drove Fred Jr. there once a month to get his hair cut. (Inmates learned to shave and cut hair at the Barber Shop and School. They practiced on a grinning skull, and two of the inmates awarded licenses would be pulled to work in the officer barber shop.)

Fred Sr. would show his son around. Archie, a Mason and gun enthusiast like Fred Sr., shook the boy's hand. Fred Jr. petted the warden's dog. They visited the death house and Fred Jr. sat in the chair. His father made him get out, said it was bad luck.

The ride to OSP in the blue Mercury took almost an hour. Amish country. Horses and buggies. Church service held in a barn. The radio played but Fred Sr. wouldn't allow the new music. They talked but he no longer talked about the war. He talked about the Soviet space dog, the new conveyor system in the powerhouse—inmates didn't have to shovel coal anymore. He mentioned the new social worker and Fred Jr. said they'd been taught to say *Negro* or *colored*. Fred Sr. mentioned the girl who lived two houses down and his son said nothing and listened to his father's car. Four hundred horses with in-block combustion chambers, a water-flow intake manifold and three two-barrel carburetors. Fred Jr. knew all of its component parts and what they did and should sound like because he was what they called mechanically inclined, and at home in the workshop he'd made of his room he would stop time fixing clocks, watches, his mother's toaster, her blender, electric fans, typewriters, a discarded adding machine he'd found and restored to use; anything with moving parts, anything but the radio that sat playing on his desk, and what didn't need repair he would dismantle anyway, solve its mystery with his mind in his hands, the new music in his ears.

He'd built an amateur crystal radio set and not only conversed with other ham operators and monitored international broadcasts, but he listened to signals from space, from the satellites, Sputnik and Vanguard and Explorer, beeping and humming to him about cosmic rays, magnetic fields, the shape of the Earth. He was also a fair carpenter, had made bird-houses, simple furniture, a wagon for his paper route, executed projects from school and others of his own design. In shop class he excelled; in math, English, history, science, his performance was average. He was small and slight and poor-sighted, and as an athlete a father's disappointment—made barely passing marks in the gymnasium. But he had inherited a predilection for firearms and, as if to fill a gap in paternal affection, been given one of his own, a Colt Woodsman .22 pistol with a long barrel and walnut grips. Fred Sr. had taught his son how to zero the sights and adjust the pull, that the way you squeeze the trigger is the most critical component of accuracy, and Fred Jr. was already an accomplished amateur marksman. He dismounted and cleaned his own arm using flannel patches and a knobbed wooden bore brush, and when he was done he would, against the onset of rust, fill the frame of the piece with gun grease, cover it in flannel, then wrap it in two thicknesses of manila drawing paper.

The radio singing Zing! Went the Strings of His Heart, asking Who Knew Where or When?

But during the ride to his last haircut at OSP they barely talked at all, for they had reached that stage in the relationship between father and son which is composed largely of silence. Fred Jr. brought his yo-yo. He sat on the metallic vinyl of the front seat, almost as big as their living room sofa, and listened again to the engine. He wasn't sure when he would be listening to his own, but he knew it wouldn't be a station wagon; it would be a Plymouth Fury or a Chevy 210, and he would wax it with Zip Wax and tune it himself, and he would tune it so well it wouldn't make a sound, she wouldn't even hear it as it slowed up alongside her like a big fish in clear water, and when she turned and looked at last she would see the black chrome shining at her, the sun burning in it as if the one in the sky were secondhand, and she would shine back then and he wouldn't have to say a word, wouldn't have to ask where she was going because her destination was his, always had been, they'd only lacked the means of getting there, and then she would be sitting no more than a foot of green vinyl away, not two doors down, in the passenger seat but not a passenger, looking through the windshield, through the glass at whatever they passed, and it wouldn't really matter where she looked because it would always come back to him on a curve of light.

Only the radio, doing their talking for them.

They parked in the lot under the hard winter sun and went in through the administrative office. They went through the bullpen because you had to go through the bullpen to go anywhere at OSP. Two turnkeys in a bulletproof cage with gun ports and mirrors, controlling everything. There were four barred steel doors in the corners of the room, and only one could be opened at a time. Sometimes the turnkey outside the cage would pat Fred Jr. down as a kind of joke. He didn't pat down Fred Sr.

He opened the door and they went to the barber shop.

Marble floor, high ceiling. Only one inmate worked the barber shop on weekends and 59631 stood there sharpening his straight razor on the stone. Fred Jr. liked the sound it made:

ssk, ssk. The stone had a corner missing. Fred Jr. was first. 59631 used scissors and a comb and Fred Jr. liked the sound the scissors made, but not as much as he liked the sound of the stone. Except for that the haircut was silent because inmates were not permitted to talk to family members. When he was done, 59631 took off the bib, bunched it up and dusted off Fred Jr.'s neck, then helped him out of the chair. It was Fred Sr.'s turn.

He sat in the chair and 59631 tied the bib on, then reclined the chair with a foot pedal so that Fred Sr. sat tilted back not quite staring up at the ceiling. 59631 stropped the blade on the leather strop hanging from its nail behind the chair. The straight razor had a wooden handle and was made of Sheffield steel, not stainless, which rusts and won't hold an edge. He used a badger-hair brush. He twirled it rapidly in the soap cup and Fred Jr., standing in front of the chair with his yo-yo, Rocking the Baby, Splitting the Atom, liked this sound as well. When he was done brushing the soap on Fred Sr.'s face, 59631 asked, as he always did, "What'll it be today, sir?" and Fred Sr. replied, "Same as always," same as he always did, and 59631 nodded and put his left hand on Fred Sr.'s forehead, something he didn't always do, brought the blade under Fred Sr.'s jaw and cut his carotid artery. Blood sprayed onto Fred Jr.'s glasses, the red veil through which he would from that moment on see this new unfathered world, through which he saw the inmate draw the blade across his father's throat, slicing the Adam's apple and larynx and cutting through the jugular vein on the other side of Fred Sr.'s neck, the yo-yo sleeping at the end of its string, Fred Sr.'s arm burrowing like an animal under the red-soaked bib, then rising, and though Fred Jr. never saw the gun he saw the shape of its barrel through the cloth as his father shoved it under the barber's chin without looking, damage done. The shot boomed and, tall as the room was, a hairy, bloody clot of scalp and skull appeared almost instantly on the vaulted ceiling, along with whatever motive 59631 may have had, slowly unpeeled itself, and landed on the floor next to the inmate's body with a sound like someone dropping a wet rag. The next sound came from far away, the clank of the wheel lock turning in the bullpen.

The yo-yo swung like a pendulum, slowing.

Fred Sr. tried to stand with his hand looking for his throat, the red spreading in a great wet fan below his neck but the foam on his face still completely white. He looked at Fred Jr., at his flesh and his blood, moved his lips but his windpipe was cut and whatever those words might have been bubbled soundlessly from that ragged new mouth and were lost. He sat down then like a man who has said his piece.

The funeral was on Valentine's Day. It was very cold and snow drifted. The casket was draped with a flag and rode a caisson drawn by four caparisoned horses. Two of the horses were saddled but had no riders. The ground was covered. The mourners kept stumbling over headstones on their way to the grave site, but only the living complained. The sun came and went, came and went, the sky opening and closing as if to admit some souls and refuse others. The flag was folded thirteen times and presented to the widow. The retching of grief interrupted by gunfire, a three-volley salute.

"And when that song has been sung," the chaplain intoned, "and you're standing on that other shore . . ."

The bugler blew taps fifty yards away.

Afterward the warden put his hand on Fred Jr.'s shoulder. Archie put his hand on his head. He was married now and had found another way to work.

She was no longer two doors down. She was gone.

In college Fred supported himself as a stock boy, a dishwasher, as someone who left a number in the student union and would do small repairs for five dollars. He took part-time work at the dog pound. He majored in history and minored in engineering, but school bored him and his grades were poor save for those he earned in celestial navigation, an elective requirement. The instructor claimed to be a direct descendant of Leif Ericson, had sailed from Iceland to New York on the replica of a Viking longship. He had long fair hair and blue eyes, and his class, with its considerable female enrollment, followed him eagerly back through millennia to the beginning, to wayfinding, the ancient practice of Polynesian sailors who had crossed vast seas without benefit of chart or compass. They studied astronomy and the instruments of navigation, from the crude latitude hooks of the South Pacific and the kamal of Arab desert traders to the quadrant of Columbus, the nocturnals and astrolabes, sextants and octants. They learned about dead reckoning and speed made good, how to find Venus by daylight. They named the bodies of the celestial sphere: Acrux, Aldebaran, Alpha Centauri.

"One day this will become a lost art as well," the instructor said. "Science will give us eyes in the sky, eyes we haven't earned."

Fred sat listening as someone sighed behind him, scratches and bites on his arms and face: he ran the gas box at the pound. A shiny sheet-metal cube, five by five by four. One side was removable and in it was a small window of reinforced plastic. If he couldn't talk them into it, he used a catch pole or snare. Put them to sleep, as parents tell their children and perhaps themselves. A hose ran from the exhaust pipe of the dog-catcher's van. When the box was at capacity—two dozen, give or take, of the unwanted, the feral, the very old, or the very sick—Fred would get in the van, turn the ignition key, and, foot on pedal, open the tables of the *Nautical Almanac*. Rows and columns, latitude and longitude. Practice problems. Sometimes he heard them wailing and struggling, clawing, biting each other and themselves, bouncing off the walls of the box until, plotting sheet in lap, he floored the pedal to speed the arrival of the final silence, found the true bearing of the body, and plotted a line of position.

Acrux, Polaris, Rigil Kentaurus.

The sun, the moon.

You are *here*.

When it was done he would turn off the engine and get out of the van wearing a mask with a charcoal filter, turn four toggles on the gas box, and remove the panel. They would be covered in urine and feces and often blood and he would remove them one at a time, unless the jaws of one were clamped to the fur and flesh of another and he was unable to break this death grip, and so would put both bodies in a single plastic bag and they would accompany each other into the hopper with the rest. A truck took the hopper to an incinerator. He cleaned the box with ammonia and warm water.

All of them weren't always dead.

Behind him, whispering and giggling.

He suggested to his supervisor reducing the number of animals per procedure, was told of quotas and necessary evil—some of them were better off anyway. Near the end of the semester he presented a design for an improved apparatus featuring a control panel, multiple compartments, utilizing a mix of gases from pressurized cylinders that would induce anesthesia before terminating vital functions. His supervisor said he would pass these plans on to someone at the Department of Agriculture, then ordered Fred back to work. Fred returned to the van and prepared for finals.

The professor announced that the final would be held on his own boat, a thirty-foot schooner not of Viking design. Fred, who was pathologically averse to travel in any conveyance not on wheels, was unable to force himself to attend. He attempted a makeup project by building his own sextant out of acrylic, handcut mirrors, a telescopic eyepiece, and a hand-drawn vernier scale. He used Legos to fasten the frame. The instructor was surprised and impressed, admired Fred's ingenuity and workmanship, declared the instrument both well made and viable but not acceptable as credit. Fred was unable to complete the course and shortly thereafter dropped out of school altogether. Years later he sometimes told people he had studied celestial navigation with a direct descendant of Leif Ericson, but the only Leif most of them knew was a pubescent California

pop singer who'd had enormous international success with a
song called "I Was Made for Dancing."

There were always problems with the older machines: jamming,
misfeeds, little black spots. When there was a problem with one
of the older ones—the 914, the 1000, the 2400—you called
toll-free and gave an operator the serial number. You would tell
the operator what the problem was and he or she would try to
walk you through a solution over the phone. If you couldn't be
helped over the phone, the operator would have to page a service technician and you would have to use the 813 or the 660,
or the Kodak next door, until sometime later in the day, depend-
ing on how busy he was and how far he had to travel, when
the tech walked through the door in his short sleeves and clip-
on tie, black-framed glasses and pocket protector, carrying in
one hand a satchel full of strange-looking tools and meters,
in the other a cup of coffee. The bag looked so heavy he almost
limped with it, and he only worked on consoles.

   "The doctor is in," he might say then, cigarette in mouth,
and you would take him down the hall to the copier room to
the 914, trying not to walk in front of him, and he would tell
you what a nice office you had, the furnishings and the carpet,
the pictures, would say hello to the other employees, would
tell you his name, by the way, though you already knew it.

   "The 914," the tech would say with certain emphasis in
the copier room. Old Unfaithful, you wanted to say, but knew
you shouldn't because he might remind you then that the 914
had made Xerox what it was, and Xerox was making the world
what it would be, and the world would be in color, a hundred

and twenty clicks a minute, a computer you could put on your desk, so you didn't call it anything, you just told him what the problem was while he put on latex gloves.

He would get on his knees and take off the service panel. He would invite you in, closer, to crouch down over the paper path with him and show him where it happened, where it hurt. Smiled wider than a man who smoked as much and drank as many cups per day as he did should, which was to say at all.

No thank you, you might say. You couldn't get any on your clothes.

The world had little black spots.

"Artifacts," he called them and asked to see a sample print. You gave it to him carefully so he couldn't touch your hand, the way Jim Dolly sometimes did, and though he didn't try, and though he never looked at you quite the way Jim Dolly looked, nor said how good you smelled, you would leave him in the copier room grounded to the carpet, his head stuck in the print engine, and walk back down the hall to your desk without having ever once said his name.

Back down the hall to where Jim Dolly was waiting.

Jim Dolly was big, red-faced, prematurely white-haired—or maybe he was born that way. He liked to wear black. He took your hand like it wasn't just your hand, looked at your name-plate and used your name. He was here to see the office manager about the laser printer, the 9200, because after lasers there was no turning back, but he was early and the office manager wasn't in yet, so he could have a seat and wait, and that was fine with Jim Dolly because he was here to do that too. Jim Dolly knew how to tell time.

Fine with me, he would say like you'd talked him into it, having a seat, sitting, not getting much smaller. He would be quiet for a time. Flip through *Newsweek*. You could hear him flipping, waiting, you could smell him. You could do some filing. Do something before it was too late, then it was: he offered gum. Told you about himself, about life before Xerox: cars, insurance, commodities, ad space, even cemetery plots. But he didn't tell you about certain other things, certain misunderstandings misconstrued as misconduct; Jim Dolly would tell you some things and ask you others, in a whisper you didn't want to hear, so you asked him about the 9200 but that seemed to be what he'd been waiting for. Hadn't you seen the commercial?

What commercial?

Super Bowl ad. Monks in a monastery. You hadn't seen it? You didn't like football.

Bet you didn't like monks either.

Your boyfriend watched it though. Vikings fan.

Never had a chance.

You wouldn't know.

Jim Dolly would. Jim Dolly tell you he played college ball? Would Jim Dolly know how many copies a minute?

All-Conference.

Was that good?

It wasn't bad. Left tackle, freshman. No big deal. Not a happy ending though. (Dividing air with the edge of his hand.) Helmet to knee. Now it was made of plastic.

Wasn't everything anymore?

He couldn't tell you how many operations.

Could he tell you how many goddamn copies?

If he did he'd have to take you to lunch.

Not necessarily.

Jim Dolly wasn't no monk.

So how many?

Seriously.

Seriously you believed him, and then the office manager got in. Jim Dolly spat his gum in the ashtray and spent the rest of the morning in the office manager's office. Even behind closed doors you could still hear the whisper. Then Xerox took them both to lunch. Then they sat in the conference room for the rest of the afternoon; the tech did the install two weeks later. Still flush with his commission, Jim Dolly lingered at the account like he always did after a sale, glad-handing the help, passing out his card like another form of promiscuity, paying compliments you couldn't afford to accept. Calling the tech Freddy, saying, "Guess who's buying your lunch today, and it ain't me." Looking closely at him, saying, "You look like you need some titties in your face. We'll take the Linc."

Within fifteen minutes they were sitting in a leather booth in a dark room downtown, and a girl Fred wouldn't look at was asking them what they'd like to drink. A piano was play-ing somewhere.

Jim Dolly laughed. "When I said topless I didn't mean the roof caved in." He ordered a gin and tonic. Fred had coffee.

"Live a little," Jim Dolly said.

"This is how I live," Fred said.

Jim Dolly watched the waitress head for the bar. "I should give her a tip just to put her shirt back on." He looked apolo-getic. "It's better in the evening."

"Happy hour?" Fred said.

"Happier than this," Jim Dolly said. "Rest of the band shows up too."

She came back with their drinks, one under each breast.

"He wants a little cream with his coffee."

"Black is fine."

"I think he's blushing," the waitress said.

Fred felt his face. "Just a little warm in here . . ."

"Red as a baboon's ass," Jim Dolly said and raised his glass. "Fuckin Raiders."

"Who?" Fred said. So they toasted Xerox instead.

"While it's still around," Jim Dolly said.

"Why wouldn't it be?"

Jim Dolly made a face at his drink. "Friggin nail polish remover."

"I heard revenues . . ."

"You see any of that let me know. Revenues and profit ain't the same thing—we're spinning our wheels here. Rochester's buzzing like a beehive but they're not putting out any new toys. Can't agree on anything." He broke ice with his teeth. "Haven't had a new product line in how many years."

"The Star."

"The Star. Typewriter with a TV sitting on top. You gonna pay sixteen grand for that?"

"The 9700."

"Half a million. And you need a tech onsite full-time just to keep it running. It'll never pass beta." Jim Dolly looked around the room and waved. "We should be going smaller, not bigger. Our desktop's a joke. And don't look behind you: here comes Canon. Here comes IBM, the Japs—the *Japs*. We might have to drop another one."

Fred looked down at his menu but didn't pick it up. "So what's good here?"

"Open your eyes, man. Sure isn't the gin." The waitress came back and Jim Dolly ordered a whisky and soda for Fred. "Live a little more," he said, put his glass back on the tray, told her to pour it back down the toilet and ordered a drink like a chemistry lesson. Then he gave her a buck and told her to go drink some milk.

He looked at Fred. "Know what we need?" and someone in the booth behind them said, "Hey bigmouth."

Jim Dolly turned his head halfway and then back. "We need another whatshisname."

Fred picked up his coffee. "That narrows it down."

"Whatshisname . . . Chester."

"Hey big time," the guy in the booth behind him said. "How about you give her a break? She's just trying to make a living here."

Jim Dolly turned his head halfway again. "If she's got mouths to feed I hope they're on the bottle." He turned the rest of the way. "Otherwise they must be starving to death." The guy laughed. He said something else and Jim Dolly laughed and was Jim Dolly, and Fred wondered if they knew each other.

He lit a cigarette. Jim Dolly watched with disdain, as he did in the presence of vices he hadn't acquired. "Carter, Carson, you know. The guy in his living room."

"It was his kitchen," Fred said.

"In fucking Queens for Christsake. Wherever the hell that is."

"You don't know where Queens is?"

"I know where the fuck the point is he started out, what? Rubbing a piece of paper with his handkerchief, sprinkling some magic powder on it?"

"Sulfur," Fred said. "Sulfur and lycopodium."

"Yeah lickapo my point is he couldn't get even arrested for what? Five years? Ten? IBM wouldn't give him the time of day. How much you figure he's worth today?"

"He left most of it to charity." Chester Carlson had licensed the patent to Xerox before it was Xerox—twenty thousand shares, but his ambition was to die a poor man.

"Well you know how much trim he must've taken down?" Jim Dolly said. "Try giving that to the Goodwill."

He'd practiced Zen meditation. Built a Buddhist monastery.

"Doesn't make him a monk," Jim Dolly said. "Here we go."

She came back and put down their drinks and stood at the table, waiting. Jim Dolly looked at her. "You know you just gave a whisky and soda to the next Thomas Edison?"

"Yeah?" She nodded and looked at Fred. "Is Mr. Edison ready to order?"

Fred tried his drink. The piano played one note at a time. "Can you give me a minute?"

"Give us a minute," Jim Dolly said, and she went away again.

"How do you know about that?" Fred said.

"What is it, national security?" Jim Dolly said. "So you have a hobby. We're just two guys talking."

"I don't have hobbies." He had a couple of patents pending. Small stuff. Specialized. He also had a tendency to let things slip.

"Stereo helicopter mapping system," he mumbled, and Jim Dolly tried to follow till his eyes glazed over.

"What's the thing on TV?" he interrupted. "The thing that slices and dices."

"I forget," Fred lied.

"See what I'm saying?" Jim Dolly said. He beckoned at the darkness over Fred's shoulder. Fred gave the whisky and soda another chance and Jim Dolly reached into the lining of his jacket. He took out a card. He seemed to be whispering for some reason. "Know what this is?"

"I have one," Fred said, and in fact had several.

"A ticket," Jim Dolly said. "Anywhere you want to go. Wild card." It was also a passport, a blank check, and a free pass. When the waitress came back he tried to slip it under her breast but she took it without looking at it and said, "Thanks, now I can open a topless copy shop. You gentlemen like some lunch?"

"That actually ain't a bad idea," Jim Dolly said. "Go ahead."

Fred looked her in the face. "What do you recommend?"

"It's a friggin steakhouse," Jim Dolly said, and Fred liked his bloody. Jim Dolly told her to burn it and ordered a double. They had another toast.

"You know he didn't invent the light bulb," Fred said.

"Bullshit," Jim Dolly said. He kept looking around the jazzy dimness, restless, widening his eyes and nodding at someone he knew, or thought he did, or wanted to know. Drumming the tabletop to some beat that had nothing to do with the piano, shaking the booth till the guy behind him tapped his shoulder: "Hey Buddy Rich, can you save it for the solo? You're spilling half my scotch here."

When Fred got back to the account he told the office manager he needed to break in the developer on the 9200. He said it would take an hour or so, his hand over his mouth. He shut the doors and ran five thousand more copies of a flyer he'd laid out the previous weekend. It wasn't stealing if the clicks were already paid for.

At five thousand feet someone touched his shoulder. He pulled his face up out of his lap and saw the airfield mechanic standing over him, looking at what used to be scrambled eggs on the front of his coat. Looking like, Are you sure you're up to this? And though of course he wasn't, here he was. Making sure.

He was seatbelted to the jumpers' bench, next to the door. He'd gotten some on the harness.

The cabin was cold. His ears popped. The engine buzzed and everything buzzed with it. They seemed to ride a bumpy surface of air. The pilot, a gun owner like the mechanic, looked over his shoulder and shouted something. The plane banked, a traumatic shift of gravity. It straightened and the pilot shouted again. The mechanic looked out the window, signaled to Fred. Fred did not want to unlatch his belt, did not want to stand. When he'd managed it, one hand on the cold metal of the frame, the mechanic hooked the lanyard of his harness to the anchor cable overhead. Pulled one of the boxes from under the bench, pushed it stiffly with his foot to the door, six inches at a time. He grabbed the handle and looked at Fred and Fred closed his eyes and the mechanic opened the door.

The drone of the engine filled the cabin with a cold blast of mile-high air. Fred felt his hat jump off his head, the sudden brightening through his eyelids. There was no escaping it. The mechanic tapped his shoulder again and when he looked the lid was off the box. The color was Cosmic Orange and the print black; rubber-banded in bundles of five hundred. He tried not to see the blue in the corner of his eye, beyond the threshold, let alone the vast green squares bound by gray bands of roadwork, traffic like lines of code; let alone the shiny metal of ponds, scattered rooftops congealing into a town, their own burgeoning shadow darkening six blocks at a time. Impossible. He felt his stomach trying to squeeze emptiness out of itself and heaved, fought it. The mechanic shoved a bundle at him. Fred let go of the frame. When he pulled the rubber off it came alive, a handful of paper tongues. The mechanic gestured impatiently and, without looking, Fred stuck his arm out over the earth and thought the wind would take it off. Don't throw them, just open your hand. His sinuses pounded. A sudden thin trail of confetti if you'd looked up at the sound of the plane, or if you hadn't, nothing till they came fluttering gently down into trees and yards and onto sidewalks and car tops, lawns, lots, public spaces, falling like the leaves you were raking, so that you looked up now and saw them in the sky and your first thought was monarchs heading south, not the

Second Amendment (with quotes from Thomas Jefferson and Clint Eastwood appended) coming at you out of the blue in Halloween colors.

The mechanic had done this over the Ho Chi Minh Trail out of a converted Cessna. Ten to thirty per hundred square meters, he said, but they only had a hundred thousand.

After the first bundle he took them out of the box himself but still wouldn't look. When he'd lost count he couldn't feel his face anymore. He and the mechanic took turns. The plane hauled to port, starboard, the lanyard grew taut like a leash, slackened. Five boxes, just over fifty pounds apiece. The mechanic dragged them out from each side of the cabin in an alternating rhythm so as not to unbalance the plane. Five boxes, four counties. Some of them blew back inside.

When they returned to the airfield a sheriff and someone from the FAA were there. A week later Issue 7 was voted down in one of the largest turnouts in state history, and Fred picked up his coat at the dry cleaners.

DESCRIPTION OF A PREFERRED EMBODIMENT

Combination embodying an index mirror rotatable
about a predetermined axis and bringing a
sighted object into juxtaposition with the line
of sight of the optical system at the center of
the horizontal mirror of an arcuate informational
grating concentric with the axis of rotation of
the index mirror and an index arm rotatable in
consonance with the index mirror, a light-
emitting diode at the proximal end of the index
arm arranged to project a beam through the
reference grating at the distal end of the arm
onto the informational grating, and a phase
detector arrayed at the proximal end of the
index arm to receive the beam refracted through
the conjuncted gratings.

They'd stayed in touch, and the two of them went shooting together as they might have gone fishing or golfing had Fred been given to either pursuit. Both belonged to the same club, participated in the same competitions, frequented both indoor and outdoor ranges with spotters and referees, practiced on both stationary and moving targets. Sometimes, though, they preferred a less formal setting and would meet at a location roughly halfway between the city and the prison the warden administered—where he'd once been a guard. A post-industrial badland, desolate aftermath of a place where things had once been milled or made, signs admonishing trespassers now unreadable with rust.

"Behind the back," the warden would say, and they'd park at the edge of a slow road, step over a chain sagging between two canted posts, and roam the ruin. Walls crumbled waist-high, sprouting rebar, gutted automobile chassis festooned with weeds like some hybrid nest, rusted fixtures in rusted cement where machinery once stood . . . Assembly plant, Fred thought, tool and die, and the warden didn't particularly care; he was just looking for things to put holes in.

His feet were still flat but only Fred still used his nickname.

Long silences, low hills, scrub, a pond more or less in the middle that was a breathtaking poisonous blue not even algae could survive. The place looked war-torn. Fred wore his suit. Occasionally they came across other visitors there for the same purpose, or riding dirt bikes, or seeking some diversion not apparent and maybe for the better. Children playing at soldier. Rarely were greetings exchanged or distances closed; if you weren't alone in this place, as a courtesy you would pretend you were.

Stop, shoot, move on. The warden's wife packed them a lunch.

"That wall."

"You mean what's left of it?"

"That brick in the corner."

"Which corner?"

"The one with the brick. In the wall."

Inhale. It is easier to aim high and lower the weapon to the target than the other way around. Hold your breath and steady the piece.

A chunk of brick gone in a burst of red powder. The sound crackling, fading, traveled, faded.

The warden's shot went wide. Fred said, "Just about put that one in orbit."

"Windage," the warden said, and they walked on. Followed a line of railroad tracks till they disappeared in the ground as if bound for the underworld. Fred carried his Woodsman, the warden a .45 Ruger semiautomatic, and though the latter was an avid hunter he and Fred shot at no living thing, and this also by unspoken agreement.

Fred had shot to kill only once in his life. He was a boy in his own backyard; a common blackbird out of a tree with his .22. When he'd gone to where it had fallen its wings were in disarray and there was a perfect round drop like red fruit at the tip of its beak. The feathers, iridescence in black. Uncommon in death.

If only he'd known.

The warden was talking about a different bird.

"Caught one of the old boys in East Block cooking pigeons in his cell," he said. "Ran a line right to his mattress springs."

"You don't feed your guests?" Fred said.

"I'm told it didn't smell half-bad. Maybe I put it on the card." He looked at Fred. "Maybe he should put in for a patent."

"He'd better have a lot of time on his hands."

"All day and a night, as we say," the warden said. "But I guess you should know."

"I guess I do," Fred said.

The warden coughed. "You and your projects."

"I like to keep busy."

"There anything left to invent?"

"Not until somebody invents it."

"So what is it this time?" the warden asked.

Fred waited. They had not fired a shot in a while. "Kind of a sextant."

"Don't we already have those?"

"This one's electronic."

"Well it's about time," the warden said. "And what do we do with it again?"

"Find your way," Fred said. He didn't mind; he knew what the warden said, and what he thought, and how to figure the difference.

"Well," the warden said, and they stopped again. "Where the bodies are."

They stood on a low rise, over the blue pond that seemed to be the epicenter of the calamity no one would explain. Its depth was also unknown and the subject of local legend. Around them they could see only the no-man's-land men had made, and the sun getting low. There was no need to pretend now.

"Think you can invent yourself someone to share that big old house with?" the warden asked. "Even Frankenstein had his bride."

"Did you see the end of the movie? And that was the monster, not the maker."

"I thought they were one and the same."

Fred looked into blue death. "They turn from me."

"Maybe it's the way you look at em. Maybe give Buddy Holly his glasses back. Hell, let your hair dry out—looks like you change your oil with it. And put some meat on your bones, they like a little more to look at."

"I guess you'd know."

The warden laughed. He had been married more than thirty years and his bones were buried in it. No children. "I just think that's a lot of house to be knocking around alone in. Ever thought about selling?"

She'd taken two jobs to keep it after he passed. "I promised her."

Passed, he'd said. *Passed away*, they say. Something you do in your sleep.

The warden cleared his throat. "Sometimes my mouth springs a leak and I plug it with my foot," he said. "That's not what I came here to talk about."

There was a large flat boulder near the edge of the pond. A spatter of bird shit, almost in the middle like a bullseye.

"I know why you came here," Fred said. He looked at the gun. "That cannon you've been lugging around must be getting pretty heavy about now."

"Since you mention it," the warden said. He raised the pistol, took aim at the white patch on the boulder, and pulled. The comical poof of a squib load. Black smoke rising from the breech, the rich smell you either love or you can cover your nose with the Bill of Rights.

"Don't you ever just want to go bowling?" the warden said. He looked like he needed to sit.

"Windage," Fred said.

"Smart-ass," the warden said. He pulled back the slide with a handkerchief and looked down inside the weapon.

"Yup," he said. "Goddamn black powder."

———

"The smoke," the warden said, his back to Fred. He unzipped his fly. "The smell."

Fred turned around. The Colt at his side, pointing down.

"I couldn't begin to tell you what it smelled like," the warden said. "I just thank God the family wasn't there."

He watered a dead tree.

"Thank God," Fred agreed. Then he said, "I understand there was arcing."

"Arcing." The warden shook and zipped. "There were flames coming out of his ears like road flares. Like he was something out of hell."

Fred turned around. "I guess some would say he was."

"Would you?" the warden asked.

Fred looked surprised, then shrugged. "I'm a guy who fixes copy machines."

"You're a guy who drops messages out of the sky."

"I believe in some things."

"Well wherever they're from, wherever they're going, they're mine till they get there," the warden said, "want em or not. I can't let it happen again. Believe that."

Fred heard the dogs, wailing and whimpering. Cruel and unusual. Not uncommon.

"When we tried to get him out of the chair it came off his bones like he was a slab of ribs."

"Amperage," Fred said, toeing an empty shell casing on the ground. "What now?"

The warden sort of mumbled. "Department of Corrections investigation."

"Keep it in the family." Fred kicked the casing away.

"Whosoever brings trouble to his house will inherit the wind—or something like that," the warden said. "Last thing I want is some board of inquiry busting my balls, touching the place up with their white gloves." Action News had been bad enough, chasing him to his car like he was some scammer bilking widows. He set the Ruger on the rock and opened the paper bag his wife had given him. "I've met the governor once and wasn't planning to do it again. I hear his wife likes the ladies. Ham or salami?"

"Doesn't matter to me," Fred said. He reached in the bag.

The warden said, "I'm not sure how this all is going to shake out, but you can bite a big chunk out of my ass and there's still plenty to go around. I've got to look ahead."

"Got another one lined up?"

"Take your pick," the warden said. "They're all on borrowed time."

Someone's brother, someone's son.

Humanity. Amperage.

"You never know when a warrant's coming through," the warden said. "Whoever it is, I'm supposed to see him out, and right now I don't even have the furniture to do the job. Chair looks like it's been in World War Three. You couldn't use it for kindling, let alone." He took a bite. "I guess yours is ham."

Fred unwrapped the sandwich. The warden's wife had cut off the crusts.

"The thing is," the warden said, "it's like you say: we want to keep this thing in the family."

"Anyone figure out what went wrong?"

"We've narrowed it down to the sponge or a bad electrode."

Fred looked at the pond. "Bad electrode would reduce the voltage. What's the drop?"

"You're asking the wrong guy. You'd have to take it up with my maintenance supervisor."

"Maintenance. What about your electrical engineer?"

"Engineer." The warden might have spat if he hadn't been chewing. "All I've got is a plant chief who doesn't even know how to run a 110-line in his own house. Had to ask one of my guards. That chair was built by the inmates themselves I don't know when—turn of the century, maybe? Used the wood from the old gallows. Leg stock is an old rubber army boot with a strip of copper, helmet looks like a hair dryer made of tin. That's the state of the art." He looked at the ham. "There are no specialists, son. Better eat that before I do—I'm sorry but I get hungry when I'm upset."

They sat on the rock and ate facing the sun. Distended and red, its motion perceptible, like a ball of blood sinking under its own weight. The blue pond blackened with the dying light, as if showing its true color.

The warden looked at Fred. "What did you say your line of work was again?"

The Census Bureau had eliminated inventor as an occupation in 1940.

"Anyone ever show an interest in that whaddyacallit of yours?"

A letter from GE. A nibble.

"Find your way," the warden mused and looked ahead. "Well not to rush, but we wait much longer we may need it."

Fred chewed and swallowed. He wouldn't have minded the crust.

First, the legs.

White oak, kiln-dried. Who cared what it looked like? They might. He'd done his homework, taken Polaroids. Ran his hands over boards in the lumberyard, feeling for flaws. The smoothness of it, the muscle. Whorls in the pattern like small galaxies of grain.

He'd made a rocking chair for his grandmother once.

The smell of basements. He'd tiled the floor, finished the walls, hung fluorescent tubes though for wood he preferred tungsten. Washer and dryer at one end, sink, the furnace with its tentacles of ductwork. Everything else was workspace: table saw, drill press, jointer, shaper, all the shelves and their plastic tubs filled with hardware, spare parts, bits and pieces. Round blades hanging on nails, circles of teeth. Miter boxes, an acetylene tank as tall as he was. He was always adding shelves. Two small windows and a drain in the sloping floor. He was sure he'd emptied the ashtray but it was always full.

He cut the legs from two-inch stock. Each pass a momentous encounter—is it the blade that screams or the wood? Sawdust in small drifts on the floor. A smell of newness, a part of the world coming apart, reconfiguring, finding another form. No wonder it sounded painful. He wore goggles over his glasses, a dust mask, chiseled square tenons in the tops of the legs and routed grooves in the sides to capture the tongues of the corbels. He drilled high-pitched holes in the inside faces for the pins that would connect the legs to the seat frame. He worked without plans or drawings but there was never any doubt about the joinery. No one was watching.

He'd covered his cup but tasted wood dust in his coffee. He'd laid the pictures in a row on the bench, and the ones the warden had given him. A reminder. The ashtray smoldered. He doused it with the dregs of his cup.

He left only to go to Mass. He believed in the body and soul and the occasional necessity of evil. It was not a perfect world, but the next one would be. You helped what you could help. He would be the middleman.

He added a padded backrest, adjustable. Civilized.

He drilled out the mortises at the drill press, squared them off with a mallet and chisel. He cut the corbels, the rails, the stretchers and slats, the wooden washers, the dowel pins and panels. In the interest of common decency, he assembled the frame. He pinned and glued the back slats to the stiles, then chiseled the ends of the dowels flush with the frame. The arms captured the leg tenons with through mortises and sat a quarter-inch proud of the shoulders of the legs.

The seat was made of Plexi, perforated—no indignity of diapers, catheters—a removable drip pan underneath. A seatbelt made of aircraft nylon with a quick-release latch. Ankle electrodes turned of naval bronze built into the leg stock, one for the left, one for the right. He'd done his homework: most chairs used only one contact, they were passing current through only half the trunk. That was no way to treat a human being.

He believed in certain things, and torture wasn't one of them. (Excepting certain cases where innocent lives were at risk.) Whatever pain had filled their days would not attend their death.

He'd calculated the voltage and the amperage, the number of applications and the interval between them. He allowed for the dissipation of adrenalin. The second one would be the last.

The helmet was not attached. It was made of leather and lined with copper mesh and sponge. He tried it on and looked like an Inca high priest or Depression-era halfback. The sponge not man-made but the skeleton of a creature that resides in large colonies at the bottom of the sea. He'd been able to obtain only small pieces of it, had to sew them together by hand, but he had doubts about the conductivity of its artificial counterpart. Just look at the pictures.

The chair was big because men had grown since back when the first one was built. It had three legs.

He drank coffee and emptied the ashtray. Felt it in his back and shoulders. Broke night.

The diner was named for its owner's mother and never closed. Chrome, glass block. The mayor was a regular at breakfast. When Fred covered nights he would sit at the counter with the shiftworkers and clubhoppers who didn't have jobs in the morning, drinking coffee and smoking, waiting for his pager to go off. Maybe a little dessert. Brenda knew she didn't have to ask but Brenda wasn't in. Her replacement was a thickset, scrubbed-looking woman with square shoulders and gray hair. They must have pulled her off the day shift, but Fred didn't go there days. She gave him a menu in her pink uniform, told him the special was tuna noodle, with a bun. He gave it back.

"Maybe a little dessert," he said and flipped his cup. "A little later." She nodded and tilted the pot. Two steelworkers sat at the counter. One was a grinder and one was an electrician, and although Fred knew their names, he wasn't sure which went with whom. The electrician ate corned beef hash and stared straight ahead, chewing without blinking. A radio played in the kitchen.

"Brenda sick or she hit the lotto?" Fred asked.

"Oh she's sick," the grinder said.

The electrician swallowed. "Sick of having guns pointed in her face."

"There was a holdup?"

"Don't you watch the news?"

Fred opened his hands. "I'm asking."

"Guy come in yesterday with pantyhose on his head," the waitress said. "Made everyone lay down on the floor. Cleaned the place out—register, wallets." Her voice went up a note. "He took Brenda's wedding ring."

"Too bad His Honor wasn't there," the grinder said. "You left out the gun. Sawed-off."

"You were here?" Fred asked.

"It was in the paper," the grinder said. "I was here it might've been different."

"Yeah, you wear your pantyhose where no one can see it," the electrician said.

"But I hear the guy looked a little like you," the grinder said to Fred.

"Yeah," the electrician said. "I heard he poked holes for his glasses."

Fred thought. "I wouldn't use a shotgun," he said. You would want one hand free. And he would have worn a mask.

"You mean that's your face?"

The waitress had gone to the window. She came back with steak and eggs for the grinder, well done and over easy. Then she went unhurriedly to the other end of the counter and took a puff off a cigarette she had parked next to the warmer. She blew smoke out the side of her mouth, looking at some sort of booklet. She made marks with her pencil. She was very neat and scrubbed-looking.

"Tell me my horoscope?" the electrician said. "Sagittarius."

"It's not that kind of book." She showed it to them. "This tells you how to pick numbers in your dreams."

"Yeah, in your dreams," the grinder said.

"You dream of a rabbit, that's two forty-nine," the new waitress said.

"Freddy doesn't believe in playing numbers," the grinder said.

"Oh no?" the new waitress said. "Are you religious?"

"Tell her why, Fred."

Fred lit another cigarette. "I don't want my life drastically altered by an act of dumb luck," he said, his little speech. "For better or for worse."

"You're deep," she said. "But it has numbers for your job, your name, the weather, days of the week . . ." She spoke flipping through it.

"Is there smart luck?" the electrician said and the waitress looked at him. The door opened. Everyone turned thinking shotgun and pantyhose but it was a young couple wearing motorcycle jackets. Mohawks. One of the steelworkers grinned and the other shook his head. After she told them the special was tuna noodle with bun, the new waitress got a bottle of Tabasco for the grinder and wiped down the counter. She lifted the coffee pot off the warmer and wiped off the bottom, and the warmer hissed slightly when she ran the damp rag over it. She rinsed the rag and wrung it and put it back in her apron with the dream book and brought the coffee pot back to Fred. She took her time but she got there.

"Pulling a double?" Fred said.

"Today was my day off," she said.

"Nervous?"

"Wouldn't you be?" the grinder said. "Even the roaches are hiding."

She shrugged. "The owner's in the back."

"Watering down the ketchup."

"He's making it worth my while," she said.

The cook came out from the kitchen and swept the floor. Said the NFL had gone on strike at midnight. Heard it on the radio. Then he went back to the kitchen, flipped the broom and stirred the chili with the handle.

"Amen," Fred said.

"Is that good?" the new waitress said.

"Puts us out of our misery," the grinder said.

"What do they want anyway?" the electrician said.

"Fifty-five percent."

"Fifty-five percent of what?"

"I don't know but that's how much they want of it."

"Hell with em, maybe they'll show Canadian," the electrician said.

"It was good enough for Theismann," the grinder said.

"What are they talking about?" the new waitress said.

"You tell me," Fred said.

"I hate sports."

"Amen."

"You know what game I like? I like Trivial Pursuits. You know that one?"

"I'm familiar," Fred said.

"He's familiar," the grinder said. "Freddy's got a foot in the door."

"Just his foot?" the electrician said. "I hear he's good with his hands too."

"What are you guys on about?" The waitress looked at Fred. "Are these friends of yours?"

"They know my name," Fred said.

"Just ships that pass in the night," the electrician said, and the grinder said, "All you pass is gas."

Fred lit another one. "Brenda coming back, do you know?"

"What am I, chopped liver?"

"With bun," the grinder said.

"Gentlemen," Fred said.

"Uh-oh," the grinder said.

"Just talking about the special, Freddy."

"All you can eat," the grinder said.

"All right," the waitress said, "okay," but they were done anyway and when they left they tipped her well, as if to pay for the privilege. Fred stayed. The punk rockers left. A bus driver came to lay over in the parking lot. She took a cup of chili out to her bus and Fred stayed, his back to the dark. Traffic dwindled . . . The booths were empty, the owner somewhere in the back, the pager never made a sound; the night had made a place for them.

They smoked. She put the old pot on the other warmer and made a fresh one. Refilled the ketchup bottles, wiped down. Stacked menus.

"But what was I saying?"

The ceiling fan spinning in his coffee.

"You're going to drink yourself an ulcer," she said.

"Already have one," he said. "Comes with the territory."

"And what might that be?" she asked.

"Actually," Fred said, "I'm thinking of going into business for myself," and he looked at the lemon meringue.

A blue stain can be found on the surface of the wall. Prussian blue is a complex compound of ferric-ferrocyanide, a stable inert transition metal complex. The occurrence of color is an electronic transition from a low-spin $Fe2+$ ion in a carbon-coordination center to a high-spin $Fe3+$ ion in a nitrogen-coordination center. (Artists who have used this pigment include Gainsborough, Constable, Manet, Van Gogh, and Picasso in his Blue Period.) According to the official literature, this was a delousing room, or a storage room for disinfected materials. The color occurs nowhere else on-site.

Things were slow at first. At first it was just the two of them in square footage on the near west side. To the left was a dry cleaner, to the right a guy who smoked cigars and did your taxes at a flat rate. There was a palm reader across the street and thrift stores and strip bars up and down and aimless men and women who blew by like tumbleweeds in slow motion. Hardly anyone ever came in—it was not that kind of business—but rent was cheap and there was room to grow, though things were slow until Indiana.

A National Engineering helmet cost fourteen hundred dollars.

After Indiana they hired a machinist and a draftsman. Later they took on a part-time secretary, a heavily made-up acquaintance of Jim Dolly's who spent the majority of her brief day on the phone, under a monumental wig, engaged in what seemed to be installments of some epic conversation. She was soon replaced by someone with actual experience, a competent, handsome woman in her early forties who shared the carpeting and imitation wood up front with the draftsman and a dartboard bearing the likeness of the president of Libya. Besides answering the phone and typing letters, she received the mail, kept the books, disbursed the payroll, would have administered the benefits had there been any, and sometimes attracted winos and other vagrants who would stop at the storefront to leer at her. One of them once put his tongue out and pressed his lips against the glass right under ɔɴɪ ,ɢɴɪяɘɘɴɪɢɴɘ ɹɐɴoɪɫɐɴ Then Jim Dolly (who'd also wrestled in college, Division II) was standing over him, applying a kind of modified nelson hold, wrenching his arm up behind his back and pushing his face against the glass till his nose bled, then dragging him out of sight, offstage, reappearing a couple of minutes later even more red-faced than usual, straightening his clothes and brushing himself off. Letting himself in and leaning on the edge of her desk the way he sometimes did.

"I look out for my own," he said, though had it been a woman loitering at the window he might have ushered her away more diplomatically, might have reappeared after a longer absence and in quite another state, having had a frank but sympathetic conversation (perhaps even driving her to a rehab facility or shelter), and would not be leaning on the edge of the secretary's desk as he was now.

"Tell me you didn't hurt him."

"Just had a few words."

"What's that on the window?"

"He was French kissing plate glass. Would you believe I gave him my handkerchief?"

"No. Why don't we just move my desk?"

"My office is a little small."

"Seriously."

"Door's locked. We need to look like a serious business."

"But look what happens. What if he comes back?"

"I wouldn't worry about him." The dartboard hung above and just beside the corner where the draftsman worked at his high table, smoking his pipe. Jim Dolly pulled a fistful of darts from the colonel's face and said, "Let's talk about it at lunch."

"I'm part-time, I don't get lunch—not to mention medical."

"You knew that going in."

"Should I talk to Fred about it?"

"Go ahead, it's his candy store," and Jim Dolly threw hard and fast, steel points piercing the board like nails from a nail gun. The draftsman in his high chair, with his ruling pens and protractor, straight edges and French curves, smoked his pipe. He didn't look up.

"At least put up blinds," the secretary said, and there was a piercing whine from the back of the business. A sort of grating.

Four point one six milliseconds in a National Engineering chair. Cost of electricity: thirty-one cents.

The machinist worked in a shop in the back. He was a short, thick-armed man who couldn't sit for long periods of time because of a medical condition. Grim-faced and stoic, with a fringe of red hair around the shiny dome of his scalp, apparently more adept in the uses of power tools than the practice of personal hygiene, he dealt almost exclusively with Fred because Fred was where the ideas came from, and because he'd known Fred's father and grandfather, a machinist like himself, and because, like the draftsman, he did not respond to winks and dirty jokes.

The noise stopped, started again.

"Tax guy's been complaining," the secretary said.

"About the smell?"

"He's a working man, he breaks a sweat. About what do you think?"

"I don't hear a sound," Jim Dolly said and looked at the draftsman again.

"Are we zoned for a machine shop?" the secretary asked, because she knew something about these things, and Jim Dolly said, "Hell if I know," because he didn't, and then he asked her if she felt like taking a walk to the liquor store, though he wasn't really asking.

"Which one?" she said. There were two within walking distance.

"Take your pick," he said. "Ronrico 151. Bacardi if they don't have that."

"You're going to bribe him with a bottle?"

"That or hit him upside the head with it," Jim Dolly said, because if Jim Dolly didn't know a thing he knew a way around it; if lending institutions proved reluctant to qualify them for a small business loan, he knew of what might be called alternative sources of investment capital, and he knew what kind of sticks the tax guy smoked, knew that Cubans went with rum, even if they were from China, and that was why he and Fred were partners, forty-nine/fifty-one.

"Let me wash my hands," he said and put the last dart in his pocket.

The secretary called them the Skipper and Gilligan, but only to herself. When a call came in she would route it to one or the other, but because Fred spent so much time with the machinist and the draftsman, and still worked part-time for Xerox, and because Jim Dolly was a salesman and not a silent partner, it was often he who picked up and then you might hear him pulling his weight, being upfront about the markup— he sometimes found a use for the truth—twenty percent, but that included consumables, hands-on training, certification and support; that included dignity and decorum, and lately propriety and correctitude as well because Jim Dolly had added a thesaurus to his stock of the tools of persuasion.

He sold a Collapse Kit to the State of Delaware, a metal frame with handles on each side, to be worn by the inmate in the event of a breakdown on the way to the scaffold. Lowered his voice and dropped hints about the Trailer, a mobile facility still in the works.

Jim Dolly used a different voice if the one on the phone belonged to a woman not his ex-wife, or to an associate in one of his collateral ventures—promotions, over-the-counter stocks, sapphic pornography—and, though it was not that kind of business, once he even had visitors, two serious-looking men who were polite though not excessively so, one wearing a suit, the other jeans and a silver satin jacket. Jim Dolly accompanied them off the premises to what he called lunch, and though he returned after only a brief absence, he seemed no longer to have an appetite, appearing instead to have a great deal on his mind, and he instructed the secretary that the next time anyone came calling she was to tell them he was in Kentucky on business. There is always a bigger fish.

He went down the narrow hall that let off the front room to wash his hands. Fred's office was next to the lavatory and later he would knock on Fred's door and say, "Let's go grab a tax deduction," and sometimes Jim Dolly went alone and came back hours later, reeking and jovial or reeking and belligerent, or didn't come back at all till the next day. Fred took lunch at the diner named after someone's mother as often as possible. Brenda had returned and the waitress who had subbed for her was back on days. He still thought of her as the night gal.

But things were slow before Indiana.

There'd been a riot. The inmates had barricaded themselves in the death house and held six guards hostage. No one was killed but they'd knocked over the chair, shattered one of the arms and torn off the electrodes. The warden sent pictures. It could have been worse, he said, but most of them were superstitious and wouldn't touch it.

Fred's only stipulation was that the chair be shipped to his business address; when it was ready he would deliver it personally. A deadline was negotiated, a handshake over the phone. The warden called OSP for a reference and a contract was sent through the mail.

It would be needed again within the month. There was a surcharge for rush jobs.

The repair was not especially difficult but they had to use fresh wood to replace the arm. The chair was old, they all were, and the oak had darkened over time; the color of the new wood didn't match. Fred covered the whole piece in three coats of epoxy and dumped his ashtray. Shook his head. It would last forever but he would have preferred a natural finish.

NASA had painted the space shuttle with it.

They rented a U-Haul cargo van, secured the chair to the inside frame with ratchet straps and covered it with a furniture mover's blanket. Fred insisted Jim Dolly accompany him to Indiana—it would serve him well, he insisted, to see where their products were put to use, and Jim Dolly suggested that in that case they should consider expanding their line of merchandise. He salaciously offered examples, and Fred tried to smile.

They drove six hours through mostly rural flatness; a succession of small towns, each a name passing from memory before the next was in sight. Roadside stands, billboards defending the unborn. Jim Dolly couldn't drive because his license was under suspension. He brought a pint, wore sunglasses, told Amish jokes. Was oblivious to scenery that didn't include a golf course. Fred wasn't bad company but he had trouble conversing and driving at the same time. He would take his eyes off the road and look steadily at his passenger as he spoke, and after a while Jim Dolly faked sleep in order to discourage conversation. Then he wasn't faking.

They stopped once for gas and once for dinner at Denny's. Fred had coffee and asked the waiter if the beef tips were marinated; he could not have marinated beef tips because of his ulcer. Jim Dolly, groggy and somewhat drunk, asked for the free Grand Slam breakfast (Jim Dolly could eat breakfast all day!) insisting it was his birthday. When he couldn't furnish legal proof he enlisted Fred as a witness, who could not on principle corroborate this claim, then demanded to speak to the manager, who apologized but said it was a matter of strict policy. He showed them where it said so on the menu.

"We'll get it back," Fred said—he would not lie to order, but charging travel expenses to a government contract was another matter.

Jim Dolly, glaring at diners whose heads had turned at the dispute, said nothing, and though his appetite seemed unaffected, he remained sullen and indignant and barely spoke again till he was almost done eating.

"They do anything different?" he asked, and the line cook hit a bell in the window.

"Who?" Fred said.

"With a woman, I mean," Jim Dolly said.

"Two jolts, same drop." Fred thought. "Not sure about the current—I understand she's a small gal."

"Right." Jim Dolly nodded. "I just thought they'd do something different."

"Took three for Mrs. Rosenberg," Fred said.

"That's not what I mean."

"You mean protocol?"

"I mean a woman. I don't know."

"She's no walk in the park," Fred said.

"So I heard," Jim Dolly said. "Hell hath no fury, right?"

"Angel dust," Fred said.

"That's what I heard," Jim Dolly said. "That shit, they snap handcuffs on that shit. Pull out their own teeth."

Or pick up a tree ax, Fred recalled. "And heaven has no rage . . ."

"Jesus," Jim Dolly said. "And both of em?" He sounded kind of impressed.

". . . like love turned to hate."

"Bet I know what went first. My old girl just called a lawyer."

"I understand she's born again," Fred said.

"Bet he was too," Jim Dolly said. He thought. "But still. I don't know."

Fred said, "We didn't create the market."

"Still," Jim Dolly said. "A woman."

"A human being," Fred said. "That's why we're here. You want his and hers hardware?"

"You're not funny," Jim Dolly said.

"I'm not trying to be."

"I mean, even if I was for it."

Fred looked at him. "You're saying you're against it?"

Jim Dolly wiped his mouth. "Sure I am. You didn't know?"

Fred drank some coffee. "I guess we never discussed it."

"So? I play the harmonica too. Does it matter?"

"I don't know." Fred drank some more coffee. "I guess not necessarily."

"Bet your little ass it doesn't. Matter of fact, it's my angle."

"That so?" Fred chain-lit another one.

"Think about it." Jim Dolly frowned, fanned the air. He stood and looked for the men's room, left Fred to think about it and pick up the bill.

The governor of Indiana left a ten-percent tip. Fred used the men's room after Jim Dolly, then got a cup of coffee to go. Jim Dolly wanted to drive but Fred talked him out of this as well. He wasn't kidding about the harmonica. They didn't talk much. Fred glanced back when he could to check on the status of their cargo. The blanket was secure but the shape unmistakable. Suspended in its dark web, riderless, the road and country falling away behind it through the back windows into nothing.

By dusk they were in Michigan City. It was too late to get into the facility but the deadline was first thing in the morning. Fred hadn't been in a prison since his father was a guard. They found a motel with a bar and grill across the parking lot, got a six-dollar room with no television, and unwound, each in his way. Everything was the same color. Fred pulled up the armchair, opened his briefcase and sat with notes and agenda spread out on the bedspread before him. Jim Dolly lay on the other double with his jacket off, eyes closed, mouth open, almost as loud as the air conditioner.

At eleven he sat up abruptly and mechanically like something programmed for nocturnal activity. Thumped into the bathroom rubbing his neck, peed, ran water, came out smoothing his hair and reaching for his jacket.

"Think I'll run across the way for a minute here," Jim Dolly said and breathed into his hand. "Grab a drink?" The question was a formality.

Fred stretched. "It's been a long one. Think I'll just catch the news."

"Troublemaker." Jim Dolly put on his jacket. "Don't wait up."

"Take it easy," Fred said. "We've got a show to put on tomorrow."

He'd forgotten there was no TV. The pillow was round and stiff, like sleeping on a football, but he didn't wait up. A woman laughed and woke him. He lay there blinking, turned his head. Jim Dolly's bed was empty but held the shape of his body as if he lay there invisible. Fred looked for a clock that wasn't there. He'd taken off his watch. A car door slammed.

He was cold.

He looked in the bathroom, went to the window and discreetly parted the curtain like he didn't want to be seen. The lights across the parking lot were still lit to the bass thump of country music. He turned off the air and stepped outside. The night was cool. The van had grown a skin of moisture, the windows frosted blind. Drone of defective neon and the streetlights like gallows. Nothing on the highway. He started for the bar and grill and then heard the woman laugh again.

He stopped and looked at the van. It moved.

The ice machine dumped ice under the stairs next to the office but Fred kept his eye on the van. It was rocking gently, fore and aft, like a kid's ride outside a discount store, a rocket you drop a dime into. He went around behind it but did not try to see into the windows. The woman was making other sounds now. He heard Jim Dolly now: "I can adjust the . . ."

"Sure," she gasped. "I can't believe it."

"I told you."

"*Shhhit.*"

"Put your leg through . . . break this sonofabitch in."

The leaf springs started to squeak. Fred stood there till he heard a car coming down the road, then hurried back to the room as if he would be caught at something.

He drove to Kentucky alone. This time the trip was longer but went by faster. He pulled into a parking lot like any other except for the blue state flag. The state seal was a picture of two men embracing, one a frontiersman, the other in city clothes like a politician. Fred passed beneath them and walked in the front door, into X-rays, a metal detector, a visitors' log passed back and forth under a bulletproof window. He was searched and questioned, then escorted to the superintendent's office by an old corrections major who never said a word. The superintendent was waiting for him with the chief of maintenance. Everyone shook hands, and they asked Fred if he'd taken 71 down.

"Forty-two," Fred said. "U.S. Highway. I like to see things." He'd spent the night in Louisville.

"Lou-a-ville," the chief of maintenance said.

"Is this the South?" Fred asked.

"Depends whose office you're in," the superintendent said and led the way. He and the chief of maintenance carried walkie-talkies, and each an outsize gut like another occupational accessory.

Pale green corridors, guards in a glass bubble, monitors throwing gray light up in neutral faces. They looked up reluctantly, as if everything they needed was there on closed-circuit.

Words exchanged, fishing trips and family. A door slammed open and slammed shut, led to other doors, stairs; a courtyard, a gate, the yard.

"We're safe," the superintendent assured him. "Try not to make eye contact."

The sky was the same blue you saw from the freeway but now you were trapped under it. Walls, wire, towers, dark corners in broad daylight. Fred in the middle. He looked at the ground, red clay, heard the mild rubber of handball, the clank of weights. He smelled smoke and lit one. Moved past men knotted together by race, religion, age, affiliation unknown. Muscle and ink. Alone or in groups, they watched without looking and were watched in turn from above, the guards with small mirrors for eyes.

The chief of maintenance had tried to plant grass but it grew thinly and in patches.

"Rock's just too close to the surface," he said, breathless.

"Makes it harder to tunnel out," the superintendent said. "You really should check out the raceway if you have time. Or Lake Barkley this time of year."

"There's always the caves," the chief of maintenance said, "since you like to see things."

"I'll start here," Fred said. "Where's the death row yard?"

"You're in it," the chief of maintenance said. "Eye contact."

"We've mainlined them into the general population," the superintendent said. "Everyone here's either CP or life and fifty. They've got nothing left to prove—haven't had a single fatality on my watch."

"Cut your throat soon as look at you," the chief of maintenance muttered. (And they looked.) "There's always something to prove."

"A couple-three stabbings, fights—schoolyard stuff," the superintendent said. "But we're not taking any chances. No one knows you're here."

"They know," Fred said. "They know everything," and they came to a black stone building, six-sided, like a mausoleum with a forty-foot chimney.

"Well that's a good thing," Fred said, looking up.

"We don't want to flush it into the sewer system," the chief of maintenance said, "but I guess you know all about all that." They went in.

Black-stone cool. In the center a squat metal capsule like a submersible, built for depths where light won't reach and alien fragile creatures live out their lives in crushing dark. Rust eating through the paint. Two oval windows slanted like eyes, insectile, an oval door with a wheel lock and six toggles. It was open five inches or so and the chief of maintenance grabbed the wheel. The door screamed open the rest of the way and Fred stepped inside.

"These damn things," he said, as if wearily familiar.

A steel chair bolted to the floor, a lead bucket beneath it. Fred sat, produced a notepad and pencil.

"You sure you want to do that?" the superintendent said.

"Got to check it for comfort," Fred said and wrote something down.

"Well?" the superintendent said.

"A rubber pad would help."

The chief of maintenance pointed to the bucket. "We fill it

90

up with sulfuric acid, eighteen percent solution. Then we drop in the briquettes."

There was a trip tray under the seat. Their voices had a metal edge.

"I've designed a gas generator," Fred said. *Cylindrical vessel containing hydrocyanic acid, boiled by an electrically heated water jacket*, the catalog said.

"A nitrogen burst system to clean the pipes afterwards—how do you clean up?"

"Ammonia and bleach," the chief of maintenance said. "Coveralls, gas masks . . ."

"Gas masks?" Fred said. "You're lucky to be alive. You should be breathing oxygen."

The chief of maintenance looked at the superintendent. "It's not like we do one a week," he said, and the superintendent hadn't done one at all.

"Glad to hear it," Fred said, and he scribbled. "The air in the chamber should be preheated to prevent condensation on the walls. This will expedite cleanup. What about clothes?"

"The coveralls are rubberized," the chief of maintenance said.

"I mean the body."

"Well that's a bit of a problem."

"Don't give them any. They can kill you as well."

"You're recommending I conduct an execution in the nude?" the superintendent said.

"Just the inmate," Fred said and tried a smile, but all they saw were bad teeth and waited for them to hide again.

"A pair of boxer shorts," he said. "Shave the body hair for good measure."

"I thought dignity was your watchword," the superintendent said.

"It's one of them," Fred said, "but whoever built this thing didn't have dignity much in mind. Or efficiency," he said. "Or safety. In the end it's about how they go, not what they wear. Clothes are clothes. This thing's about as bad for your health as it is for theirs." He stood. "Let's take a look at these seals." He ran his hands around the edge of the doorway, the windows. "Gaskets are shot."

"We coat them with Vaseline," the chief of maintenance said.

"They should be replaced," Fred said. Neoprene, Teflon, pickled asbestos. "As an added precaution the chamber should operate at a negative pressure." He recommended two pounds per square inch.

He'd designed a vacuum pump.

"Anything else?" the superintendent asked.

Gas detectors, alarms, proper ventilation, emergency breathing apparatus, first aid . . . Goddamn things.

He tapped the hull with his knuckle and it rang.

"How much is this party getting to run me?" the superintendent said.

"Depends," Fred said. "At this point I'm not sure what would be more cost effective: refurbishing the old unit or outright replacement." He told them he had a fully designed model on the drafting board—a two-seater—but not that it would run them two hundred thousand dollars.

"Let's go back to my office," the superintendent said.

When they stepped out of the building a shriveled old man no taller than Fred stood waiting for them. He was thin and pale and shirtless, ribs and veins, and his hair was cut short except for a narrow ribbon of it that hung between his shoulder blades. Dark purplish growths erupted from his chest and face like overripe fruit. He was looking at Fred and Fred looked back and saw an old man who was still in his twenties.

"Are you Mr. Death?" the ancient boy said.

"My name's Fred," Fred said.

The superintendent raised his walkie-talkie but didn't use it. "Stand down, William," he said. "You know what'll happen."

The inmate stepped obediently back and to the side. "I won't make any trouble, sir, you know me. I just wanted to ask Mr. Fred here something is all."

"I'll talk to him," Fred said.

"That's my call if you don't mind," the superintendent said, and he looked at this boy like a parent who understands he must treat each of his children differently. Then he looked at the other inmates. The chief of maintenance seemed to be shaking his head.

"All right," he said then, "what have you got," and made some kind of gesture to the guns above and behind them. The chief of maintenance stood back with a handkerchief over his mouth.

The superintendent wouldn't let them shake hands.

"I hear you're some kind of executioner," the young man said. "Somebody in the yard called you that. No offense."

"I'm surprised you hear anything at all since nobody knows I'm here," Fred said. "I'm an engineer and a consultant. I design, build, and sell hardware. Some training. I don't wear a hood, and I don't push the button."

"I thought it was a lever."

"Doesn't matter if it's a daisy chain as long as it works," Fred said. "My job is to make it easier for everyone. I didn't create the market, but if that's where you're headed," and he nodded slightly toward the black stone he'd just stepped from, "better for your sake I'm here."

The young man considered this. "Be straight with me then," he said. "Not like her," and he seemed for a moment to be looking somewhere else. "She told me to close my eyes, left me on a swing in the playground—I just kept waiting for the next push . . . Mamaw and Papaw raised me up, gave me love, but he wouldn't give me twelve dollars for a squirrel gun. I waited till they were asleep in their bed . . ."

"All right now," the superintendent said. "What is it you need, son?"

"I just mean I'll take what I got coming, sir. And if your gas don't do me this monster will." He waved his hand over his face and chest, the burgeoning sores. "Caught it in Fayetteville—unless you can get it from a woman. Anyway, no one bothers me now. Guess we'll see what comes first."

"Sounds like you've made peace with it to me," Fred said.

"I didn't say I wasn't scared."

"Then what can I tell you?"

"Well I've heard things, sir. About guys shaking, beating their heads against the pole, eyes bugged, foaming at the mouth like dogs . . . that don't sound so easy to me."

"Cyanide gas has to be breathed to do its job," Fred said. "When inhaled it is instantly fatal. Don't fight it and it won't hurt."

"So in other words you all couldn't do it without me."

"William," the superintendent said, "that's not a question."

"I suppose you could put it that way," Fred said.

The young man looked into the ground. "Can you give me a way to go?"

"That's on you," Fred said. "Don't fight it. When you're strapped in listen for the pellets dropping in the bucket beneath you."

"I don't know . . ."

"You'll hear them dissolving."

"Like Alka-Seltzer," the chief of maintenance said without irony.

"When you hear that sound," Fred said, "close your eyes and count to three."

"Fast or slow?" the young man asked softly, and the superintendent said his name again.

"Count to three and take a deep breath," Fred said, "and when you open your eyes you'll be standing on the other shore. You can clear your lungs there and draw fresh breath. Someone will call your name, your true name." And the old boy stood intent as if listening for it now. "You can lay down your cross then, William," Fred said. "Follow that voice and go home."

The young man looked like he wanted to step forward, but wouldn't cross the line the superintendent had drawn. He looked thoughtful. "So I'll get my push?"

"Show us how to die and you might teach us how to live," Fred said. He put a hand in his pocket. "You should talk to your clergyman."

The young man shrugged. "Chaplain Dan just says punks ain't in the book."

"Stand down now, son," the superintendent said, and raised his walkie-talkie again. "Time to go on about your business. We've all got things to do."

The young man was already backing up. "Yessir, sir. Sorry to hold you all up. Thanks very much for your time, Mr. Death-fredsir." He turned back into the yard and what business he had left there. He turned back and they could just hear him, speaking softly to himself, repeating a phrase like the lost child in the children's story chanting there's no place like home. But they couldn't hear exactly what his version was, and then it was lost in the general murmur of the yard.

They walked back through the yard toward the gate. "So how many of these affairs have you sat in on, Mr. Death?" the superintendent asked. He seemed impressed.

"Fred," Fred said. "I've never been invited."

She said she liked to be scared so he took her to a double feature at the drive-in. In the first one five college kids rent a cabin in the deep woods. The virgin, an archaeology major, stumbles upon a manuscript bound in human flesh, its text inscribed in blood. She recites a passage and invokes a horde of evil spirits. The cabin is besieged, the students possessed one by one, transformed, impaled, beheaded, shot, burned, bludgeoned, dismembered, the archaeology major raped by sentient trees. Only the dropout survives—or does he?

"That was twisted," she said happily at the intermission. "Are you hungry?"

Fred offered to go to the concession stand. She'd screamed up an appetite and ordered a list of items that she qualified with a large Diet Coke. It was a long walk.

He negotiated the parking lot, tried to avoid speaker wires stretched between cars like booby traps, arms stuck out of windows ending in cigarettes. People walked their dogs. They sat on car hoods reclining against windshields, peered from the backs of station wagons, dangled legs from tailgates, deployed lawn chairs and blankets and blasted heavy metal from auxiliary speakers. Reek of beer and varieties of smoke. There was a playground in front of the screen and during the intermission it was overrun with brightly lit children. They flooded the slide, the seesaws, crawled through tunnels, climbed. They swung on the swings, disappearing in darkness at the height of the arc. Distended shadows cavorted on the big white screen at his back like the tableau of a feature not on the marquee.

During the day it was a flea market.

The restrooms were in the same building as the concessions. They smelled of piss and mothballs and worse and not a single toilet was flushed. Fred in his suit standing over a porcelain trough next to a guy in an Iron Maiden T-shirt, each with a cigarette stuck to his lower lip.

"Think the poor bastard made it?" the guy said.

"Bet he makes it to Part Two," Fred said. He tried to speak without breathing.

"They like to leave you hanging."

"Like to set up the next one," Fred said, and the other guy left without washing his hands as if already on his way to the box office.

The line in the concession stand snaked around two long steel rails. Pinball and video games, the light heavy and yellow with grease. You could almost see the kid from Kentucky here, playing *Pac-Man*, pulling on an Icee the size of a fire extinguisher. Fred bought hot dogs, fries, popcorn, a shake, Coke, dispensed ketchup and mustard and liquefied cheese from huge jugs equipped with plungers like detonators. Outside he joined the audience returning to their vehicles, purchases carefully arrayed in hands and arms like offerings. There was a shoving match in the gravel.

He got back to the car just as the floodlights over the screen went dark and there appeared an animated countdown to the next feature.

"I thought those devil trees got you," she said and took things off his hands.

"What's this one about?"

"'Death is just the beginning,' it just said." Again.

This time the agent of resurrection is a serum that glows in the dark. A decapitated zombie lurches around campus with its head tucked under its arm. Comes upon the dean's daughter strapped nude to a table. Uses its tongue but not to talk.

"He ain't shy," she said. "Don't rescue her just yet!" and a hundred horns agreed. Fred heard an invitation and spent ten minutes insinuating his arm around her shoulders. He touched her knee, found a bulge and cupped it. She pulled at her shake. A scent came off her he couldn't quite define. He reached in as if to find its source, groped like someone feeling for change in a sofa. She drew the line.

"We can go to my house," he said. "No one's there." No one ever was.

"I have certain rules," she said, open and shut.

Fred fell back. She had her rules, her honor, he had what he had. He rolled down the window, lit a cigarette.

"You understand," she said.

"What's not to?" he said.

"Is there garbage?" she said, and he took her empty cup and dropped it in the back. She reached for his zipper.

"I thought—"

"There's other things we can do," she said and commenced bringing him back to life as well.

3. *To calculate Rope Length, Subtract Chin Height from Scaffold Crossbeam Height and add Drop Distance from Drop Distance Table.*

4. *Using three-quarter (¾) inch Manila hemp, mark rope at Rope Length and cut additional seven (7) feet.*

5. *Boil rope for one (1) hour and stretch while drying to eliminate all spring, stiffness, and tendency to coil. Dry thoroughly.*

6. *Make loop as shown from Standing Length to Running End. Distance from A to B should be approximately eighteen (18) inches. Distance from C to Running End should be approximately thirty-five (35) inches.*

7. *Wrap Running End six (6) turns. No extra rope should remain.*

8. *Pull Running End to tighten loops, then lock loops and form Knot by pulling down at D and pulling up on Running End.*

9. *Slide Knot up or down Standing Length to adjust size of Noose.*

10. *Lubricate Knot. Melted paraffin is recommended.*

He was invited to Holman for dinner. Made four states in eighteen hours. The top of Alabama was pine trees and hills, the bottom mangrove swamps, palm trees, alligators, a dog-sized species of rodent like a cross between a beaver and a rat. In between, the state was a vast sideshow: congregations of snake handlers, a moon rocket at a rest stop, a tiny museum whose sole display was Hitler's typewriter, the woman who'd been struck by a meteor; there was the birthplace of Sun Ra and Hank Williams's grave, an underground dance hall with a seven-acre lake. He passed tar paper shacks, houses on stilts. A derelict mansion among strange-looking trees like deformed giants in suits of leaves. Near the Gulf he was briefly lost, got on Highway 64 and crossed a river officially called the Styx. Passed the Isle of Bones.

The regional director of the Board of Corrections lived across the street from the prison in a big white house. Piazzas, a small lake out front, bald cypress hung with Spanish moss. After a tour of the facility, dinner was barbecued catfish and squash casserole at a big oak table in the dining room. An elderly dark-skinned woman in a maid's uniform served them. The night was hot and a fan hummed in the window. After the prayer the regional director apologized.

"We've got central air but it's on the blink again, I'm afraid."

"If you like I could take a look at it after dinner," Fred said.

The regional director's wife lowered her fork. "The warden used to live here. He's probably getting even with us for pulling rank. Anyway," she said, "we couldn't possibly allow a guest." Her voice was soft and lilted the lump of his surname. On the drive down he'd heard other people you couldn't make head nor tails.

"Fred," Fred said.

"Could we allow Fred to pass the greens?" the regional director's son inquired. An enormous crew cut kid, so big he had to sit with one leg off his chair.

"You've got arms," the regional director said and gave his son a look.

"He certainly does," the regional director's wife said and asked Fred if the meal was to his liking.

"Never had anything like it."

"Just ain't enough of it," the regional director's son said. He looked at Fred. "Guess you do a little cookin of your own."

The regional director gave his son another look and cleared his throat.

"I'm sure Fred doesn't want to talk shop," his wife said, more to appease her husband, it seemed, than admonish her son.

"I defer to the custom of my hosts," Fred said.

"What's that mean?" the regional director's son said. "I'm a redneck."

"Can we just pretend?" the regional director said.

"I'm sure Fred knows better," his mother said.

"I think everyone knows something the next fella doesn't," Fred said. The world's wisdom came in bits and pieces.

The regional director's wife didn't appear to have heard. She was younger than her husband and looked at her son as though they were alone. "Not everyone was put here to invent the wheel," she said.

"Amen," the regional director said.

"I was put here to anchor the O-line," the regional director's son told Fred and stuffed his mouth. He was sweating. Bones cracked.

"Easy," his mother said, "you have all year." She looked at her guest. "You believe he's just a freshman? U of A."

"Damn redshirt," her husband grumbled.

The regional director's son looked hard at Fred. "Tigers or Tide?"

Fred looked back. "How's that?"

"Auburn or U?" the boy asked impatiently.

"I'm sure he doesn't have a dog in that fight," the regional director said. "For Pete's sake."

"Buckeye?" his wife said. "Wolverine?"

"What's a seven-course meal at Auburn?" the regional director's son said.

"We've heard it," his father said.

"A six-pack and a possum," the boy said, and the maid appeared with a pitcher of iced tea and refilled his glass. She refilled his mother's from another decanter. She had worked this house for twenty years, supported her family and put a child through school filling glasses and serving dinner, was

respected and called ma'am in her own community, and though
she too knew something the next fellow didn't, she shared
nothing and retired to the next room to sit and read by the
light of a small lamp until called for.

"Getting a little low on the grits," the regional director's
son said loudly and to no response.

"Getting a little deaf in her dotage," his mother said.

"Depends who's doing the talking," his father said.

"I don't suppose you played sports in school?" the regional
director's wife asked Fred. Her son made a sound.

"Don't suppose you ever had your head flushed in a turlet?"
he said, and his father thumped the table with the butt of his
knife. "You'll have to excuse my boy, he has trouble thinking
and chewing at the same time." He spoke to his food. "Any more
noise like that and he'll be chewing shoe leather for dessert."

"I'm not sure that's punishment," the regional director's
wife said, and her son said nothing but stuffed his mouth as if
against the coming privation.

"Fred's a competition shooter," the regional director said.

"Well that's just guns," his wife said. "I mean something
physical." She performed delicate surgery on her fish.

"I did the best I could with what I was given," Fred said.
"I have my interests."

"Putting bad boys to bed early," she said.

"I make things," Fred said.

"Y'all hear about the Auburn alum got pulled over for
speeding?" the regional director's son asked.

"Cop says, 'You got any ID?'" his mother said.

"Tiger says, 'Bout what?'" her son said and something flew into the fan. The maid returned to the kitchen. Fred asked the regional director's wife if she minded living across the street from the prison.

"You mean 'the facility'?" She hooked her fingers. "I sleep like a baby," she said, lifting her glass as if to say she had help. "But my friends say they could never."

"You have friends?" her son said and touched a small pouch of loose flesh under her chin. She took his hand and put it on the table.

"Personally I think they like coming here—makes them feel like they're doing something dangerous."

"No one ever stays," the regional director's son said.

"You can't see much from here," his mother said, "but I hear things. I hear them playing. Basketball, mainly, and I know what a home run sounds like." Her hand still covered her son's. "That perfect *crack!* Right in the middle of it all," and her voice became both intimate and far away. "Haven't heard one in a while. You don't suppose he—" She looked at Fred almost suspiciously. "How do you get into that line of work anyway? Doesn't seem to be much competition."

"Well that ain't healthy," the regional director's son said.

"Just born to it, you could say," Fred said.

"Who could be born to that," she wondered.

"Say a friend of the family, then," Fred said. Say one thing led to another.

A grandfather clock somewhere struck the hour. The regional director's son raised his hand from the back of the classroom. "I have a question," and there was a hopeful silence.

"If you had your choice," he said to Fred, "what way would you pick?"

Fred paused, expecting another censure. Then he swallowed some coffee and said, "Pistol shot to the back of the head."

"Good Lord," the regional director said.

"All I've got is the Kenmore in the kitchen," his wife said. "Do you know Sylvia Plath?"

"Not personally."

"You've been in the kitchen?" the regional director said.

"If it was me?" his son said.

"Eating yourself to death is not an option," the regional director said.

"Eating ain't what I had in mind, but in present company I'll go with the one where they shoot you full of drugs and you just fall asleep. Seems like a no-brainer to me."

The father said nothing.

"Not as easy as you think," Fred said. "The State of Texas has done it forty times and I'd say eighty percent of them were botches."

"Damn Longhorns," the regional director's son said.

"You've got at least three drugs involved and it's not easy to administer them in the proper dosage with the correct timing—especially by hand. How would you like to suffocate, slowly, but you can't tell anybody because you're paralyzed and everybody thinks you're asleep?"

"It's not all it's cracked up to be," the regional director's wife said.

The regional director's son had cleaned his plate. You couldn't tell if he was listening.

"Well I've got a little room left," the regional director said. "Anybody for pecan pie?"

"Just one more question," the regional director's son said and put down his utensils and clasped his hands, affecting a scholarly brow. "Does it take more juice to fry a colored person than a white one?" And something broke in the kitchen.

The regional director was an avid collector of guns, and after dessert he showed Fred some of his rarer pieces: a French palm pistol dating from 1802, an assassin's weapon that looked like a yo-yo with a barrel; a German handgun that was hardly any bigger with four short barrels, one placed on top of the other. They were just for show; the regional director couldn't have fired these relics if he'd wanted to, as the ammunition for them no longer existed.

After the guns there was billiards, and then the regional director took Fred to the verandah at the back of the house to remind him why he was there. Held a glass of brandy and smoked a cigar; Fred drank from his bottomless black cup. It was the hottest night he'd ever known. The porch light showed him a few palmettos but could not further penetrate a muggy darkness filled with frogs and crickets and other sounds he couldn't begin to guess. One of them was a deep bellowing moan you could feel in your breastbone, and Fred was sure the wood rail under his hand was vibrating.

"Either my boy's still hungry," the regional director said, "or that's a bull gator looking for a girlfriend."

"Think he's headed our way?" Fred said, half joking.

"If he'd have gotten here a little earlier we could have had stew for supper."

"I don't suppose it tastes like chicken."

"More like pork actually. But he's probably a mile off. It's rattlesnakes you want to watch out for."

Sheet lightning. It was hurricane season.

Somewhere in the house they heard the regional director's wife laughing at the television, then a car with a bad muffler pulling up out front. The horn played a school song, there was more laughter. The voice of the regional director's son. Then a car door slammed and the muffler roared off, trailing obscenities, a rebel yell.

"So what do you think?" the regional director said.

"Boys will be boys."

"That's not what I'm talking about."

"It's not just a piece of paper," Fred said. "I put my name to it and something goes wrong, I have to live with that. Not to mention what it would do to my credibility."

Something snapped and he jumped. The lantern-like device on the porch that lures insects with light and kills them with voltage. Patented in 1932. It snapped and flickered, and then in vast amplification another round of lightning blue-lit the sky, as if a far greater scourge were being checked at the world's threshold.

"Looks like a bad one's on the way," the regional director said. "Here's the best I can do: we let you make minimal repairs now, just enough to bring us up to speed for the twenty-third. We carry out the protocol as scheduled, then let you go ahead with full replacement."

Fred put out his cigarette. "Can I sleep on it?"

"If you do it'll be at a motel. Say yes and you can have the guest room. I wouldn't wait too long though; out here we get hail that'll crack your skull."

Out front, across the street, the prison was silent.

ATTORNEY FOR PLAINTIFF: Sir, in your professional opinion, is the electric chair of the State of Alabama in adequate repair to perform a safe, humane, and efficient execution?

STATE ATTORNEY: Objection. The witness has already signed an affidavit. He's just trying to get even with the State for rebidding his contract.

COURT: Counselor?

ATTORNEY FOR PLAINTIFF: Your Honor, a stipulation of the witness's contract provided that he supervise and consult during the execution of my client to ensure that the equipment perform optimally—it has already been demonstrated to malfunction in the past. In annulling the agreement the State has disallowed this participation, thereby exacerbating the risk of another botched procedure.

PLAINTIFF: Can I say something?

COURT: No, that's why you have an attorney. The witness may answer the question, preferably in layman's terms.

WITNESS: The condition of the hardware notwithstanding, I'm concerned with the State's plan to use three jolts of electricity during the procedure—especially the two-minute application of two hundred and fifty volts at the end.

ATTORNEY FOR PLAINTIFF: Wouldn't this just finish the job?

WITNESS: On the contrary. Even if the first applications cause brain death, the lower voltage might act as a defibrillator, restarting your client's heart and leaving a brain-dead vegetable strapped in the chair. And if the electrodes were to fail again, the state would have no means of completing the sentence.

PLAINTIFF: Can I just say something?

COURT: Counselor, please restrain your client.

ATTORNEY FOR PLAINTIFF: No further questions.

Fred's expert witness fee was five hundred dollars. And in South Carolina. And in Oklahoma.

Jim Dolly saw to the punch. The secretary had decorated a tree in a corner of the front office, hung a wreath at the door, and sprayed artificial snow out of a can. She drew the recently acquired blinds. There was a meat tray and gift exchange, there was music. The tree was fragrant. Jim Dolly brought a guest, the woman who'd originally held the secretarial position. She professed no hard feelings, as though this were her prerogative, and drank so much of the punch she even tried to dance with the draftsman, admitted to hard feelings after all, spent the last half hour or so kneeling in the bathroom. Fred brought the night gal. The machinist, having received the gift of cologne (in a set that included eau de toilette spray and deodorant stick) from an anonymous giver, stood near the bowl. Outside, another four inches fell.

The office closed early on New Year's Eve and was closed on New Year's Day. Everybody but Jim Dolly came in the day after that. He didn't call. "Just like last year," the secretary said, and Fred remembered, but Jim Dolly didn't come in or call the next day either. The secretary dialed his home number and no one answered but a machine. She left a message.

"He came in last year," she muttered. She worried about people. The draftsman looked up and looked back down.

That afternoon Fred got in his Buick and drove to the far west side. The sun was out but it was fifteen degrees and even the light of the new year looked frozen, the snow and ice incandescent.

Jim Dolly lived in a high-rise condo overlooking the arctic desolation of the lake. The building stood a couple hundred yards off the street and was occupied mainly by singles and retirees. It was self-contained as a moon base: six elevators, two swimming pools, a tennis court, putting green, sauna, weight room, handball and racquetball courts, a film society, deli, restaurant and lounge; there were tenants who hadn't left in years. There was a receptionist and security guard in the lobby, and a warm and spacious foyer that was as far as they'd let you get.

There was a phone. A panel of buttons and numbers and Fred pressed the button next to Jim Dolly's number. The foyer was carpeted. Fred pressed the button again. A kid came in delivering groceries and the receptionist buzzed him in. Fred pressed the lobby button and spoke to the receptionist. He asked about Jim Dolly and watched her tell him over the phone that she wasn't permitted to discuss the comings and goings of tenants but would be happy to take a message. She didn't sound happy. The guard looked elsewhere.

Fred drove once around the lot looking for Jim Dolly's

Lincoln. He didn't see it but there was an underground garage he had no access to, and he followed a slow-moving truck equipped with a salt spreader back out to the street, keeping his distance and glad he believed in undercoating.

When he got back to the office the secretary looked up like she'd been waiting for him. She told him to call the bank. Also waiting were two serious-looking gentlemen in Jim Dolly's office. Polite but not excessively so.

At T + 7 seconds the applause is over. The ship begins to roll. It has cleared the tower, cleared the sea, and we can hear Houston and we can hear the wire-thin radio voice of the crew: the commander, the pilot, the first and second mission specialists. "Roger your roll," Houston says, and the vehicle turns on its long axis, the shuttle swinging around and leaning back, arcing away from us, all fire and white and sky.

At T + 15 the second mission specialist says what sounds like "Fuckin hot," and that's all we hear her say. "Oookay," the commander says a second later, and Houston says, "Roll program confirmed." We are switched to another camera then, perhaps airborne, a longer lens, the better to track this furiously burning progress.

"There's Mach one," the pilot says at T + 40 seconds and at T + 53 Houston says, "Velocity twenty-two hundred fifty-seven feet per second, altitude four point three nautical miles." At T + 1 minute, 7 seconds, all we can see of the ship is the white column of its trail and the coronal brilliance atop which it rides, a meteor returning to its origin, and Houston says, "Go to throttle up."

Another camera and we see the vehicle again, flattened, grainy, and the commander says, "Roger go at throttle up!" at T + 1 minute, 10 seconds. Three seconds later the pilot says, "Uh-oh." We hear a loud burst of static, almost a roar, and even after the ship is no longer a ship, consumed by its own suddenly engorged exhaust, upward progress momentarily unchecked, even then Houston continues to report velocity (twenty-nine hundred feet per second), altitude (nine nautical miles), downrange distance (seven nautical miles), and it is not for another twenty-five seconds, when what remains is a thick trail of white forked like a two-headed serpent of smoke, and a tiny unaccounted-for fragment of the stack darting crazily across the utter blue, jetting smoke and flame as if skywriting an epitaph in some deranged longhand, not until T + 1 minute, 38 seconds that the voice of Houston says, "Flight controllers here looking very carefully at the situation," that he says, "Obviously a major malfunction . . ."

He says, "We have no downlink."

The Department of Corrections called. New Jersey? Delaware? The draftsman couldn't be sure; he didn't like answering the phone. He and Fred took turns because they no longer had a secretary. Nor was there a machinist and they now worked out of Fred's basement, but the commissioner of the Department of Corrections was on the line and he needed a machine.

They'd passed a bill. The statute forbade the participation of doctors. Fred put on his wool-blend topcoat and his felt hat and drove to the library.

The main branch was downtown, a big gray block of granite and terra cotta next to the old post office and more or less a repetition of it. Just inside the main entrance, beneath the two-story ceiling and cordoned off with velvet ropes, stood a scale replica of the terrestrial globe, six feet across and turning imperceptibly, once every twenty-four hours, like the planet to which you were so precariously attached with all its other inhabitants and their dreams and diseases and this blue reproduction, turning. Fred stood before it and cast his modest shadow on the Western Hemisphere, stamping his galoshes.

The restroom stank of homelessness. In the Popular Library heavily layered men and women falling through cracks landed momentarily in upholstered chairs, looking through magazines, some talking back to them, nodding over them as if in agreement. The old man at the Information Desk looked vaguely disappointed in Fred and said, "Science and Technology." This was Literature.

Down a winding flight of shiny stone steps and through an underground passage, a gallery of local history and progress—on one side the heroes of commerce, on the other men and women of color and their inventions: the traffic light, the gas mask, the carbon light bulb filament, the potato chip. Old photographs staring through an afterlife of dusty glass.

In Science and Technology Fred scrolled through microfilm, a stream of white print in a field of blue, occasionally stopping the blur to write down numbers. Euthanasia. Phlebotomy. Sodium Pentothal. R726.H86.

He took an elevator.

On the third floor he haunted the aisles and stacks, grabbing at spines, loading his arms. Some as old as relics, bindings cracked and peeling, shedding their leaves. Fred sat in the middle of a long table with banker's lamps, the light in the tall windows a cold, graduated blue. Dusk. Besides him there were just the young librarian and a few scattered patrons, one a thickly bearded man in a parka, wearing a dirty woolen cap, scribbling furiously in a notebook surrounded by obscure texts as though drafting an extremist manifesto. He moved his lips.

Truth serum—sodium pentothal—really just a potent sedative. Half-life of about twelve hours. Fred wrote it down. Used medically to induce coma at a dose of one and a half grams. What would, say, five grams do, he wondered and wrote it down.

They left one by one. The bearded man muttered: "Goddamn bill of attainder."

Pages yellowed, parched; sometimes they almost crumbled in his hand. The smell of them. Curare smells like nothing. It is extracted from a vine that grows in the Amazon. Witch doctors boil the leaves and roots, native hunters tip their arrows with it. Its synthetic equivalent: pancuronium bromide, a muscle relaxant derived by witch doctors in white lab coats. In the spaces between the lines Fred saw streams of molecules, flooding the neuromuscular junction like an army of officials waving their warrants, blocking the binding action of acetylcholine, preventing the contraction of muscle fiber. You stopped breathing.

Malouetia bequaertiana. The librarian laughed softly into the phone.

He could find nothing about lethal dosages and consulted

the protocol for putting down unwanted animals. Pentobarbital would pretty much destroy the respiratory system without any help, but imagine the righteous outcry. Better to stick to the medical literatures, to potassium chloride.

The procedure and equipment shall be designed to ensure that the identity of the individual actually administering the lethal substance shall be unknown even to said individual.

The bearded man was gone. The windows shiny with night. She sounded like she was in love.

You get potassium from eating bananas, also from South America. In larger doses it affects the conductivity of the cardiac muscle. Fred looked at waveforms.

His coat draped the back of his chair. The heart stops, filled with blood.

The young librarian said goodbye but didn't lower the phone. She pressed a button, cleared her throat of all affection and her voice filled the building, announced the library would close in twenty minutes.

Two days later Fred called his friend the warden at OSP and asked if he was still raising livestock in Minimum.

"Having a pig roast?" the warden asked.

"Furthering human progress," Fred said.

"How much hog does that call for?"

"Two hundred pounds should do."

The draftsman owned a van. He and Fred took out the backseats and covered the floor with old carpeting. At the farm the inmates covered the carpeting with straw and loaded the pig on a ramp. A big Yorkshire, pink and muscular, it balked at the top of the incline but they fooled it by holding a wooden board in its face. Then they leashed it to a frame stanchion so it couldn't get at its fellow passengers.

The draftsman drove. The pig commenced pissing and shitting as soon as the van was in motion. They opened the windows.

"You're going to enter history," Fred told the pig. He sat with a box of corn-cobs in his lap. "All you have to do is go to sleep."

The pig farted.

They checked into a motel on the Boulevard, just north of where it becomes the Strip. A double was thirty dollars and there were free adult movies and a wedding chapel and a complimentary continental breakfast. Neither Fred nor his draftsman had been to Las Vegas before, though the draftsman occasionally spent weekends in Atlantic City.

They rose early and went to the lobby, but all that remained of breakfast were a few pieces of fruit and some complimentary burnt coffee. In the van they headed south, drove past palm trees and signs familiar from the neon montage of movies and television, redolent of spectacle and exotic possibility, but at this hour looking like decorations the day after Christmas. Crooked bits of plastic spelled out the names of entertainers, performers either born to this place or reborn to it, working the end of the road.

It was already hot. The mountains were solid and close in the early light and there were underground nuclear detonations just sixty-five miles away.

They turned left on Convention Center Drive and drove toward the big silver dome. There was a hassle with the

parking lot attendant; they hadn't scheduled a slot at the loading dock. If Jim Dolly were there he would have told the guy
to tell it to Andrew Jackson, or Johnnie Walker, or just backed
him off. The last time with Jim Dolly had been Chicago, and
there'd been flashing of bills then too (though Fred knew now
where they'd come from), and drinking and glad-handing and
whoring and altercating, while meanwhile Fred manned the
booth, attended conferences, made notes, nursed a social drink,
went to bed early. His fifty-one percent.

He did not like asking for favors; they would carry it in
from their parking space. They had less than two hours to set
up but they were displaying only one product.

By ten the convention was in full swing. Men, mostly, with
name badges and plastic cups in their hands visited booths
where every conceivable device and application was promoted,
brochured, demonstrated, guaranteed: a dozen varieties of
handcuffs, restraints, portable cages, things made bulletproof,
knifeproof, flameproof; shields, visors, helmets, uniforms for
both guards and inmates, riot guns, tranquilizer darts, a multi-
purpose billy club that could spray Mace, deliver an electric
shock, transmit an officer-down but could it still just plain
knock the shit out of someone? A small metal vehicle about
the size of a shopping cart that was actually a one-man tank,
rolling almost noiselessly across the carpet. Women in scanty
modified guard uniforms with caps, fishnet, patrolled the room,
pouring champagne and proffering trays of hors d'oeuvres.

Some of the vendors offered their own refreshments, and
these were visited by a derelict of Shoshone descent who
seemed to have wandered in straight out of the desert. He wore

a dirty Hawaiian shirt and had long graying hair, no teeth, burnt leathered skin that looked as though it could deflect a knife blade and had done just that. He reeked of booze and old sweat and worse, and when he approached the women with the trays they veered off and gave him such clearance he could only stand with his hand empty and his eyes full, watching them pass.

Close to noon a small crowd had gathered in front of National Engineering, Inc., drawn by the gurney with its single armrest, the IV stand, the EKG machine, the black boxes. They were waiting for a demonstration but Fred and his draftsman could not recruit a single volunteer. It was an aspect of the industry that saw little light at these events, and beyond the matter of propriety, there was that of superstition.

The Indian approached. He stopped, looked about, pointed a finger at Fred. "You know a guy put out a little spread . . . wings, something," he advised, "guy could pull some business."

Fred looked at him, then looked away. Then he looked back at the visitor and said, "You help us out and I'll get you so many wings you can fly out of here."

"What're you selling?" the derelict asked, apparently unfamiliar with the theme of the event.

"Dignity," Fred said.

"And hardware," the draftsman said.

"I gotta sign something?" the man asked. The draftsman gave him a release form and he affixed to it a name which in English has no translation.

They laid him down on the gurney and secured his arm to the rest with an elbow splint. Fred noted the tracks of an old doper. It would have been necessary to perform a cutdown, make an incision in the neck or groin, lift out a good vein and insert the needle, and Fred, now a licensed phlebotomist, was qualified to train prison staff in just this procedure—it was part of the package, though he chose to not yet share this with his audience. Instead they covered the Indian with a gray woolen blanket and taped the IV line from the drip stand to his arm, covering it with a bandage so you couldn't quite tell it drained into a pail under the gurney.

"Saline solution," Fred explained to the growing crowd. "Makes it easier for the body to accept the drugs when we administer the cocktail."

"Cocktail," the volunteer repeated, eyes closed. "Happy hour."

They strapped him in with four sets of straps. The draftsman ran another line from a T-valve in the IV to a fitting at the bottom of the first black box.

The deputy warden from Mississippi looked at the volunteer and asked what was his crime.

"See his shirt?" someone said. "Does the condemned have anything to say?" someone said and at this a woman in the crowd spoke up against such exploitation, and when the man with her offered to take his place, the Shoshone lifted his head and spoke quite clearly on the score.

"Go find your own fuckin gig," he advised. "Guy's trying to make a living here."

"This is the delivery module," Fred said when the couple had gone, and opened a panel in the first black box. The syringes, upright, two rows of three.

"One set's backup," he explained, and the operations manager from Oklahoma asked, "What's your power supply?"

"Twelve-volt battery," Fred said. They'd taken it out of the van. "Rechargeable. In case of a power failure, the procedure can still be carried out. If need be it can complete six cycles at fifteen-minute intervals before it has to recharge."

"Hear that, Texas?" Oklahoma said. "Think you all can keep up now?"

Fred went to the other black box and stood to one side of it. The draftsman stood on the other and from under his breath Fred told him to get rid of his pipe. There were two keys in the front panel and two buttons. Fred faced his prospects.

"The death warrant has been read," he announced, and the volunteer seemed asleep, at peace and breathing evenly. "At a signal from the warden, or other designated event coordinator, the control module is armed."

He turned one of the keys, and the draftsman turned the other. A red light came on.

"The machine is now armed," he said, "but the cycle has not yet begun." He pressed a button above the key. The draftsman pressed the other one. The red light went off and an amber light came on.

"A computer inside the control module is now deciding which of us actuated the delivery," Fred said. "Once the decision is made it is erased from memory. It will never be known."

"My brother-in-law was playing the two-bit slots at Bally's last night?" the deputy director from Oklahoma said in a low voice. "Double Diamond, five paylines. Hit three on the diagonal, paid out twenty-five thousand quarters. Son of a bitch."

"Odds are still better at the tables," the operations manager said. "But what's worse: knowing or not?"

The amber light on the machine was replaced by green. "The call has been made," Fred said, and he went back to the first black box. The draftsman stayed where he was. The man in the gurney snored.

"The delivery module is armed," Fred said. "From here everything is automatic." A slender steel piston hung above each syringe. The draftsman said, "Foxfire one," and the first piston dropped as if on command.

Fred cleared his throat. "Fifteen cc's of ten percent sodium thiopental to induce a state of unconsciousness." You could hear liquid dribbling somewhere. When the syringe was empty the State of Texas raised his arm.

"Where I come from we do it by hand," he said.

"I'm aware," Fred said.

"We have a problem with bolus," Texas said. "Can your machine give a bolus?"

Fred explained how his machine could not give a bolus.

"We see some gasping and choking too."

"I recommend ten cc's of antihistamine," Fred said. "Before." Looking at his stopwatch. When he looked up the second piston dropped.

Foxfire two. The draftsman was late but there hadn't been much time to rehearse.

"First two's the worst two," someone said. The volunteer made a sound with his tongue. Fred stood in front of the gurney and demonstrated terminal breathing. Closed his eyes. A showstopper.

The man whose name has no English translation lay still.

Florida pointed to the EKG machine. "You forget to plug that in?"

"The electrocardiogram is part of the protocol mandated by the statute," Fred said. During the actual event it would be wired to the inmate and monitored by a state-appointed physician, or prison staff trained by Fred himself; he was certified for this as well.

Red, yellow, green, like a traffic light running in reverse. The Indian said "Checkmate" before the draftsman could say anything. The last one dropped. The EKG machine sat still and blank, but Fred had sample printouts on which someone's heart had inscribed its last moments. He showed them the waveforms, the smooth curves of normal sinus rhythm, then the idioventricular, its fading complexes. Then a straight line.

For the encore he demonstrated the manual overrides to be used in the event of a system failure.

They gave three more demonstrations that afternoon, attending to their stand-in between performances. After the last the State of Missouri approached and said, "How do you like your steak?" and New Jersey invited himself along. The draftsman had trouble waking up the volunteer. As he and Fred unbuckled the restraints, a security guard approached with a young woman in denim who seemed unaffiliated with the event. She wore a beaded necklace and her dark hair in two long braids and no expression on her face which, if you looked closely, might have borne some resemblance to the man who'd been executed by proxy four times that afternoon and whose mortal remains she might have come to claim. She never said a word, but Fred and the draftsman stepped aside as she snatched the blanket to the floor, knelt and revived the sleeper with a few words whispered in his ear, then led him through the parting crowd and away while Fred replaced the blanket to cover the stain he'd left on the mattress.

That evening they had prime rib at the Golden Steer on Sahara, where Sammy Davis Jr. had dined when they wouldn't let him eat in the casinos. Then Fred and his draftsman walked the pyrotechnics of the Strip, looked for souvenirs, dropped back into the crowds. There was a full-contact karate tournament at the Sands, but New Jersey had given them tickets to a magic show. They passed the Last Frontier, the Dunes, the Flamingo, the Tropicana; crossed the boulevard in front of taxis and limos edging impatiently forward, the traffic light so short-lived this might have been yet another game fixed in favor of the house.

In the casino they kept moving, past red felt and green, dealers raking and cutting in bow ties and vests, proving and washing and riffling, standing at empty tables shouting, "Three ways to play, four ways to win"; players standing or hitting, doubling down, splitting pairs, watching wheels, sitting on folding chairs in the keno lounge like revivalists in a prayer tent; men and women of every means and physical description surrounded by the same mountainous dark, a thousand ghost towns, the fossils of shark teeth eighty million years old. The House.

Cigarette girls and waitresses with trays full of cleavage and free drinks that weren't really free. You had to go through the slots to get to the theater; they still had time before the show. There were penny slots and there were machines in the high-limit lounge that cost a hundred dollars a spin. The draftsman played quarters. Fred left him sitting in front of the reels and went to the men's room. The guy standing at the urinal next to him was unshaven and red-eyed and looked to have slept in his clothes if at all. He was tapping the tiled wall with his forehead and muttering.

"All the stacks are in so there's no turning back. He goes all in and I call. He has sixty-five, flops the straight!" He tapped a little harder and stopped. Looked at Fred.

"Gimme ten bucks," he muttered Fred's way.

"I'm a little short myself," Fred said.

"Gimme five."

Fred stood there and shook. "Sorry."

"Fuck you."

Fred thought. "Same to you."

The guy laughed and said, "Gimme a cigarette," and Fred gave him one and when he left the guy was still standing in the urinal as if caught in its grip, muttering, "Who goes all in with a high pair?"

The draftsman was still pulling the lever. Fred watched. Circus music, fixed eyes, clatter and jingle of modest payouts. Fred watched and his mind worked. There were progressive jackpots now, they were probably using microprocessors. A guy could use something small and slender, work his way up the payout chute, trip a microswitch . . . but he was only amusing himself. He was an honest man.

A great burst of joy at one of the tables.

The draftsman stayed with the same machine. He won almost two hundred dollars, put it all back in, and probably would have kept going but it was time to see the magician.

—*Wie heissen Sie?*

—*Wo kommen Sie her?*

—*Was wollen Sie?*

—*Darf ich das Innere ihrer Maschine besichtigen?*

—*Was ist ihr Antrieb?*

—*Haben Sie eine Nachricht?*

The phone rings. The wind is howling. The phone is ringing and you pick up the line. You hear the wind, speak into the phone. The voice that issues from the static and hiss is unfamiliar, but you have waited all your life to hear it. It is old and trembling and speaks with a French accent. It knows your name. You are being called upon to testify—a man is on trial for what may be his life. The charges: corrupting history and defaming the dead. The wind howls. It asks only a moment of your time.

How did you get this number? you ask back.

From the warden in Mississippi, the Frenchman says across the lake of ice. But he is not a lawyer, he is a scholar, an expert in ancient texts and documents; he teaches at a small university you could not possibly have heard of. You picture a small wizened man, even smaller than yourself, wearing a bow tie and perhaps a pince-nez. He is not a lawyer but he is part of the defense team. The defendant's name begins at the end of the alphabet. It is also unfamiliar but the Frenchman has questions of his own: he asks about your background, your vocation, your expertise.

Fred was happy to oblige. He talked for almost an hour, chain-smoking, and he could tell the Frenchman was chain-smoking at the other end, listening. Fred would have kept talking had the Frenchman not interrupted; he would have to cut the call short. He apologized. They were very eager to meet him, he said, but the defendant was not permitted to travel. He invited Fred to Toronto. He said they would pay his airfare and accommodations.

"I don't fly," Fred said and asked if he could bring his fiancée. A date was agreed upon.

She insisted on separate rooms.

They took the Buick, another six-hour drive. They drove into a blizzard so heavy they couldn't see the taillights in front of them. Fred walked them through it, kept close to the guardrail; they couldn't see the markings of the road either. Niagara Falls was half-frozen, great white beards and tusks of ice hung in a mist as still as themselves. At the border a guard asked them what the purpose of their visit was.

"We're practicing for our honeymoon," she said in her seat.

"Professional reasons," Fred said.

The guard let them in.

She liked Toronto. The city was bigger than they'd expected, and cold, but the weather was clear. The people sounded almost American but were slightly nicer. The black people sounded like the white people. Distances were measured in meters and kilometers and the paper currency was exotically colored, as if there were nothing it couldn't buy. She liked it but Fred didn't; it reminded him of a parallel universe in a science-fiction film. Everything seems identical to where you come from until you begin to notice subtle but sinister discrepancies. They had colour instead of color.

They had rickshaws.

"*Aboat,*" she said, tickled. "There's just something *aboat* it."

The rooms reserved for them did not adjoin so they had to settle for one with two doubles. She said they could hang a blanket up between them like in what was that movie called? They relaxed for a while, watched Canadian content. She let him sit on the bed with her, on top of the covers. Fred looked at his watch. He put on his coat and they dry-kissed and he took the elevator down into the lobby and went out into the street. He had no luck hailing a cab and climbed into a rickshaw operated by a big tanned middle-aged man wearing a headband and shorts and sandals in February. He threw a blanket over Fred and headed off toward the office building where they waited. Fred closed his eyes at the intersections.

He walked to the end of the long hall he had been walking down all his life.

A door. A secretary in a cramped office, stacks of folders on her desk.

"They're waiting," she said.

They were waiting for Fred in a small conference room. Carpeted, a table, no windows. He recognized the Frenchman immediately, who was remarkably close in appearance to the man he had pictured over the phone. He took Fred by the shoulders and kissed his cheeks and whispered something in his own language. The lawyer shook his hand. She was an elegant, severe woman, headmistress or someone who trained horses, and here she was called a barrister. She introduced him to the defendant. The defendant spoke with a German accent and there was a yellow hard hat resting on his lap.

"People like to throw things once in a while," he explained, shaking hands. He was a big man with a large belly and a smooth pink face. Thinning hair. A square white bandage was taped to the crown of his head, and he peeled it half back to reveal a patch of discolored flesh. Stitches. "I hope no one throws anything at you."

"Me too," Fred said. "Why would they?" He took a pack of cigarettes from inside his jacket and the barrister asked him politely not to smoke. Fred complied. He believed in the innate goodness of women.

Her client asked him if he believed in UFOs. Fred asked him to repeat himself. He looked at the barrister, who did not look back.

"Flying saucers?" Fred said. "Well," he said. Flying saucers. "Can't say I've seen one myself but I guess anything's possible."

"What if I told you," the defendant said, "that what we think of as UFOs are in reality highly advanced Nazi aircraft, designed and built near the end of the war but still operational today, flying reconnaissance missions out of secret bases in the Antarctic?"

"Well," Fred said. He cleared his throat and spoke carefully. "I guess you could call me a show-me kind of guy."

"Then I show you." The German took a fat old briefcase out from under the table. He opened it, lifted a sheaf of paperwork and fanned it carefully out before Fred.

Articles. Photographs and drawings of Nazi UFO prototypes. Something that looked like a sombrero with an Iron Cross on the bell. An official UFO Investigator's Kit complete with a pass, spotting chart, a list of questions to ask the crew upon landing. A scale model for only four-fifty plus postage. A proposed expedition to Antarctica to find the South Polar Opening (secretly stumbled upon by Admiral Byrd), leaving from Buenos Aires in a chartered jumbo jet. Cost of reservations: nine thousand, nine hundred and ninety-nine dollars.

"I'm in the mail-order business," the defendant explained.

"People buy this?"

"I can't keep up."

"And you believe it."

"As you say," the defendant said, "anything is possible."

"Until proven otherwise," the barrister said.

Fred wanted a cigarette. "Where is this going?"

"You've heard of Atlantis?" the defendant said.

"This is going to Atlantis," Fred said.

"Mr. Z," the barrister said.

"Atlantis," the German said. "Evidence now points to the Mediterranean Basin. Underwater ruins, rock core samples that

prove the Strait of Gibraltar was once an isthmus, the Basin
a fertile river valley like the Po or the Euphrates." Cave paintings that depicted a great advanced civilization—tall, blond,
blue-eyed—flourishing until some great cataclysm, probably
an earthquake, destroyed the Gibraltar land mass and turned
the valley into a sea, drowning the great city.

"What if I told you there were six-foot-tall Aryan mum-
mies found perfectly preserved in Outer Mongolia?"

"I think maybe I'd rather you didn't," Fred said and briefly
grinned his stained grin. The Frenchman's eyes pleaded with
him for patience.

The Seven Sisters of Eve. Sanskrit manuscripts containing
plans for flying machines, automobiles, high-tech weaponry,
and communications.

"Mr. Z," the barrister said.

The defendant held up a hand and looked at Fred. "Are
you with me so far, *mein Freund*?"

"I have no idea where you are," Fred said.

"You would like hard evidence," the German said. "Documentation. Photographs, perhaps?"

"I'd like a Chesterfield," Fred said. "Evidence of what
exactly?"

The barrister had a manila folder. A stack of eight-by-ten
photographs. She laid them on top of the pile before him. Old,
black and white. Aerial reconnaissance. Some sort of compound. A camp.

"I don't see any flying saucers," Fred said.

"Do you see any gas chambers?" the Frenchman said.

"You consider yourself a skeptic?" the defendant asked.

"You could say I'm on the pragmatic side," Fred said. His glasses needed cleaning.

"So." He said it with a *z*. "What do you think of the six million?"

"The six million."

"*Endgültige Lösung*," the barrister said with a fair accent. "The camps. The gas. The Hollow Cause."

"The Holocaust industry," the German said.

"Industry," Fred said.

"You name it," the barrister said.

"Reparations, for one," the defendant said. "Five thousand deutsche marks per Jew—you do the math. Not to mention free real estate: a homeland for Israel and half of Europe to the communists. Not to mention entertainment: books, plays, movies, operas, and all of it propaganda. Surely you've heard of the diary of Anne Frank?"

"A fraud," the Frenchman said. "Written in ballpoint ink. Ballpoint did not come into use until the fifties."

"I wasn't aware," Fred said.

"But you believe," the defendant said. "You accept the official story."

"I believe what I was taught, I suppose. Never had reason not to."

"But the numbers," the barrister said. "The six million."

Fred looked at her. "Six million is quite a figure."

"But you've never really thought about it," the defendant said.

"You can smoke in the hall if you like," the barrister said. "Then we'll talk numbers."

"*Böse Angewohnheit*." The defendant was something of a health fanatic. "Would you like to borrow my helmet?"

So they started with the numbers. Arithmetic: between three and four million fled Europe between '33 and '45, less than three and a half million remaining in occupied territory. Documented. Not even Einstein could get six out of three and a half. By the end of the war less than four hundred thousand inmates had been registered to Auschwitz—a synthetic coal and rubber plant.

"Gutta-percha," the Frenchman said.

"Why would you slaughter your own labor force?" the defendant said. "Why would you strain your resources shuffling millions of refugees about Europe in the midst of such desperate military and economic straits, fighting a full-scale war on multiple fronts? It defies logic, and no more logical people have ever lived." He said something else, in German. The sound of logic.

They moved on to the names. Not just the big ones, the headliners, but the supporting cast as well: Heydrich, Hoess, Gerstein, Rassinier—the former inmate who debunked claims of gassing at Buchenwald—Fanslau, the S.S. major-general who took a personal interest in the welfare of labor camp prisoners, who once had a guard shot on the spot for slapping a pregnant inmate. Hundreds of letters written on his behalf by former inmates (photocopies on file), never admitted as evidence at Nuremberg just as cross-examinations by defense attorneys were not permitted. So-called confessions of former S.S. officers extracted by beatings and torture (medical records on file), the so-called memoirs of Hoess and Eichmann communist-Jewish fabrications. Fictions of human soap and handbags made of skin. Doctored photographs, burnt corpses from Hamburg and Dresden (the real holocaust!) superimposed on concentration camp negatives. Accounts of *Einsatzgruppen* and *Sonder-kommando* but no surviving eyewitnesses, no documentation, and never a single written order to harm a single hair on a single Jewish head. The Madagascar Plan, superseded at the Wannsee Conference by the Final Solution—not extermination but *Arbeitseinsatz im Osten*—labor assignment in the east.

It was on file.

"The only gas you will ever find in the so-called death camps," the defendant said, and he imitated a fart. Fred felt a fine spray. No facilities ever found at Dachau, Buchenwald, Bergen-Belsen. So all eyes turn to the east, to Auschwitz-Birkenau, Majdanek, Treblinka, Sobibor, where nothing could be disproved because the Soviets did not allow inspections for ten years. Till they'd had time to make alterations, when they needed to make a case for something worse than themselves—as if anything could be worse than Stalin, Mao, Pol Pot, the North Koreans, their countless millions of corpses.

Of course they were starved to skeletons—saturation bombing by the Allies had destroyed German supply lines. Of course there were mountains of bodies and burning pits—typhus outbreaks were rampant near war's end and all the doctors needed at the Russian Front.

But the bulldozers were British. Also on file.

"The smell of burning rubber has been compared to that of burning flesh," the defendant said.

"Gutta-percha," the Frenchman said.

"The Red Cross was permitted full access," the barrister said. "Not a trace of mistreatment reported, let alone genocide. They even forced the Nazis to install new plumbing in the showers. There was an inmate swimming pool, nine thousand parcels a day received by prisoners. There are copious memoranda."

The Frenchman said, "We're not saying this was paradise."

"But no worse than American internment camps for the Japanese," the German said.

"We were at war with the Japanese," Fred said and thought of his father.

The defendant stifled a belch. "In 1936 the Zionist leader Weizmann declared war on Germany on behalf of the world's Jewry."

"Actually, that needs looking into," the Frenchman said.

"What can you prove?" Fred asked.

"We don't have to prove everything," the barrister said. "But where there's smoke there's reasonable doubt."

"You don't have to believe us," the Frenchman said.

"Perhaps better you don't," the defendant said. "Ideally it's better you don't believe a thing."

"Then of what use am I?" Fred said.

Everyone looked at everyone else.

"There has never been a definitive forensic examination of the camps," the barrister said, "especially of the facilities in question. Someone familiar with the various modes of execution would be required—particularly gas chambers—and who knew such an expert even existed?"

Fred wanted another cigarette.

"You will go as an officer of the court," she said.

"Go where?" Fred said, and they looked at him.

"I have this thing about planes," he said.

"You have the fear of flying?" the Frenchman said.

"I have the fear of crashing," Fred said.

"Then I will row you there myself," the defendant said. "As an officer of the court, you will find what you will find. I will accept it. The proof, as they say, is in the pudding."

"What exactly are you accused of?" Fred asked.

"I'm in the mail-order business," the defendant said and emptied his briefcase out on the table. Amid the UFO miscellany were other literature, books, pamphlets: *The Hollow Cost: A Myth Exposed* . . . *The Shoah Must Go On* . . .

"Falsifying history," the barrister said, "spreading false news . . . among other charges."

"I didn't know you could go to prison for that," Fred said.

"Depends who is doing it," the Frenchman said.

Fred looked at the pictures again. He looked at pictures, maps, photostats, correspondence, communiqués, journals, minutes, marginalia, notes scrawled on napkins. Copious memoranda. All that day and part of the next. She was not happy about being left alone so much but she understood. She shopped a little, watched pay-per-view movies in their room. There was a mini-bar, and they haggled with the front desk over it at checkout. When they got back there was much to do and not much time.

Passports. Reservations. A marriage certificate.

White oak, quartersawn. A hundred board feet of it. He made a pot of coffee and cut the legs first. He cut outer wraps so the grain figure would show on all four sides of them, then angled the table saw and bevel-ripped the edges of the wraps and cut angled grooves in them for the leg splines. He cut the splines and the cores and dry-assembled the legs, planing the cores till the wraps were flush and the legs square. Then he took them apart and put them back together with glue and clamps and while the glue set he cut the rails, top and bottom and center. He fit the table saw with a dado blade and cut grooves in the long edges of the rails and made cheek cuts for the tenons, trimmed the tenons and chamfered the edges with a block plane. With an unlit cigarette in his mouth he took up his pencil and marked the center and ends of an arch in the bottom rail of the footboard, then drew the arch with a fairing stick and cut it with a handsaw and then sanded the arch and sanded the rails. He sanded and stained as he went along, dark walnut, and the smell of the finishing oil began to smell better than the coffee and he made a fresh pot before he cut the filler slats and before he cut the spindles he made the workpiece for the notches that would hold them.

Sixteen for a double. Eighteen for a queen. Twenty-three for a king.

He kept pulling it out of himself, kept running out of room for it. Had to lay the side rails across the washer and dryer because they were over seven feet long.

The windows grew dark when he wasn't looking, then light, and he lay down on the old wood-dusted couch and woke up wood-dusted himself under windows that were dark again. He thought he'd heard someone knocking but no one ever came there on weekends; it was either a dream or someone whose dreams he'd torn apart with his saw. He'd asked her not to call. A clock ran silently on the wall but he was outside time and the only space of which he was sensible was that in which he worked; there was a toilet in the basement so he didn't have to leave till it was done. He made more coffee and lit another cigarette and cut the tops and subtops and center slats and corbels and sanded the corbels with a sanding drum fitted to the drill press. He assembled the headboard and the footboard with the glue and clamps, and when the glue had dried he stained the parts he couldn't stain before, and when the stain dried he topped it with a clear finish, three coats, napping between coats and sanding with 320 grit.

He worked through the weekend with the phone off the hook and it was getting to be another day again when he took it upstairs one piece at a time. Then the hardware, the angle iron, the mating fasteners and pan-head screws. He put it all in the master bedroom, his parents' room—it hadn't been used in years. The windows threw slabs of light on the floor, the boards ticked. A bureau, a chiffonier, two night tables, a chair. Now this. He put it together in the empty space in the middle, the light peeling up off the floor, bending and rippling over him. It warmed him as the work did. When he was done he dragged on the box spring and mattress and wanted to lie down on it and sleep, but he had not built it to be alone in. He heard his draftsman walking up the front porch, coming to work.

Valentine's Day. Fred wore the suit he wore on the road, his bride the dress she'd worn to someone else's wedding. Pink double-knit. No best man, no maid of honor. The warden exercised the power vested in him by the state, in his office, his secretary the only witness.

You sit in seat B and cross yourself. Rolling, rolling like an outsize bus with five hundred riders looking for a lost road. You hope they never find it, watch the demonstration in the aisle. She points out the location of the emergency exits, demonstrates the deployment of the oxygen masks, and attaches one to her face (make sure yours is properly fitted before assisting your neighbor, your blue-faced bride, gasping for air like a landed fish), says you can use your seat cushion as a flotation device in the unlikely event of (but landing cannot be the right word). You watch it again in German. Your draftsman sits next to you on the aisle, for his bladder.

You recall your only other flight, too many years ago, the tiny cabin, the planetary curve of the ground, try to think of it as an initiation, but now it seems like a dry run in which you used up your allotment of luck. If there's a first time there has to be a last, so you cross yourself discreetly again and look out the window. The flaps open and close, and it feels like the first time again.

The flight attendants patrol the aisles, checking seatbelts, latching luggage bins. One of them is a man and you think of male nurses and switchboard operators. They are asked to take their seats. He can't help you, either.

The plane slows, turns sharply, a ninety-degree pivot. Stops, but not for long. Everyone is facing the same direction. The rumble of the engines, with you so long you no longer notice it, returns with accumulated vengeance and becomes a roar that drives you ahead with utmost urgency, burning distance like a fuse, turning speed into velocity and your body into a problem of physics. It reaches an ultimate level and stays there, everything trembling and rattling, the windows, the seats, the backs of heads in the long tunnel of the fuselage. You would cross yourself again if you were willing to let go of the armrests, so you close your eyes and are heartily sorry for offending and things change right away; the cabin lurches again and your seat tilts back, though you know it is not just your seat. A smoothing of the tremor beneath you, a floating in your stomach and groin and then the whine of hydraulics, the landing gear and the doors that seal them into the great body as though they won't be needed again. You turn your head to reorient yourself in the dark, and when you open your eyes you are following your wife's gaze through the window and along the great wing. The plane banks, your weight shifts to the left and the earth tilts toward you like a table off which all the objects are about to slide: streets, cars, green of yards, blocks of roofs and grids of blocks, lives lived as remote and unknowable as the atoms of matter. A pit that is next to you and below you, and though you don't suffer from vertigo or any particular fear of heights, you turn your head and look around the cabin for an object on which to fix your eyes and anchor yourself, find it in the flat gaze of some celebrity stranger peering from a magazine in the seat pocket in front of you. The flaps align.

Already puffs of vapor that you recognize as shreds of clouds are bursting against the windows—you swear you can hear them. The cabin still angled back, still climbing, but a soft bell rings and symbols light up on the bulkhead: you can smoke but you can't leave your seat. Fair enough. The pilot's voice welcomes you to the abyss with a German accent, nasal through the cabin speakers but confident, authoritative, full of altitude, knots, ceilings and weather. You find the language of aeronautics reassuring and feel no immediate need to imagine a destination. Now the pilot is speaking German and sounds older, grave, and you wonder if he flew in the war, Messerschmitt or Stuka, and you wonder about *his* allotment of luck, or justice, do some quick arithmetic and realize it is not likely, but you don't know if you'd rather it were.

They were to meet their translator in Frankfurt.

Less than two hours into the flight the captain announced they were over the ocean. Finally they'd leveled off—for a while there seemed no limit to how small things could get. Fred leaned over his bride's lap, looked out the window and studied the wing. It was very long and bent and flexed in the wind as if to beat, birdlike. The sun they fled flattened itself upon it, molten orange, and below, the clouds in streams and rafts. Below again, six or seven miles, the other abyss, more black now than blue, smooth, metallic, reflecting nothing. There were no islands. Looking down for one, Fred found instead recollection of an incident he had seen in headlines, though he couldn't remember exactly when: a defective cargo door opening on a flight over the Pacific. Explosive decompression, five rows of seats ripped out of the business section and into the void along with nine of their occupants, still strapped in, embarking on the journey for which there is only one class of passenger.

Everyone else had gone on to Honolulu. He stopped looking.

His wife's hand was on top of his. The light on the wing had dimmed, no longer a glow but a ghost of pink, paling as you looked, and Fred realized that at six hundred miles an hour heading due east they were traveling through time as well, into the night of the future.

"I thought they'd never," the bride said; the attendants were trundling carts up and down the aisles, stopping at each row to speak with the captain's accent. What would you like? *Was hätten sie gern?* Fred chose a meal that looked like an abstraction of food: a rectangle of chicken breast with dark squares of pumpernickel and cubes of butter. Salad and coffee. When he was done he reclined his seat and smoked, terror deferred, watching the cabin steadily darken around the tiny overhead lights. The muted roar, the sustaining hum and hiss. His briefcase of bones in the bin overhead. The distant chiming of a piano. A stewardess spiraled up the coil of steps at the head of the cabin, into the piano. A man and a woman and a young girl sat in front of him, ostensibly a family. The parents spoke infrequently and mainly to each other, in whispers. The girl would sometimes turn around in her seat, sit on her knees with her arms on top of the backrest and study the aft cabin. The fourth time or so she did this she looked directly at Fred and said, "Are you a chain-smoker?"

"He sure is," Fred's wife said.

"That's why I'm sitting here," Fred said. "This is the chain-smoking section."

"It sure is," Fred's wife said.

"I hope it isn't bothering you," Fred said.

The girl shrugged. "I like the smell." She glanced at her parents, then whispered, "Can I have one?"

Fred didn't say anything.

"I have some gum, cutie," Fred's wife said. "Would you like some gum? Where are you going?"

"I was just kidding," the girl said, somewhat annoyed. "We're seeing my grandmother in Dresden. She smokes too. She's a communist."

"I'm sure she's a very nice person," Fred said.

"She's dying," the girl said.

"We're so sorry," Fred's wife said and sounded like she'd been grieving for days. She was like that, you just had to push the button.

The draftsman drank his dark beer and stood.

"It's nobody's fault," the girl said. "She's just old. What are you going to do in Germany?"

"Just stopping over," Fred said and for a moment was saying so to the girl who'd lived two doors down. He'd found no one else to haunt him.

The girl looked at Fred's wife. "Are you related?"

The bride was silent. The draftsman had gone to the bathroom.

"Actually, we're on our honeymoon," Fred said. "We're going to Poland."

The girl looked at them dubiously.

"Official business too," Fred said. "Sort of a professional visit, you could say."

The girl looked thoughtful. "Like a mission?"

"You could say that," Fred said. "We really can't talk much about it though."

"Are you a spy?"

Fred's wife perked up, a different button. Fred said he wasn't a spy.

"You don't look like one," the girl said, and Fred's wife laughed outright. The draftsman returned to his seat.

"Well, I guess I'd make a pretty good one then," Fred said.

"You look like Mr. Clarke," the girl said. "He teaches special ed."

"Well that sounds important," Fred's wife said.

"The retarded," the draftsman said.

"I'm sure he's very nice," Fred's wife defaulted.

"He yells a lot," the girl said. "He got in trouble but we're not supposed to talk about it."

Parental whispering turned her head to the seats next to her. A brief, quiet exchange. Then she turned back to Fred and his wife, smiled apologetically and waved and sat back down facing front.

"Excuse me," Fred said as if she were still there and got up for the first time and stepped into the aisle. He'd been drinking coffee nonstop since the cabin service had started.

The adventure of the lavatory, a narrow booth of polished metal and plastic wood. The fixtures made him think of prison hardware. The dry metal hole, one hand on the bulkhead, unpracticed aim. A burst of blue liquid. When he came out they were just starting the movies. Fred's wife bought a pair of headphones and said, "Turn out the light."

The first one was a romantic comedy. Cher's mouth moving in German. Fred's wife didn't like subtitles but she'd seen it before and knew just when to cry. Then she fell asleep. An extraterrestrial hunter landed on Earth in search of human prey. This time the subtitles were in German and she still wore the headphones, but the carnage required no translation and Fred watched in silence and smoked. He couldn't find her hand. The credits rolled. Only a few lights remained in the cabin. Blankets and pillows had been distributed, the draftsman had drunk himself to sleep. The bride snored softly. Fred leaned over and looked out the window.

The moon was full and somehow they were flying above it. The cloudscape over which it shone endless and unbroken, corrugations of silver and gray and ice-blue light. It looked as solid as the moon; everything was made of everything else, and along the horizon, just beyond the lunar corona, there were stars. Fred looked for his familiars: Acrux, Aldebaran, Alpha Centauri, but he could find nothing he'd been taught, as if they'd wandered into a region of sky so remote the constellations were as yet unmapped.

A red signal flashing at the end of the wing.

Was wollen Sie?

Fred had not missed Mass in his adult life. He and his bride rose early and had coffee and tea and chocolate biscuits in the hotel café. They were staying near the old city, surrounded by cathedrals and crypts, museums, palaces, Gothic arches and stained glass. The water in the hotel was tepid and there was hardly any toilet paper; they were glad they'd heeded the German's advice and brought their own. This was a land of not enough.

After breakfast they put on their scarves and coats and hats and gloves and walked along the garden that circled Old Town, half covered in snow. They were dressed in cheap off-brands that seemed to come out of the factory secondhand, and few people took them for foreigners till they spoke. Fred wore a tie. They cut through what looked like a campus, passed a statue of Copernicus with thick curly hair and an astrolabe. Fred explained who Copernicus was. His wife said he looked like a rock star, or a fag. Then they reached the medieval market square in the middle of Old Town. Ten acres of brick and ice, the bitter wind that scoured it clear of vendors and stray dogs now hurrying worshippers toward morning service at the basilica. Horses pulling a small bus clopped by, pigeons sat in stiff official ranks atop walls and power lines. They passed the town hall tower and the statue of a great poet, but Fred didn't know who the poet was. Behind him a long building with twenty arched entrances taking up almost one side of the square. Merchants had come there to sell and trade and spend nights six hundred years past, and you could still buy things—jewelry, embroidery, costume dolls and lace. Some of the shops took hard currency, dollars or deutsche marks, while others stood empty with their proprietors standing out front, arms folded, merchants of want.

She would meet him there after Mass. She wasn't Catholic. He reminded her to look for batteries and their mouths bumped, closed tight to the wind.

The basilica was almost as old as the square and named for the Virgin. The entrance was flanked by two towers. One was taller than the other and there were white birds flying around it. At noon a trumpeter would emerge in the belfry and sound his horn, and would do so every hour after. He would not finish, though, because when he'd played it six hundred years ago to warn of the Tartar invasion, he'd been shot in the throat with an arrow just halfway through the song. Fred went inside.

In the entrance he put his gloves in his hat and dipped his fingers in the baptismal font. The water was cold but it made you new again. Forehead, breast, left shoulder, right. He walked down the long central aisle through the nave, candles on each side, the vaulted blue ceiling lit only by high windows. The only electric light came from the chancel and he found an empty pew as close to it as he could get. He knelt, sat, looked up and ahead, under the sky of stone.

The altar was fifty feet high and carved of wood and gilded and painted in many colors. In each wing were carved three panels telling three stories, one above the other, but the biggest was in the middle: five apostles marveling at the Assumption of the Virgin into Heaven, the folds of their robes like a turbulent sea in arrest.

It was cold. When the choir sang the hymn rose in pale mists. The priest was young. All made the Sign. The Greeting, the mass murmur of the response—the clenched crowded sounds of the celebrants were foreign but needed no translation; Fred knew where they were going and followed softly under his breath. The Kyrie, the Gloria, a stout old woman in black smiling through tears. The brief silence in which you could ask of Him what you would, and Fred asked for His blessing as an officer of the Canadian courts, that the truth he sought be disclosed to him in whatever form He saw fit, that He see fit to provide them with toilets that weren't hopelessly clogged, and he was going to ask that the good people of this country be delivered from the heel of oppression, amen, but the priest was already praying, collecting their petitions.

Someone wheezed behind him, struggling for breath as though that too were in short supply. Emphysema, maybe bronchitis; people were not well here. The pew filled with late-comers but Fred didn't look up till the Rite of Peace. He turned to his right and shook someone's hand, he turned left and the old woman in black kept smiling and did not see him. The priest took communion, the choir sang. The worshipers filled the aisles in long lines. Fred joined them hastily, looking at his watch— they had a train to catch. He kept looking at it till someone nudged him: your turn. He knelt before the distributing min-ister and heard Latin.

"Amen," he said and put out his tongue.

Ite, missa est.

He hurried back to the merchants' hall with the taste of Christ dissolving in his mouth. She looked frazzled with lan-guage but had managed to buy an ashtray, a stack of doilies, batteries for the video camera.

"Zwotty," she said phonetically, "zwotty." She said there was a colored guy talking Polish and the novelty of it had not quite worn off. "Are you hungry?" she asked. He was but there was no time—they could eat on the train. They went back to the hotel lobby where the draftsman and the translator were waiting for them. The translator was a tall man pushing seventy in a fleece vest and fisherman's cap. He was German but born and raised in Lodz, spoke Polish, German, English, French, and Yiddish. Upon the invasion he was arrested by the Poles, then liberated by the Nazis, drafted, and later shipped to North Africa to serve under Rommel.

"A good man but uppity," he told Fred. (And overrated, in his opinion.) His entire unit was captured by the Americans and he spent the remainder of the war in Iowa, working in a cannery with twenty other POWs, opposite an American woman whose name he'd not forgotten. He passed her a note before he was shipped back to Europe, a sheet of paper folded eight times.

"You didn't drink the tap water, did you?" He'd already explained that Europeans did not drink tap water.

They squeezed into a taxi standing outside—taxis were not permitted to cruise here. A stout white box that looked like a refrigerator on wheels and felt like it: the heater was broken. They headed for the depot northeast of the old city. It was a short drive and there was no more Renaissance stone, only the brute ugly lumps of the people's architecture. The people whose architecture it purported to be were lined up for blocks in the shivering cold, not taking communion but waiting their turn to buy soap, vinegar, tobacco. *Spirytus*.

"Vodka," the translator translated. Ninety-six percent alcohol. *Solidarnosc* posters on telephone poles and walls.

The train left on time. They sat opposite a gray-haired man in a suit reading a newspaper, and a soldier listening to Elvis Presley through headphones. There were soldiers everywhere. The gray-haired man was drinking tea.

"Where did he get that?" Fred's wife wondered, and the translator leaned forward and spoke.

"He says he brought it with him," the translator said, and they saw a thermos beside him.

"Isn't there a dining car?" Fred said.

The translator leaned forward again. There was a buffet in Carriage Seven, "full of kettles, and the kettles full of nothing," the translator said, finding a line worth quoting. He and the gray-haired man spoke for a while. They learned there would be a dining room at the hotel, that the gray-haired man was a teacher who made the equivalent of a hundred dollars a month, that it would cost him a month's pay to keep his three-room flat in coal through the winter. He said the Auschwitz hockey team was in first place, that one of his sons played wing. The other had been run over by a tank during martial law in '81.

"How awful for him," Fred's wife said into the cup of her hand. Her stomach growled. The soldier sleeping to "King Creole."

There were many stops. The ticket inspector came through. The translator dozed and they woke him and he translated, rolled a cigarette and smoked it through a wood holder inlaid with tiny gold beads. He'd had it since the war. The draftsman lit his pipe. He sat next to an Australian girl who was traveling alone around the world and didn't mind the smell. Snow squalls buffeted the train and they rode past frozen polluted streams, hay fields, the flat plain in exact squares portioned out by some commissar of equity. Greenhouses, outhouses, horse-drawn carts with truck tires, a tractor in a field, driverless. Another old woman in black with a sack on her shoulder.

The teacher sneezed or said something as they pulled in.

"How was that?" Fred's wife said, as if it might have to do with food.

He recommended they visit the town, time permitting; there was a kosher vodka distillery, a synagogue housing the Jewish Center.

"Oswiecim," the teacher said again.

They took two rooms at the hotel. It smelled like sulfur and gasoline. The desk clerk was a young man with bad teeth and a mustache like Walesa. He gave them their keys and a bottle of water for each room. Then he asked in Polish if they had any bubble gum, but they had chewed all they had on the train.

"Thankyouverymuch," he said. Elvis again.

The rooms bare but clean, beds with iron rails, radiators, wash basins. The bathroom down the hall, and the smell.

"That smell," she said.

"Naphthol," Fred said. "Kills bugs dead." But he wasn't sure where he'd smelled it before.

They took a late lunch. The dining room looked like a cafeteria but the waiter wore a short-waisted jacket that was no longer white. There were no other diners and no menu and only one item being served: sour cream soup with a slice of boiled egg at the bottom of the bowl. A warm carbonated drink that tasted vaguely of apples. They barely finished.

"Like it already came back up," the draftsman said and it stayed with them, the taste they would take in their mouths through the gate, under the wrought-iron welcome.

The translator kept nodding off during the meal. When they'd done he retired to the room he was sharing with the draftsman to take a nap. He suffered from gout and fallen arches, and since there were English-speaking tours and he had been so useful already, they decided to let him rest.

The hotel had once been the officers' quarters. It had also been the administration building, a reception center for inmates, and a brothel. The adjacent wing was now the visitor center. There were restrooms in the basement but they were still in Poland and women carried half rolls in their bags. Upstairs was a bookstore, an information desk, a small theater, the exhibit hall. Walls hung with photographs, paintings, drawings, maps. Memento mori. Someone had tethered a desiccated figure to a barbed-wire fence post, the arm crooked at a right angle to form a familiar shape.

Fred's wife stared. "Is that supposed to be . . . ?"

"Work of art," Fred said.

"So what's it doing here?" the draftsman said, and they went into the theater.

Fifteen minutes of black-and-white footage the Soviets had shot when they'd liberated the camp. Fur-hatted soldiers escorting communist political prisoners to a version of freedom, one of them a woman named Olga. The film showed every half hour.

But the camp was not unpleasant. The barracks made mostly of red brick, the roofs thick with clean blankets of snow. They called them blocks and gave them numbers but there were wide avenues of crushed brick and granite between them, plowed and lined with poplar trees, and except for the sentry boxes and barbed wire it might have been a rustic apartment complex or a summer camp in the off-season. The guide wore a two-piece blue uniform similar to that of the Salvation Army. She took them on a short detour around the back of the kitchen to show them the fence. A sign said HALT! STOJ! And the guide explained that the fence had been electrified. She showed them the porcelain insulators connecting the rusty wire to the fence posts that leaned inward, scythe-like, at the top, and said inmates had been known to end their misery by walking up to the fence and grabbing it with both hands.

"I'm going to the fence," she said they would say, and everyone knew what they meant.

One of the American students, a tall girl with round glasses, wrote it down in a notebook, a mitten in her mouth.

"What's the drop?" Fred said.

"I'm sorry?" the guide said.

"Voltage," he said.

"This I'm not sure," the guide said. "Enough to kill you," she said then and another of the students suddenly declared he'd had enough of World History II, "I'm going to the fence!" and stepped forward and grabbed the wire, convulsing violently with his head thrown back, mouth and eyes wide open, his performance so credible no one risked laughter till his teacher snatched him away by the back of his coat collar and apologized.

The guide issued a warning. She had a wide pretty face and unshaven legs.

Block 4. Baby clothes: tiny shoes, dresses, bonnets, sleepers. Schematics and models and canisters of pellets, bolts of cloth and a shirt, said to have been woven of human hair. For sale during the war.

The barracks were heated.

"You can smell it," Fred's wife said.

"It's turning to powder," the Australian girl said, her voice thick like she was choking on it.

Behind the glass, some of it was still in braids. The light was dim, they could see themselves in it.

"It's all gray," the kid from the fence said. "I thought it doesn't age."

"Everything ages," his teacher said.

"Is evidence of exposure to cyanide gas," the guide said.

"Has it been analyzed?" Fred asked.

"By Forensic Institute in Krakow." She said it *Crackoff* and the kid who'd gone to the fence repeated it like a dirty word.

The girl with the glasses and notebook asked how much, and the guide told her how many.

"One hundred forty thousand," she said. She said the Russians found fifteen thousand pounds of it packed in paper bags and the girl wrote it down.

She asked about skin. Lampshades.

"Was in Buchenwald," the guide said.

Shoes. Half a roomful like a clearinghouse of plunder—men's, women's, children's, unpaired, all time-dyed to the same neutral monochrome but for the scattered flare of red leather. Pyramids of empty luggage, suitcases marked with names as though further use were expected of them. A display of prosthetic limbs like spare parts for automatons, wooden arms reaching, hands open, legs bent at the knee as if removed in the act of prostration. Striped uniforms, a knot of eyeglasses like a tumbleweed of wire and glass, dentures, hairbrushes, toothbrushes, cans of shoe polish, prayer shawls, wristwatches, gold and silver fillings—mined from corpses en route to the ovens, she said.

The tall student with the glasses and notebook raised her hand and asked the guide if she belonged to the Communist Party.

The guide tried to smile. "This is not part of tour."

"Would it be the Party's position," the student asked anyway, "that what happened here is as much the ultimate product of capitalism as it is the logical outcome of ethnic persecution?" She sounded like she was reading. "Perhaps even more so?"

The guide had blond hair pulled back in a tight bun. "Party has no official position here," she said. "It does not concern with logic and production. It is share the opinion of the world that this was crime against humanity."

"What are they talking about?" Fred's wife whispered.

"Ideology," Fred said.

"Dead is dead," the draftsman said, and Fred blew his nose.

He was just finishing when he heard the guide's voice, dribbled on his shoe and zipped, hurriedly kicked white snow over the yellow.

"You are lost?" she said.

"The men's room was . . ." He stopped, saw it between them and the wire: a big rectangular shape in the ground, metal ladders curving up out of the sides.

"If it were summer I could take a dip," Fred said.

"What is 'dip'?" the guide said.

He gestured toward the rectangular shape. It was empty but for snow. "I didn't know there was a swimming pool here."

"This is not swimming pool," the guide said. "Is reservoir for fire brigade."

Fred walked to the other end. A tall pedestal with a ladder attached, behind that a shallow basin with drain and fixture as for the cleansing of feet.

"A reservoir with a diving board?" he said.

"If it was swimming pool, then for political prisoners only," she said. Some of the rest of the group were gathering about.

"Well which is it?" Fred said.

"Is under study," the guide said. "By Museum Committee."

"What is that?" one of the students said.

"It looks like a pool," another one said. The girl with the notebook seemed to be sketching something. Cameras were not allowed.

"Possible reservoir," the guide said. "Not part of tour. But while we are here," she said and pointed to the double row of tall trees that ran the length of the camp behind the barracks. The wind picked up and two of them leaned into each other as if exchanging a secret.

The Black Wall was not black, it was gray. Portable. Three joined panels made of logs and covered with cork. Like an altar. There were red and white roses in front of the Black Wall.

To protect the bricks of the courtyard, the guide said. They'd stood facing it, their backs to the rifles.

"Can I touch it?" Fred said.

"To touch is not permit," the guide said and asked for a period of silence in memory of the twenty thousand (estimated) inmates who'd stood there. Fred faced the wall, his back to the silence. It did not occur to him to think that this was the last thing you would see before the true and final blackness took you. That you might not hear the shot that pushed you into it. It occurred to him to say, "Where are the bullet holes?"

"Is reproduction," the guide said. "Not original artifact," and a snowball flew from somewhere, exploded on the cork.

The guide said, "Medical experiments."

"Why are the windows covered?" the Australian girl asked. Sheets of plywood, also painted black.

"Symbolic," the history teacher suggested. A word scrawled on a blackboard.

"Who's that?" one of his students asked. She was looking at a display in front of the covered windows, at the photograph of a man in uniform. Dark-haired, aristocratic.

"Hello," another girl said. "Can Tom Cruise play him in the movie?"

"There's a movie?" Fred's wife said.

"Camp physician," the guide said. "Was call him Angel of Death." She recounted his experiments: dye injected into the eyeballs of children in an attempt to change brown to blue; amputations and mastectomies performed without anesthetic; subjects exposed to ruinous extremes of temperature, to mustard gas, malaria, typhus, shot in select limbs, wood shavings and ground glass rubbed into the wounds to initiate infections

157

of tetanus and gangrene; an attempt to create Siamese twins by sewing the veins of children together.

Children were a special interest of his, the guide said. And twins and dwarves and gypsies.

"Of little or no scientific value," she said.

"Can we go inside?" someone asked.

"Is not possible," the guide said. "We go now to punishment block."

"Thank God," Fred's wife whispered, for the dark angel was still at large and you might find yourself seized upon entering, strapped to a table or into a chair in a sealed chamber, the air gradually pumped out till you couldn't breathe, till your ears bled and your eyes popped forth as with cartoon amazement, in order to study the effects of high altitude on Luftwaffe pilots. Or for the hell of it.

They'd put the priest in Cell 18.

An inmate had turned up missing. In order to discourage further escape attempts, ten men were selected at random and condemned to the starvation cells. Only one of them asked for mercy. The priest, who had been arrested for hiding Jews in his friary, volunteered to take the man's place.

The tiny cell was locked. Through the bars they could see candles and a plaque on the floor the priest had knelt upon, starving, praying. The missing man was found drowned in a latrine. The priest was made a saint. The guide did not know what became of the man whose life had been spared, only that he was not a Jew.

Fred crossed himself.

The draftsman listened to his stomach and said, "We should all be saints."

Snow crunching and cracking ice, labored white breaths. Blocks 21, 20, 18, devoted to the victims of other nations, to the Dutch, French, Hungarian. Someone asked about homosexuals and the guide seemed not to have heard. They passed the open space of ground used for roll call, and she told them an inmate standing in the back row had given premature birth during morning muster, had buried the squirming infant alive on the spot, pushing it into the mud with her foot, then covering it like a dog burying a bone. Across from this a mass gallows for political prisoners that could hang twenty at a drop, and Fred regarded its construction critically.

"What's a political prisoner anyway?" his wife asked. Her eyes were dry. There seemed to be no buttons for this.

"Swim team," the draftsman said.

"Whatever they want it to be," Fred said, and his wife said, "You always have an answer, in your furry little hat."

You went in through the back. The sun was low and the snow almost blue. The door was open. A light hummed over it. A sort of vestibule and you turned right into a room filled with ceramic urns. Empty. She called it the laying-out room. She said the urns had been filled with ashes and could be returned to relatives and loved ones for a fee. You turned left. The door was made of wood and opened inward.

A narrow chamber maybe fifty feet long, maybe a third as wide. Floor of poured concrete, a large vase of flowers in the middle. Walls and ceiling of stucco. Beams overhead, naked bulbs between them. As they filled the room the echoes faded. It was cold enough to see your last breath here. Fred looked up. Four square holes in the ceiling.

The guide told them these were the vents through which the pellets were dropped. They were framed in wood.

"How old is that wood?" Fred asked.

"This I'm not sure," the guide said.

```
Four (4) square roof vents exhausting less
than two (2) feet from the surface of the
roof. No fans, no sealant, no gaskets, no
stack, no heating mechanism, no circula-
tion system, high humidity, floor drains
that would leak into the camp sewer system,
wooden doors that open inward, inhibiting
the removal of decedents.
```

She called their attention to the walls, cracked and crumbly, gray and stained, to the marks she said were scratches, scratches made by their nails, she said.

There were other marks as well: broad, straight, deliberate. Fred pointed and said, "There used to be a wall there."

"Yes," the guide said.

"And there."

"Yes," the guide said. "For lavatories."

"Lavatories in a gas chamber," Fred said.

"It was convert to air raid shelter in '44," the guide said.

"When was it converted back?"

"After the war."

"So this is a reconstruction," Fred said.

"It is a manner of speaking," the guide said.

"It is or it isn't," Fred said.

"A restoration, yes," the guide said. "As it was." She looked around. "Does anyone more have question?" She looked at everyone and repeated herself. No one said anything and they went to see the *krema*, oven mouths full of flowers.

Mortar, brick, concrete, sediment. Hammer, chisel, auger bit and brace. A mattock you could hold in one hand.

The second camp was much bigger. You could take an unguided tour.

Bride and groom, draftsman, translator. Maps and plans, official literature, what passed for blueprints from the State Museum. They took the tracks through the mouth of the gate-house. On one side the women's camp—long wooden huts like horse barns—to the right only chimneys remained, a field of cairns. Then the *Rampe*, the siding where selections were said to be made, *Links oder Rechts*. They made one of their own, broke a lock: steam ovens, showers, a blue stain on a wall. He took up his auger and drilled: "Control sample."

His wife stood watch. Sometimes she held the camera. A road cut the camp in half. (They'd found a restaurant at the bus depot.)

It falls to the floor and crumbles. He puts it in a sandwich bag.

"I am bagging," he says on tape. On YouTube.

The road ran north to Mexiko, the tracks went west toward Kanada—they'd stored stolen clothing there. He carried a black valise. The men's camp, the gypsy camp, some kind of cart in the distance, bumping and swaying over the icy grounds. The tracks ended in flowers: cross section of bed and rails, flat and abrupt like the stumps of amputation. They pointed to the monument, official art. Beyond this, the ruins of the *krema*.

A man and a woman rode the cart. She stepped off with a trash bag, bagged trash. Frozen flowers, burnt candles, a beer can—people had no respect. Words were exchanged, the custodians moved on. The translator wouldn't say what had been said.

The snow squalled and the rain froze. The weather was on their side.

They consulted the printed matter, ducked under yellow tape. The roof and walls of the undressing room gone, it looked like an empty basement. The crematorium reduced to rubble— *German demolitions team*, the booklet said, but the ground that it called a roof was only partially collapsed, a ragged hole in its middle just big enough.

Seven from I, seven from II, but they took only four samples from III. His wife was to whistle if someone came near. He worked with the utmost respect.

Brick and mortar, plaster and paint. Sour-flesh smell of old wet wood. He hammered and chiseled, swung the mattock, scraped, put things into zippered bags, wore a dust mask. The draftsman carried them in his backpack, took pictures and drew them; the translator diverted a guard . . . They photographed, taped, measured length and height, widths and depths of gray empty spaces.

But often they seemed to be alone.

Breakfast at the bus station café: hot milk, bean soup, a mushroom omelet. Then vents and ducts and valves.

Standing around the hole in Krema 11. It was barely big enough.

"You don't know what might be down there," she said. She squatted behind the privy on the path. The women's room was foul, the Sauna in good repair. The draftsman kicked in the door and limped the rest of the day.

"Sixty-one feet," he says on tape. "Sixty-one feet from the rear."

Drains, pipes, trenches, rabbets, blowers, baffles, and gaskets. The Sauna, where children saw parents stripped naked (according to the provided literature). A long wall splitting a long hall in half, a side for each sex. She sat on a bench, said she wasn't going to the next one . . . Steam ovens protruding through the wall, gaskets. He hammered away like Van Helsing, but he meant to bring something to life. He calculated and counted, inspected and plumbed, looked through windows, peepholes, grilles. Examined and estimated, distinguished between, decided on the color of ash: oyster gray.

The draftsman bore truth on his back, limping.

"As you can see, a rough-cut hole," her husband says, sitting on the edge, legs gone at the knee. Excuse me down there.

She thought she'd seen something running past the barracks. She might have been mistaken. She hated to complain.

So much of it wasn't even there. The buildings of Kanada gone, the White House a wooden square in the snow (they were saving the Red House for last). They took the road past the ash pond to the fence. The pond was frozen, they looked through the wire: Mexiko.

Eight from iv, four from v. Twenty-five pounds but they were almost done.

Chimneys, retorts, urns, showers, washrooms, anterooms, morgues, booths, rooms not mentioned in the official literature, and rooms that seemed other than what they were said to be.

Camp extension, the booklet said. *Unfinished*. Not even tracks in the snow, but what could live there?

Women had smuggled dynamite from the factories. It said so in black and white. They would smuggle the samples through Customs in their dirty laundry.

Finally, the path through the woods. (The next day she sat in the car with her crosswords—they forgot to leave the keys, she couldn't feel her feet.) It was getting dark. A mass grave, another burning pit, a gate and another long road. Houses filled with families and light—there must have been some mistake. Follow the signs. Another fence, an enclosure like someone's backyard. A marble marker in Hebrew and English, but the Red House wasn't there.

Finally, he lowered himself into it, disappearing down the hole.

"Leave the light off," she says.

He sits on the edge of the bed, in the smell of sulfur and gasoline. Piles his clothes on the chair. The room is cold, the floor feels like marble. The blanket, coarse and stiff, covers them like a lid.

"Your glasses." He forgot, feels himself grin, his face expanding sheepishly in the dark. Drops them where he hopes his clothes are. He can't see her anyway. The radiator comes on, thumps and clangs like someone beating it with a pipe. She says words he can't hear through the racket but they smell like their last meal: sausage, cucumber, duck blood soup. He tastes it again, lurches forward on hands and knees.

"No," she says, "that's not." He tries again. She is still in her gown.

"That hurts," she says. Hurts them both. She says she has something she can use.

Let her, she says, help him. Dishpan hand smoothed with oil. It finds a fit and he moves forward again. At the same time it is a sinking, a different disappearing.

"There," she says, and he tries to suck the word off her tongue. It is the last sound she makes before the departed awake. The wind wailing through its narrow mouth in the window, snow and ice pelting the glass like little stones. The squeak and clank and clang.

"Oh," she says. "*Oh.*"

She says nothing and he is lying somewhere next to her. They hear the radiator spitting and dripping.

"Trap must be full," he says and draws smoke. She says something. She says something which becomes part of the wind, which sounds like something else, the feral howling of what the desk clerk warned them about.

Just trying to scare them, thankyouverymuch.

Their train leaves for Warsaw in the morning.

NO. 041062671Q4
IN THE COURT OF QUEEN'S BENCH OF ONTARIO
JUDICIAL DISTRICT OF TORONTO
BETWEEN:
HER MAJESTY THE QUEEN
- V -
_____ Accused

PROCEEDINGS
Toronto, Ontario 1st March, 19__
Transcript Management Department
5th Fl North, 10036 University Street Toronto, ON
(780) 427-6181

Proceedings taken in the Court of Queen's Bench
of Ontario
Superior Courts Building, Toronto, Ontario
March 1, 19__ 2:00 P.M. Session

The Honourable Justice _____
Court of Queen's Bench of Ontario

_____ For the Crown
_____ For the Accused
_____ Court Clerk

Ivan L _____, sworn, testifying:

Defence, examining:

  Q: Good morning, sir.

  A: Good morning.

  Q: What is your name, sir?

  A: My name is Ivan L_____.

  Q: And what is your occupation?

  A: I am a professional embalmer and funeral director. I also manage and operate the largest crematorium in North America.

  (Objection.)

  Q: Would you care to rephrase that, sir?

A Canadian one-dollar coin had eleven sides and was brown as an American penny. They called it a loonie. Fred's wife found this name amusing till she learned it referred to the dignified aquatic bird floating on the coin's reverse side, which undermined its charm for her. It was funnier when it made no sense.

  A: My name is Ivan L _____. I manage and operate what I believe to be the largest crematorium in North America.

  Q: Would you also say it is the most efficient?

  (Objection.)

  Q: Would you say it is one of the most efficient?

167

(Objection.)

(Brief discussion off the record.)

Q: Let me put it to you this way, Mr. L _____:
how do you get a hundred Jews in a Volkswagen?

EXHIBIT P-1: FILE PROVIDED

Q: And when did you arrive at the camp?

A: December, nineteen hundred forty-two.

Q: Are you Jewish?

A: Not that I know of.

(Laughter.)

THE COURT: Order.

Q: Why were you there, then?

A: I have sexual intercourse with a Polish man.
Sexual relation with not-Aryan was consider . . .

(Consults with Translator.)

TRANSLATOR: A political crime.

Q: Did you wear a badge of any kind?

A: A triangle, half red and half black.

Q: What did it stand for?

A: Anti-social.

THE COURT: Must have clashed something awful
with the stripes.

THE ACCUSED: ().

Q: How long does it take, then, to burn a
human body?

A: About an hour and a half under optimal
conditions.

Q: But children burn faster than adults.

A: That's correct.

Q: And Jews burn faster than gentiles.
(Objection.)

Q: And skinny people faster than fat people?

A: On the contrary. Human fat is very good
fuel—it ignites instantly at high temperatures. A
person with little or no fat is very difficult to
burn because they consist mainly of wet tissues.

There was a heavy metal club and a subway station under the hotel. They thought they would take a train to the court-house. They thought they would go to Osgoode Station but boarded on the wrong side. Found themselves at Finch, the end of the line.

A: On the contrary, the refractory bricks
won't tolerate it. A cool-down period of at least
an hour between cremations is required. The
burner must be turned off and air blown through
the chamber. But with the older coal-fired units
it's not so easy. You can't just turn coal off.

EXHIBIT P-2: DANDELION

Q: You were picking flowers in a concentration
camp?

169

A: Well . . . at Raisko. For work. They use the dandelion in production for . . . (consults with Translator).

TRANSLATOR: Synthetic rubber.

Q: Did you ever see any smokestacks in the camp?

A: I saw them but they are very far away, very tiny. Maybe five kilometer away. They are smoking but I couldn't say they are in the camp or no.

Q: Did you see any movement of prisoners, of the yellow stars, toward the chimneys?

A: Only the ones already who was dead.

Q: There were bodies about?

A: Yes. Hundreds, thousand maybe. Dead of black fever, the typhus. And some who taken their lives at the electric wire. They taken them away by the wheelbarrow.

Q: But you didn't see living prisoners being taken toward the smokestacks.

THE CROWN: Objection.

THE ACCUSED: [].

JURY: *Happy, happy birthday to you!*
      Happy, happy birthday to you!

They ate lunch at a Mexican restaurant. It was not an authentic Mexican restaurant but one link in a chain that had begun in the States and crossed the border. Fred's wife found its presence reassuring. She would say "America" like some exile an ocean from home, and she ordered the seafood chimichanga.

They were joined by the barrister and several other witnesses. The defendant begged off, complaining of stomach flu. They sat in a large booth surrounded by salmon-colored stucco, canned mariachi music, faux balconies bristling with flowers. Fred ordered a steak and asked the waiter, whose name was Steve, to make sure the meat wasn't marinated. His wife allowed herself one margarita, and the barrister asked for a glass of water. It was someone's birthday. When someone was having a birthday in the Mexican chain restaurant, the waitstaff and busboys would surround the table and sing a birthday song, clapping their hands. They couldn't sing "Happy Birthday to You" for fear of copyright infringement. When it was over they would get back to work, resuming their former expressions.

Someone was coming to the table. His name was not Steve. He wore black pants and a white shirt and was holding a glass and must have been bringing the barrister her water. No one really noticed him till he was almost there—they were watching the besieged celebrants and the circle of employees singing and clapping their hands. The man whose birthday it was wore a sombrero.

You look good! You look good!
You look fine! You look fine!

When the man dressed as a busboy got to the table, you could see it wasn't a drinking glass in his hand but a jar, that the jar had a lid, and that the lid wasn't screwed down because the man simply lifted it off before tossing the contents of the jar in the barrister's face. Then you saw that it wasn't water the jar had contained.

Happy, happy birthday to you!

Happy, happy birthday to you!

Olé!

The barrister rolled out of the booth, face in hands as with some great despair. The man whose name was not Steve and who was dressed as a busboy ran out of the chain restaurant like someone who had not paid for his meal, and this was at first what some patrons thought was the case. One of the character witnesses, a friend of the defendant who had spent time in a Swedish mental institution and ordered the Grande Burrito, ran out in pursuit. No one else at the table had been splashed. The barrister writhed on the carpet in her business suit, not making a sound. Fred knelt uncertainly at her side and called for a doctor. His wife joined him, discreetly tugging the barrister's skirt down.

Years later the chain would be struck by the largest outbreak of hepatitis A in U.S. history and close its doors, though a restaurant remains open in Austria.

IN THE COURT OF QUEEN'S BENCH OF ONTARIO
JUDICIAL DISTRICT OF TORONTO

ENTER EXHIBIT

Sample No.	Results
880386.17	ND*
880386.18	ND

880386.19	ND
880386.20	ND
880386.20D	1.4
880386.21	4.4
880386.22	1.7
880386.23	ND
880386.24	ND
880386.25	3.8
880386.25D	1.9
880386.26	1.3
880386.27	1.4
880386.28	1.3
880386.29	7.0
880386.30	1.1
880386.30D	ND
880386.31	ND
880386.32	1,050

*ND = None detected

Q: What is the difference between a Jew and a pizza?

A: About 1200 degrees Fahrenheit.

(HISTORICAL FACT #4)

DEFENCE: What is the difference between typhus and typhoid?

WITNESS: Typhus is a disease of the blood vessels caused by the human louse. The louse bites the skin, then defecates into the wound.

The bite itches. When you scratch the itch, you force bacteria into the bloodstream. It spreads throughout the body and eats away the lining of the blood vessels. As a result it can cause pneumonia, gangrene, exhaustion, shedding of the skin, death.

Typhoid is different . . .

THE COURT: Nature's bounty. Which one kills more people?

WITNESS: Typhus, by far.

THE COURT: Proceed.

DEFENCE: Is there a cure?

WITNESS: There is now. In 1945 there wasn't.

DEFENCE: That's when you arrived at B _____?

WITNESS: Yes, on the second of May. I was still a medical student.

DEFENCE: What was the condition of the camp when you got there?

WITNESS: Bodies everywhere. I would estimate between three and five hundred people a day were dying of disease. Even the British were getting it. There were fires burning everywhere at B _____ —the clothing of the dead was burned to kill the lice, which migrate from the dead to the living. There was a terrible smell throughout the camp. You could smell it perhaps three miles away.

DEFENCE: How were the bodies disposed of?

WITNESS: The British used bulldozers to push them into these huge mounds . . .

DEFENCE: So this surreal footage we're all
familiar with, piles of skeletal bodies being
bulldozed into mountains of corpses . . .

THE CROWN: Objection.

THE COURT: Goddamn lawyers.

Q: And what is *your* name, sir?

A: I have no name. That, also, is lost to the past.

THE COURT: He doesn't look Jewish either.

Q: What is your occupation?

A: I was chief of the Arawaks before Columbus came, before
we were enslaved, put to work in the gold mines. Before we were
kidnapped, taken to Spain and put up for sale, infected with
smallpox, raped, mutilated, hung, burned at the stake.

THE COURT: An outrage.

A: The Spaniards would cut off the legs of children who
ran from them. They made bets to see who could cut one of us
in half with one stroke of his sword. They took infants from
their mothers' breast and used them for dog food.

THE COURT: A gross miscarriage. Sir, you're in the wrong
venue. Bailiff, take this man to Small Claims.

(Discussion off the record.)

Q: And then what?

A: My wife was taking a bath . . . she was
washing herself . . . down there (witness loses
composure briefly). We ran out of Irish
Spring . . .

Q: What did you do then?

A: I called Rabbi Feldman. We discussed it well into the night . . . and we decided there was only one thing to do. So we hopped the fence at Greenwood Cemetery and had kevurah for the four bars.

Q: Would you favor exhuming the grave for DNA testing?

A: I think some things should remain a mystery. (Says Kaddish.)

THE COURT: Does the Crown wish to cross?

THE CROWN: We don't need soap, My Lady. We have the truth.

[ENTER HISTORICAL FACT]

Q: So there was an order?

A: In my opinion.

Q: A specific order.

A: That is another matter.

Q: Aren't you a historian?

A: In my opinion.

Q: So there wasn't an order.

A: The order was oral.

Q: What were the exact words of the oral order?

A: No one knows . . . We have only reflections.

Q: "So what began in 1941 was a process of destruction not planned in advance."

A: Correct.

Q: "Not organized centrally by any agency."

A: Correct.

Q: "No blueprint."

A: Correct.

Q: "No budget for destructive measures."

A: Correct.

Q: "They were taken step by step, one step at a time."

A: This is what I said.

Q: "Not so much a plan being carried out, but an incredible melding of minds, a consensus, mind-reading by a far-flung bureaucracy." Correct?

A: Perhaps "mind-reading" is a bit excessive . . .

Q: But this is what you said, correct? A wink and a nod, correct?

A: I said nothing about any order not existing.

Q: Aren't you a historian?

A: I would describe myself as an empiricist.

Canadian football differs from the American form in that there are twelve players on a team as opposed to eleven, and the season runs from June to November; in that the field is one hundred and ten yards long and sixty-five yards wide; in that the end zones are twenty yards deep and the goalpost positioned on the goal line; in that the line of scrimmage is never closer than one yard from the goal line; in that each offence (Can. sp.) is allotted three downs to convert as opposed to four, and the team against whom a field goal has been scored has the option of either receiving a kickoff or taking possession on its own thirty-five-yard line.

In a further departure from American rules, Canadian football provides for a single-point score called a *rouge*, but no one is sure what that is.

Q: Welche Musik spielen sie am liebsten fur neue Ankunfte?

A: Ravel, Waltzer.

Q: Und fur die Insassen, die arbeiten gehen?

A: Irgendwas von Mozart.

THE COURT: Gesundheit. Now can you hum a few bars of "Lili Marleen"?

THE ACCUSED: ().

From the Testimony of Ivan L_____

A:
It's very difficult.
Human bodies
Do not burn completely
In open spaces.
The torsos and bones
Are especially hard to incinerate
And tremendous amounts of fuel
Are required.

The heat is constantly escaping
Into the open air
So it's very hard to concentrate
All the heat
In one area.

CROWN: And what is your occupation, sir?

WITNESS: I'm a photogrammetric engineer specializing in aerial triangulation, digital mapping, and rectification of photographs.

THE COURT: May we call you Chuck?

CROWN: This photograph was taken at a scale of one to ten thousand. Can you see the map of the kremas? (Enter EXHIBIT.)

WITNESS: Yes.

CROWN: These patches, do you have any idea of what they are?

WITNESS: Hard to tell. They're not shadows, but they have no elevation. I'm not sure what they are.

CROWN: Could they be vents?

WITNESS: It would be hard to say. These pictures were taken with a very long focal length, it's hard to determine the height of things based on stereo, the geometry involved in stereo. I couldn't say for sure.

THE COURT: Zzzzzzzzzzzzzzzzzzz.

Q: What about this one?

A: Looks like a swimming pool.

Q: A swimming pool? How can you tell? Is there water in it?

A: Yes. Based on color tone and the casting of shadows along its edge, I'd say there's water in it.

Q: Was it used by the inmates?

A: Oh, yes. And there were other recreational activities as well. Soccer, handball, fencing . . .

Q: Apparently the Commandant was a great believer in physical fitness.

A: Yes, but he was also a cultured man. A great lover of art and music.

Q: We've all heard about the orchestra.

A: Not just one . . . everything you did, you did to music. And he provided a fully equipped studio where artists could paint and sketch. Inmates could take classes in drawing and sculpture.

Q: What about this one?

A: I believe I see the theater.

Q: They showed films at A_____?

A: That was at the cinema.

Q: Were plays performed at the theater?

A: Plays, opera. I saw *Die Fledermaus* there, and *The Magic Flute*.

Q: What was this building?

A: Let me . . . (Witness puts on glasses.) The library.

Q: Also for inmates?

A: Yes. Some forty-five thousand volumes, I
understand. We had some lively discussions
there . . . politics, philosophy. The Commandant
was one of those Hegelians, you know, always with
the big words . . . but a real team player. Did I
tell you he put in flush toilets?

Q: And this?

A: The sauna.

Q: One more . . .

A: That would have been the brothel.

Q: There was a brothel at A_____?

A: Yes, next to the dental clinic.

(Objection.)

THE COURT: (Waking.) Ma, it's just
underwear . . . I can explain . . .

Q: Can you tell me what I am now holding in my
hand? (Enter EXHIBIT.)

A: Yes. It is a marriage certificate.

Q: People were married in the camp?

A: Oftentimes worker inmates fell in love and
were married . . . by the Commandant himself.

Q: But surely you couldn't start a family
there.

A: Many children were born in the camp, in the
maternity ward of the hospital. There was also a
childcare center where inmates could leave the
little ones.

Q: So inmates could receive medical care?

A: I myself was treated for the cl—the gout.

Q: Can you tell me what I am now holding in my hand?

A: Gelt. I mean, money. (Enter EXHIBIT.)

Q: German currency?

A: The camp printed its own. When we were paid, we could spend it as we liked . . . cake, ice cream, extra toiletries at the canteen . . .

Q: One more question: Did you ever witness any mistreatment of Jews in the camp?

A: Only once, when I was whipped by an S.S. woman . . . blond.

THE COURT: Did you have a hard-on?

THE CROWN: I know I do.

Q: Are you saying you're Jewish?

A: Jawohl—I mean, I am not a Zionist. Ask me about the coupons.

Montreal has more churches than houses and is sometimes called "The City of Churches."

A: "Never before has an event been so deeply sensed by its participants as being part of an epoch-shaping history in the making. Never before has a personal experience been felt to be so personally relevant. The hyperhistorical complex may be described as ethnocentric and egocentric. It is why most memoirs and accounts are full of preposterous verbosity, graphonomic

exaggeration, dramatic effects, overestimated
self-inflation, dilettante philosophizing,
would-be lyricism, unchecked histrionics,
unconfirmed rumor, bias, apologies, partisan
attacks. The question thus arises whether
participants in such a world-changing event can
at all be its historians and whether the time
has already come when valid historic judgment,
free of partisanship, vendetta, and ulterior
motive, is possible."

    THE COURT: Not on my watch . . . Hyperwhat?

In Toronto there were only two places where you could buy
beer: state-run liquor stores or the Beer Store. At the Beer Store
they bought a carton of Heineken. When they got back to the
hotel they discovered the carton consisted of ten bottles instead
of twelve, and that instead of containing twelve fluid ounces,
each bottle contained eleven and a half. They decided that this
was not a problem; she just wanted to have something around.
There was no room in the mini-bar but she liked it at room
temperature anyway.

    Q: I hold in my hand Cassell's English-German
Dictionary, 1957, twelfth edition, updated 1968.
    A: I am unfamiliar with this volume.
    Q: It defines Entwesung to mean "disinfection,
sterilization, extermination of vermin,
delousing." I put it to you that Entwesung refers
to pest control.

A: The prefix ent means "to negate." And
wesen . . . May I see this book?

Q: My Lady . . .

THE COURT: Got something to hide, Counsel?
(To Witness) Mind if I look over your shoulder?

A: "Reality, substance, essence, being,
creature."

THE COURT: "Living thing, organism, state."

A: "Condition, nature, character, property."

THE COURT: "Intrinsic virtue, conduct,
demeanor."

Q: If I could get that back . . . ?

A: "Air."

A: "Way."

A: "Bearing."

THE COURT: And while you're at it, look up
creeping fescue.

Judicial notice had been taken. The jury had been instructed.
There was no need to prove that which could not be the subject of dispute among reasonable persons. No need for witnesses, testimony, descriptions, heavy accents, etc., for stories
that always begin and end the same way (and how else can
they begin and end?). No further deposition required, no
experts, scholars, translators, perpetrators, journalists. It was
on the books, as it were, the jury instructed to that effect.
Installed in their wooden chairs as in a loge at the opera, they
would not have to hear about, be subject to, suffer the imprecations of, be reduced to, bear with, hear out, be haunted by,

put upon, put off, smell what could no longer be smelled but only evoked. It was a matter of record. There was ample documentation, no burden of proof—not to mention what need not be said. (*So you suffered*. Life is suffering. *So you watched loved ones die*. Whom has love kept alive?) And it would be something of a relief then, really, to be spared the painstaking detail, the broken-English allegations, the palsied limbs and voices, the unblinking candor, the obligatory tears, the inaccuracy of memory and permanence of same, the imperfections of translation, the lapses, recoveries, second-handing of experience, the dignity of composure and indignity of its loss, the figured speech and sly maneuvering of counsel, to not be manipulated, have one's buttons pushed, look in the eye of or be looked in the eye by, be moved or unmoved, unchanged, unforgiving, not to mention not having to hear the unspeakable, think the unthinkable, unsee the unseeable, envy (yes, envy), ponder, blink, sigh, doubt, etc., et al., at al., i.a., not to mention ad infinitum, ad absurdum, ad nauseam, ad perpetuam memoriam.

It was officially remembered, as it were.

So noted.

Sie schauen gut, Sie schauen gut
Sie blick fein, Sie schauen fein
Happy, happy birthday to you

DEFENCE: I put it to you that it cannot be reasonably true, in that crematorium chimneys do not belch flames.

WITNESS: There are many accounts of a substantially similar nature.

DEFENCE: Have you considered what happens to a chimney that belches flames?

WITNESS: I imagine—

THE COURT: Witness! Do not imagine, please!

EXHIBIT P-4: UNAMENDED, ORIGINAL VERSION OF INFORMATION NUMBER 14476777

Q: The Polish-Soviet investigation committee produced the four million figure?

A: Yes.

Q: Would you say that's a false figure?

A: I would say it's inaccurate.

Q: Hoess produced the 2.5 million figure.

A: Yes.

Q: The War Refugee Board produced the 1.7 million figure.

A: I'm not sure whether—

Q: That figure is correct?

A: It's within reason, yeah, but still a little high.

Q: And you produced one million.

A: Yes, but with much more information than was at their disposal.

The electric light bulb was invented in Canada. So was the baseball glove.

THE CROWN: Objection.

THE COURT: Overruled.

DEFENCE: Objection.

THE COURT: I'll allow it, order. (Gavel.) Anyone who finds this testimony distasteful, unpleasant, or emotionally draining is free to stick their head back up their arse. The witness may proceed.

THE ASHES: (

[ENTER CANADIAN CONTENT]

).

```
WITNESS: I love Jews.

THE CROWN: I quote: "Many countries of the
Anglo-Saxon world, notably Britain and America,
are today facing the gravest danger in their
history, the danger posed by the alien races in
their midst. Unless something is done in Britain
to halt the immigration and assimilation of
Africans and Asians into our country, we are
faced in the near future, quite apart from the
bloodshed of racial conflict, with the biological
alteration and eventual extinction of the British
people as they have existed here since the coming
of the Saxons. In short, we are threatened with
the irrecoverable loss of our European culture
and racial heritage." Are these not your words?

   THE COURT: Odor in the court!

   WITNESS: I was having a bad day. Notice I
didn't say anything about Jews.
```

The CN Tower is the tallest free-standing structure in the Western Hemisphere. The stairs to the main level consist of 1,776 steps. They are for emergency use only. The indoor observation deck has a glass floor two and a half inches thick. Fred's wife refused to put her weight on it, so Fred went in alone. He stood on top of 1,122 feet of space and looked down, a cartoon figure who has stepped off a cliff but has yet to appreciate the untenability of his position. He saw a parking lot. (The tower once housed a discotheque called Sparkles which boasted the highest dance floor in the world.) There was a revolving restaurant that completed a full rotation every seventy-two minutes, but lately they were getting takeout and taking it back to their room.

The tower is struck by lightning forty to fifty times a year.

```
THE CROWN: Are you a chemist, sir?
WITNESS: Technically speaking . . .
THE CROWN: Yes or no, please.
WITNESS: I have had basic training at the
college level.
THE COURT: Are you a chemist, yes or no?
WITNESS: No, ma'am.
THE CROWN: Are you a physicist?
WITNESS: No.
THE CROWN: Are you a toxicologist?
WITNESS: No.
THE CROWN: Are you a historian?
WITNESS: I minored in history at the
undergraduate level.
THE COURT: That's a no.
CLERK: So noted.
THE CROWN: Are you a statistician?
WITNESS: No.
THE CROWN: Are you a forensic archaeologist?
WITNESS: I'm not sure what that is.
THE COURT: Me neither. How about a
philematologist?
THE CROWN: Are you an engineer?
WITNESS: I believe I have the required
```

background and training both in the classroom and
in practice to perform my function as an engineer.

THE CROWN: Do you have a degree in
engineering, sir?

WITNESS: Well, I would question what an
engineering degree is.

THE COURT: I wouldn't. Do you have a degree
or no?

THE WITNESS: I was unable to complete my
studies due to financial hardship.

THE COURT: Let the record show the witness
practises engineering without degree,
certificate, or licence.

CLERK: So noted.

THE CROWN: Yet you felt qualified to conduct
this . . . investigation.

WITNESS: I conducted it.

THE CROWN: Chemistry, forensics, toxicology,
engineering–all disciplines pertinent to this
proceeding, yet you can claim expertise in none
of them.

THE WITNESS: Well, I would question what is
meant by expertise.

THE COURT: I'll bet.

WITNESS: Anyone who's gone to college for two
years has the necessary math and science to
practise electrical engineering in the state of
O _____ and to do what I did in the field.

THE CROWN: How much research did you do?

WITNESS: As much as I could in the time I was allotted . . . I could build a crematory with what I've learned. I ran a bone press.

THE CROWN: What kind of research materials did you use?

WITNESS: Maps, floor plans, original blueprints . . . the bulk of them from the official archives at the camps.

THE CROWN: These don't look so official to me. I would suggest that all you did was procure tourist materials available at any souvenir kiosk.

THE COURT: Archives my ass.

WITNESS: I did not go there as a tourist.

THE CROWN: I would suggest you went there as an amateur, a fraud, and a trespasser. My Lady, the methodology of this inspection, if it can even be called that, is ridiculous and preposterous and I ask the Court to determine this witness not be allowed to provide expert testimony as the paucity of his training in all relevant areas, as well as his unsuitability to comment on questions of engineering, is unequivocal.

THE COURT: Let the record show the witness has . . . paucity? (Gavel.) Now why did I just do that?

CLERK: So noted.

EXHIBIT P-4: AMENDED VERSION OF INFORMATION
NUMBER 14476777

A: Sample One showed no detection Sample Two showed
no detection Sample Three showed no detection Sample Four
showed no detection Sample Five showed no detection Sample
Five duplicate test showed no detection Sample Six showed no
detection Sample Seven showed no detection Sample Seven
spike recovery test indicated one hundred and nineteen percent
Sample Eight showed no detection Sample Eight duplicate test
showed one point nine milligrams per kilogram Sample Nine
showed six point seven milligrams per kilogram Sample Ten
showed no detection Sample Eleven showed no detection
Sample Twelve showed no detection Sample Thirteen no detection Sample Fourteen no detection Sample Fifteen showed ten
point three milligrams per kilogram Sample Sixteen showed
one point four milligrams per kilogram Sample Sixteen spike
recovery test indicated ninety-six percent Sample Seventeen
showed no detection Sample Eighteen showed no detection

THE CROWN: Are you a chemist, sir?

WITNESS: I have a doctorate in analytical
chemistry from Cornell University.

THE COURT: Bingo!

THE CROWN: Tell us about Prussian blue.

WITNESS: I graduated first in my class at
Harvard, summa cum laude.

THE COURT: Oh Lawdy!

THE CROWN: So the absence of color doesn't necessarily mean cyanide radicals aren't present?

WITNESS: I also have a full professorship at Cornell. I sit on the boards of DuPont, Procter and Gamble, and Clairol.

THE COURT: Let the record show the witness sits on boards.

CLERK: So noted.

WITNESS: My heroes are Marie Curie and Gaylord Perry.

THE CROWN: So by the time they got to you the samples had pretty much been reduced to powder, is that correct?

WITNESS: Correct. I also enjoy sailing and tennis, and consult with the government on a number of projects which I'm not at liberty to discuss. Go Tribe!

THE CROWN: Would you say, then, that their integrity as samples was pretty much compromised?

WITNESS: What was the question?

THE COURT: What's the difference between a Jew and a louse?

WITNESS: About three hundred parts per million.

THE COURT: Good enough for me. (Gavel.) Mexican, anyone?

DEFENCE: If it's all the same to My Lady, we'll stick with the cafeteria.

IN THE COURT OF QUEEN'S BENCH OF ONTARIO

FINAL JUDGEMENT

> BAILIFF: All rise.
> THE COURT: Has the jury reached a verdict?
> FOREMAN: We have, My Lady.

They'd come from everywhere—from the city, the provinces, the States; from across the ocean. They'd traveled by car, bus, plane; they'd walked, biked, hitchhiked, hopped trains. They were skinheads and militant Jews, Klansmen, militant blacks, communists, revisionists, homosexuals, libertarians, survivors, survivors of the dead, defenders of free speech, civil rights activists, groups without affiliation, people who just wanted to hurt things and people who were there to watch things hurt. It was somebody's birthday. The street in front of the courthouse had been blocked to traffic and the demonstrators gathered there with their signs and banners and megaphones and effigies, some in gas masks, facing the line of Mounties who were there to keep them off the courthouse steps. No ceremonial red but black leather, crash helmets, the long white batons held crosswise and end to end to form a single rail. It was the twentieth of April.

Rank sweetness of horseshit in the street. The sky a cold spring blue, elm trees blossoming in spite of everything.

The defendant appeared on the courthouse steps with his defense team, the Frenchman, Fred and his wife, a dozen other witnesses and sympathizers, everyone in yellow hard hats like a cadre of building inspectors. The Crown had not yet emerged. The barrister's bandages were off, ragged pink patches of new skin on her face. The skinheads took up a low one-word chant, their voices a percussive thump like a blunt instrument. A bass hum of disapproval, cheers, applause. The riot squad stood as still as the trees.

They started down. Local news teams closed in. The defendant turned to Fred and raised his voice. "You and the missus can ride with me," he said, not for the first time.

Fred looked around dubiously. "I don't think we'll all fit." Wasn't there a rear exit?

"First come, first serve," the German said, and this was the extent of the plan. A microphone bumped his mouth. Shouted questions he answered in motion: only the beginning . . . they had not heard the last . . . would not be silenced, he assured them, and then the crowd, friend and enemy alike, drowned him out. His lip was bleeding.

Fred's wife held on to his arm. The police pushed the demonstrators to the curb, opening a path on the sidewalk. The demonstrators pushed back and the passage narrowed, then opened up again. The air felt thick, crowded with cries. On the street mounted officers floated above the roofs of parked cruisers. A single reporter and her cameraman still dogged the defendant, who by now was only trying to get away. What car? Fred saw something red burst on the side of the reporter's head, felt it wet on his face, saw someone wearing a handkerchief like a bank robber. He wondered if he was her enemy. Then he looked ahead and couldn't see the defendant anymore.

In the street someone was burning a flag.

The Mounties surged back toward the steps and knocked Fred off his feet. His wife yelled his name and helped him up, his glasses under his nose. When he put them back on he saw a pair of blue-jeaned legs under a huddle of cops, white helmets clicking together. The demonstrators flooded the sidewalk. Some of them ran up the courthouse steps, though Fred wasn't sure now exactly what they were demonstrating. He'd thought they might come after him but they seemed more interested in each other; he was a reason to fight. He couldn't hear himself yelling. Couldn't get alongside her so he pushed her ahead of him across the sidewalk. He was no longer sure which way the hotel was, they just had to get off this block. In the street he looked to his right. Another contingent of cops were advancing in a wedge, gas-masked, prodding the demonstrators before them with the long white batons. Behind them the tear gas squad, riot guns slanted across their chests, moving in slow lockstep like a dream parade of the faceless. The retreating crowd solidified around him, a hard grip of backs and shoulders going nowhere. A woman was screaming. He saw his wife driving herself toward the other side of the street; either she was just beyond this knot of bodies or too strong for it. A horse trotted between them. The hard muscle of the mob relaxed and he could move again. A man with a long beard spat in his face. Fred would have preferred a blow, realized he was somehow still wearing the hard hat. A skinhead grabbed the beard and smashed the man's nose with his forehead, and Fred, who did not condone violence unless absolutely necessary, was about to thank him when a cop appeared behind the skinhead, got a baton under his chin with both hands, and dragged him off. The crowd flexed again. Fred felt himself lifted off his feet like a piece of something in a sea. He couldn't see her, nor hear her, nor hear himself saying her name. They were pressing in from all sides now and it was getting hard to breathe, let alone believe.

This was not making history, this was being crushed in its coils.

This was losing yourself.

Every day is someone's birthday.

Probably the tear gas saved him. A sound like a car back-firing but muffled, and the crowd let him go for good. An acrid smell. He heard the sound again, closer, and his eyes began to sting. He could just see a plume of white drifting in when they shut so tight his head hurt. He had a handkerchief somewhere, went down on all fours like he'd dropped it but didn't they say it was lighter than air? Someone stepped on his hand, he had to beat on someone's leg. He crawled. His skin burned. His eyes felt like wounds. His nose too full to breathe with, he sucked air through his mouth but it was made of fire and he coughed it all out, inhaled and coughed again, deep retching ejaculations that turned him inside out like some damage to his deepest self. He listened for her, tried to sort her out of the shouting, crying, the laughing horses, shattering glass, the coughing and choking, rattling of metal. He crawled with his face inside his shirt. The street was covered with snot. Then he was sitting on the other side of it, another casualty on the curb with a rope of mucous a foot long pending from one nostril.

He managed to open one eye. A canister rolling by, dividing into three pieces, each one exploding. Nonlethal. He turned and tried blindly to rise, endless tears pouring forth like some inexhaustible grief of which he were only a channel.

```
Dear Fred,

First, let me apologize for taking so long to respond to your
inquiry. It took considerable time for the dust to settle
after the rec room incident of last month, and I'm afraid all
my time was consumed dealing with the matter at hand. I'm
happy to say that order has been restored, and though the
tragedy was regrettable, I believe the Institute is all the
stronger for it. I do hope the delay has not caused you too
much inconvenience.

In regards to your proposal, I'm sorry to say that we're going
to have to pass. The Board of Corrections here as well as the
state budget office have deemed the bid too expensive and have
opted instead to refurbish the existing facility. The contract
has already been awarded, though I'm not at liberty to say to
whom. I'm sorry that things had to work out this way. I found
your visit enlightening, and I assure you the outcome would
have been different had I more say in the matter.

If I can be of further assistance, please do not hesitate to
call on me at any time.

Sincerely,

Bill A. A _____
```

The icebreaker was at a lounge equipped with a brand-new karaoke machine, an interactive entertainment device Fred found intolerable. He did not attend. The next evening there was a formal dinner at the Holiday Inn, and Fred was there with his wife. The banquet room had a flowing fountain in the center, chandeliers and a twenty-foot ceiling and was accessible to the handicapped. Silk draperies in school colors hung from the ceiling and the tables had matching skirts, with china, silverware, crystal glassware, and balloon bouquets for centerpieces. Maître d' service, an open bar, live music, a menu of full-course meals—all courtesy of the Mystery Guest, about whom there was no want of speculation.

Fred and his wife sat at a table near the fountain with two other couples and two empty chairs. To their right another husband and wife of whom which was the alumnus Fred would not have guessed had the woman not been wearing a name tag. Thin-faced and blushing, she gave him her hand and said they'd had algebra together.

"It's all right if you don't remember," she said. "I remember everything—I can't help it." She brandished a yearbook.

"Some kind of syndrome," her husband said, "there's a name for it," and they exchanged occupations.

"Freelance engineer," Fred said, and she asked what kind of engineering, and he said he specialized in punitory hardware, then waited to be asked to elaborate but wasn't.

The man to his left was more familiar. He'd been voted Most Likely to End Up in Prison and this was in fact where he'd been. He didn't say why or for how long but he'd also lost the use of his legs in a motorcycle accident and sat in a wheelchair wearing a leather jacket, a fringe of hair combed over his scalp, next to his girlfriend, a sweet-natured young woman not half his age with long yellow hair and pitted cheeks and a tattooed snake coiled around her jugular vein.

The band played songs without words, blue tremolo, sleepwalking out of the past.

Orders were taken: chicken, steak, or fish. Before dinner was served, the class vice-president, who'd resumed the endless martini he'd begun at the icebreaker, rose unsteadily to applause and whistling and stood behind the podium under the welcoming banner, fourteen feet of canvas screenprinted in school colors. The class vice-president welcomed his classmates, attempted a joke playing waistlines and hairlines off inflation and recession, honored the dead (whose graduation pictures were displayed on the wall behind the podium and included the class president, a demise no one would speak of), raised his glass to the missing, hoped to see everyone at Cedar Point the following day, and raised his glass again to the Mystery Guest ("Thank you, whoever you are, and keep em coming"), finally returning to the table he shared with the surviving class officers and the empty seat beside him.

Lights lowered, candles lit. The band played ballads during the meal. After each song the diners would look up and applaud, and this was also the opportunity to look around, just happy to be there or hungry for the shock of recognition, the unkindnesses of time, perhaps stealing a glance at the man who'd been voted Nicest Eyes (Male) and his youthful (male) companion. Some of the tables called to each other in recollection, bursts of merriment as oppressive as only the happiness of others can be. But everyone pondered the running question of the Mystery Guest, whether he or she had been voted Most Athletic, Most Intelligent, Nicest Smile, Class Clown, or anything at all, had succeeded in Hollywood, real estate, the computer industry, some endeavor which could not be admitted to publicly, or had simply dreamt a winning number. For all anybody knew the enigma was sitting among them now, or perhaps watching from the wings like Gatsby, waiting for that right moment to reveal not only his or her identity, but also a greater design of which this generous repast was only a prologue.

Someone had to be Heimliched. A program too close to a candle caught fire.

No one called to the table at which Fred and his wife sat,

though it was not without conversation. The woman with whom he'd had algebra kept remembering things, disgorging bits of the past between bites. The girlfriend of the man voted Most Likely to End Up in Prison kept asking, "So how does it *feel*?" but nobody asked, "Didn't I see you on TV?"

"You should say something," Fred's wife said, near the end of her chicken breast.

"That's not why I came here," Fred said.

"It's not?"

"Say what?" the woman who'd had algebra with him said.

"If you hadn't waited so long, they could have put it in the program," his wife said.

"How's your chicken?" Fred said.

"You could still ask."

"Ask what?" the woman said.

"Everybody going to Cedar Point?" the girlfriend of the man voted Most Likely to End Up in Prison asked instead.

"Why not?" the husband of the woman who'd had algebra with Fred said. "You're never too old if someone else is paying for it."

"No Blue Streak for me," the man voted Most Likely to End Up in Prison said.

"I can't go on anything spinny," the woman who'd had algebra with Fred said. "One ride and I'm done for the day. Up and down and around is fine, I just can't do anything that spins."

"There's a name for that too," her husband said to no one and Fred's wife said, "What about just miniature golf?"

A waiter came with more champagne. "None for me," Fred's wife said. She was diabetic, thank you. A recent development.

"One or Two?" the girlfriend of the man voted Most Likely to End Up in Prison asked. "My auntie's Type One," she said and seemed grimly proud. Her voice turned grave. "Every thirty seconds, a leg is lost to diabetes." And a brief silence ensued, as if they awaited the drop of a limb.

After the main course the class vice-president made the rounds, lurching from table to table with a glass, squinting myopically at name tags. He came to Fred's wife and squinted at her chest and asked who her homeroom teacher was.

"It's not me, it's my husband," she said, pointing.

"Gonna do a little dancing?" the class vice-president asked.

"I have to watch my feet," she said. "I'm Type Two." It seemed to have given her life new meaning.

"Try the cheesecake," the vice-president said and bumped his way to the table where the class sweethearts sat. He was in auto parts.

"Maybe a sliver . . ." Fred's wife said, and everyone else ordered the mousse. Fred had another glass of champagne.

Then there were games, contests, prizes. They matched the baby picture to the graduate, answered trivia questions, raced to unscramble the names of the top ten songs their senior year. A slideshow. Lip-syncing. The music started again and there was dancing. The girlfriend of the man voted Most Likely to End Up in Prison wheeled her boyfriend out in front of the band, took both his hands and turned him in half circles, slow, then faster. She let go of him and swung her hips around the chair, clapping, then climbed into it and straddled him, danced in his denim lap. The man who'd been voted Least Likely to Succeed watched through a video camera, and the husband of the woman who'd had algebra with Fred said, "Think there's anything going on down there?"

"You can always ask him," Fred said, and the husband of the woman with whom he'd had algebra said, "Someone should run over *my* legs."

Fred and his wife slow-danced once, in the summer wind.

When she'd gone back to the table in deference to her disease, he drifted to the edges of the room and stood at the margins of conversations, right hand opening and closing, waiting politely to be noticed. When he was they were kinder than he'd expected, than perhaps he'd hoped they would be. Some of them seemed to remember him or were polite enough to pretend. They seemed to want to be impressed: "Are you the guy?" but no, hadn't seen it—heard about it at the icebreaker. Was he there? They consulted the program. They were all in the same boat now, and it was a lifeboat, without apparent capacity; there was always exactly room for one more.

The woman who'd been drum majorette said, "*60 Minutes*, right?" and Fred didn't bother to correct her; perhaps there wasn't room for everything. She was drunk. Then someone thought to ask if he was the Mystery Guest.

"If I was I wouldn't want to spoil it for you," Fred said, and they nodded. He was another kind of mystery—a stranger who'd been on TV. But the question renewed the topic of the evening, and after a few minutes he was able to slip away under its cover as discreetly as he'd arrived, picture untaken, glass empty, heading back toward his wife who sat with the husband of the woman with whom he'd had algebra.

"They won't know who you are if they don't know who you were," a voice said en route, and Fred, slipping past empty tables, turned.

The speaker was not familiar to him. If they'd shared any classes, even a homeroom or study hall, Fred could not recall. A man sitting alone at an empty table. He was not familiar to anyone else either for he wasn't in the yearbook, had not participated in any activities, had not distinguished himself athletically nor academically. He'd never missed a day of school, had posed no disciplinary problems nor achieved social distinction, and graduated with no honors other than Perfect Attendance. He'd changed little, perhaps least of them all. He lived in his parents' home, was adequately employed, had never married, hardly traveled, had neither suffered nor celebrated in excess. Like most of the class he had not been voted Most Likely to do or be anything; fading into oblivion was not a category on the ballot, but oblivion was where he'd begun.

"Excuse me?" Fred said.

"I thought you held your own," the man who hadn't been voted anything said.

"I think they're a little drunk."

"20/20," the man said, a little impatient now. "You didn't embarrass yourself."

Fred thanked him and bent down to see if he was wearing a name, but there was no tag, no introduction, no offered hand.

"I took it off," the man said. "I know who I am."

"Well good for you," Fred said. "We should all know this."

"They didn't mention Toronto."

"Toronto," Fred said, and here needed no explanation. "No, they didn't. Guess they decided it was a little off point." The point was a botched electrocution in Florida. He'd been sought out, consulted, interviewed. Stone Phillips called him "chief" off-camera.

"That's an interesting way to make a living," the man observed.

"Everybody's good at something," Fred said.

"So how's business, Mr. Death?" As if suit and glass were cloak and scythe.

"A little slow these days," Fred admitted, nodding his head, and said, "Fred."

"You're a doer, not a viewer," the man said. "That's something my mother says."

"And what do you do?"

"Watch TV."

"I mean for a living."

"Everybody's good at something," the man said, and that was the extent of it.

Fred nodded. He looked across the room to where his wife was but couldn't tell if she was looking back.

"They didn't say anything about the Report, either," the man said.

"You've read it?" Fred said.

"I never read books," the man said.

"You watch TV," Fred said.

"I read every word," the man said.

"Well I guess maybe it's more of a pamphlet?" Fred said.

"It's more than a book," the man said with the condescension of the utterly powerless. But he seemed to understand that the author is sometimes last to know.

"Well thank you," Fred said. He waited. "I don't suppose you're the . . ."

The man shook his head and might have smiled. "If I was it'd be a different kind of party."

Fred started to ask and stopped. He looked across the room again.

"You don't have to stay," the man said.

"Just looking in on my wife," Fred said. "She has a condition."

The man kept his eyes on Fred. "Just nature taking its course."

"Something else your mother says? Or is it your father?" Fred said. Must have been the champagne.

"Dad's got a mouthful of dirt," the man said. "But then I guess he would know." There was a commotion across the room, and Fred looked back toward the corner he'd just left. A shout of disgust, uneasy laughter: the woman who'd been drum majorette seemed to have thrown up, and the man voted Least Likely to Succeed was looking unhappily at his shoes. Fred turned back to the man who'd read the Report; he wasn't looking that way, nor was he looking at Fred, who remained a moment longer, said, "Well say hello to . . ." and left it up to him, then returned to the table where his wife sat and stayed there the rest of the evening.

Eventually the class vice-president was unconscious, head down at the officers' table. Some of the balloons had broken free and floated up to the ceiling, rolling around on invisible currents like disembodied thoughts. Beneath them a slur of voices, laughter, sobbing, apologies, just one more for the scrapbook, for the road. The band broke the spell with songs of the present, like an alarm clock in a dream. The evening was drawing to a close—four hours and thirty years gone by already—but almost no one had left, and they'd all but forgotten about the Mystery Guest. Then the woman voted Most Likely to Become a Teacher ran in from the parking lot, said a long black limousine was pulling up outside.

"Thank you for calling National Engineering, Inc. All lines are busy. At the tone, please leave your name, number, and a detailed message, and someone will get back to you as soon as possible."

[Tone.]

[Hangs up.]

[Tone.]

[Breathing.]

[Tone.]

"*Blut und Ehre. Heil!*"

[Tone.]

"This is for Fred. Hi, Fred, this is Sue at Jiffy Cleaners and Tailors? Your clothes are ready. One suit, one shift, two sweaters, one comforter. We couldn't do much with the ink but we talked about that, okay? We're open Monday through Friday, nine to six, and Saturday, ten to five. Okay, thank you."

[Tone.]
[Squealing sound.]

There were two of them. They never looked at him. He didn't know what color their eyes were. He would steal glances just to see, and when he did they weren't looking back. They were both of medium build, but one of them had olive skin while the other was pale—a redhead. Go figure. They were younger men, though it was hard to tell their ages exactly—early thirties, he guessed, but thirty wasn't what it used to be. It was hard to get a good look; he was at the counter and they always took a booth. He had to turn his head on some pretext, and of course you couldn't stare. He observed them in increments, put them together in pieces: denim, chinos, sunglasses, sideburns. Brown leather. They were casual. He tried to listen for an accent when they were conversing or kidding the waitress, the one who'd taken his wife's place, but they seemed to keep it short, to maintain a volume so you couldn't be sure. Probably trained that way.

He'd see them at the diner. Might have seen them somewhere else but he couldn't be sure, they were good at being anybody. When they left and the gal who'd replaced his wife refilled his cup, he'd ask her if she knew them. Said he was just curious, said they looked familiar. Couldn't remember her name.

Q: What was the name of Christopher Columbus's dog?
She stuck her thumb, squeezed a drop onto the strip. A drop was all it took, and any finger would do. She got home late and couldn't just go right to sleep, so she sat in the kitchen

watching tapes, sticking her thumb. She sat with her feet up. You had to take care of your feet—it was a matter of every thirty seconds. She kept them clean, kept her nails trim and used lotion but not between the toes. She wore custom-molded shoes with special inlays, arch straps and collars. (You couldn't sit on register.) At home she sat in the kitchen with her face in a thirteen-inch screen, drinking Diet Coke with them up, her back to the front room, in her smock.

Unwinding, rewinding. She put the strip in the meter.

He sat in the front room with the little people, her little friends, in front of the twenty-five-inch. He liked to smoke in the living room, liked doing his work to the news. Things were not his fault. (Her back was not to *him*.) He'd gotten her the machine so she could sit in the kitchen and not in his smoke; for her black-and-white was color enough. He made the tapes for her—she liked the old ones best—*The Saint*, *The Fugitive*, *Highway Patrol*. She loved Broderick Crawford's no-nonsense gravel, she loved hating the one-armed man, and who doesn't love an English accent?

She hit Rewind. Things happen so fast: one second you're at the wholesale club buying twelve pounds of ground sirloin, getting lightheaded, the faces around you blurring and babbling. Then you're lying on your back in a white room, a pale figure leaning over you, but instead of the voice of light she heard a scolding Filipino accent: "You blood is too much sweet! Is too much sugar!" She could barely understand him. But before the whiteness there was nothing, not even that. Everything just stopped, then started again in a new way—for good, and barely in English.

a) Pinto

b) Isabella

c) Leonardo

d) Bubbles

She took out the strip. She took out the tape. She could open the fridge without getting up. The pens were in the fridge with the Diet Coke. The pens were better than needles because you just had to click them, only they wouldn't go through cloth. You had to take them out fifteen minutes before so it wouldn't sting. She took out a Diet Coke. She checked her feet with a mirror. She checked the numbers on the meter and put in another tape.

She opened the can.

"*Bonanza!*"

The little people lived on a shelf.

He said he was going to get her a new machine, one that played discs instead. Progress was constantly being made, things being improved upon, like it or not; you just had to wait till the price went down. He kept up. He had a computer. It was in his office in the living room—more of a nook really, a nick in the wall—and it was equipped with something what did he call it again? but at night when he was in bed and she wasn't ready to sleep, or pretend to, or for what he was ready for, she could go into the living room and sit at his desk, and she would dial a number without dialing, press Enter and enter, ride long-distance lines to other cities, houses, rooms, to mornings and afternoons where other people sat before other screens that lit up their faces—though you couldn't see them—perhaps their lives, playing the game. In the game they would answer questions that tested their knowledge of past and present events, of persons living or dead, of Christopher Columbus and the Seven Wonders of the World, and more than one player played, they would each take a turn, and it was almost like having them over except better in that they weren't, in that they couldn't smoke or eat or drink things you would have to get them, and they wouldn't have to see you and smell your feet and think thoughts about you, everyone was their essence, particles lighting up screens, faces, voids: UPANYWAY, BIGBRO, MRCOFFEE, QUIZARD.

She was FREDSGIRL. He took care of her and she took care of her feet, collected the little people. She liked the boy and girl people—Dearly Beloved, Smart Little Sister, A Star for You—and especially the ones from the Inspirational Collection—Celestial Dreamer Music Box was perhaps her favorite, though if anyone asked she would of course say she loved them all the same.

Q: *What is Charles Bronson's real name?*

The answering machine was next to the computer. He needed it for business purposes, but he didn't get so many business calls these days. He watched a lot of news. People left other kinds of messages, but he wouldn't let her hear the kinds of messages they left. She wanted to unlist their number. He told her to let him worry about it, she had enough on her mind; her feet, her blood, her trouble sleeping; what she wouldn't tell him and what he wouldn't hear.

She had her own name. She moved from machine to machine.

At Revco she would pick up the microphone and say, "Price check on Register Two," or "Security to Zone One."

Broderick Crawford would say, "Ten-four! Ten-four! Ten-four!"

A golf course and a village of outlet stores had been built over the ruin where they'd once gone plinking, so they went to a firing range instead. There were twelve bays but on Sunday, if you were a member, you could have the whole range to yourself for an hour and you could bring a guest. The warden was a member. He was trying not to be a warden. He'd retired and grown a goatee and had brought along a case of pistols of mostly foreign make: Ruger, Norinco, a Bulgarian-made Makarov, two Berettas. He seemed to have given up on revolvers entirely.

Fred brought one piece, a short-barreled .32 that had belonged to a veterinarian. It was not a weapon designed for long-range accuracy and the warden looked at it and said, "It's been a while, but isn't that what they used to call a Saturday Night Special?"

"Nineteen-year-old kid took out Franz Ferdinand with one of these," Fred said. "If it was gun enough to start World War One . . ." He kept it pointed at the floor. "In a defensive confrontation you want something that's easy to use."

"You want something that's not gonna blow up in your face," the warden said.

"Things have a way of doing that anyway," and they stood at the firing line, the partitions narrow like doorways without doors. The warden leaned back.

"Well?" he said.

"Well what?" Fred said.

"I'm told it makes me look like Colonel Sanders."

"I thought that's what you were going for," Fred said and slipped his goggles on over his glasses so that he looked like someone whose vision was so enhanced he could see wavelengths invisible to the average person. "I see a couple of guys at the diner just about every time I go there. The other day I saw them at the Shell station."

"Couple guys," the warden said.

"I'm not sure," Fred said, "but I think they were at the wholesale club too."

"Well it's cheaper to buy in bulk," the warden said.

"Could be," Fred said. "Could be routine surveillance, harassment—you know they're experts at psychological warfare."

"They."

"Mossad," Fred said and slipped on his earmuffs and shot six rapid rounds into the silhouette at the back of the range. The warden raised his Beretta and fired almost in unison as if at a common foe, and in the aftermath of humming blue air there was the smell of the Fourth of July and the targets dancing to stillness. They reeled them in.

Fred studied the wounds he would have made. The warden said, "Maybe you should bend your front knee a little more."

"In a defensive confrontation," Fred said and the warden turned his back on the rest of it, went to the long table at the long window behind which the rangemaster sat. He lifted the Colt from its case—his lone American arm—and asked after Fred's wife. As if there would be any change of subject.

"Still at the till," Fred said. He pushed out the cylinder of the revolver and the spent black powder casings rattled onto the floor like loose change. "Three to eleven."

"Not a bad thing," the warden said, a little unsure. "Keeping busy . . ."

"She's not doing it out of boredom," Fred said. "Told me the other night a van pulled into the parking lot and just sat in the back corner with the fog lights on. No plates. Drove in circles for about five minutes, then flashed the brights through the storefront and took off. Said it felt like they were winking at her."

The warden looked at him. "Well you know, if you need a little help."

"All I need is to make an honest living, thank you, like anyone else." And he inventoried familiar grievances, then added some new. The phone calls.

"'They' again," the warden said.

"I've made enemies," Fred said.

He'd sat in courtrooms making statements before God, against people just trying to do a dirty job.

"That's not what I'm talking about," Fred said. "I thought you were on my side."

"Just saying," the warden said. "I believe the word is *repercussions*?"

"Tell it to my ulcer," Fred said. He used a speed loader, this time the plus-P rounds—flat-nosed, hard cast, shoot somebody in the face and they'd lose more than their smile. Clipped a fresh enemy on the hanger and sent it back. "Feels like I swallowed a hot coal."

"I might have you beat there," the warden said. His Colt was also a .32 but it was an automatic made in 1903, its body embossed with swirling patterns like vines. It held eight rounds and he pulled the trigger in a slow deliberate way, the way he spoke, as if every sound made in the hour were part of one con-versation. Fred rapid-fired as before, and this time he pushed the retrieve button first so he could shoot a charging target, a darkness in the shape of a man growing at him from the back of the range.

The rangemaster knocked on the glass. "Shooter!" She spoke through an intercom. "Hey Dirty Harry. Do that again you can go shoot beer cans in your backyard. We have rules here."

The warden walked back to the table again, put down the Colt, and took up the Makarov. He came back to his bay slowly, pale and wheezing.

"You all right?" Fred said.

"Just acting my age."

"That's nice-looking iron."

"Don't let's get started on iron." He put in a clip. "Made in Bulgaria. Cold War shit."

"Looks like James Bond."

"I guess you should know," the warden said, "being a man of intrigue now and all."

"I'm not making it up," Fred said. "You should listen to my answering machine."

"But you wouldn't take anything back."

"It's out of my hands—I'm told I've been translated into four languages."

The warden either smiled or winced. "Sounds like someone needs an agent."

"I'm not in it for the money," Fred said.

"I didn't say you were . . . Told by whom?"

"They wouldn't let me testify. People have a right to know."

"And what if you're wrong?" the warden said, more or less to himself. Then to himself: "Human beings in cages . . . like some ungodly zookeeper . . ." He looked up. "Went in for my annual last month—I tell you?"

"There's iron in brick," Fred said. "That's what makes it red."

"Says he wants to do some more tests."

"Ferric-ferrocyanide."

"I love the way you say that."

Fred kicked brass across the firing line, down the lane. "Soaks it up like a sponge. No so-called expert is going to tell me . . . I believe the word is *perjury*?"

"There's iron in white brick too."

"They got to him," Fred said. Then they'd gotten to Missouri, Delaware . . .

"There's iron in blood," the warden said. "Think I'm feeling it now."

Fred came back a little. "What?"

The warden started, stopped. Decided against. "Maybe next time we shoot skeet."

"These days I only want to shoot what's coming at me," Fred said.

"Well how about it then," the warden said, and they riddled the rest of the hour. When the rangemaster tapped on the window behind them, Fred turned with such intent it seemed the confrontation he'd been rehearsing was finally at hand. Their time was up. They went through two doors and the next party was waiting in the gun shop, an old guy and two kids who must have been his grandchildren. Boy and girl.

"Time to teach em how to protect their loved ones," the old man said, like there wasn't a moment to lose.

"You too?" the warden said.

"That was a short hour," Fred said.

"You get to a point where even the bad time flies," the warden said.

Fred handed in his goggles. "So how did your checkup go?" he said.

He walked up to the counter in his three-piece suit, asked for a cup of coffee and told the kid at the register he was interested in the management position. A woman in a light-blue shirt with golden arches on the breast pocket gave him an application and asked him if he needed a pen. Fred said he didn't, and filled in the blanks in the smoking section while he drank his coffee.

They called him a week later. He wore his other suit. The first assistant manager came to the counter and shook Fred's hand. He was dressed like the woman who'd given him the application but wore a dark-blue tie and told Fred to come around back. Next to the restrooms a door said EMPLOYEES ONLY and the first assistant manager opened it and let him in. There was a time clock by the door, then a stainless-steel walk-in freezer and a stainless-steel sink where a kid stood mixing Mac Sauce. The sauce vegetables and the sauce base came in separate containers and the formula was a closely guarded secret, like that of Pepsi-Cola or the ink used for printing money.

"I thought it was just ketchup and mayonnaise," Fred said.

"I didn't hear that," the first assistant manager said. You could smell the grease trap. A cockroach disappeared.

Hamburger buns in big plastic trays stacked eight feet high. They squeezed past them to the restaurant manager's office. The restaurant manager sat in a chair studying Fred's application, looked up gradually as if tearing himself away. He was a stocky man with thinning red hair and also wore a blue tie but his shirt was yellow. He did not rise, probably due to his bulk and the size of the chair, but gave Fred his hand and a first name and told him to sit. The first assistant manager stood in the doorway. The office was tiny.

The restaurant manager looked at Fred squarely. "Takes balls," he said.

"How's that?" Fred said.

"Switching tracks like this at your age," the restaurant manager said. "Takes some real stones. My hat's off to you."

Fred thanked him. "It's not like I have a lot of choice," he said. He had not thought of it in terms of genitalia.

"If it's any consolation," the restaurant manager said, "Ray Kroc was fifty-two when he sold his first shake machine to the McDonald brothers."

"I didn't know that," Fred said, unconsoled.

"You didn't go to Hamburger U," the first assistant manager said.

"There's such a place?" Fred said, fairly amazed; perhaps next he'd see the Hamburglar on *America's Most Wanted*.

"Oak Brook, Illinois," the restaurant manager said, but he was looking at the application again. "You're some kind of engineer?"

"I've done engineering-related work," Fred said.

The restaurant manager frowned slightly. "Well we ain't smashing atoms here, this is fast food. Any management experience?"

"I've run my own business," Fred said. "It's all there."

The restaurant manager moved his lips. "I see references in the corrections field." He glanced at the first assistant manager and grinned. "You go over the wall or under it?"

"I'm a contractor," Fred said. "I design, repair, and maintain certain facilities . . . some training . . . It's a very specialized field."

"I'm sure," the restaurant manager said and looked again at the first assistant. "I used to be a teacher. High school—the young and the useless." One day one of the useless little bastards had asked him what was the use of history. "So welcome to the private sector."

"I'll give it my best shot," Fred said. "Like I say, I don't have much choice. Government contracts have a way of drying up." They stopped returning your calls.

"No shit," the first assistant manager said and they both looked at him. "I mean the government and all."

"Shift change," the restaurant manager said abruptly, and the first assistant manager gave him a puzzled look, then went away.

"I taught him social studies his junior year," the restaurant manager said.

"Small world," Fred said.

"Straight D's."

"Grades aren't everything," Fred said.

"My point is if he can do it," the restaurant manager said, and Fred nodded. They weren't splitting the atom, and Fred nodded again. You started at the bottom, Management Trainee. In this capacity learned all the jobs, working alongside the kids who flipped and seared meat, shot tartar sauce out of a caulking gun, passed free food to their friends through the drive-thru window, groped each other in the cooler. Then you were a Second Assistant Manager and there was paperwork and training new employees and staying till three in the morning closing and cleaning, dumping putrefied grease that smelled like the final corruption of matter, which you wouldn't have to do as First Assistant even if you couldn't get days, for you would be more concerned with building sales and controlling costs, honing leadership skills, controlling profit and loss line items, and always, always, whether you were Trainee or Restaurant Manager, which you would eventually become because luck was not a factor, it was simply a matter of hard work, patience, and the availability of positions, always maintaining Quality, Service, Cleanliness, and Value (QSCV), and Ensuring That A Respectful Workplace Exists In The Restaurant.

"That means no grabass to you," the restaurant manager said.

"You don't have to worry about that," Fred said.

"I'm not worried," the restaurant manager said.

"Define Q," he said.

"Quality," Fred said.

"Quality is doing the right thing even when no one's looking," the restaurant manager said.

"You come up with that?" Fred said and turned. The first assistant manager was standing in the doorway with a plunger.

The restaurant manager groaned. "Not again."

"I've done a little plumbing too," Fred said but couldn't remember if he'd put it on the application.

The first assistant manager waved the plunger at him. "You'll get your chance."

"Just give him the tour while I make the call," the restaurant manager said. He scribbled on the application and they shook hands one more time.

The restaurant was divided into management zones. The Grill Zone smelled like reconstituted onions. The hamburger patties were frozen solid and made a wooden clacking sound when you slapped them down. The dressing table stood behind the grill (mustard adds spice, ketchup adds moisture, they taught at Hamburger U) and there Fred was introduced to a management trainee, a tattooed and crew cut woman of about thirty who neither spoke nor offered her hand but bared all her teeth for about a tenth of a second. The first assistant manager said, "Right," and showed Fred the Drive-Thru Zone. Then he guided him to a door at the back of the building. On the way they passed the walk-in where a girl was cleaning the stainless with a sponge, the metal in her mouth the same color.

"Go with the grain," Fred said, already managing her, psyched by the tour, "stroke down, not up," and smiled his yellow smile. She looked at him through a faint reek of vinegar.

They went outside. It was mild and sunny but Fred still smelled reconstituted onions. Walking across the parking lot the first assistant manager asked Fred if the restaurant manager had said anything about him, and Fred replied, "Only the good stuff," and the first assistant manager said, "If they take you on I'll tell you why he quit teaching." They reached a wooden enclosure in the corner of the lot. Inside were a dumpster and an incinerator and now all Fred smelled was garbage. A man about Fred's age leaned on a shovel before the furnace with a cigarette in his mouth, watching a blue plastic milk crate melt in the flames.

"What'd I tell you about that?" the first assistant manager said.

"What you tell me about what?" the man asked the flames.

The first assistant manager grinned at Fred. "Guess what zone this is," he said and tugged the cigarette from the man's lips. He lit one of his own, pulled up another plastic milk crate, a red one, and sat.

"How long have you been doing this?" Fred asked either of them.

"About three years," the first assistant manager said and stood suddenly.

"Watch this," he said and picked up the red crate and pushed it into the incinerator. Presently it began to sag and puddle, melding slowly with the blue in the great heat, becoming something unspeakable. Mesmerizing.

Something ran under the dumpster.

"Thank you for calling National Engineering, Inc. All lines are busy. At the tone, please leave your name, number, and a detailed message, and someone will get back to you as soon as possible."

[Tone.]

"Hey Fred, pick up. Pick up, Freddy, I want to talk. You know who this is? Don't you want to talk? Pick up. We need to clear up a few things. Hope this isn't a bad time for you . . . should I call back? Maybe I should stop by instead so we can chat in person. Pick up. Pick it up, you fuck. You busy? You got your little prick up that pig's ass and you can't come to the phone? [Music.] Knock that off! [Music stops.] Jesus, I can smell it from here. Take a break. Pick up. Jesus, I'm doing you a favor . . . Okay, be that way. [Recites address.] I get that right? Ready or not, motherfucker, here we come."

[Tone.]

[Hangs up.]

[Tone.]

[Child, unintelligible.]

He was sitting at the counter when they came in. He didn't have to see them to know who they were. They took the booth behind him and to his left—he didn't look but that was where they always sat. The waitress hurried over with her coffee pot.

"My husband said the same thing," Fred heard her say. "Is that good or bad?" He didn't hear the answer but it made her chuckle. It always did. "You guys." He glanced over. One of them was wearing a baseball cap. The waitress came back around the counter. Fred finished his cup but when she swung the pot his way he held up his hand.

"You're kidding," she said.

"In a minute," he said and slipped off his stool and walked over to the booth. His hands were at his sides.

They didn't look up till he said, "Gentlemen." The one without the baseball cap had red hair and was dunking a tea bag.

"I hate to interrupt your breakfast," Fred said, though they hadn't yet been served, "but I'd like to ask you something." They glanced at each other but neither of them said anything. Finally, he could see what color their eyes were.

"I'd like to ask you," Fred said, trying to maintain a volume, a tone, "why you're following me."

The guy wearing the baseball cap glanced at the other one, then looked at Fred. "Excuse me?"

The one who was dunking the tea bag began, "He wants to know" and the other one said, "I heard what he wants to know." His eyes moved but not his head.

"You think we're following you?" he said after a moment's reflection.

Fred took a breath but didn't speak.

The men in the booth looked at each other. The one dipping the tea bag sort of shrugged. (A world of information in a gesture: training.) He did not seem especially perturbed. Curious, even, as to how this might play out. The other, having assumed the role of spokesman, looked back up at Fred.

"Is this a joke?" he said.

"Do I look like I'm joking?"

"So humor me: why do you think we're following you?"

Fred shifted his feet. He would play along for now. "In this country there's a thing called the First Amendment."

The man wearing a baseball cap nodded. "Which one is that again?"

"Religion?" the man dunking the tea bag said. He seemed to be trying to count.

"And speech," Fred said. "That's what concerns us here."

"Right," the man in the baseball cap said. "So how about the freedom to drink my coffee without some pencil-neck accusing me of some paranoid shit I don't even know what he's talking about?"

"Mikey, Mikey," the one with red hair assuaged. He poured honey in his tea. And *Mikey*, he'd called him. A name too thoroughly believable. "Let the Greek handle it."

"I'll handle it."

"We don't want you to handle it."

"Wait a minute." The one whose name was purportedly Mikey looked suddenly at Fred. "Is this some hidden camera shit? Is that what this is? Is Allen Fuck gonna come out of nowhere and shake my hand? Do we sign something?"

"Show's been off for years," the other one said.

"I thought they brought it back."

"You're thinking of the other one. On Fox."

Fred nodded, smiling. "Okay," he said, nodding and smiling. "Okay. Now that that's out of the way." He stopped nodding and smiling and then his hands started shaking. "Now that we're past that," he said, "I'm going to have to ask you to stop."

"I'm about to ask you the same, my friend," the guy wearing the ball cap said.

"I'm not joking," Fred said.

"Neither are we."

"I've got nothing against you people."

"Well that's a relief," the one now drinking his tea said.

"'You people'?" the other one said.

"It's in the bricks, I didn't put it there," Fred said. "I understand you're just following orders but I'm asking you to leave her out of it."

"Who?" one of them said. "What bricks?"

"You know who. I'm the one you want."

It had grown quieter in the diner. An autographed picture of Telly Savalas hung over the booth. Fred looked out the window. Their van was parked where it usually was. Carpet Kings. Probably full of surveillance gear.

The strap chafed his armpit.

The waitress came back with two plates of toast. White, wheat. She set them down, looked at the three of them a little uneasily, and said, "I didn't know you guys knew each other."

"Me neither," the one with the wheat toast said.

"Somebody thinks we do," the other one said.

She didn't understand. She looked at Fred.

"Mossad," he said.

Her lips formed the letter *M*.

"Moe Howard . . . mo money . . . ," the one with white toast said.

"Mos*sad*," the other one said. "Kinda like the Jewish CIA, right?"

"Israeli intelligence," Fred said to the waitress.

"There you go," the one with red hair said. "Is the manager around by chance?"

"I'll see if Dimitri's still here," the waitress said and backed away.

228

"Or is it JDL?" Fred said. His jacket was unbuttoned. In a defensive confrontation there is not always time to unbutton your jacket.

"What's that, a radio station?" the one without the base-ball cap said.

"Maybe he wants us to follow him," the one wearing the baseball cap said.

"Or," the other one said, "maybe he wants to follow us."

"He's not my type."

"Said he's the one we want."

"He's got a wedding ring."

"Don't they all."

"Looks a little shaky to me," the one whose alleged name was Mikey said.

"Must be nervous."

"He's making me nervous," the one who'd been called Mikey said, and the one who'd called him that said, "They don't want to make you nervous."

The waitress came back with the new owner. He was a tall handsome Greek in a sport jacket who spoke night-school English and had provided a nonsmoking section, added a children's menu and Telly Savalas. Changed everything but the name.

"Gentlemens," he asked everyone, "everything is how?"

The man with the baseball cap looked at the other man. "So how is it?"

The man with red hair and white toast tilted his head. "Ask whateverhisnameis."

"Fred?" Dimitri said to Fred.

"They've been dogging me for weeks," Fred said.

"Docking?" Dimitri said.

"Bothering him," the waitress said, "he means."

"Maybe months," Fred said. His hands were now rock steady. "Don't let the red hair fool you. Or the van. I won't even go into the phone calls."

Dimitri looked at the men in the booth. "Did you ever said him anything, this man?"

The man with red hair looked at the waitress for clarification, and then so did Dimitri. She shook her head like it weighed a ton.

"Fred was on 20/20," she whispered into the booth.

"He's gonna be on disability if he don't stop hairussing people," the man with the baseball cap said.

"He's giving you twenty years," the other one said. "Twenty years and fifty pounds."

"I can't even drink my coffee."

Dimitri told the waitress to go look after his customers.

"Guys, I am sorry because this," he said down into the booth.

"Well that's a start," one of them said.

"It was just a matter of time," Fred said.

"Fred," Dimitri said, "go to have your coffee. You have your coffee and let my customer be alone. If no, you have coffee in Dunking Donut. Understand?"

"I was having coffee on that stool before you ever set foot in here," Fred said, as if that superseded mere ownership. But it was very quiet in the diner. The kind of silence it takes a lot of people to make.

"If I've made a mistake," Fred said and the guy who wasn't wearing a baseball cap sighed and reached into his jacket. Fred steps back and reaches into his. Cross draw. The guy without the baseball cap is closer and he shoots him once in the fore-head. It is all one movement and Fred swings his arm to the left and shoots the other guy twice in the chest. The guy with the baseball cap slumps and lowers his head and his cap falls in his lap. The letter *M* tattooed on his bald spot. Telly Savalas grins, spattered.

"Gentlemens," he says, "your breakfast is at me."

"Does that mean what I think it means?" the one with the hole in his head said. He put back his wallet.

SOFA & LOVE SEAT
Beautiful sofa and love seat, Carolina blue, excellent condi-tion. Originally paid $1200, will take best offer.

$30 TOASTMASTER MODEL TOV200 4-SLICE
Easy-clean, nonstick interior. Bake, broil, toast, defrost, reheat, and top brown. 30-minute timer with stay-on fea-ture. LED power indicator. Full range temperature control. Slide-out crumb tray. Rack advances when door is opened. Includes wire rack, back pan, and broil insert.

Firm. Cash only.

ELECTRIC CHAIR
Authentic, full scale, never used. Being sold for non-payment. THIS IS NOT A FAKE. Solid oak construction, nylon restraints, adjustable seatback, leg electrodes, and

more. Once in a lifetime opportunity, ideal conversation piece for the well-heeled collector. Original value 35K, make offer. Helmet not included. Will go fast.

The next one was from a guy who called himself Hans Raeder, though he didn't sound German. He apologized for tying up the business line ("but in a way this is all of our business"). It took him a while. "But yeah," he said, said he heard strange noises on his phone—Zog was listening. He thanked Fred for writing it. Did he know the Three P's? He would have gone to Toronto but he'd had surgery (strangulated hernia). He said he was a big fan, said he wasn't alone. He sneezed. Took him a while but he got around to it ("I don't know if I'd call it a rally exactly"). But there would be speeches, potluck, social- izing, maybe a raffle. He could talk about the Report, they could talk about Zog. They would listen to whatever he wanted to talk about, and they would compensate him for talking about it. Wouldn't exactly say they were rolling in it ("We have house notes like anyone") but they would love to have him, if he would have them.

He asked if Fred ever heard strange noises on the line. Did he know how to use a multimeter? Did he know hernias are congenital? Did he know Eve had sex with the serpent to create Jews?

There would probably be a raffle.

He sang a song in German.

The next one was Sue from Jiffy. They still hadn't picked up their clothes.

———

His wife's cousin had acreage south of Norwalk, right off 61. Recreational property. He gave Fred directions over the phone. Go right in, he said, there were wild turkey and whitetail deer.

"I shoot nothing that lives," Fred said.

Go right in, his wife's cousin said, just like that. Not everyone was against him.

Fred called the warden, told him where it was. The warden said he'd try and make it. "If I'm late start without me."

Fred pulled off 61 South in the early afternoon. A winding county road, then a road with no name or number but a sign that marked it as a dead end. Bumpy and narrow, leaves and branches pressing against the windows like a mob of uncertain sympathy. If you met someone coming the other way . . . but somehow you knew there would be no one. At the end there was barely room to turn around, just an opening into the woods and another sign with its rusty declaration: PRIVATE PROPERTY. He turned off the engine and waited.

Or had he said he'd try and fake it?

He waited for most of an hour, started to nod off . . . the last letter . . . Zog, a giant with one eye, a long arm. He snapped out of it and got out of the car, walked around it looking for scratches. He stood by the sign. If it was private property, why not a gate? A lock? He looked back up the way he'd come, listening for traffic on the county road. Not everyone was against him, but if his phone were tapped . . . It had been a while since he'd pulled a trigger. He went back to his car, got the Colt out of the glove box. If the warden came he could honk his horn, but he was starting to think the warden wouldn't come. The way he'd sounded over the phone.

Fred went into the woods, wearing his synthetic suit. It was cold but walking didn't help. The footpath was wider than he'd expected. Trees, trees, bushes, grass, bare branches against the bright sky like veinwork. He almost stepped on a caterpillar. Heard something—a rustling, snapping—something of size and weight, but it seemed to come from no particular direction. His wife's cousin had said there were deer, and turkeys could be aggressive in the breeding season.

If a tree falls in the forest . . . how did it go again?

He came into a sort of clearing; the path forked around a patch of tall grass the color of straw with a big rock in the middle. Something sat atop the rock, looking at him. He heard the sound again. This time it was behind him and he spun, the hammer cocked.

If you shoot a tree in the woods, and no one is there . . .

The tree looked back. It was not a tree.

The warden was wearing a denim barn jacket and a hunting cap, but he did not have a gun. He was staring at Fred with a hand on his thigh. His lips were somewhat pursed, like someone trying to whistle or form a word, one that begins with the letter W. Something was oozing between his fingers. He still did not make a sound, but his cap said THE KING HAS RETIRED.

"You hear that?" he asked.

"What?" she said. "I was dreaming."

"Listen."

They lay on their backs and listened together. The night was mild, Indian-summer warm, the window open. Sounds of traffic on distant unknowable errands, the snarled snarl of a catfight, then only their own voices speaking up into the common darkness where the ceiling had been.

"Was that it?" she said.

"Maybe something bumping in the garbage cans."

"Cats," she said. "A raccoon."

"Maybe," he said.

"One tried to follow me up the porch the other day," she said. "Big as a little bear."

"But what was I dreaming?" she said.

His head was turned toward the nightstand on his side of the bed. The small drawer in it.

"You should get rid of that thing." She could see what he was thinking in the dark.

"Accidental discharge," he said.

"He could have pressed charges," she said.

"A flesh wound."

"Your best friend."

"Tell me about it," he said. "Says it's still not as bad as chemo."

"That a joke?"

"Ask *him*," Fred said, and silence resumed. He felt her turn onto her side; the wall of her back. He couldn't think of anything else to say, so he put his hand on her hip.

"Let me sleep," she murmured.

He took his hand away.

"You could leave it," she said.

"Tomorrow," she could barely say.

"Tomorrow," he said.

"I can't help it."

"You don't have to help anything," he said, and then he smelled it.

"You smell that?" he said.

"The usual," she said.

The smoke alarm in the hall went off.

"9-1-1," Fred said calmly, as if according to a plan, and swung his legs out from under the covers. He put on his glasses and got the gun out of the drawer and took it toward the bedroom door.

Three beeps and a pause, over and over. She groped for light on her nightstand.

"Where is it?" she said. He flipped the switch by the door and went out into the hall. Squinting, she found her own glasses, the phone, the buttons.

The dispatcher sounded like a customer service rep. He asked Fred's wife where she was calling from.

"I think we're on fire," Fred's wife said. "We need the fire department."

The dispatcher asked her if she saw flames. Fred came back into the bedroom.

"Did you see flames?" his wife said.

"Smoke out the wazoo," he said. "Are they on the way?"

"Is the fire department on the way?" she asked the operator. She listened and looked at Fred and said, "He said they're on the way," then: "What color is the smoke? he wants to know."

Fred took the receiver and hung it up. "Come on," he said and gathered the comforter off the bed. "Downstairs." The phone rang. They coughed almost simultaneously in response.

"Don't answer it," he said. "Come on."

"My feet," she said and stepped into a pair of chenille orthotic slippers, and kept stepping, following Fred out of the bedroom. The phone kept ringing behind them. Already a lambent glow at the end of the hall, at the top of the stairs where the smoke alarm was. A slow-changing gray shape like a genie rubbed from a lamp. When they got there they started coughing uncontrollably and covered their mouths with the blanket. Downstairs, yellow flame had fed its way across the living room carpet to the stairs and was starting to climb the risers. Its tongue on the banister, the brown starting to blacken, smoke like a dark river pouring up the ceiling of the passage, gravity defied.

"My little people," she choked out, for this was what she sometimes called her Hummels, and the heat rose in slow drafts to their faces. There was a fire extinguisher in the kitchen though she had suggested the bedroom.

The keening above them was such now that Fred jumped and swung at it with the butt of the revolver. Failing that he took aim and she covered her ears and he shot out the alarm like some alien device that had attached itself to their home.

"You're gonna shoot the fire too?" she said, and now they could hear it.

They went back down the hall to the bedroom in a throat-burning, eye-blinding fog and shut the door. The phone was still ringing. Fred bunched the blanket at the foot of the door, but smoke was coming up through the heat register and he covered it with a pillow, still coughing, nose running, eyes crying. The floor was warm under his feet. He went to the phone

237

and again took aim, but his wife said his name so he knocked it off its cradle. Then he opened the other window looking out onto the porch roof.

"Should we lay down?" his wife said.

He crawled out onto the roof and she asked what he was doing. He turned around and reached through the window. "Come on."

"I'll wait here," she said, looking to the phone, its tinny imprecations.

"That floor'll go any minute." He choked, turned and spat. "We have to."

"My bathrobe," she said but might have felt or heard something under her slippers and lurched forward and gave him her arms. He fairly dragged her out onto the roof over the porch, and they knelt together on the rough granules of the shingles and listened for sirens. Instead they heard someone say, "You up there, Fred? You should see your dining room."

Their next-door neighbor's son stood near the foot of the driveway below. A pasty thirtyish kid who lived in his parents' garage where he drank beer and played the electric bass, unaccompanied. He was only drinking beer now and sounded it, and in the burgeoning glow from the house you could see the label of the can.

"Never mind that," Fred said, "call 9-1-1."

"You didn't call?" the neighbor said. "I thought I heard a shot."

"You hear any sirens?" Fred said. "Make the call, please. You have a ladder?"

"On it," the neighbor said but stood staring into the house as if under the spell of the flames. He started to raise the can as if in toast.

"Just get the goddamn ladder!" a voice from up the drive yelled and the thirtyish boy went grumbling up toward the garage. He'd been married once for a month.

The lights went on in the house on the other side. Things were bursting inside somewhere below them. Fred looked at the crab apple tree that rose from the lawn, branches overhanging the roof. He still had the gun. Suddenly, he felt crosshairs on them.

"Let's go," he said.

"Go where?" she said. "He's getting the ladder."

"The tree," he said. "We're sitting ducks out here," and grabbed for her meaty arm. She snatched it back, but only so she could use it to crawl dutifully behind him as he moved crouching down the slope of the roof. When they were enfolded in branches she hauled herself up by his pajamas, stood with her hands on his bony shoulders. He tried to shove the gun into his waistband but it was too heavy, so with one hand and bare feet he stepped into the tree, into its florid blossoms and promised bitter fruit. Something flew out of it then and made for the moon, shrinking against that big pale disk as if crossing the void to reach it. He told her where to put her feet.

"I don't know," she said but tentatively exchanged one set of limbs for another. Then they stood on boughs he hoped could be stood upon, on each side of the trunk, clinging to it and to each other as they had rarely done in marriage. Fred's feet were sticky with sap.

He could see the orange glow inside the house dawning like a terrible truth and then the flames that were its source, illuminating the porch and the front lawn and the small crowd that had materialized on its edge, haphazardly dressed, some of whom had seen him on television and were his audience once again. No one looking up.

"Someone get a ladder!" he shouted.

"Oh my God," his wife prayed, eyes closed. She couldn't stop shaking.

"In the tree," someone said.

"You okay, Fred?"

"Both of them . . ."

"My Celestial Dreamer," his wife murmured, and inside the house, stripped of paint and charred to one color, her little friends were popping like toy grenades.

"Where's a ladder?" someone said.

"Wait for the firemen."

"Where the hell are they?" Fred said and there was a loud crack just below them and she was gone. A violent rustling, whipping and snapping, then a scream and a thud and a groan, then nothing. He couldn't see. He cried her name and climbed down in the dark like he was twelve years old again.

"Is that a gun?" someone said when he was almost to the crotch of the tree. It was, and when he tried to hang-drop the last four feet with one hand, he fell to the ground and it discharged harmlessly into the dirt on impact.

The onlookers screamed and scattered in their bathrobes and sweat suits, leaving just a few of their number behind, leaving Fred's wife and the man she'd landed on lying prone under the tree. Her leg was bent at an angle nature had not intended, her head in his lap as though he would provide comfort in oblivion. The flames cast their shadows on the lawn in lurid animation.

"Don't shoot," someone said, and Fred saw the son of his next-door neighbors standing in the driveway, holding the ladder. It stood straight up into the night.

—Maintain eye contact. Look at individuals, not an anonymous blur. Establish credibility and rapport with your eyes.

—It's OK to hold notes in your hand. However, make sure your notes are well organized and not too bulky.

—Use humor freely. A little humor can go a long way. Anecdotes, humorous exaggeration, and gross under-statements about your topic help get and keep your listeners' attention.

A big room with a wooden floor. The kind of space people fill with smoke while they elect union stewards, hold wedding receptions and wakes, celebrate First Communions. A clock on the back wall. Unfolded chairs. A man with a hundred keys on his hip. The floor had not been waxed but it was clean, and the windows were caged. There was no stage but a riser consisting of a wooden frame to which carpeting had been nailed. A microphone with stand. Fred wished there was a lectern; he wanted something in front of his body, a place to put his hands. He wished there was a lectern instead of the banner tacked up on the wall behind the riser, but he supposed people were entitled to an opinion (though wasn't his more than that?) and his back would be to it when he spoke.

He and his wife sat in the front row with the man who

called himself Hans Raeder, an audience accumulating slowly behind them. Her leg was in a cast. The man who called himself Hans Raeder was less diffident in person than he was on Fred's answering machine. Paunchy, in his late thirties, he wore a beige sort of uniform with the banner in miniature around his arm, a square black smudge under his nose. Though the effect was closer to Oliver Hardy than what might have been intended, he was an affable and considerate host and warmly greeted all arrivals, most of whom he seemed to know, and some of whom brought trays and bowls covered with aluminum foil. He was especially solicitous of Fred's wife, providing an extra chair as a footrest (it was crucial to keep the leg elevated), and for whom he had his son fetch a can of Diet Coke. His son was a big skinhead who wore a nylon bomber jacket and a T-shirt transformed with safety pins and permanent marker.

"Name of my band," he explained, shaking hands though he seemed to regard Fred with some suspicion. His band, White Lightning, had loaned their PA system to the event. He said he'd tried to read the Report but found it too full of scientific mumbo jumbo.

"I threw a desk out the window in Chemistry," he said.

"No one was hurt," his father said.

"Only book I ever read was *Lord of the Flies* in juvie."

"Maybe I can clear some things up for you today," Fred said with doubts of his own.

"We'll see," the kid said, but he didn't seem to need things cleared up. There seemed to be beer on his breath. "I guess I'm more the man-of-action type. How many niggers does it take to turn on a TV?"

"We just need to focus his ideology a bit," the man who called himself Hans Raeder said and turned to the man ringing with keys.

Fred turned his head every time the back door clanked open, marked the progress of the minute hand above it. When it had crept almost to the top of the hour and the rented seats seemed as full as they were going to get, the man who called himself Hans Raeder suddenly bounded onto the stage and grabbed the microphone, his back to the red and black and its crooked cross. He raised his right arm stiffly, clicked his heels together and shouted two words; somebody shouted them back, and some- body else giggled. The microphone squawked. Preliminary remarks (a less colloquial version of his son's joke; a reiteration, for the benefit of newcomers, of the Three P's), and then the Report. He held up a copy and told the audience how many thousands more were thought to be in print—nobody knew for sure—and that it had been translated into French, German, Spanish, Russian, Swedish, perhaps other languages of which he was not aware. He read from the introduction, written by the English historian who'd testified on behalf of the defendant in Toronto, and this was the first Fred heard that such a preface existed. Even before calling him by name, the man who called himself Hans Raeder referred to Fred as the new Galileo, the new Tyndale—which latter comparison he was eager to explain—and as a would-be martyr whose persecutors, cower- ing once again behind the last letter of the alphabet, had recently tried to burn alive as they had the heretics of old.

"Without further introduction," he said finally, "what they didn't tell you on 20/20," and Fred rose and took the stage and shook hands with the man who called him the new Galileo and the new Tyndale. He adjusted the microphone stand and stood alone before the audience clutching his sheaf of refutations, one hand in his pocket, his suit still reeking of smoke as if he'd been delivered fresh from the stake.

He looked at them.

Wide Slavic faces, first-generation, second. A biker chewing gum. A baby on a lap. More men than women, more scattered than gathered, they looked back: machinist, nurse's aide, forklift driver, truck driver, cashier, assistant manager, idler. People. Skinheads in the back row, snickering, jostled each other like boys in pews. The man who called himself Hans Raeder stepped back to keep an eye on them, confiscated something in a paper bag. He read your gas meter with his mustache and haircut, and a few of the audience wore homemade uniforms similar to his. Others dressed as though they'd come straight from church, with petitions that could not be answered there. People. Most looked fundamentally decent, honest as you or I, but fed up, unappeased, even afraid, forgotten, and now they all looked at Fred as if to see was it he who had remembered them.

The Guide to Public Speaking said the maximum audience attention span was thought to be about twenty minutes.

So he started with himself. Stammered briefly through background and profession, through a shriek of feedback like some piercing objection. He spoke of his father. His mouth strayed from the mic. Then the call from the Frenchman, the meeting in Toronto, the trip to Poland and the forensic tour of the camps—to the best of his knowledge the only such inspection ever performed. He had not wanted to forget anything, it was all there in his notes, but he couldn't forget the waning of time and attention, pages were shuffled, and then the trial was over and only the Report remained, as if it had been the real purpose of his mission all along, and he read a short excerpt describing the chemical properties of Prussian blue.

"Ferric-ferrocyanide," he intoned, and some of the audience nodded with reverence if not comprehension, while one of the skinheads made a snoring sound and the man who called himself Hans Raeder gripped the back of his son's neck.

Then life after the Report: the conspiring, discrediting, slander and libel. The undoing and undermining, loss of livelihood, blackballed and blacklisted against any chance of employment. His wife, a Type Two diabetic forced not only to work a job detrimental to her health but also made the subject of the vilest threats and harassment imaginable . . .

"And now, most recently, an attempt on my life resulting in the loss of the home I was raised in and bodily harm to the person who means more to me than anyone else on Earth. And, to add insult to injury, bad faith to good, our insurance company has denied our claim, blaming faulty wiring and unpermitted work."

Make sure your gestures are large enough for everyone to see, and Fred threw up his arms, suddenly inspired.

"I was going to say," he said, "that the rest is history. But on reflection, looking out upon your assembled faces here today, I would rather say," he said, "that the rest is the future."

One of the skinheads belched.

At first they kept to their seats. Though the applause was as generous as this congregation was capable of, it wasn't until the man who called himself Hans Raeder, banging his hands together like slabs of raw meat, whistling with his tongue against his teeth, stood and encouraged them with upward sweeping motions that others followed suit. Emboldened, and though he hadn't intended to, Fred waited till they were sitting again and then asked if anyone had any questions. The accustomed silence out of which a hand then rose, and a man in a windbreaker affiliating him with the pipefitters' union asked Fred if he'd received any royalties from the myriad printings of the Report, and Fred replied that he hadn't, nor was he in it for the money to begin with, eliciting another round of applause, another interval, and though this wasn't a group that readily yielded appetite to attention and most of them had yet to eat lunch, another raised hand (why did they call it Russian blue?), another (did he think the Fuehrer was still alive?), another, and then a woman with a voice full of country warmth asked Fred if he had any children, and if so were they being bused, and Fred said he hadn't, but while he didn't consider himself political, he did believe that people should be allowed to educate their families as they saw fit, regardless of race, creed, or other considerations drowned out in another burst of acclaim, not quite another standing ovation.

About twenty minutes later, after the man with the keys had whispered in his ear, the man who called himself Hans Raeder leapt onto the stage, clapping just a bit more rapidly than before. He took the microphone from its stand and put his arm around Fred's shoulder. He praised Fred's speech, praised his courage and conviction and the selfsame qualities in Fred's wife, who self-consciously lowered her Diet Coke, her leg up as though she were watching videos in her kitchen. The man who called himself Hans Raeder then with great reluctance said he'd have to cut the Q&A short—they'd rented the hall for four hours—but he encouraged the attendees to stick around; a modest buffet was being provided, potluck, with beverages, and there was going to be a raffle in which first prize was a Naugahyde recliner. There were also copies of the Report for sale, the proceeds of which would go to the guest of honor and his wife against the financial hardships imposed on them by (did he have to say it?), and Fred was so taken with the reception he'd thus far received it didn't occur to him to ask if this was in addition to the speaker's fee he'd already been promised.

"But before that," the man who called himself Hans Raeder said, "before that I'd like to ask each and every one of you here, except for Fred's lovely beloved here, who can't for obvious reasons, but everyone else here today I'd like to invite you to join us in a little march around the block here now, to show our support for Fred and each other, our Pride in Preserving the Purity of our heritage, our unity in our common brother- and sisterhood. We don't need a permit if we keep it on the sidewalk, people. We've made a few signs, feel free to grab one, and remember this is a peaceful demonstration—we are a peaceful people," he said, unless, and someone muttered something about marching on an empty stomach, and one of the unruly contingent from the back tapped their putative leader's paunch and said, "Don't look so empty to me," at which the man who called himself Hans Raeder simply said, "So let's keep it single-file and leave room for pedestrians," and then turned to look at Fred.

The man who called himself Hans Raeder looked at Fred then like a suitor on the verge of proposal: "And I would like to ask our guest of honor here to join me at the head of the line as honorary parade marshal. We would be privileged to have you if you would accept this invitation," he said, "but of course you're under no obligation."

The chair had been donated. There was macaroni and beef.

A rough order of march assembled itself off to the side, near the fire exit. Fred alongside the man who called himself Hans Raeder, still holding his notes instead of a sign. His wife stayed exactly where she was and in no want for company; the majority of those in attendance chose not to participate though all had limbs intact. Someone pushed the panic bar. The day so brilliant with promise it hurt to look at it. The leader raised his right arm in salute, left hand on his belt, and commenced singing a German children's song in a rich and gifted baritone. A boy goes out into the wide world alone, comes back to his family a man. Fred had heard it before. Behind him a guy in a denim vest wore a Wehrmacht infantry helmet and held a flag and tried to sing along, though he didn't seem to know the words. They set off in a ragged file through the fire doors, not to escape a blaze but to enter one, a retinue of roughly a dozen apostles, youth bringing up the rear with a song of its own.

You have to start somewhere, and at first you say yes to everything, but after a while you can pick and choose—there was plenty to choose from on the answering machine, and only so much of him to go around. No more neighborhood gatherings then, no more paper plates, beans and franks; let the bingo halls and backyards become hotel convention rooms and auditoria, his appearances now lectures and conferences. They wanted him to tell his truth in the suburbs too, not to mention Columbus, not to mention Chicago. He was invited to appear on panels, he was invited to Birmingham and Houston. (There was talk of New York.) He was still preaching to the choir, but the choir evolved with the changes in venue, became educated, professional, politically sophisticated, though sometimes still the red-and-black flashed like a flesh wound (a blond-haired girl with a beret, her khaki breast jutting like artillery), still sometimes the tattoos, suspenders, and Doc Martens, but now strictly for purposes of security.

"I came, I saw, I chiseled," he said.

And they paid. Honoraria for his appearances, compensation for lodging and other travel expenses. The Institute told him to keep his receipts—not that he wouldn't have done it for free; after all, they listened, money was a technicality. Standing before and above, if not of, the upturned, nodding, sometimes smiling assembly, he saw himself being heard and understood, his thoughts becoming words becoming light shining on smooth blank faces, and those faces ripening in that light. He got better at it. Loosened up, forgot about his hands, improvised. It was okay to repeat yourself as long as you made it different each time: the boiling point of hydrocyanic acid, life as the son of a prison guard, the sabotage of his vocation by

Zionist conspirators . . . "and the rest, as they don't say, is the future." He would look up and see meaning being made; there were no strangers out there, only friends he had yet to find. He cracked dubious jokes and they burst like a studio audience on cue, as if his jokes didn't have to be funny—they were funny before he told them, his listeners laughing before he arrived, just as they were already nodding and understanding. He didn't have to understand them back, and who is to say this isn't love?

"At this point I'll have to schedule my own execution just to break even," he said, and that bland upturning erupted. He was no longer funny by accident.

He'd come to enjoy the routine as well, the motions. Long drives accompanied by AM talk, FM oldies, empty stretches of interstate green, the federal highways (a farmer fetching his mail at roadside, you could see his face and wave). Then the outskirts, the corporate limits, innerbelts and outer; Holiday Inn, Super 8 Motel, T.G.I. Fridays. The proximity of airports, planes roaring within arm's reach overhead (they seemed a good omen as long as you weren't on them). Parking lots, luggage, the bright dusted lobbies and clerks in company colors, the waiting, Lysoled stillness of rooms upon entering and finding the switch, the formal stiffness of the sheets, four different kinds of towels. Even the oily soap that never quite comes off, as if you can never be too clean.

"I'm suing the Anti-Defamation League for defamation of character," he said. He appeared on a talk radio show like those he heard on the road, the kind devoted to government conspiracy, alien abduction, the moon-landing hoax, JFK in a wheelchair on a Greek island.

Someone said he should think about a manager, an agent, but he was a regular guy. Fred. He knew what he knew.

"If a tree falls in the woods and there's no one around to hear it," Fred said, ". . . well they make books from trees, don't they?"

Sometimes they took him out to dinner afterward. Afterward there was mingling, handshaking, congratulations, introductions. Nursing a drink and smoking in a smoky drink-filled room. They gave him their cards. There was photographing and videotaping, sitting at a table signing copies of the Report, printed at a retail copy center (a hundred clicks per minute) and staple-bound, foreworded by the British historian who'd testified in Toronto. In Houston he signed one for the blond-haired girl with the armband. He also signed her copy of *Mein Kampf* and a picture of her holding an assault rifle. She seemed confused that Fred was right: "I thought we *wanted* them dead." She leaned over behind him, her chest prodding his shoulder. He did not have to understand her either.

"'To Ingrid,'" she instructed.

"Are you still in school?" Fred asked. She said she was taking inhalation therapy at community college. The woman behind her worked as an office manager. She had two copies of the Report and her hair was cut short, with a wash of gray like a kind of grace. She asked Fred what he was doing after the signing—did he know Houston? She offered to show him around. A little shyly, it seemed. A slight stammer.

"I'm having dinner with my wife," Fred said.

"Bring her along," she said. A half smile, what might have been. "I'll show you both the Space Center."

His wife was back at the room with her leg, drawing blood from her thumb. She was sometimes uncomfortable at these functions.

She left him her card but he had no use for it. It was taken off his hands by the British historian who'd prefaced the Report, who was considered in some circles to be not a historian at all. He'd written books saying the Final Solution was someone else's idea, that while a visionary leader tried to expand his country's sphere of influence, subordinates did what they thought he wanted; that Churchill was a racist, alcoholic, warmongering, whoremongering coward; he'd written about Rommel, Himmler, Heydrich, Goebbels; debunked the diary of Anne Frank, moralized on the firebombings of Dresden and Hamburg, described the Hungarian uprising of '56 as an anti-Jewish rebellion. He'd edited the memoirs of Eichmann, refuted the authenticity of Hitler's purported diary (till official opinion swung the other way, whereupon he reversed his position on the *Today* show). He had been barred from entering Germany, Austria, Canada, South Africa, and New Zealand, and Fred shook hands with all of it.

"Fuck's sake, New Zealand," the British historian said. "I didn't even know I wanted to go there." He raised a glass. "Here's hoping Mexico doesn't show me the door—now that's where the party is." His face, often seen through the lens of a tumbler, was handsome in a lined, world-weary way, and Fred's wife would have adored his accent.

The Report was a turning point of his life, he told Fred.

"It's all about the brick," Fred said. "I have no politics."

"Thank God," the British historian said. "Ever been to the U.K.?"

"I have this thing about flying."

"That's why God invented drugs," the British historian said. "You've got to see the stones, man. You won't be the same."

Fred knew that *hang* came from *henge*. He looked at the trilithon before him, rough greenish sandstone twice as tall as he was. Two uprights joined at the top by a lintel—like an ancient gallows. Or a doorway. The grass was muddy. Some of the stones were roped off but he ducked under as he had elsewhere. You couldn't touch anything.

There were voices, he looked around. The rain had congealed into a gray mist like an emanation of the ruins. No one was sure of their purpose but it must have had something to do with death; there were holes in the ground where other stones might have gone, but instead they'd held burnt human bones. They'd found other things. A ditch formed a ring around the site 350 feet across, and in the ditch were flint tools, fragments of pottery, the bones of animals and of human beings again, now unburnt but broken.

He didn't think they'd hung people five thousand years ago. *Gallows* also meant *torture*.

"Rock group," his wife said, more than once. She would rather have seen Big Ben, the changing of the Queen's Guard. She wanted to hear people sound British.

The ruins didn't speak but reminded her of another place.

The Slaughter Stone, Altar Stone, Station Stone, Heel Stone. What remained of the bluestones stood in the inner circle but not in the center. Some of them weighed four tons or so and had been transported from a quarry nearly two hundred miles away. But the stone in the middle was thirty feet high and weighed twelve times as much, and how had they moved that one, and who were *they*?

Voices; there were people about but in the mist you couldn't see them.

"Don't get under that thing," his wife said, but the lintels didn't just rest on the uprights; woodworking methods had been used, tongue and groove in stone, joinery Fred knew better than he knew himself.

Who were they?

"Giants from Ireland," the British historian said. He raised a flask to them. "They brought the stones from Africar—they were said to have healing properties. Then King Arthur decided he wanted them brought here as a monument to his knights—Uther Pendragon is buried here, so the story goes—so Merlin cast a spell on the stones that made them weightless."

"Couldn't the giants stop them?" Fred's wife said, but she just wanted to hear him talk.

"That's the Irish for you," the British historian said. "Probably sleeping one off."

They'd found other things as well. In the ditch, in the mound. A decapitated Saxon.

Or it was a UFO landing site. Or a place of ancestral worship. Or it was a gatepost to parallel worlds.

The British historian pointed to the northeast portal, the one they'd come through. It had been aligned so the midsummer sun would rise there, so that there the midwinter sun would set. He said *solstice*, *equinox*, *latitude*, and these were words Fred knew the way he knew *miter*, *mortise*, and *tenon*.

"In June this place is crawling with hippies," the British historian said, but it was November and there were no white robes to be seen. The Heel Stone leaned toward them through the mist just outside the portal, eyeless, a crack like a frown in a face. It leans through the Ages—Stone and Bronze and Iron. There was a fence behind it, and behind the fence was the highway that ran between Amesbury and Winterbourne Stoke. You could feel the vibrations under your feet.

A beer can was wedged in the crack.

Fred reached for it.

In the evening the British historian showed them Chelsea. He showed them the statue of Thomas More and the headquarters of the football club. They saw the home of Oscar Wilde and he took them down King's Road where Mick Jagger and the Beatles had lived. It rained bitterly. They sat in a famous pub, drank a pint. The British historian, who'd been drinking most of the day and was just starting to show signs of it, was also famous for being late and by the time they got to the Old Town Hall there were barely ten minutes to go before Fred was to give his presentation.

A news crew from Thames Television was there. So were a small contingent of Metro police officers who remained outside the building in custodian helmets and shiny black macs. So was the Frenchman who'd called him from Toronto—had it been five years already? six?—who would not only precede Fred onstage but had arranged for him to speak in Cologne. He pressed his face to Fred's but there was no time to talk; the British historian was already onstage, a little unsteady, making the introductions.

"Without fur ado," he said, "I give you," and shook the Frenchman's hand, for he did not believe men should embrace.

"It is my great honor," the Frenchman said not thirty minutes later, "to give you," and Fred stepped behind the podium to the greatest reception he'd ever known. He stood under the ornate ceiling of the Main Hall, the dimmed chandeliers, the rain clamoring against the great dark windows as in accord or condemnation. His wife sat in the front row but he couldn't see her. He recycled a joke from the repertory, let the audience make it new, then thanked the Frenchman and recalled the first time he'd heard his accent . . . late January, dead of winter . . . He noticed them looking off to his side and then the British historian was standing next to him.

"Excuse me," Fred said. The British historian whispered into his ear and Fred looked at him and looked back at the audience. He apologized and said he would be right back and followed the historian offstage.

In the anteroom a man in a long white slicker stood with three policemen.

"Terribly sorry about this," the chief inspector said, "but may I see your passport and some identification?"

Fred gave him his passport and his driver's license. The chief inspector returned Fred's license but kept his passport and Fred asked what it was about.

"I'm terribly sorry, sir," the chief inspector said, "but I'm afraid I must ask you to accompany us to the station."

"Am I under arrest?"

"Not at all," the chief inspector said. He was sorry again, frightfully this time. "Orders from the Home Secretary."

"Is my passport not properly stamped?"

"Absolutely, sir. I'm sure it's just a lot of bother, but I'm afraid the law requires that you remain with us till we've cleared things up," the chief inspector said.

"What if I refuse?" Fred said.

"Then we'll have to place you under arrest." With all due regret.

"What do you call this?"

"You're being detained on suspicion."

"On suspicion of what?"

"If you would just come this way, sir."

Fred gestured vaguely, no longer sure where things were. "My wife."

"She has a serious illness," the British historian said in a fair impersonation of sobriety, though he couldn't seem to remember exactly what the illness was.

"Very good, sir," the chief inspector said and sent one of the officers to collect her.

They rode to the police station in an unmarked van. At the station they were installed in a visitors' room with no other visitors and the chief inspector asked Fred if he wished to call the American consulate.

"I don't want to talk to anybody unless they can get me out of here," Fred said.

"Very good, sir, but I'm afraid you'll have to stay with us until your status has been determined."

"But I'm not under arrest."

"Not at all, sir, you're being detained till we've determined your status. Would you like some coffee? Tea perhaps?"

"I don't drink tea," Fred said.

"Do you have anything I could snack on?" Fred's wife said. She described her condition. She said she didn't always get symptoms.

"Very good, then," the chief inspector said. "I'll see to it." And he left the room, deferential as a butler.

She did not like his accent as much as the British historian's, and they did not hear it again.

They had tea and coffee and biscuits. The station personnel were polite and accommodating. They waited. Plastic contour chairs and thin stained carpeting, no television and nothing to read. Fred's wife kept her legs up on one of the chairs.

She used the bathroom. Used the loo. They made "ma'am" sound like "mom."

Just before midnight a young woman came in and sat down. She looked Indian, subcontinental, but sounded like everyone else. She wore a yellow poncho and a resigned look, as if she'd done this before. Took off the poncho but not the look, asked if they could spare a fag. Fred's wife smiled;

259

people were always asking each other for fags. Fred gave her one of his.

Just after the young woman the deputy chief inspector came in with two policemen. He was a younger version of his superior, portly and red-cheeked, without mustache, but his manner was identical. He apologized and told Fred he was under arrest.

Fred's wife said, "Oh."

Fred asked what he was being charged with. The policemen stood to either side of him.

"To be perfectly honest I'm not sure," the deputy chief inspector said. "I've just received orders from the Home Office."

"I demand we be allowed to leave the country," Fred said, now standing. His foot seemed to be asleep. He swayed. The two policemen took his arms and didn't let go.

"I'm afraid that isn't possible just yet, sir. Would you like to speak with the duty solicitor?"

"I'd like to speak with the American consulate."

"Very good, sir, that will be arranged. Now if you'll just come this way."

"My wife," Fred said.

"We'll look after her, sir," the deputy chief inspector said.

"You look after *him*," Fred's wife said, and when they'd gone she cried for a time. The girl who'd asked for a cigarette called her love, consoled her with a copy of *The Sun*.

They searched him and booked him and put him in a cell. Gave him a blanket. The cell was unheated and damp and he sat on a cot wrapped in the blanket. He got up and paced for a while, trying to warm himself, then sat back down. A mouse crawled out from under the cot. Fred looked at the mouse and it ran back under the cot. About an hour later they came and told him the under-consul was on the phone.

They took him to a large office filled with desks. Civilians sat in chairs by some of the desks looking blank or nervous or defiantly bored. Some in handcuffs, some drunk. Characters with colorful language. Violin stories. *No bovver. It's him what give em to me. Share it up.* Men, mostly, in blue tunics and white shirts, typing. They sat Fred down and handed him a phone.

"What's the problem over there?" It was good to hear an American voice, but either he'd just woken up or he was slightly drunk.

Fred said his name into the phone.

"Well that's a start. What's going on?"

"I'm under arrest."

"And what do you want me to do about it?"

"Well . . ."

"So what did you do?"

"Nothing."

"Right. So what do they think you did?"

"They're saying I'm in the country illegally. Or I might be."

"Might be. You have a passport?"

"Yes."

"Is it stamped?"

"Yes. I showed it to them."

"And they arrested you anyway."

"I'm calling from the police station."

"Right. Now what aren't you telling me?"

"That's it. I came here to give a speech. My passport is in order."

"What kind of speech?"

"I can't go into it over the phone. Can you come to the station so we can talk in person?"

Fred wasn't sure but he thought he heard the under-consul say, "In a pig's ass."

"Excuse me?"

"I know what kind of speech it was, you son of a bitch."

Now he was sure. He lowered the receiver and looked at the policeman whose phone he was using. The policeman didn't look back. Fred could hear the under-consul's voice. He lifted the receiver and said, "I don't think I care for your language, sir. Let me remind you of something."

"My father landed at Normandy," the under-consul said. "He lost a leg at Omaha Beach so you could make speeches."

"My father served in the Pacific."

"He must be turning over in his grave."

"He probably is," Fred said. "I'm an American citizen."

"Making speeches for the cocksuckers who took his leg."

"It's your job to help me."

"Don't tell me my goddamn job," the under-consul said. "You want help? Here's some advice, citizen: next time you go to a foreign country, don't go around breaking their laws. And if you do, call a goddamn lawyer."

The under-consul hung up. Fred stared at the phone. He stared at it till the policeman at whose desk he was sitting took it gently away from him.

"I demand to speak to the duty solicitor," Fred demanded softly, though he wasn't quite sure what the duty solicitor did.

"No problem at all, Your Lordship. We'll ring him for you straight away," the policeman said. "Meanwhile I'd be honored to escort Himself back to his quarters till such time as his arse can be got hold of."

They took him back to his cell. There was another man there now, snoring on the cot, up to his eyes in the blanket. Fred wondered how colorful this character might be. He sat on the floor with his back against the wall and wrapped his arms around himself, within the colder embrace. When they came back for him his teeth were chattering like some wind-up gag from a novelty shop. They took him back to the same large office but sat him at a different desk and gave him another phone.

He heard a yawn still in the duty solicitor's voice. "How can I be of help, sir?"

Fred asked him exactly what a duty solicitor was. His teeth kept chattering.

"I believe what you call in the States a public defender," the duty solicitor said.

"Well what are my options here?"

"Depends," the duty solicitor said. "What's the charge?"

"There doesn't seem to be one."

"No charge then? So why do you suppose you're being held?"

"I don't want to go into detail over the phone . . . they're saying I'm in the country illegally."

"And who might they be?"

"I'm not sure . . . Home Office?"

Fred wasn't sure again but thought he heard the duty solicitor say *fuck*. He would have preferred *blast*.

"Hello?" he said.

"Yes," the duty solicitor said. "Is your passport in order, then?"

"Yes."

"And do they know this?"

"I gave it to the chief inspector."

"Ah," the duty solicitor said. "Well then, Fred—Fred, is it?"

"Yes," Fred said.

"Yes," the duty solicitor said. "I'm afraid there's nothing I can do for you then. Fred."

"Nothing you can do," Fred said. He found himself almost assuming the duty solicitor's accent. "Why can't you do anything?"

"You haven't committed a crime."

"I know that, but," and it stopped there. There was no more thought. Only sounds in imitation of it. "There must be something."

"I'd advise you to call the American consulate."

"The American consulate."

"That's right, sir." He didn't say *Fred* anymore. "It's his duty to help you."

"His duty," Fred said, and the duty solicitor said something else. He kept talking but Fred held the receiver away from his head, let the voice drain into the air like emptying a cup. Then he hung up and they led him back to his cell. Stopped at the lavatory on the way because the cell had no toilet. He wanted a cigarette. He asked after his wife but they seemed not to know who he was talking about.

He tried to sleep but could only sit there hugging himself, jacket buttoned to his neck. He heard his cellmate masturbating in his sleep a yard away.

"Fur coat and no knickers," his cellmate muttered, humping the cot with great oneiric passion.

He did not know what time it had become when the two men from the Immigration Department came to see him. They wore suits and got him out of his cell and had him taken to an interrogation room. There was a table with a microphone and tape recorder, acoustic tile, and he sat across the table from the men from the Immigration Department, punch-drunk and shivering. His teeth were chattering again and in his head sounded like a jackhammer breaking up a sidewalk.

One of them said, "You don't have to make a statement if you don't wish to."

When he could manage it, Fred told the tape recorder his name. One of the men from Immigration asked his date of birth and Fred said, "Why? You sending me a card? I'm an American citizen. I demand to return to my homeland immediately."

The men from Immigration said it was not possible for him to leave the country at this time.

"I have been falsely arrested and illegally in prison," Fred said into the microphone. Certain words didn't seem to make it out of his mouth intact. "I'm an American citizen.

"I legally entered this country through Dover," he said. "I am in a cell without toilet facilities . . . I haven't slept in two days."

"We suggest you call the American consulate at this time," one of the men from Immigration said. "Or the duty solicitor. Charges may be brought."

"I've been placed in a cell with a criminal who may or may not be aware of my occupation," Fred said. "Vermin . . . I entered in Dover. My blanket has been . . .

"What kind of charges?" he said.

"That has yet to be determined," and they handed him an immigration form. He bent his head toward the microphone and raised his voice, though they'd told him this wasn't necessary.

"My wife has also been legally detained," he garbled. "She suffers from serious medical, and I have not been permitted to see her."

The men from Immigration looked at each other. "Your wife is being seen to," one of them said.

"If you're deported she may have to stay behind," the other one said.

"And your rental car."

"You won't be permitted to leave through Dover," the other one said.

"No sir, that won't be possible. You'll have to sort out through Heathrow."

"Or Gatwick."

"Would it be possible for me to have a cigarette?" Fred said, and one of the men from Immigration spoke to the guard. The guard gave Fred a cigarette and a light.

Best fag he'd ever had. The guard was a Marlboro man.

"I have been served with form IS-151-A," the tape says. "I've been diagnosed with a gastric ulcer and the situation is very painful. I am incarcerated with a possible violent criminal, and have received no help from the embassy."

He gathered himself then and spoke carefully: "At this point I'd like to be allowed to see my wife. This is my statement."

They brought her to the interrogation room from wherever she'd been. The men from Immigration whispered to the guard and left. She looked pale and shaky and Fred, galvanized, reached across the table and spoke.

She yawned. "I was trying to sleep," she complained.

"Are they treating you all right?" Fred said.

"Two chairs sure ain't a bed," his wife said. "People coming in and out. They don't call it a waiting room for nothing."

"Are you using your pens? Have they given you something to eat?"

She pulled half a sweet roll from her sweater pocket, wrapped in a napkin. "I'm saving this for an emergency." She put it back. "They gave me some word puzzles but some of it's weird. What's a lorry?"

"British for truck," Fred said. "Just hang on a little longer. I think I know who's behind this and they can't hold us forever."

"Those people," his wife said.

"In the waiting room?"

"The other ones," she said. Her eyes were closed and she seemed almost to be talking in her sleep, in touch with the unguarded truth. "It's because of them. They aren't right."

"They've helped us," he said. "Paid our rent."

"God help us from their help. I don't want to owe them anything."

"Listen," he said. "Sometimes things are complicated."

267

She didn't answer. Her eyes were still closed and she was nodding. Her skin looked an awful gray.

The guard stepped forward and put a hand on Fred's shoulder. "Sir. At this time."

"I'd like to speak to the American consul," Fred said softly.

"Well bloody hell," the guard said, and Fred's wife lifted her head but still didn't open her eyes.

"Bloody," she said, dozing.

The under-consul sounded like he was still asleep himself. "This bear be good," he said. "Who is it?"

"A taxpayer," Fred said.

"What?" the under-consul said. "Who is this?"

"You know damn well who it is," Fred said. "Just thought I'd return the favor and ruin your night, you fucking lackey." He did not approve of foul language but under the right circumstances he became quite fluent.

"Is this the Nazi-lover?" the under-consul said, and Fred thought he heard a woman's voice in the background.

"I don't love them any more than I love you, you worthless son of a bitch," he said. "But I'll say this: they pulled their weight. And when I get back I'm issuing a formal complaint to the State Department, I promise you."

"You want a formal complaint?" the under-consul said, and Fred wondered again if he had been sleeping in drink. "Try this." He heard the woman laughing, then another sound, sharp and terse, which he didn't fully recognize till the under-consul had hung up.

He'd forgotten to mention his wife. When he got back to

the interrogation room she was gone. They let him use the lavatory again, then took him back to his cell.

He asked for a blanket. Around four thirty they gave him one and he dozed in broken stretches over the next couple of hours, his dreams reiterations of the previous evening. He tried to give his speech, tried to gather up his papers scattered among the big black stones, a sound coming from the cracks in their faces. He rarely dreamed.

When he opened his eyes there was light coming into the cell through a small window he hadn't known was there. His cellmate was sitting up on the cot, bald-headed with a black eye, staring at him over his coffee.

"And who the fuck might you be?" Fred's cellmate inquired. He seemed to be smiling but you couldn't tell if this was due to good humor or because he had no teeth.

"A trespasser," Fred said. "Tourist . . .

"Political prisoner," he said then. The man looked at him. "Fred."

"Right," his cellmate said. "How do you take your coffee then, Fred?" You could hear the other inmates being woken in the other cells, clang of clubs on bars.

Fred said he liked it black and his cellmate nodded. "I like it black every chance I get," he leered, then shouted, "Well bring fucking Fred a bloody cup! Fuck sake!"

By eight o'clock his cellmate and all the other prisoners were gone, taken to court. Fred heard new inmates arriving, but no one else was brought to his cell. He asked about his wife but there was no reply; the day-shift personnel didn't seem to know what to do with him so they pretended he wasn't there. He asked about his wife once an hour on the hour, when they made their rounds, but the only response he got was a lunch consisting of a breakfast someone hadn't eaten. Eggs, toast, sausage. He was very hungry but his ulcer wouldn't let him near it. He left the tray sitting on the floor and the next time he looked at it the mice had taken an interest in the eggs.

At one o'clock he demanded to see his wife and twenty minutes later they came back and opened his cell and took him back to the interrogation room. She wasn't there but another official from the Immigration Department was and he invited Fred to sit down. Fred sat.

"Where is she?" he said.

"First let me say it has been determined that you are in the country illegally," the man from Immigration said, "in violation of a ban by the Home Secretary."

"What ban . . . who?" Fred said.

"The ban that was in place before you arrived," the man from Immigration said.

"Just let us go home," Fred said.

"I'm afraid we can't do that," the man from Immigration said. "You'll be held until you can be deported."

"Where's my wife?" Fred said.

"In due time, sir," the man from Immigration said.

"I entered this country in Dover with a valid stamped passport," Fred said. He said this like he was making another statement, though the tape recorder was gone.

"Technically you are not in the country illegally," the man from Immigration said.

"So I've heard," Fred said.

"But an official determination has been made that you are, and that is the law," the man from Immigration said.

"Who made this dermination?" Fred said. It was getting hard to form words again. "The Imitation Department?"

"The decision was made very high up in the Home Office," the man from Immigration said. "Much higher than my ladder will reach, so to speak."

"What about my wife?" Fred said, and somebody knocked at the door. Fred turned when it opened but it was another policeman, asking to speak to the man from Immigration. The man from Immigration frowned heavily, excused himself, and went out into the hall with the policeman. When he returned he sat down and sighed, still frowning.

"I'm afraid," he began, and now Fred was afraid too.

"I'm afraid you won't be able to see your wife right at this moment, sir," the man from Immigration said. "It seems there's been a bit of a complication."

"Complication," Fred said. "Where is she?"

"In hospital, I'm afraid," the man from Immigration said. "It appears she was found unconscious in the lavatory."

Lava tree.

Fred looked at him.

"I assure you, sir," the man from Immigration said. "I've been informed she's resting comfortably and appears to be in no danger at this time."

"I demand to see her this minute," Fred said.

"You shall see her as soon as it can be arranged, sir," the man from Immigration said. "But first I must tell you we've contacted French Immigration about your possible deportation to France."

"I don't want to go to France," Fred said. "I want to see my wife."

"Nevertheless," the man from Immigration said, holding up a hand, "if France refuses, the next step would be to try Belgium. Do you know where Belgium is, sir?"

"Goddamn suburb of France," Fred said. "She went into shock," he said. "Is that what happened?"

"If Belgium won't have you, then Germany," the man from Immigration said.

"Too much insulin . . . or is it too much sugar?" Fred said and seemed to be talking to himself. Or was it not enough?

"Germany," he said to himself.

"If Belgium won't have you," the man from Immigration said.

He had commitments in Germany. Cologne. He could not think about that now.

"If Germany will have you," the man from Immigration said, "the Hamburg ferry runs twice a week. The next one leaves Tuesday."

"Never mind Tuesday," Fred said. "What about my wife?"

"Tuesday is three days from now," the man from Immigration said. "Legally, we can hold you for up to five. Plenty of time for her to recuperate."

"She's a Type Two diabetic," Fred said. "What happened?"

"You have my word she's receiving the best of care," the man from Immigration said. "It's merely a precaution, really."

"Your word," Fred said. "Cologne."

"Hamburg," the man from Immigration said. "If Germany will have you."

Fred sat in the green room at Sat.1 with a faith healer and a therapist who specialized in optimizing the sexual pleasure of the overweight and obese. His wife wasn't there. Production assistants or whatever they were scurried in and out with headsets and clipboards, and on monitors they could see the host chatting up the audience and announcing today's guests. She seemed nervous. The show was live.

"*Meine Damen und Herren,*" she said to seven and a half million people.

The producer approached, an irritable, impatient man who treated the guests like incompetent employees and his employees like necessary evils. He advised the therapist she looked pale and the makeup girl cheerfully applied the final shades of pink like the flush of some permanent embarrassment. Another girl with a headset and clipboard escorted the guest from the green room to close but muffled applause. She re-entered the world on the monitor screen and Fred and the faith healer became two of the seven and a half million.

He didn't understand a word. His translator, the man from the National-Demokratische Partei Deutschlands, had not been allowed in the building. The studio would furnish a translator and the interview broadcast via digital delay. Another kind of miracle. The faith healer turned to him. She asked him in German if he spoke it and he understood just enough to shake his head.

"Your name," the faith healer said. "I have thought perhaps."

"My great-grandfather," Fred said. "Or maybe the one before that. Anyway I don't speak a word."

"*Grosse Grossvater*," the faith healer said.

"Yes," Fred said. "How long have you been healing the sick?"

"I am having my gift from *zo* high," the faith healer said and held the palm of her hand about two feet above the floor.

"My wife has diabetes," Fred said. "I should have brought her along."

"*Ach so*," the faith healer said. She pointed to the monitor. "She is not?"

Fred shook his head. "She's back in the States right now. The trip was a little much for her."

"She has not needed me," the faith healer said. "I am for the one without medicine. Faith work best . . . *wenn Hoffnung nicht in der Weise ist.*" She looked at him intently, as if she would make him understand with her eyes. As if it were he who in some way could benefit from her powers.

Fred nodded. On the monitor was a soap commercial in which you could see all of a woman's breasts.

"And your work?" the faith healer said.

"In a way you could say we're in the same line," he said.

"I'm sorry?" But she was looking over his shoulder now. He turned and saw the producer behind him and behind the producer three uniformed police officers. One was a woman who spoke some English and told Fred he was under arrest.

Once again he found himself asking what he was being charged with. The policewoman's English failed her here and she exchanged words with the producer. He nodded and looked at Fred.

"You are under arrest for incitement to hatred and defaming the dead," the producer said, with such relish and authority he might have pronounced a verdict and passed sentence as well. Laughter and applause from the studio audience. The faith healer looked at the floor. Fred was replaced by a pre-taped segment.

In Mannheim some of the trusties were Jews. They delivered the meals. They would come into his cell and taunt him, make threatening near-miss gestures, have "accidents" with his food and just leave it there on the floor. Slices of dark bread, cheese. He began to fear for his safety. He had nothing against them but he would give what he got. In Mannheim you were allotted a broom and dustpan, and he took his broom and sharpened the handle into a rough point on the edge of his window. Now when they came into his cell he held it with both hands, the bristles tucked under his arm like the stock of a rifle, backing carefully away from the door, telling them how to move and where to put his tray. The trusties affected great amusement at this, but they kept their mouths shut and stopped having accidents with his food till the guards took his weapon away.

They'd given him his own cell: a bed, a chair, an enamel-covered table on which to eat and write. A sort of metal cabinet that functioned as locker and wardrobe, a sink with mirror, a toilet with curtain. The window had bars but you could turn the light on and off as you pleased. The cells were equipped for cable and there was a built-in radio that played two stations.

The trash can had a lid. Some inmates had boomboxes, color TV. Fred bought a coffee pot from the prison store; the man from the National-Demokratische Partei Deutschlands had given him the money (and an English Bible), and this was the last visitor Fred had. The only time he turned on the radio station he heard an angry kid rapping in German.

The walls were three feet thick. Fred wasn't sure how old the old prison was, but its dank resounding passages echoed those his father had walked, haunted him with footsteps, and sometimes he heard other things, or thought or dreamed he did, echoes of suffering, martyrdom, breaking bones, consigned to stone. But when he asked who'd occupied the cell before him, he was told of a minor tennis star serving time for tax evasion.

The man from the NPD had translated the Report into German. He taught French and English in high school.

They called it investigative custody. *Untersuchungshaft*—awaiting trial. He was in his cell twenty-two hours and forty-five minutes a day. Mornings they let him out in the yard, where he heard German and a dozen other languages, fragments of English though never its American dialect. In the yard was the red-faced bigamist from Munich. There was the kid of seventeen or eighteen whose nose always ran and who'd gone around taking a crowbar to parked windshields, finishing the argument he'd started with his girlfriend. He spat every time he finished a sentence, as if to rid himself of words. The African whose father, a U.N. ambassador, had waived immunity to teach his son a lesson, who hung out with the Spaniard who wore Hawaiian shirts and claimed to eat the cockroaches with whom they all shared their cells.

The red-faced bigamist went around with a small dachs-hund under his arm. It had one blue eye and one brown. Once, during a dispute over soccer, the dog became aggressive as if with its own opinion, escaped its owner's grasp, and was itself booted like a penalty kick nearly the width of the yard. It sur-vived but afterward dragged a leg and urinated blood, and restrictions were placed upon inmates having pets.

He'd seen the young vandal shivering outside one morning and loaned him his jacket. The kid disappeared and later Fred traced him to the infirmary, found out he'd been sent away for detox. He did not see his jacket again till one of the trusties wore it into his cell, a size small.

Mostly he just chain-smoked with himself.

The judge had let him keep his watch. They gave you tooth-paste and a toothbrush that wasn't sawed off as in American prisons; a comb, shampoo, soap, razors, two towels, and a face cloth. If you didn't like the razors there was Gillette in the prison store, and you could buy coffee or tea, honey or lemon oil, sardines or chocolate; you could buy paint and brushes and inmates of an artistic turn sometimes sold or traded for their work in the yard, meticulous carnal depictions, roses and hearts bound in barbed wire—another kind of pornography— and Fred had use for none of it.

A river ran some two hundred meters away. He never saw it but could hear the gulls, and out on the grounds he heard crows cawing and sometimes the cooing of doves.

Most inmates were allowed one five-minute phone call per month, but Fred was in investigative custody and wasn't allowed any. He was permitted two thirty-minute visits but the

Amtsgericht had final approval and would permit neither the Frenchman nor the British historian. (A guard would sit in on visits, an official listener who not only sometimes participated in conversations but suggested changes of topic.) No limit was placed on mail as long as the letters were written in German or English. If you got a letter in German you could ask someone to read it for you in exchange for chocolate or cigarettes; you could ask the bigamist from Munich.

"She is leaving you for the postman," the bigamist declaimed loudly in his corner of the yard. "His *Päckchen* is bigger and he make delivery in the rear." Fred wrested the letter angrily back and, though he did not approve of violence unless necessary, thought with guilty satisfaction of the little dog, airborne and pissing blood.

But he never heard from his wife and there was no one who could translate this silence. He wrote to her and she didn't write back. He wrote to the British historian, the Frenchman, the German national for whom he'd gone to Toronto. His pen dried up—he'd bought it at the prison store for thirty-five cents—and he did not buy another.

He bought antacids; his ulcer was having its say and the news wasn't good. The prison *Doktor*, a grouchy son of a bitch with a thick white mustache, advised Fred to avoid stress and watch his diet, but do so here and you would watch yourself starve to death. One hot meal a day, at noon. At night the dark bread, five slices or so, and two of cheese or sausage. Then nothing till noon the next day. He was always hungry but they knew what they were doing; starvation affected the memory, thinking—he would be unable to mount a proper defense. The

Spaniard who claimed to eat cockroaches said they were high in protein, gave you short bursts of manic energy. Like a drug, he said, and asked Fred why he was there.

"I told the truth."

"This is why you have no friends."

"There are worse things than being alone," Fred said.

The staff was efficient, humane, fair. They could not be the children of men who threw children into ovens.

Church services every Sunday, Protestant or Catholic. The sermons were in German but at first Fred was not deterred; he attended both until, perusing the Bible the man from the NPD had given him, he found the passage of Corinthians in which Paul advises against prayer in a foreign tongue.

A sharp, chemical taste. Bitter. And their legs would get lodged in your teeth.

He was thirty-four days in Mannheim when the local court lost venue of his case. It was transferred to the *Landgericht*, a grim concrete block of a building with a steel upper story, vertical slits for windows. Fred was granted a new bail hearing and someone had gotten him a lawyer, a tanned heavyset character from New Orleans with a shaved head and an eyepatch. The man from the NPD was allowed to translate. The state attorney, himself a rising star, argued strenuously that Fred was a flight risk, in the end no less dangerous than the bomb-builders and pipe-swingers he would incite.

"My client should be so accomplished," Fred's lawyer said dryly, having represented a busload of just such miscreants, and in the end the *Vorsitzende Richter* allowed Fred to post bond.

After the hearing they stood out in the cold in front of the courthouse, a Baroque palace across the street. Trolley tracks. The lawyer from New Orleans wore a black leather trench coat and a suit and tie and an aftershave so strong even the northern wind could not entirely dispel it. He smelled like home.

He scratched irritably under the eyepatch, as if he wore it only for effect, then handed Fred an envelope.

"There are thirty-three extraditable offenses listed in the treaty between this nation and ours," the lawyer said in that accent that wasn't just Southern. "The one you've been charged with ain't one of em."

Fred waited for a trolley car to pass. "What's in the envelope?"

"What envelope?" his lawyer said.

Fred boarded a Lufthansa 747 in Frankfurt the next morning, a nine-hour flight during which the blinding white sun never set, as if time were suspended and all destinations deferred. By early afternoon he was standing without luggage on the porch of the duplex they'd rented after the fire. He tasted the bitter taste jet lag left in his mouth, and everywhere a slight shimmer as of objects superimposed upon themselves. The mailbox was empty. The lock had been changed. He knocked, listened, looked around, then shimmed the latch with a credit card that served no other purpose.

He wasn't home anymore. She'd taken everything except the carpet it had come with. There wasn't even a smell. He walked slowly through rooms like a prospective tenant and couldn't hear himself. He looked for a note and found none, only his mail stacked on the kitchen counter. He took stock. Considered. Sat on the living room floor with his back against the wall. It was cold but he barely noticed this either; he was Fred, international fugitive, man of destiny, flipping through his mail, but at first the only envelope he opened was a certified letter from the clerk of courts containing his wife's Complaint. He thought for a moment of the guy who'd organized the rally, the man he'd marched with, but really he hadn't seemed her type.

And what had become of the Buick?

He was suddenly very dizzy, like a kid who's been spinning in place and just stops. He hadn't slept at all on the plane, hadn't slept well in weeks. He lay down on the living room floor of an American duplex with his mail pillowed under his head, and didn't wake up even when the landlord arrived with a family of three looking for an extra bedroom. It was the child who discovered him and, after trying unsuccessfully to rouse him by pulling his coat and lightly kicking his leg, went back to the kitchen and reported to his parents that a homeless was sleeping on the floor in the big room.

So many towns named for saints. The sun went down early, but when it rose it pulled temperatures with it into the fifties and sixties, and there was so much still green that winter here was just a cool wet summer back east. When Fred arrived a partly furnished room in North Hollywood was waiting for him, and so was a used Ford Escort. (It was understood he would take over the car note and the rent, month to month, or week to week.) No phone. Tall leggy palms like something out of Dr. Seuss. The job was an hour's drive through the mountains to an office parkway in Santa Clarita. Paved black driveways, bougainvillea, pine, a tree with the bark stripped off and the trunk white as bone. An amusement park across the interstate. Fred wandered an arrangement of single-story white buildings with polarized windows, company names and addresses stenciled in identical white lettering. He finally had to ask the groundskeeper where Parametric Solutions, Inc., was.

The door was propped open. He walked in on a new carpet, under a drop ceiling with rectangles of fluorescent light. Two rows of desks as in a classroom. Two rows of people at the desks talking into phones, some wearing sweaters or coats or hugging themselves because for some reason the air conditioning was on. Almost no one looked up. A big guy approached Fred like he was going to tackle him. He wore crisp white sleeves and a tie and had gelled his thinning blond hair. He brought himself to a halt and said, "Tell me you're here to fix the compressor."

"I'm here about the consulting position?" Fred gave him the letter. The big guy looked at it moving his lips, looked momentarily disappointed, then shook Fred's hand. "Welcome aboard," he said. "Cold enough for you? We're working on it," and he took Fred into his office. He was the office manager.

At the phones they were asking questions.

"You'll start on the phones," the office manager told Fred.

"I was under the impression it was a consulting position."

"I'm sure it will become that," the office manager said, leaning around a computer, "but everyone starts in the call center." He passed a W-4 across his desk and two or three sheets of paper stapled together. A list of questions.

"Some kind of survey?" Fred said.

"You could say that."

"What is it for?"

"My guess is some kind of demographic thing. Establishing a possible test market?"

Fred looked at the office manager.

"I know," the office manager said, "I know. This is just the way he works. He doesn't show his cards all at once." He leaned in and folded his hands. "Let me tell you something: he may not know himself. Yet. He believes in discovering needs, not inventing them."

"Who is he?" Fred asked.

"A genius."

"You've met him?"

"Not yet." The office manager looked suspicious. "Who did you talk to?"

"Some of his people. That letter came in the mail." Along with his wife's petition.

"It's just the way he works." The office manager leaned back. "You may have already seen him, shook his hand somewhere without knowing it. I was pitching minor league ball when they called me. You've heard the expression 'fisher of men'? Well add women . . ." He smiled warily, as at a joke he was too fond of repeating. "Anyway, he's a genius, okay? But everyone starts on the phones. We're working on the AC—bad compressor or something." He said the handsets were also just temporary; computers and auto-dialers were on the way. Socializing with the other associates during business hours was not encouraged. He did not use the word *employee*.

Fred sat down at a desk near the back of the room. The light over his head was bruised with dim patches like bad news on an X-ray. A list of numbers. A stack of answer sheets. The phone had a lot of buttons and the office manager showed him which ones mattered. Fred studied the questions. Listened around. He went over the questions again and dialed a number.

"Hello?" a woman said.

"Hello," Fred said. "Am I speaking to the head of household?" You were supposed to sound like you were smiling.

She sighed. "Depends who you ask." She didn't sound like she was smiling. "Who is this?"

Fred recited the name of the company. "Feel free to end the call at any time."

She laughed cruelly. "Okay," she said and hung up.

He dialed the next number. This time, when he said, "Do you have time to answer some questions?" he did not extend the option of ending the call.

"What kind of questions?" A voice of uncertain gender, of a certain resignation.

"What kind of questions do you most enjoy answering?" Fred asked. "a) Those with yes or no answers? b) Those involving quantities and measurements? c) Personal preference questions? d) Multiple choice questions? or e) No preference?"

"It would depend."

No preference. Fred made a mark on the answer sheet. "What is the size of the household?"

"You mean how many people?" the voice said. "Four if that's what you mean."

"How many people in the household are over the age of eighteen?"

"Three."

"Three?"

"Make that two. Sometimes I think he—"

"Two."

"Yes, sometimes I think . . . How many questions did you say?"

Fred wrote two. "Feel free to end the call at any time." It seemed safe to say. "How many household members use public transportation?"

"One."

"Male or female."

"She takes the bus."

"What is her favorite color?"

After a second the voice said, "I guess that's kind of a gray area," and laughed with an abandon out of all proportion to its wit.

"Should I put undecided?"

"Kind of a mint . . ."

"Can you be more specific, please?"

"Can we come back to it?"

"Do any of the household members who use public transportation and are over the age of eighteen have any physical impairments?"

The voice asked Fred to repeat that one, then it said, "She gets migraines."

Fred made a mark. Migraines were not on the list. "Do you have any pets?"

"Sure. Nosebleeds too."

"How many hours of television would you say the household watches per week? On the average."

"Aspirin doesn't help. Maybe she should get a CAT scan or something."

"Do you listen to more than one radio station?"

"Can we come back to that one? Maybe sometimes you're just better off not knowing."

Fred made a mark.

"Do you have a favorite radio station?"

"Classic rock." Slightly affronted, as if somehow Fred should have known.

An old trestle spanned a dry wash a hundred feet or so from Parametric Solutions, Inc., and Fred took his breaks on it, smoking. The second time, a woman was standing there, doing what he was doing. She seemed annoyed at his presence. Everything looked combustible. He stared down into the dirt, flicked an ash into his hand and wondered aloud how far away the ocean was. She didn't wonder back, and when he looked up she'd gone. A small cloud of smoke dissipated. He went back to his desk and looked up at the ceiling tiles. Water stains. Leaky return duct maybe, but he kept the thought to himself and continued asking strangers questions. Driving home in the evening he was still asking them: Does the household eat its meals together? Do you feel safe in your neighborhood at night? There was no end to them, it seemed, and if there were would he then hear the questions not on the list?

He didn't like the Escort. It drove like a bumper car. Rush hour resembled some mass crawl from catastrophe, motorcycles splitting lanes at a hundred miles an hour.

The apartment building, actually a residential motel, was a two-story stucco rectangle built around a courtyard with a swimming pool. No palm trees on the premises but a twenty-foot fence with an electric gate. Razor wire. The gate let onto a parking lot but it was first come, first served; when the lot was full you could spend twenty minutes looking for a space on the street. If other employees (who were not referred to as such) from Parametric Solutions, Inc., lived there, Fred never saw them. He'd expected some of the tenants to be aspiring actors or screenwriters or stand-up comics, practicing lines through thin walls, but many were migrant workers or day laborers who stood at intersections or in parking lots at certain hours, holding signs or selling fruit or flowers or offering themselves to passing traffic. Next door was a middle-aged man who wore a cowboy hat and tank top and tattoos he'd gotten in prison doing time for armed robbery. He'd had a bit role in a *Lethal Weapon* iteration.

The courtyard was the scene of great social activity in the evening. Laughter, mariachi, drinking and dancing; the drained, uncovered pool filled with people, lawn chairs, a barbecue grill. People left their doors open. Fred didn't, though he watched for a while from the balcony. When he went back into his studio efficiency, he could not bring himself to walk on the carpet barefoot.

He slept two feet from a noisy full-sized refrigerator. Kids roamed the property at night, banged on doors and ran away.

Beyond the motel there was little evidence of the Industry. Once Fred drove past the Warner Bros. lot and it looked like a beige penitentiary with figures of cartoon animals muraled *en gigante* to the wall. The shield of blue and gold.

After nearly a week of cryptic interrogations over the phone, he got up one overcast morning, walked a block to his parking space and saw a man there looking at the Escort. A red kerchief was tied around his neck.

"Can I help you?" Fred said. The guy spun, then jumped into the passenger side of a pickup truck idling in the middle of the street. Fred watched it pull out, tried to get a license number. When he got back to work an hour later the associates of Parametric Solutions, Inc., were standing outside on the sidewalk or sitting in their cars. They were watching the groundskeeper scrape the company name off the door with WD-40 and a razor blade. The windows were dark and Fred walked up to the glass and put his face to it. The desks were still there but the phones were gone, disconnected lines lying across the carpet like severed umbilicals. Fred turned to his former coworkers, who could now also be referred to as unemployed. Two of them were holding each other. A man who seemed attired too impeccably as a woman to be called a crossdresser said, "You know as much as we do."

"They said they make me administrator," a man with a strange accent said. His voice was filled with murder. The office manager was nowhere in sight.

Fred drove back to his apartment. He found the letter he'd shown the office manager, went down to the payphone by the rental office. Someone was there—someone always was—so he walked down the street to a gas station and called the number in the letter. A recording said Parametric Solutions, Inc., was being relocated, to bear with them till the new address could be made available. Even the recording sounded skeptical. Fred left his number and stood at the payphone for an hour. That night there was another party and he watched from the balcony in the cold. Below him two young women stood talking, holding cigarettes and green bottles. One of them, migrant or aspiring or both, dark of hair and eye with Spanish blood, looked up at him and smiled for perhaps one second, then resumed her conversation, her gray smoke, her green glass, but when Fred withdrew from the rail he was also backing away from the brink, for sometimes one second is all that is called for. Then you can hear the music.

The next day it rained and he stayed inside, running out of groceries. The day after that he drove to the gas station and put five dollars in his tank, then sat in Dunkin' Donuts nursing coffee and studying the letter. There was an address. Barstow. He went back to his apartment but when he tried to open the door he couldn't key the knob; it was twice as big as it had been in the morning. They'd put something on it, a big metal shell that spun loosely when you turned it and didn't open anything.

The ex–armed robber was sitting on the balcony reading something called *Our Lady of the Flowers*. "I can get you in if you need your effects," he offered.

"Wouldn't want you to get in any trouble on my account," Fred said. His neighbor told him to suit himself and Fred went down to the manager's office. A sign said she would be back in an hour—unless she got the part, Fred thought. He got in the Escort, already cast in his role. All he could do now was drive to the address on the letter. He didn't care who owned what anymore, only who could pay him his week's pay.

Heading up 14 he looked in the rearview mirror and saw a pickup maybe three lengths back. Then two. He slowed to let it pass but the truck slowed as well, kept a steady distance. Vast arid hills and outlet stores on his left. He wondered if it was the truck he'd seen by his car the other day, and when he turned left onto the frontage road it followed him into desert outland like an alter ego. He kept turning left, then a right, on roads unmarked and unpaved, the body of the car leaning like it would detach itself from its frame, and when the dust had somewhat settled he'd lost the truck and himself in the Mojave. It wasn't hot outside but the sun was starting to cook him through the winter cool and he rolled down the window. Kept looking in the mirror. He hated the Escort now, hated anti-lock brakes and power steering—they were for people who don't know how things work. He hated the desert. When he was on blacktop again he pulled over and it stopped. He went into the glove compartment but the map was locked in a room in what was now the past. The desert started again on its own terms.

He sat a while trying to think his way to 58. Looked up. Someone was coming and then the pickup truck pulled off about a hundred feet behind him. The man with the red kerchief got out and headed off the road, tugging at his zipper. Got behind a cluster of squat trees with leaves like bayonets. Fred took his keys out of the ignition, got out of his car, and walked back toward the truck. He heard a loud buzzing sound and wasn't sure if it came from the telephone lines overhead or some other kind of life.

The driver was a skinny kid with a baseball cap turned around on his head. "Hola," he said to Fred though he didn't look Mexican.

"Why are you following me?" Fred said.

"Whatever gave you that idea," the kid said.

"I saw you back in town, looking at my car. Now here we are. I suppose you're a fisher of men too?"

"More a fisher of cars," the kid admitted. "Let's back up a little. It isn't your car—not since you stopped making payments." He picked up a clipboard, displayed the top sheet through the window. Fred barely read it, just saw the word DISCHARGE stamped in the middle.

"This can't be right," he said. "I haven't even had a chance to make a payment." Then he heard an engine start.

"Doesn't look like you're gonna get one," the kid said, and Fred turned and the Escort was already pulling away, the man no longer behind the trees behind the wheel.

"He can use a slide hammer faster than most people can use their keys," the kid said.

"You sons of bitches," Fred said.

"I know, I'm sorry," the kid said genuinely. "Let me give you a ride back into town."

"Go fuck yourself," Fred said.

"You don't mean that," the kid said.

Fred spat and started walking. The truck walked with him.

"Who's fucking who?" the kid yelled. "You'll die out here."

"You'll just have to live with that," Fred yelled back, and in the end the kid got in the last word without saying anything and was gone. Dust settling quickly in still air. Gone.

Fred walked. He stopped. The desert had him to itself. It wasn't as smooth as it looked driving past; it was cracked and pebbled like something falling apart from neglect. It made a sound in the bushes: *ssk*, *ssk*, in front and behind and then to his side. Small cacti with flowers that bloom at night. He started walking again. Greasewood. Distant vague mountains.

Shirt without tie. The sun a generalized whiteness overhead so you couldn't tell east from west. He thought about putting his thumb out but there were no other cars as yet.

You had to be somewhere to be someone, and if he was still around when the stars came out maybe they would tell him who he was.

"And they just left you there?" the documentarist said. He sounded incredulous, but then he always did. He'd already apologized for it; he was just a born skeptic, but of course he gave everyone the benefit of the doubt.

He had a Ph.D. in philosophy. Roger Ebert had called him a genius, a faculty Fred now equated with deserts and dispossession.

"More or less," he said. When the documentarist pressed him for details, he mentioned getting picked up by the highway patrol, then became vague.

"I guess you could say I went underground."

The documentarist nodded. He'd had to hire a private detective to dig Fred up. "But why would you need to?" he said.

"Figure of speech," Fred said. He shrugged. He did not want them knowing who his enemies were just yet, nor his friends; there were other things to talk about. There were numbers.

The producer said little, ordered nothing. Sketched on a napkin. She wore a blazer and black turtleneck, black-framed glasses. The documentarist wore an oxford shirt.

The waitress came by with the coffee pot and the documentarist held up a hand. Fred nodded. He was drinking coffee in

his hometown in a place called Friendly's, which was bright
and well managed and boasted twenty-two flavors of ice cream
but wasn't named after anybody's mother.

The documentarist asked him if he had an agent.

"People in my shoes don't have agents," Fred said. People
in his shoes took them off to sleep on a cot in an unused jani-
torial closet. Threw them at mice.

"How are you making a living these days?"

"I'm in security."

He was in a polyester uniform twenty hours a week. A large
private university he wouldn't name.

"Not that I'd exactly call it a living," he said. "Which reminds me."

The documentarist nodded again and looked at the producer, who finally spoke. She sounded like her last name, and
her last name sounded like money. "We'll agree to a one-time
fee but there won't be anything off the back end. All the other
subjects have accepted the same terms." She hesitated a little
before calling them subjects.

"Frankly," the documentarist said, "my films just don't
make bank."

It was true. He was often regarded as the foremost documentary filmmaker of his generation, etc., but Cannes, Toronto,
Roger Ebert notwithstanding, he could not exactly call it a living either. He'd made a film that had exonerated a man on
death row but otherwise barely turned a profit. He'd made a
film about a physicist in a wheelchair who could neither move
nor speak but could explain the origin of the universe, yet

which knowledge was not worth a fraction of the fee the documentarist commanded directing beer commercials, blue jean commercials, commercials for Exxon, Target, Nike, the kind of ad shown during the Super Bowl or the Academy Awards; people talked about them in cafeterias and cubicles the next day. They did not talk about quantum mechanics, and it would remain to be seen if they would talk about Fred.

"How much?" Fred said, and the producer slid her napkin across the booth as if to show him her sketches. Fred looked.

"How many other subjects are there?" he asked. He didn't hesitate.

"Three or four," the documentarist said. "I haven't narrowed it down yet."

"May I ask who they are?"

"I'd rather you guys didn't know about each other just yet," the documentarist said. "What you each have in common is an unusual occupation and a powerful conviction about what you do."

"Well I don't do it much anymore," Fred said and, using the producer's pen, drew another picture on the napkin and pushed it back across the booth.

This was only to be expected. The documentarist leaned in without looking at Fred's numbers and said, "Why is it I get the feeling you're holding out on us?"

"Things may have slipped my mind," Fred said. "I'm sure it'll all come back to me before the camera starts rolling."

"It might be to your advantage if things start slipping back in now," the producer said.

Fred thought. "I could use an advance," he said.

They signed their names to it, shook on it, and the documentarist picked up the check. He'd had the eggs Benedict; Fred, dry toast and coffee.

Fred had been professionally assured that the accident on his wife's cousin's acreage had, in the long run, made no detectable medical difference. Still, no one would talk to him at the funeral. He was on his way home in a slightly used Buick Park Avenue (silver, gray interior, 3.8 V6, cash) when he saw a Starbucks sign outside Ashland and pulled off into an outlet mall there. He cruised around looking for a parking spot and a place where he could nurse a cup and bury the warden again, alone. The mall was the size of a small town, with blocks and stop signs, and he realized he was driving across the barrens to which they'd once taken their guns. As if he'd been drawn there.

He recalled a movie about a subdivision built over a tribal grave site. Here were stores that sold Levi's, women's lingerie, household items, sporting goods, and none seem troubled by restless spirits. Still, he got his coffee to go.

At first all he had to do was talk. The documentarist would ask a question and Fred would answer. He had his doubts. "I'm not much on conversation," he confided to the documentarist, which wasn't strictly true, but he found the stare of the lens inhibiting. "I might need a little priming . . ."

So the device.

The device consisted simply of a video camera, a projector, and a two-way mirror. It enabled the subject to look at both

his interviewer and the camera at the same time, and it worked
so well the editor privately joked that another invention would
be required just to shut Fred up. The documentarist had developed it expressly for this film. It gave Fred a face to talk to and
when you saw the movie he was talking you right in the eye,
his head twelve feet tall. Patent pending.

Genius, some said again (though some insisted it was just
a variation on the teleprompter), a revolutionary advance in
the field; the interviewer didn't even have to be in the same
room with the subject, nor was he when Fred said things like
"I studied celestial navigation with a direct descendant of Leif
Ericson," or "When I was fourteen my father's throat was cut
right in front of my eyes."

At first there were three others: the lady lion tamer, the man
who wrote fortune cookie fortunes, and the man who built
life-sized statues of famous figures (the Virgin Mary, Mao) out
of Legos. But after certain facts came to light and the Report
began to exert its inexorable pull, shaping the film around it,
the other subjects were displaced, squeezed out, tentatively to
be reunited in a future project with a composer who made
music with insects, a deaf-and-dumb detective, or some as-yet-
undiscovered eccentric. They still hadn't changed the title.

Additional footage was required: the old prison where his
father had worked and died (closed), the old Catholic grade
school (a housing project), the house he'd grown up in and
watched burn down (a community garden). Fred driving
through the new world the old neighborhoods had become. The
second-unit kid in the passenger seat with an old spring-wound

workhorse, sixteen-millimeter, loaded with high-speed black-and-white reversal.

A Baptist church that used to be a bank.

"Third/Fifth Federal," Fred said.

"You don't have to talk," the second-unit kid said, under the dashboard for the angle. (The documentarist had quickly noted Fred's inability to speak and watch the road at the same time and decided to record his narration as voiceover.)

"Used to be a high school."

"Used to be a five and dime."

"Used to be they couldn't set foot in this neighborhood without somebody taking a shot at them," Fred said. Now there was no getting out.

Smoking, coffee, three packs a day, ten or fifteen cups—black, he'd said. Make it six, the documentarist said, make it twenty or thirty, with sugar. A family restaurant rented after hours, a corner booth, a thousand feet of him from every angle and distance: pouring, stirring, sipping. (He didn't take sugar but the documentarist insisted.) The makeup girl wore black, had black lips in a face so white it was almost featureless. Dabbed something cool and creamy on his skin: concealer, foundation, even eyeliner. Final touches. Then the lens like a gun barrel inches from his lips as he blew smoke in profile. The window a sheet of light. Three in the morning, five hundred frames per second. Humming like something in a machine shop.

But when he was talking the camera was padded and stared mutely.

"At your age you should think about a moisturizer," she said.

Sets were required. Carpenters. He'd thought this done only for Hollywood fictions, but here they were, staging reenactments in re-creations of reconstructions. Here he now sat in a white room with three walls, venetian blinds, in the chair he had placed in the classifieds, best offer. He strapped himself in under the white-hot light, blinded, sweating through the countdown, but the button they pushed was the one on the Arriflex. He'd lowered himself into the black hole of Krema II, but the subterranean chamber in which he found himself now was an abandoned basement on a street named New York Avenue, where every other house was boarded up, and it was better lit and warm; he did not have to grope and crawl among fallen beams and rubble. A puddle at the bottom, he dipped his hand in and brought up a chunk of masonry. Again, the documentarist said, again, as if next time it would come up gold. He didn't remember doing it in the camp, but he remembered the documentarist saying they would get to the bottom of things, the truth, even if they had to make it up.

The chair had survived the fire, untouched.

They gave him a hammer and chisel. He chipped plaster and brick from an abandoned basement wall, his hands glowing, uninvited locals providing unsolicited "security."

"Do you have any regrets?" the documentarist asked, sitting in another room. The producer never asked him anything. She sat in a room in another state, counting.

Fred liked being on set. Most of being on set was waiting, a manageable ennui, not quite hearing every word of the endless consultation that preceded every take, but he was patient and comfortable and shown every consideration. Craft service knew about his ulcer. The makeup girl smiled at his jokes. It was a small crew, union and non, but he liked watching them, the way they spoke to each other and the way they didn't have to. He liked the camera assistant, and the camera loader, who also clapped the clapperboard and replaced magazines like ammunition in a firefight (a thousand feet lasted eleven minutes); the key grip, who solved everything with duct tape; the gaffer; the best boy, who was a girl; the assistant to the director, who was not the assistant director with her big mouth and hat to the back, who seemed more in charge of things than the director himself.

He liked craft service: roast beef, chicken parmesan, pasta with clam sauce, red or white.

They shot him on a scaffold, tying a noose around a sandbag, pulling a lever and dropping it through a trapdoor. The gallows had been hastily assembled and he was not allowed to participate in its construction. They shot him hanging a sandbag twelve times.

He wore the leather electrode helmet and he sits there like Knute Rockne with eyeglasses, discussing the relative conductivity of human flesh. At the editing table the documentarist decided it was over the top but made the footage available as a deleted scene on the DVD release.

He hadn't seen her in five years. The hearing lasted ten minutes. She didn't want anything except for it to be over. She had a lawyer but only to draw up the paperwork. She had an artificial leg below the knee. Fred represented himself.

"I only want what's best for her," he told the judge.

The leg had a silicone sleeve and was almost indistinguishable from its counterpart. Fred thought of the roomful of limbs at the camp.

The five of them sat at a big table in a large room with dark wood-paneled walls. There were windows in the walls but the wood was very dark and the light seemed far away. She'd brought her ostensible fiancé with her, a tall wrinkled apparition who leaned on a cane and had a narrow fringe of white hair clamped around the back of his skull. A pair of miniature American flags were pinned to the lapels of his suit, and he wore the blue garrison cap of a Veteran of Foreign Wars. The lawyer whispered in his good ear and he uncovered his spotted scalp.

The judge asked that they demonstrate in what way their union was irreparably damaged. She did most of the talking. She bore no ill will and attributed their undoing mostly to the crowd with whom he'd cast his lot. She didn't look at him once.

"They used him," she said. "And he used them back."

"He consorted with the enemy," the old man blurted and pulled something from his pocket. "I served under Bradley, Omar Nelson," and he began reciting a list of campaigns. The judge, who'd earned a Purple Heart and a metal plate in his head in Korea, instructed him not to speak unless spoken to.

"I want what's best for everyone," Fred amended, and so did not say his wife's fiancé looked as though he might have marched with Sherman as well.

"Took this off a rifleman at Bastogne," the old man said. He threw a faded cloth insignia patch on the table like a scalp. "Used my combat knife, hand to hand. So foggy I never saw his face."

The judge ordered him out of the room.

"*I'm* what's best for her!" The old man glared at Fred as he stood, shrugging off her lawyer's arm. He had to return to collect the breast eagle.

After they signed the decree of dissolution, the judge said it would become final one month after date of entry. Neither party could remarry for a period of six months. She reclaimed her maiden name as though in place of her lost member. Outside Fred skulked in a doorway at the top of the courthouse steps, watching the woman he had courted in a diner that had long since served its last customer help the old man down to the sidewalk. She managed very well, considering. Eventually they arrived at an old but well-kept Lincoln sedan parked dead center in front of the building. Gun-metal gray. Low compression, Fred thought, but probably it rode on air. A parking ticket flapped under the windshield wiper like a dead leaf, and the old man plucked it out and threw it into the street without looking at it. He got in the passenger side.

The documentarist put him in a cage. It resembled a bird cage but was big enough to hold a man. The chair was inside.

"What's this about?" Fred said.

"Trust me," the documentarist said. "Watch your head."

"Can I get something in writing?" Fred said, crouching as he got inside.

They strapped him in like some four-eyed astronaut in a Value City suit. The makeup girl put cool moist things on his face with a soft brush, chewing now instead of smiling, and this always put him in a trance of cooperation. The gum popped and snapped in a faraway way.

The documentarist reached through the bars, put his hand on Fred's shoulder.

"You've been a good sport about this," he said.

"I'm a team player," Fred said. "I just don't get it."

"You'll understand better when you see it in context," the documentarist said. "You might say it's a metaphor."

"I might not," Fred said. "Things are what they are."

"There's a hotspot on his nose," the documentarist told the makeup girl.

The AD hollered.

The building had once been a foundry. It had no power so they'd brought their own and the cage stood on a hydraulic scissor lift. The documentarist said "go" instead of "action." The cage began to rise.

"This is your ascent, Fred," the documentarist shouted. "Look straight ahead."

Fred obliged. The arc lamps glared. A strobe would be added in post to simulate the effect of a lightning storm. He rose past a camera on a catwalk.

"Look down," the documentarist shouted, his hands cupped around his mouth. Genius needs no bullhorn. The diesel-driven generator chugged.

"Smile!" he said.

"Look up!"

Fred looked up. There was nothing beyond the brilliance of the lights, and he rose into it a little way, then stopped.

In January Fred drove to Boston to see a cut that was almost final. The producer would reimburse him for mileage. He sat with the documentarist and the producer and they watched the whole thing from three chairs in front of a flatbed editing table. Fred was in the middle. He'd thought they would sit in a smoky screening room, smoking, but the documentarist didn't trust projectors. When it was over they remained in bright silence until Fred said, "It's longer." Then he said, "It's not the same.

"The title," he said.

"We needed to make changes," the producer said.

"The elephant," Fred said.

"That was a find," the producer said.

"We still have some mixing to do," the documentarist said. "And the music is scratch." He saw nothing wrong with the title.

"But at Harvard," Fred said.

"That was a rough cut," the documentarist said. To raise funding for additional footage. Postproduction.

"More additional footage," Fred said.

"This is a much more balanced point of view," the producer said. "It's complete."

But at Harvard it had seemed complete enough and there was a great burst of applause after the screening. The Q&A had not gone quite as well, not for the documentarist, who seemed uncomfortable, even defensive, as if they'd applauded for the wrong reasons and now were asking the wrong questions. When they thanked him he didn't seem to want to be thanked.

At Harvard Fred had walked through the Yard—the snow-sagging trees, walkways, red brick buildings—and told the audience the freshman dorms looked like the barrack blocks without barbed wire. Only the students laughed. One of them had concerns about the First Amendment. Sophomore, pre-law, innate goodness and round brown eyes. She'd called Fred the most humane character in the film. Now they'd made him someone else.

"If it ain't broke," he said, "don't break it."

The producer corrected him and Fred said, "I know what I said." He turned to the documentarist. "This is what you do to raise money?"

"This is the film I wanted to make, Fred," the documentarist said.

"But the elephant," Fred said. Like some kind of goddamn sacrifice.

"The elephant's going to Park City," the producer said, and Fred said, "Then it'll be going there without me," and he signed something, and he told them how far he'd driven and how much he'd spent on gas, and they compensated him and didn't try to talk him out of or into anything else.

Nineteen days later, the temperature just above zero at two in the morning, Fred woke up and couldn't get back to sleep. As if a loud shout had woken him, but there was only the hum of the space heater and the producer's last name, silently burning a hole in his belly. He was awake the rest of the night. Before starting his shift he called the documentarist, listened to an answering machine, and hung up. When his shift was over he called again and again did not leave a message. Called his supervisor instead. A family emergency, he said—the captain was a family man. Take as much time as you need, the captain said, and even gave Fred a lift downtown to the Greyhound station.

He'd signed something.

He didn't want to take his car into the mountains.

By the time they pulled into Salt Lake Central Station, they'd boarded a number of passengers who seemed to comprise the steerage class of the festival: latecomers, the curious, fanatics of modest means who could afford neither airfare nor accommodations in Park City. And Fred. It was just daybreak. A woman hugging a battered square case sat across the aisle from him. He'd slept little in the last day and a half and this apparently made him the ideal listener: she told him she'd made a documentary short about a landless Indian tribe with only five members. One of them, her husband, rode beside her wearing a tracksuit and cowboy hat. Fred said hello and the husband nodded; he had taken a vow of silence. Their story had not qualified for competition but she was hoping to arrange her own screening in town, rent or beg a space, basement or back room, pass out tickets on Main Street. A sixteen-millimeter projector stowed in the luggage bin below. Fred dozed and she shook him awake. There were no buses into Park City—did he wish to split a cab with them? A few minutes later he found himself in the front seat of an SUV with the inside door latches sawed off. They crawled from the city in morning rush hour, then broke out into the mountains, the outer ranges the color of ash, peaks still clear of snow. There was no sun but the gray day brightened ahead. The driver was quiet as the tribesman. The woman was smiling. She looked at Fred and asked why he'd come to the festival.

He thought. "You wouldn't believe me if I told you."

"Try me."

Fred thought again. "To tell the truth."

"Well me too," she said as if challenged.

He glanced at her husband, who wore headphones. "How long's it been since he spoke?"

"Eight years," she said. He would not break his silence till the government had granted his tribe sovereignty.

"What do they do then?" Fred said, cranky and sleep-deprived. "Build a casino?"

"That isn't their way," the woman said quietly, and Fred said nothing as the mountains closed in.

They twisted through gorges and he craned his neck to look up the walls but couldn't see out of the pit. Then everything opened up again and in the distance to the right a ski ramp was fixed to the lower slope like a giant playground slide. No one was jumping; everyone was here to see movies. The mountains were empty. The filmmaker asked Fred where he would be staying, and in truth he had not thought this far ahead. He thought of the Bible he'd had in Mannheim. *The foxes have holes, and the birds of the air have nests*, but he couldn't remember the rest.

He told her he'd made arrangements.

Park City was a town of old rustic Western-style buildings and dwellings becoming rustic and Western in a modern, expensive way. Hills covered with evergreens and bare brown trees. There was snow on the ground but the roads were just plowed. The cab driver got out and opened the passenger door at the corner of a street where Swedish miners had once lived. Icicles dripping points of light. The filmmaker wished him luck though she sounded uncertain as to why. Her husband waved.

The festival box office was housed in a corner building across the street from a restaurant with an outdoor fireplace.

The fire burned but had no one yet to warm. Fred went inside. An indoor mini-mall, the box office on the first floor. It was a big room with tables and computers and people behind the tables at the computers. Everyone else was standing in a long line switching back behind posts and chains. The people at the computers weren't selling many tickets. They were constantly shaking their heads, and then the people from the line would walk away also shaking their heads, perhaps to console themselves at the fire across the street. A festival of discontent. Then a cheerful young woman in a fashionably oversized sweater said, "Who's next?" and it was Fred's turn to be disappointed.

He told her the name of the film, and smiling and shaking, she told him it was sold out.

"The board," Fred said, pointing to the big board on the wall behind the tables. It announced the day's screenings and said there were still tickets available.

"I know," the young woman said apologetically. "It needs updated. We're so understaffed."

"Standing room?" Fred said.

"Waitlist," she said.

"Weightless."

She repeated herself and carefully explained the routine.

"Doesn't sound like I'd have much of a shot," he said.

"You'd be surprised," she encouraged.

Was there a supervisor he could talk to? A manager?

"There's a coordinator!" she said as if only just realizing. "He gets in at noon."

Probably another line. Fred looked at his watch.

"What if I told you," he said then, and she listened patiently, almost sympathetically, then told him what she would ask him if he told her that.

"It's a long story," he said.

"Then all I can tell you is waitlist," she said. She seemed disappointed, as though she'd encountered this ruse before. She recovered quickly, brightening. "Or come back after noon if you want to share with someone else."

Fred lowered his voice. "I can prove it," he said and opened his wallet.

"Sir," she said, disappointed in a different way, as if he were about to expose himself which in a way he was. "You'll have to come back after noon and prove it to the coordinator." She whispered in confidence, "He's actually paid to listen."

He put his wallet back, grabbed his lapels. "This is the coat I wore to the camps."

"It certainly looks warm enough," she said. "You can show it to the coordinator. After lunch. Or—"

"Waitlist," Fred said.

"Exactly."

"Are you a volunteer?" Fred said.

"I'm a film student who loves to help people. I would love to help the next person."

"Can you at least tell me where I can get a cup of coffee?" Fred said. "Or is there a waitlist for that too?"

"Anywhere on Main Street," the young woman said. "You might meet some interesting people there."

"God save us from interesting people," Fred said, and the young woman reloaded her impregnable smile. It won every time. Then she was smiling past him, brightly and unpromising: "Next? Whoever's next, step down please!"

He left and walked up the block, drained by the exchange, passed a restaurant he didn't know was owned by Robert Redford. He didn't know who owned the restaurant but he knew who Robert Redford was—Robert Redford ran the festival and he wondered if at any moment he might turn a corner and see Robert Redford at the center of some knot of activity, calmly delegating as a good administrator does, because Robert Redford was also the Sundance Kid, a killer but kindhearted by nature, and one of the stars of one of the few films Fred liked or even remembered.

A decent, approachable man. Someone who would want to help.

He did not see Robert Redford but it was still early and there was plenty of coffee on Main Street. There were plenty of bars and restaurants, gift shops, boutiques, pizzerias, hotels, galleries, walls covered with posters, festival banners waving from streetlight poles, and he walked uphill past them into a pub and ordered a cup. He did not normally drink coffee in bars but felt a need to hide in the dark. A man and a woman sat next to him, wearing name badges on lanyards. The man was a director and the woman was a journalist. Fred smoked and drank his coffee in the dimness, smelling Bloody Marys and breakfast, watching the young bartender pour two different colors of beer into a schooner. A dollar bill was pinned high to the wall behind the bar, and along with it a unit of currency each from visitors of other countries. They fluttered like wings when someone opened the door. When someone told a dirty joke, the bartender rang a bell. Fred asked him what it would be like in there later.

"Come back tonight," the bartender said with a slight brogue, "and you can see Courtney Love show her breasts."

"Courtney who?" Fred said.

"Good for you," the man on the other side of Fred said. The bartender gave the Black and Tan to the director who was being interviewed by the journalist.

"Irish breakfast," the bartender said, but the director didn't hear.

"You've made a feature film with a budget of four hundred dollars. How is that accomplished?" the journalist asked.

"It's essentially home movie footage reconfigured into a metanarrative." The director was eating peanuts and putting the shells in his pocket. "We shot extra scenes to fill in certain gaps but I defy anyone to tell the difference. To spend money would have compromised authenticity."

"You also appear in the film. How did you like playing yourself?"

"I'm always playing myself," the director said.

"I'm always playing with myself too," the drunk on the other side of Fred said. "Come back tonight and you can see me punch out QT."

"I thought Courtney Love punches out QT," the bartender said.

"Then we have to see *his* tits," the man said, and the bartender rang the bell though it wasn't much of a joke. Fred didn't know who QT was either. He knew who Mao Tse-tung was, smiling faintly in purple from a five-yuan note.

He drank two more cups and when he left there were no more seats at the bar. Traffic had thickened and slowed steadily while he was inside, was doing little now but burning gas. He went back the way he'd come, trudging down in the same hat and coat he'd worn to the camps, but not the same boots. He passed under a ski lift, a net stretched across the road beneath it but there was no one on the lift to drop anything or fall. It was quieter here, the street lined with small houses. He didn't know where it led but it seemed to be getting away from the festival. A small park to his right. A public restroom there but the door was locked and he unzipped his pants behind it. Someone shouted. Fred didn't know if the shout was directed at him but it cut him short and he turned around, stumbled down a snowy embankment to a cinder walking path. He took it back toward town, passing under small bridges. A jogger overtook him but it was Fred who was out of breath, the air entering his lungs in thin sheets with sharp edges. On his right were lodges and houses, people drinking in a heated outdoor pool. One of them wore only a cowboy hat, and Fred looked away. On the other side was a stream, above that a busy-sounding highway, and in the trees and on the ground he saw a bird with the head of a crow, a white belly, dark-green wings, a long tail. He saw a harried woman leading children on a scavenger hunt. Every day is someone's birthday.

"Have you seen the shoe tree?" she asked almost desperately, but all he'd seen in the trees were the strange-looking birds. The ones on the ground pecking at a pale carcass.

The path took him to the bus station. He found a men's room and finished what he'd started, then sat down in the waiting room to warm up. Pale wooden walls, a Native American motif. Pale wooden racks filled with tourist information: he read a brochure about an old silver mine on Bald Mountain, now converted into a museum. It had been the site of a great disaster and was haunted by the ghosts of miners looking for body parts lost in the explosion. The shaft was fifteen hundred feet deep. The shuttle was free. For once the dead were on his side.

The bus was so crowded you could stand without hanging on to anything. Everyone else was wearing badges on lanyards. They spoke English but it was the dialect of cinema, and apparently you needed a badge to understand it. It was a short ride. The mine was a cluster of battered sheds with the roof of the hoist house peaking above them. Everyone got off the bus and went to the entrance. Fred couldn't get in. The museum had been appropriated for a filmmakers' conference and you needed a festival pass.

"What kind of conference?" Fred asked the man at the door.

"The Future of Digital Filmmaking," the man at the door said. He said nothing about phantom miners, nor the woman who'd been somehow incorporated into their legend, clothed only in her long hair, riding a horse through a tunnel two hundred feet underground.

Waiting for the shuttle back, Fred looked down on Park City from halfway up the mountain. He could see only the outskirts, a scattering of distant rooftops and then only the mountains again. A hot air balloon like a bright-colored moon hung motionless over the town, and from this height he looked dead ahead at it, on equal terms.

When he got back to the bus station he'd given up the idea of pleading his case at the box office—its purpose seemed only to turn people away—and headed instead back to the main drag of the festival. He had not seen a mob like this since he'd stepped out of the courthouse in Toronto, but this was another kind of riot. Traffic was stranded, SUVs and somehow a stretch limo, all remaining space in the street and sidewalk dense with three kinds of people: those who wore their names on strings, those who didn't, and those who didn't have to, breathing the same thin air. Winter tans. Brightly colored little phones that fit in the palms of their hands. It was getting colder, clouds were gathering, he dropped the earflaps of his cap and shoved his gloved hands in his pockets, worked his way past the theater where the story of his life would unfold. Obelisks pilastered to its façade, a figurehead of the Sphinx posing its riddle over the tiled ticket booth, over a young woman with a microphone and cameraman shining a bright light in the faces of strangers. She asked them about their clothes. She was very pretty but so was everyone else, and everyone was also handsome and beautiful and fascinating, and mostly white in black cashmere and cowboy hats and sometimes in short skirts and high heels, or wearing a badge that said I AM NOT GEORGE CLOONEY and looking like someone whose name you should know, but Fred, who was not entirely immune to the disease of celebrity, by which even the best of us are sometimes infected, Fred was only interested in two faces: the one that belonged to the documentarist, which he wasn't sure whether to avoid or confront, and that of Robert Redford, the face of the festival, weathered but unaffected, a face that might even recognize yours and the film to which it belonged, and having done so would assure it a berth at the event where hundreds would see it for the first time, at the festival he'd named for the role in which he'd starred, as you were starring in yours, and who knew what else you might have in common?

For the hell of it he was about to ask a volunteer if she knew where Robert Redford was. It began to snow. He was hungry. Someone shoved a flyer in his hands. He followed the directions on the flyer and wound up in the basement of a bar above Main Street, sitting on a folding chair next to a space heater. There was a VCR and a big-screen TV on which were showing a number of short subjects that had been deemed unsuitable for the main festival. Fred dozed through four or five of these but admission was not charged and there were free hot dogs, and he half expected to see among the tiny half-drunk audience the filmmaker whose husband had taken a vow of silence, but he didn't.

Around six he went to the Egyptian. The girl at the box office had said they would start passing out the waitlist cards an hour before showtime, so he got there well before that. He was not the first and was soon not the last. The entrances were closed. Rail barriers pushed the line to the edge of the sidewalk. The snow had stopped falling but the drifts blew hard. The cold was epic, Stalingrad or Shackleton. The line tried to keep warm by marching and jumping in place, by talking about the festival, about films and directors and juries and awards. Then they talked about how cold it was. Fred savored his secret as if it would keep him alive. He kept an eye out for the documentarist, for a limo, flashbulbs—wasn't this a premiere? The marquee bore only the name of the festival. Film students with badges appointing them crowd liaisons came out periodically to walk up and down the line, running through the waitlist drill and making sure no one needed medical attention. After a while they just walked up and down the line, then fled back inside.

When they passed out the cards he couldn't feel certain parts of himself. He knew it could have been worse, could have been the false warmth of hypothermia (bodies found naked by would-be rescuers, clothing shed in the final moments as if in preparation for the hereafter). The cards were numbered. Technically you could leave the line—you could go somewhere and stay alive and return without losing your place, but Fred wasn't taking any chances. Neither was the man in front of him. The man in front of Fred wore a hunting cap and coveralls and other layers, one of which came in liquid form and was drawn from a half-pint bottle partly concealed in a black plastic bag. He pushed it at Fred and Fred shook his head.

"I don't think that helps," he said.

"As long as it feels like it does," the man with the half-pint said and took another drink. He took his other hand out of his pocket and put his thumb and little finger together. "So long as you can do this . . ."

"So they say," Fred said but hadn't yet tried it himself.

The man looked into the street at passersby. "Seen any big shots?" he asked.

"I wouldn't know if I had," Fred said.

"Good for you," the man said. "How do you tell a local from an out-of-towner?"

Fred tried to form a smile, told him he'd heard that one in the pub.

"Well excuse me," the man said. "I just live here."

"Well that's a switch," Fred said. Then he asked the man how he made his living, his customary follow-up.

"Sucking shit out of septic tanks," the man said. A pump truck, hepatitis B shot. "Thought I'd see what all the people in black come here and freeze their asses off for. You'd think it was a goddamn funeral." He pushed the bottle at Fred again and again Fred said no thanks.

"Excuse hell out of me," the man said. You couldn't tell if he was offended or just talked that way. He looked a little unsteady on his feet. "I wanted to see that witch movie, couldn't get in. You see it?"

"This is what I came to see," Fred said. The man looked at him, leaned back as if for a better appraisal, lost a little of his balance and bumped a couple in front of him.

"Excuse me I just live here," he said by way of apology. He asked if they knew how to tell an out-of-towner from a local. Asked them if they'd seen the witch.

He reeled back Fred's way then, tilted his head toward the marquee and tried to lower his voice. "I hear this movie they show somebody getting fried."

"I don't think so," Fred said. Or was this another change? Additional footage.

"I heard he's some kind of ex . . . ex . . ." The man trailed off, tried again, faltered. "I hear he's some kinda damn Nazi."

"He isn't a Nazi," Fred said. "He's an engineer." His mouth had trouble forming certain words but not these.

"I'll kick a Nazi's ass," the man said. Then he raised the bottle reflectively and said, "I'll say one thing though."

"It's a true story," Fred said.

"Disciplined," the man said. "And clean. I'll say that. Then I'll kick their ass." And he drank to their discipline and cleanliness, or to kicking their ass.

"What do you mean not a Nazi?" he said suddenly. "The hell are we doing here then?" He looked a little suspicious. "How do you know so much? This guy a friend of yours?"

"I know the story."

"No shit," the man said. "So why do they call him Mr. Death?"

"I wouldn't want to spoil it for you."

"Mighty white of you," the man said. "Me being a local yokel and all."

"No offense," Fred said.

"I'll be judge of that," the man said and raised the bottle but it was empty.

"Well fuck me," he said. He raised the bottle again and it was still empty. Looked around.

"Time to change the antifreeze," he announced then. "Flush and fill—don't start without me . . ."

"That's what the cards are for," Fred said.

"Why you think they give us these cards?" the man said, stepping away. "Kick a Nazi's ass," he mumbled, bumping into people, excusing hell out of himself.

When he'd gone the theater staff started selling waitlist tickets at ten dollars each. The volunteers moved the barriers. One of them announced they were seating the advance ticketholders. The advance ticketholders formed another line, and when it had disappeared into the theater there was room in the lobby for the waitlist. It surged forward as one, making grateful sounds, and Fred staggered along, his feet somewhere below him, operating under remote control. The lobby was small, the doors closed just behind him. On the wall over the concession stand were pharaonic likenesses in relief and painted scarabs, and a sign on a door said the balcony was closed for repair. Fred smelled coffee but wanted nothing, just stood there in the ecstatic warmth while someone drove nails into his ears and through his feet.

Almost half an hour later the novelty of survival had worn off and the staff were still counting heads in the theater. They were shorthanded and running late. Fred watched in vain for the documentarist. A young man with a shaved head and not dressed in black came out and announced they would seat waitlist ticketholders one through seven. Fred looked at his ticket though he already knew his number. He took off his gloves. They let in more of the line from outside and the crowd shifted. The stomping of boots, melting ice. There was slush on the carpet. Footprints.

The young man with the shaved head came out of the theater and announced that no more seats were available, the screening was now officially sold out. He said he was sorry. Their tickets would be refunded at the booth. The doors were closed behind him.

It was Fred's turn to have to piss.

There was nothing Egyptian about the restroom. All the urinals were occupied so he went into a stall and shut the door.

When he'd finished and come out, he washed his hands for a long time. He washed them till everyone else was gone. Thought he heard distant applause.

He could demand to see the manager, tell them who he was. Demand they speak to the documentarist.

He could make demands.

He stood there, not looking in the mirror. When he'd left he imagined his reflection left behind, looking out.

Coming up the stairs, he heard drama that was not a soundtrack. When he was back in the lobby he saw that it was coming from the entrance. The local man who drained septic tanks for a living was standing just inside the doors, pleading his case.

"Excuse me I just goddamn live here!" He'd managed to get drunker while keeping his feet. "What was I supposed to do, piss my pants? There was a line!"

Probably one at the liquor store too, Fred thought.

"The room is filled to capacity," someone who must have been the manager said. "I couldn't let you in if I wanted to."

The whole theater staff seemed to be there, except for the young man with the shaved head, who stood before the doors to Fred's film like a St. Peter. From behind him came circus music.

"Sir, if you don't leave I'm going to have to call Sergeant Little," the manager said.

"I'll kick his Nazi little ass," the local man said. "Kick Redford's ass," and he started with Redford's manager by hitting him in the mouth with the back of his fist. The staff closed in around him. The kid with the shaved head headed for the trouble.

Fred stopped thinking and moved. He saw the boatman on the wall, stopped. The door to the balcony was closer. He kept waiting for someone to call to him but all he heard was the local man's voice in struggle: "I live here. This is my home." The door with the sign was unlocked.

He climbed the narrow stairs, climbed into the music. Opened the door on lightning. It was not a large balcony, but it was not a large house. Mr. Death rising in his homemade cage; the seats dirty in disrepair, some of them missing. He closed the door behind him and moved down along the wall, wondering if the floor would hold even him. But it made no sound nor betrayed other sign of weakness, as if he weighed nothing at all, and he sat in front and took off his hat and watched them electrocute the elephant.

It collapsed in a great smoldering pile of meat. Sounds of outrage below. Fred looked down at the backs of all those heads and wondered would he be charged with this atrocity as well. That was Edison, he would tell them, he would have his chance, and then he heard his voice and saw them hearing it: it was telling the world how much coffee he drank. He saw them seeing his huge elastic self, undulating in a shiny black pool.

He looked himself in the eye, but it was not a window, it was an eye.

He saw it for the first time again.

Home movies: his father, himself, the guards and trusties, working and horseplaying on the grounds at OSP. A reenactment, staged, fake scratches and age, but his young self looked more like him than he had.

He couldn't see his father's face.

"When I was fourteen years old," he said.

Strapped in his death chair in black and white, in a grain so turbulent he seemed to be disintegrating into the particles of being; standing at the switch, throwing it on himself, the ensuing brilliance revealing the walls of the theater, the glyphs and reliefs figured there: the jackal-headed god, the scale on which your heart will be weighed, the demon who will devour it if it is too heavy with sin, as the mind devours light and spits up stones in the dark.

His wife had declined to participate, smart girl. The camera will steal your soul if you have one.

He drove his car and drank coffee and smoked, saw himself stir himself into bits . . . The German in his yellow hard hat, iron in brick, Fred in the camp in the hat he now held in his hands. Video flattened onto film, drained of blood and color . . . Someone behind a surgeon's mask, pretending to be him, moving in slow motion like a sleepwalker. Chiseling at a wall as if to inscribe his text, his report, his book of the dead. A life . . . Faces he hadn't recognized the first time and didn't know now: detractors, debunkers, belittlers, revilers, crows and jackals wearing the masks of men. The British historian who said the Report had changed his life, saying, "An insignificant little man who came from nowhere and returned to it," but who did he mean? Wasn't he a friend? He too had been edited, remade, deformed. Only lies are larger than life.

They called him a Columbus who called the world flat.

He heard the audience cackle, protecting itself with laughter. Then it lifted its hands in a great cataract of applause. Fred's remained on his lap. He could not add to nor take from the clamor of skin, of shouted and whistled air, it was meant for someone else. They applauded with their backs to him till the credits had run. Then the other light came on.

The color of the walls—they'd thought gold was the flesh of the gods. The curtain closed over the screen. A festival moderator took the stage. Energetic in middle age, streaks of gray, a down vest. She thanked everyone for braving the weather and for coming to the festival. She introduced the documentarist and the producer, who also stood and joined her onstage, and then the house was on its feet, a bigger hand this time, not a seat left sat in out of 262.

There are fourteen judges in the Hall of Two Truths.

The moderator announced they would commence the Q&A portion of the screening. She dispatched a couple of volunteers with wireless microphones who would relay the queries of audience members chosen at her discretion.

They asked about the origin of the film and about the device. They asked about the authenticity of certain footages. The documentarist was articulate. He was funny and charming, and sometimes coy, and occasionally impatient as genius sometimes is.

Sometimes he did not understand the question.

Someone asked about the Harvard screening and the producer said, "There is only one cut."

Someone asked about the elephant and the documentarist said her name was Topsy, that she was executed at Coney Island but Thomas Edison's involvement is uncertain.

They asked about Toronto, they asked about the bricks.

Someone asked where Fred was and Fred said, "Up here."

The documentarist looked up. People turned their heads, then the rest of themselves, and a low murmur was conducted like a current through the audience.

"I'm here," Fred announced, a little louder, standing now though the balcony rail was low. The murmuring rose, then slowly abated. The producer took a step. The documentarist stayed where he was but seemed to be nodding and might have been smiling, though from a distance it was hard to tell.

The balcony at the back was now another stage. The audience had reversed itself more than seemed physically possible—filmmakers, journalists, agents, executives—their faces featureless as the backs of their heads. Fred swayed dizzily but there was no sitting down now, only falling. He stood above them at a height of seven thousand feet, within the gold walls just beyond which the wind howled, asking only a moment of your time. It would beguile your body from its clothes and from your body whatever self it concealed. He heard the stairs somewhere behind him, the door, imploring voices, but no one yet touched him, as if he could not be found. Was this what the historian meant by nowhere?

"I'm Fred," Fred said, his voice now less than the silence into which it spoke.

Nein.

Alfred Rosenberg, Nazi Party philosopher, when asked if he wished to make a final statement before being hanged at Nuremberg.

All the walls are down.

All the gates and towers, save the west tower, gone . . . The gymnasium, high school, dining hall . . . Zone Two, Zone Three, the death house, the powerhouse, the building where the band rehearsed: dust. A high fence runs across the middle of what used to be there, and on the other side stands the minimum-security wing of what is there now. You can see the inmates far away and below from the west tower, walking their dogs. A new program: they have been trained to train them for the visually impaired. You can see them but you can't take their picture; your camera will be confiscated and you will be escorted from the grounds. You will be permanently barred from returning, they say.

They say the program is a great success.

What remains: the administration building and the warden's quarters; the central guard room, the visiting room, the Catholic chapel. The east cell block and the west cell block, the laundry and showers, the infirmary—gutted but still there, preserved by the Preservation Society. Bare fixtures, peeling paint, debris. The Hole, the Box, the barber shop in the northeast wing and, on the other side, the old prison court and the isolation cells buried beneath it. A catacomb. They've left the cemetery next to the railroad tracks—you can see the headstones from the west tower but that's as close as you can get; it is still on state property, still in use. You can't take their pictures either.

The Preservation Society took the state to court, and the court took it off the state's hands. They've managed to restore whatever they've been able to raise money for, and they conduct guided tours five days a week. (Eight dollars for adults, six for children.) They've made the administration building a museum, and in a glass case there is an engraved invitation to a hanging—*His soul will be swung into eternity on Dec 8, 1899, at 2 o'clock, p.m., sharp.* Not transferable. In another case, much bigger, is the chair I built for the warden. The plaque says DONATED BY ANONYMOUS—I try not to draw attention to myself, even if it seems not to matter anymore.

The chair is still there but the warden is gone, as are the tailor shop and garage, the fishing pond . . . the lumber mill, the greenhouse, the dog who slept in the road . . .

They put it behind glass because kids kept climbing into it.

Word gets around. Now here comes Hollywood with its cameras and lights. The Discovery Channel, music videos, rock stars and rappers, performers who either belong here or pretend to. (And her younger son pretends to be one of them.) Celebrities have visited, but I won't drop any big names. You can rent out the space for parties and receptions and reunions, and once a year there is Murder Mystery Dinner at sixty-nine dollars a plate.

Once a year there is Halloween.

Twice a month, March through November, the society allows for another kind of visit. Admission is higher than usual and there is a waiting list. There is a limit of a hundred guests, and children must be accompanied by an adult. No guides, no concessions, no light but what you can carry, and the doors are locked behind you, dusk till dawn. You sign a release. You can leave whenever you want, but once you've left you can't come back. The younger one turns thirteen on the day of one of those nights, and this is our gift to him: Happy Birthday.

They call it a hunt, not a tour.

We stand in our coats in front of the front entrance. Granite pillars. Victorian. Gothic. We are not alone, but the other visitors are lugging around cameras and microphones, Geiger counters, ion counters, infrared thermometers. Gear. We carry only lanterns and spare batteries. The only ghosts I know of are the ones who follow you everywhere, and you are looking for a place to lose them.

I'm a show-me kind of guy.

"Looks like a castle," the younger one says, and so it does. A castle without king or subjects, only invaders.

Goth kids. Girls in veils and black lace.

Queen Anne. Romanesque.

They lock the doors behind us.

It is always ten degrees cooler inside. There is light and power in the administration building but tonight only the foyer is lit. The museum is off-limits. He's wearing the same baggy uniform he usually wears, but I've made sure his pants are not below his waist, not under his shoes. I've made sure his headphones are in the car. This is no place for music.

We take the stairs. The steps are painted. I don't pretend to be his father, I try to set an example. I've never held a child's hand, and I've fought the urge to take the back of his neck. In the central guard room there are more granite pillars and the ceiling is almost too high for our lamps. I try to draw his attention to the spirit of the architecture, the upward thrust of its design, almost ecclesiastic, meant to inspire inmates up and out of old ways, to better ones . . . Anyway, I try to instruct.

"Where did they do the raping?" he says. He is afraid of the wrong things.

I pretend not to hear that and show him the control center instead, a two-story cage of glass and steel. Restored. Faded parquet floor, black and white squares like a big chessboard.

"What kind of cell is that?" he asks.

Not a cell, I say. The guards ran the prison from there.

"Go figure," he says, but he doesn't say whatever, and then there are other voices. A light in the chapel upstairs.

The chapel is a big room with slender round columns and balconies. Once there were pews, then folding chairs, now just bits of plaster littering the floor. The light comes from the other end, on the riser where the altar once stood. Four of them on a big air mattress—one on each corner. A tripod with a lamp hanging over the middle of the mattress, and over that a gauzy shroud like a mosquito net. But there are no insects up here, nothing lives but us, and the shroud is intended not to keep anything out, but whatever might show itself in.

"Are you a friend?" someone says.

"Did something bad happen to you?"

"Were you ever alive?"

"I don't like this EMF I'm getting."

We watch from the top of the stairs, all they've conjured so far. They are holding hands. I signal for us to leave and turn and the younger one belches at the top of his lungs—something he can do at will. His lone talent, thus far. Somebody screams. I set an example and head back downstairs. Someone comes after us.

"You don't know what you're fucking with," he warns us from the top of the steps, but we aren't the ones chanting around a shrouded light.

Back through the control room to the east cell block. Six tiers, six hundred cells. I start to tell him something about them and he stops me, says I already told him. Sometimes I think he just says that. We start up. A spiral ladder enclosed in a narrow barred cage a hundred feet high. Old paint and rust flaking off the handrail. The climb isn't making me any younger and we stop to rest with the lights off, gloves on, near the top but not the end. *Inter spem et metum.* (They used to teach Latin in high school.)

"Need a jump-start, Old School?" he says, but he sounds about as winded as me. "Aren't there regular stairs?"

Everyone takes the regular stairs. You still have to climb them.

"Is this supposed to teach me something?" he says, but whatever I tell him will be something I already told him, so I use my breath to breathe and we start up again.

We get to the top without running into anyone else, head down the catwalk along the top range. The ceiling is close, peeling flaps of paint like ranks of sleeping bats. Our lights bend over them and so do the lights of the ghosthunters, some of them tinted red to show them what white light won't. You can hear them before you see them, shouting to each other in their own language, about auras and apparitions, hot and cold readings, DVPs, EVPs, and RVPs. One of them passes us wearing a dust mask and night-vision goggles and His Bagginess snickers and gives way—it's a squeeze—leans over the rail to our left, shines his light down the drop.

Don't even think it, I say.

"I never," he says.

Get away from there, I say, let's look in these cells.

Big enough for one, they held two. Damp, rot, rust, mold—they get inside us as much as we do them, in our noses and throats, and linger. In some the frames of left-behind bunks, toilets and sinks stained beyond cleansing, dark shapes on the wall left by missing pictures. They are occupied again: click of a Geiger counter, someone unrolling her sleeping bag, someone's naked pale behind heaving in and out of the dark, and that too will get you permanently barred. I steer us past to the next one.

She tells me to try to be a friend. I tell him to be careful. These doors still lock, I say, and no one has the keys. Maybe I shouldn't have told him.

Cell by cell, tier by tier, down. We pass a guy with a tiny camera strapped to his head, a drunken biker sobbing over something lost or found. The younger one wants his picture taken behind bars, and I make a bad pun about cell phones. Tell him he doesn't have to smile, and not to flip me off. His face goes white in the flash but when we look at the shot only his hands are visible, gripping the bars out of the black.

Pictures don't lie, I say, and this is a lie in itself.

"Maybe it depends who's taking em," he says but doesn't want to try it again.

At the bottom of the block, a narrow trench dug into the floor, opening through the wall: a tunnel. The younger one gets as excited as he'll allow himself, so I don't tell him it's a fake, another kind of escape, dug for a Hollywood movie. It is meant to be a film about injustice and the unquenchable human spirit, etc., but Hollywood is Hollywood. It can't escape itself.

I tell him stay out of there. We move on, climb the west block, then up another spiral to the west tower. This is not an official tour and the tower is closed, so we stand at the parapet, looking. The lights of the new facility away and below, and we look down into the present from the past. It's cold. A young couple is out here already, smoking, ignoring us in favor of the moon. I light up one of my own.

"Gimme a puff," he says, just to say it. He doesn't approve. He asks about my father—knows my father was a guard. He asks me if my father ever used his gun.

Never said, I say; he doesn't know everything and doesn't need to.

"Anyone ever break out?"

Not on his watch, I say, and tell him all the stories but one. Then I light another.

"I thought you wanted air," he says, yawns. "How long we staying anyway? This place even smells outside."

Till we see what there is to see.

"There's no such thing," he says. "Just these losers looking for em."

Happy birthday anyway, I say. I thought it's the thought that counts.

"What if the thought sucks too?"

I admit that could be a problem.

I pinch the ash, keep the butt. One more stop, I tell him, and go to the stairs. Back down West Block, through the control room, the visitors' room, down the long slanted wing where the barber shop was. Wood floor, now the color of stone. Discolored patches where the chairs once stood. I stand in front of one and play the light over it, then through the space above and on the back wall where things once hung. The air is harder to breathe down there. Haven't breathed it since I was a boy.

"What are you looking for?" the younger one asks.

I don't have to look for it, I say.

I wait for the next question but it doesn't come. I ask him if he knows where he is.

"Do *you* know where I am?" his voice says, and the rest of him is somewhere else. I swing the light around. The barber shop is empty. I go to the doorway, look down the long hall of the diagonal. Other doorways, other rooms, lavatories, showers. He could be in any of them, or none of them. He could be in the sixth dimension.

Let's not play games, I say.

"Who's playing?" he says and wails like what he might become.

I'll leave you here, I say.

"Promises, promises," he says.

I hear footsteps. A scream far away.

"It wasn't me," he says.

I'm going to count, I say. I pick a number. He picks a smaller one, beats me to it.

I'm going to set an example he might not like.

"Boo," he says. Then he sings happy birthday to himself.

The melting point of steel is 2500 degrees Fahrenheit.

I was clipping the dog's nails when she called, said there'd been some kind of accident. It was on every channel. I didn't see much fire, just a lot of black smoke. A plane was surrounded at the airport. The commander in chief was in Florida, reading a story to second-graders. I knew steel beams were involved but didn't think it possible for open flame to get that hot. Even jet-fueled . . .

Just like the burning pits.

"Maybe it wasn't an accident," she said.

The dog and I watched them go down—back then he still knew who I was. Back then I saw it just like everyone else, over and over, just sort of dissolving from top to bottom under that boiling gray cloud, kind of neatly in a way, and so fast. Just ten seconds, like a free fall.

I finished clipping his nails. These days I wouldn't even try.

These days I don't see it like everyone else. I see the speed and precision of it, the pancaking, each floor giving way to the next with no resistance, no toppling, the little bursts of white smoke. I see something controlled, an implosion. Shock cord and thermite. A thumb on a button at a safe distance.

What I don't see I believe needs looking into. There are other mysteries: explosions in the sub-basements just before the impacts. Blackouts, evacuations, inexplicable sounds of construction going on in the weeks before the planes. The new property owner took over just six weeks earlier and promptly took out insurance against exactly what happened.

These days he moves in slow circles, favoring his hip. Sometimes when he gets up he leaves a stain.

Then there's the matter of Building 7.

But the way it goes in, sort of softly, neat, like a coin into a slot, again and again. You almost expect it to come out the other side intact, no damage done, like something that can slip through solid matter. A ghost.

You could say we met on the way to Saturn.

Back then I was still in security, made rounds at a large private university. The libraries, the Law School, the frat houses, the School of Engineering, the School of Applied Social Sciences. The School of Engineering is across the street from the natural history museum, and a narrow tunnel connects the museum to the planetarium. To her. She sits on a stool at the entrance to the tunnel, tearing tickets in half. I went once a week. She counts heads, cleans and vacuums, tells you no food or beverages allowed inside, and if the astronomer isn't there she can run the show herself. There are several; my favorite begins in silence and darkness. Then James Earl Jones says, "Can something come from nothing?" and you are engulfed in white light and sound and it is like witnessing the First Moment from a dentist's chair. Now that they've figured out how the whole thing is going to end, I suppose they'll make a show out of that too. (And whose voice will they find to tell that story? I say go with an Englishman.)

She told me to enjoy *Destination Saturn*. "Enjoy the trip," she said. I said I would, though the accommodations were a little small for my taste. I meant no offense but she took some. Said it was the most advanced midsize facility in North America. Told me the Skymaster ZKP3/S projector was the only one of its kind and could show you over five thousand stars.

I told her I could name every one of them: Acrux, Aldebaran . . .

She tore my ticket in half.

After Mars and Jupiter, the sixty-two moons and nine rings, after the winds that rage a thousand miles an hour, we went to Dunkin' Donuts for coffee. She told me over decaf with an artificial sweetener about her work, her day, how many Weight-Watchers points are in a glazed donut. I told her I'm good with my hands. Next time she checked her baggage: her father was a drunk who made her pay for his mistakes, and she'd married a man devoted to maintaining the tradition. She hadn't seen him in years and I sometimes wonder if that will change. The past is not a canceled soap opera. He left her a son; somebody else left her the younger one. Her father left her the house we live in. Died in his sleep—probably the only useful thing he ever did for anybody and all he had to do was not wake up.

I suppose he had his side of it.

The house needs work, I do what I can.

It has a basement and a garage and half a second floor, stands on a street with other bungalows, mostly ranches, a few colonials. To the right what they used to call a starter home; these days that's as far as you might get. A young couple live there with a baby, an SUV, a missing cat. He drives to General Motors in Lordstown every morning; she stays behind with the baby, waits for the cat to come home. Sometimes he waters his lawn in a softball uniform. They bowl and go to church, barbecue occasionally in the backyard with a small group of friends who look more or less like them. We are not invited. But they are quiet and clean, and in the winter he snowblows our sidewalk without asking anything in return. That is neighbor enough for me.

The wife handles the diplomatic chores. She asks what I do. I say I'm semi-retired and she doesn't pursue it. Says there are squatters in the area. I say people have to live somewhere. Says she saw the younger one cutting through their yard the other day—no big deal, just thought I should know.

She asks me if I've seen Tiger.

Only on the flyers, I say.

To the left lives a retired librarian, getting deafer by the day. All the quiet she can stand now—I drive her to the grocery store once a week. The man down the street has a flagpole in his front yard. A black dog is tied to the base of the pole and a black flag flies at the top. MIA. He lives alone. On certain national holidays he raises the Stars and Bars. The couple have complained but the neighborhood association believes in the sanctity of private property and minding their own business, so long as you cut your grass and don't let trash pile up on the tree lawn.

I see to the grass. I mulch. I've put in a new water heater, a double sink, new counters; I've painted, insulated, rewired, regrouted, almost fell off the roof resealing the chimney flashing. A young man's game, but I believe in pulling my weight. I work alone. I've tried to get the younger one to help me around but he is in need of maintenance himself. The older one used to. The older one is a straight arrow—honorable, uncomplaining, and a fair craftsman in his own right. Used to send emails and letters from whatever desert he was deployed to—he couldn't always tell us—now we hardly ever hear. He's due home later this year; her fingers are crossed and her breath held. We support the troops. She Watches her Weight. I reface the cabinets, walnut glaze.

She thinks of me as a former minor celebrity but didn't care for the film. Prefers true crime.

The younger one has blue eyes and light-brown skin. I don't ask. Sometimes his hair matches his eyes, and his clothes are so loose he looks lost in them. Spends time in the room he used to share with his brother; at the computer, in that world, one with an edge but no horizon. Wallows in video-game carnage designed by some kid from MIT, some genius making the rest of us dumber. Or he plays with the dog. Then he disappears to wherever his skateboard takes him, sometimes alone, sometimes not, and I'm not sure it makes a difference. He always comes back. Once with his hair a different color, spray paint on his hands, a water snake he caught at the park by the lake. Once in the back of a police car. Home or not, he disappears.

His friends are few, but quiet and well-mannered. They scare me.

Once he advised me to go fuck myself. She said it was nothing personal.

"Just acting out," she said, but I wanted to do some acting out of my own. Wanted to take hold of his hair whatever color it was. I sandblasted the drainpipes instead.

Did I say he's good with the dog?

She tells me not to worry about it. She says I do plenty, and by way of gratitude has let me convert the garage into a workshop. I have baseboard heating and high-security locks, weatherstripping, dehumidifiers, my washing machines. I try to keep busy. There is no longer room for the car but she doesn't mind.

Once in a while we all have dinner at the seafood restaurant in the strip mall across the street from City Hall. City Hall is a low-rise expansive building the mayor shares with the police station, court, recreation center, board of ed. We went there when they wouldn't let us marry in the planetarium. Regulations, they said, but sometimes I have to wonder what they didn't say.

It is eight minutes long, give or take. Takes seven to read the statement, more or less. He sits on the floor in front of them wearing an orange scrubsuit. He is blindfolded. His hands are tied behind his back, and his ankles are bound. (You don't see this at first.) Hair gray, receding, salt and pepper in his beard.

He moves his head like a blind man searching his dark. His mouth opens and closes, like there's something left to say. He seems unsure what's required of him.

Maybe he's just afraid.

There are five of them, all in black and wearing hoods. The one in the middle reads a kind of speech. He puts one sheet behind the other. The two on either side of him pose with assault rifles on their hips. A tableau. You can see the language you hear on the banner behind them. On the banner behind is a black sun. The one in the middle finishes matter-of-factly, like the closing of a monthly report. He hands off the speech to his right. With his left hand he pulls something from his sash, and he steps forward and they all move in with him as one dark thing.

The hem of a curtain sometimes swings in from the right. Must be a window there, a breeze. Light.

The man in the scrubsuit is taken to the floor by his hair. A zoom and the image disintegrates, then re-forms though you wish it wouldn't. When you see him again he is trying to struggle. Someone is squeezing his jaw, keeping his head up. An arm, maybe someone else's, moving back and forth. The blade is short. You can hear him through his gag like there isn't one. It comes out in dark sheets. (You can't see it on the black.) The arm is fast, working one side then the other. You can hear him longer than you would think. You hear him longer than you would think you would want to hear him. They are more than halfway through when he lets out one more gasp, almost resigned, then slackens, and everything relaxes in a way. It is just work now.

Now you hear the squealing of a pig.

Just work. (*A powered handsaw would be ideal for purposes of scission postmortem but may not be in keeping with the protocol of the ritual.*) Jump cut to the final pass of the blade. When what's required of him is lifted free you feel almost a kind of relief, though *relief* is not really the word and I do not know what the word is. It is placed on the body, on its back, and it starts to topple and someone has to step forward to right it. A tricky balance. One eye open and turned inward, like someone trying to look at his own nose. It won't stay put.

Another jump cut. One of them holds it up in both hands. It belonged to an American contractor working for a foreign construction firm. He is still winking at us.

I ask the younger one where he got it from.

He shrugs. "Somebody sent me a link."

"Can't you just watch porn like the other kids?"

He shrugs again. "Somebody has to."

"Somebody did. We're taking away your computer privileges for a while."

"We'll see what she has to say."

"She's already said it."

He doesn't shrug. I'm thinking of passwords. "What about those ragheads?" he says.

"You shouldn't say that," I say.

"Would you make it painless for them too?"

"Somebody has to," I say.

He squeals like a pig.

———

It's his time. He was once the youngest one himself, now he's older than any of us. Arthritic, obese, half-deaf, half-blind, can't hold his water, bleeds from his mouth. He is showing signs of senility. Has seizures. Spends most of his day these days at the foot of the stairs in the living room. You have to step over, go around: it's his time. One day it will be mine.

She believes they have a heaven too; I haven't thought about it one way or the other. She's asked me to take him to the vet, I said I would see to it. She asked me to break it to the younger one and I said I would do so after the fact, because the fact is I'm not taking him to the vet.

Like I said, I keep busy.

The garage door is unlocked.

I tell him this is the only way. It isn't easy—he's almost dead weight and I'm not sure age is just a number myself. He growls. I don't know if it hurts or that he just doesn't recognize me, but that's why the muzzle—his teeth may be falling out but he'll use what he has. It's nothing personal; it's what happens to love. I'll be his friend if he can't be mine.

Outside, down the ramp I built for him when the stairs started to hurt. Now the ramp hurts. Gravity. Just a few steps across the breezeway but I can't help thinking about neighbors; the retired librarian, the housewife, noses and narrowed eyes, curtains and blinds. I'd hold my breath but I need it.

His fur feels and smells like it's time, and then some.

He balks at the garage door, whines a little. Probably the collie in him wanting to talk it over. The shepherd knows it's time, let's do this thing, but collies want to think twice about everything. Maybe he knows something I don't. I whisper to him, tell him it won't hurt and to the best of my knowledge that's the truth. If he suffers, it's so the next one won't have to—the autopsy will tell. He isn't the first. Sometimes strays wander into our yard for the sake of progress; you do what you can with what you are given. When it's my turn I won't have it any other way. I'm a small man but I pull my weight. I'd like to be of some use.

I kick the door shut behind us.

I'm a Golden Rule kind of guy.

Taking the younger one to the new place. Not my idea—his are not the first pair of hands I would entrust with a weapon. His mother asked me to. She apparently believes in the healing power of guns. Thinks it might bring us closer together, might help make up for the dog; they came into the world at more or less the same time.

A forty-minute drive on U.S. 422. There's a reservoir there with a causeway running across it and people fish off the causeway, but we aren't going fishing. You can pull off the shoulder onto the grass within a certain distance of the water and they won't ticket or tow you. There is a break in the woods. Then there's an old rail line and you just follow the tracks to the quarry. It's less than a mile but even with his head in headphones, cheap sunglasses, his mouth makes it last.

Why can't we just go fishing? it wants to know. Bets there's bass in those weeds.

I don't know from bass, I tell him, and neither does he. I tell him he wouldn't have the patience anyway.

"That's what you're supposed to teach me," he says.

"I thought you wanted to shoot," I say.

"I thought we'd go to one of those target places."

I tell him I don't like those places. "Like a bowling alley with guns."

Then he says, "How do I know you're not just trying to get rid of me?"

A fair question. I leave it open. We get there.

"Awesome," he says. Awesome, they say. I say the Grand Canyon is awesome, the energy hiding in an atom. A quarry is a hole in the ground. I don't know when the last time they pulled any limestone out of it was, but these days people come here mainly to put in lead. We come in from the open end, where the tower of the old kiln still stands, the conveyor to the crusher conveying nothing. The gray-white walls rise in tiers, ledges, pocked with little black holes. There are empty casings all over the place. Weeds. An old Ford Torino rusting on its rims in the middle of the stone floor. People shoot at it or put things on top of it to shoot, and someone took the front seat out and sat it fifty feet from the wreck. Beer cans in its vicinity, a used diaper and the Sunday comics, bleached to black and white. Condoms.

She wants me to have a talk with him. The only talk he listens to comes from the little box of noise he carries plugged into his head, and it rhymes.

He murmurs something I pretend I didn't hear.

"What?" I say.

"Nothing."

This where you bang my mother? I'll make him pay for it later. Truth is I brought her here once and all she did was try to clean up.

I take off my jacket—it's always warmer in the pit, even well into afternoon. Show up too early and you're sun-blind. If someone's already here you can either leave or wait your turn—only one party shoots at a time, there is an etiquette. There is no one here now. He wants to sit on the car seat and I tell him about bugs and disease. Tell him we didn't come here to sit. Make him pay. Then I take the Woodsman out of its case. Rimfire, single action—I don't want him shooting up the place like he's killing zombies on a computer screen.

He doesn't say it is awesome. He says, "That thing looks older than you."

"It is," I say. "My father gave it to me." And he has enough sense not to have an answer.

Of course it isn't loaded. I light up.

"Smoke em if you got em," he says. "Can I have one?" and this time I shake one out of the pack.

He looks at me like I'm crazy. "Why not just put the gun in your mouth?"

I let him hold the Colt while I set up some targets on the Ford—cans (all the bottles are broken), a couple of big white stones. I tell him if he points it at me he'll be hitching a ride back home. He ponders this like a viable option. I come back and show him how to hold a gun.

"Why can't it be a Glock?" he says, the same way he wanted to go fishing.

"I don't like plastic guns," I say. "Let's work on your stance." Feet sixteen to eighteen inches apart, weak side a foot in front of the other.

"I don't have a weak side," he says.

"Bend your front knee," I say.

"I'm gonna have time to do all this when some banger's coming at me?"

"Nobody's coming at you."

"I mean in real life."

"What's this," I say, "Nintendo?"

He looks at me with pity. "Old school."

"They're all the same to me."

"My brother says they're good practice."

"Maybe you took it the wrong way."

"You've never even shot anyone."

"You want me to apologize?"

"You just strap em down and turn on the juice."

"I've never seen an execution." Then I remember the video.

"My brother shot someone."

"I don't think he had any choice."

"Freakin haji."

"That'll be enough," I say and I kick his feet apart, pull off his sunglasses. We work on the sight picture.

"Don't look at the target," I say. "Look at the sights. Put them together."

"The can is blurry," he says.

"It's supposed to be," I say. "You focus on the target, you miss."

Then I show him how to pull the trigger.

Call it a gypsy cab. Call it a limo. Call it livery, jitney, hack. I call it a service.

You might see my ad on the bulletin board at Save-More.

You can tear off my number. My rates are reasonable. I don't cruise or solicit or loiter around taxi stands. I have an ad online but I don't use my name. I have a cell phone and a Buick Park Avenue, clean, with low mileage and a lot of leg room. Gran Touring suspension. I will take you to the airport and pick you up there when you return. Same goes for the bus station, Amtrak, what have you. I drive people like the retired librarian to the grocery store, to church, to doctor's appointments, the laundromat, and I will stand in baggage claim holding a sign with your uncle's name on it. You don't have to tip. I go into neighborhoods where the licensed taxis won't go, though not without insurance, and I don't mean State Farm.

Got a rig under my seat.

I wouldn't exactly call it a living, but at my age the prospects are nil to none and I get to meet a lot of people. I got to meet Mr. Dembo. Mr. Dembo is from a small African nation that recently gained its independence and doesn't yet know what to do with it. Tonight he's wearing Dockers and a polo shirt, but when I picked him up at the airport he was in uniform: green officer's cap, brown jacket with braiding and medals and epaulets, striped green trousers. Like someone who should have been traveling in a state car with bodyguards and adjutants, but he was with one other man who wore civilian clothes and gave me the name of a hotel. I suspected they hadn't torn my number off the board at Giant Eagle. I put their luggage in the trunk. It weighed a ton.

In the car I asked him what branch of the military he was in.

"No military," the man in civilian clothes said. His accent was heavy but reassuring; he enunciated like someone with nothing to hide. "Ministry of Justice. Mr. Dembo is assistant to the deputy commissioner of Prison Services, administrative section." He took a breath. "I am his secretary."

I didn't say Mr. Dembo wore a lot of brass for a guy stationed at a desk. "Business or pleasure?" I said, and Mr. Dembo raised his hand and spoke for himself.

"I'm afraid pleasure is not in the budget these days," he said. "Though you might call this a sort of shopping expedition."

I didn't ask what he was shopping for because I never ask more than two questions in a row. I told him my father had also worked in the prison system.

"I know," he said. Then he told me what else they knew. How they knew it was no big mystery—I wasn't exactly in hiding, because no one seemed to be looking. That seemed to have changed. So I waited for why.

He asked me to take the long way around, and he would do the same. I skipped an exit. He mourned for his country in the dusk. Told me about the eastern highlands where he was born, the ancient stone ruins, eating bush rat cooked on an outdoor mud stove.

I said it sounded like a nice place to visit.

"You would be hacked to pieces as soon as you stepped off the plane," he said, then told me about the ruins of the economy, how there was eighty percent unemployment and eleven thousand percent inflation, how AIDS and cholera had reduced the average life expectancy to thirty-five and left a nation of orphans. That his country was in danger of becoming a hub for international terrorism, that crime and civil unrest had risen to unprecedented levels.

I didn't ask what had ruined their economy. We passed over switchyards and the road curved into the cloverleaf. The car curved with it. That is a chassis for you.

"Do you know what necklacing is?" Mr. Dembo asked me.

I do but wished I didn't.

"Capital punishment," he said, "has become an unfortunate but increasing necessity."

"You don't have to tell me about necessary evils," I said. Rule of law and all.

"To make matters worse, our equipment doesn't seem capable of meeting the demand."

I waited again.

"Take a simple gallows," he said. "Apparently there is more to its construction than nailing some wood together and tying a piece of rope to it. We are learning the hard way." He paused. "There have been some embarrassments."

Merging onto 480 is always a competition. Then we were part of it, the long straightaway. They'd just resurfaced the road and it was shiny as glass.

"You're telling me," I said, "there's no one in your country knows how to properly hang a condemned criminal?"

"I'm saying I'm in the market for some good old American know-how." They'd been dealing with an Englishman till he ran afoul of his government.

"The Chinese just shoot them in the back of the head," I said. Used to make the family pay for the rifle round.

"We are not the Chinese," Mr. Dembo said. "There is the matter of decorum."

"Not much dignity in a hanging."

"Am I talking to the wrong man? I understand the death penalty may become a thing of the past in this country."

Nothing would make me happier, but it's a wide world and some things never go out of fashion. I told him building a proper multiple gallows was not difficult provided you have the space. Nor a chair for that matter, nor lethal injection machine. "But what if I told you," I said, "that I was working on the most advanced, humane, and efficient form of capital punishment ever devised?"

"Nitrogen," he said after a moment. He'd done some homework.

"Better," I said. We were coming to the next interchange. There wasn't much of the long way left so I gave him the condensed version. Once I pick a lane I like to stick with it.

He excused himself and spoke with his secretary in a tongue that sounded French. Then back to me: "Intriguing, but I'm afraid we didn't come all this way to invest in a science project."

"Taking a look won't cost you anything. And since you've come all this way."

He excused himself again. Then the secretary to the assistant to the deputy commissioner said, "We will have to speak with our superior. You can be reached at this number?"

I said I could and they reached me the next morning. "We are under a tight schedule," I heard the secretary say. "How soon can you arrange a demonstration?"

"Three days?" I said.

"Two," the secretary said, two days ago. "That is the best we can do."

Easter Sunday. Best they could do. I had to go to a pet store, and they were clearly reluctant. ("It is a privilege to love something," they say, then charge you accordingly.) But I didn't have time to look, wait for something to stray my way. At least he is out of uniform; we don't get many visitors as it is, but Idi Amin walking up your driveway is something else again. I've swept the floor. Squeezed in a couple of lawn chairs. I keep a coffee pot in the garage and try to be a host, but the secretary doesn't touch it and Mr. Dembo doesn't answer. He is looking at the wireless.

"Looks like a ticket booth," he says finally.

Looks like what it was. What they call Art Deco. Mostly glass on top, shiny tin skirting around the bottom half. Scroll-work. Must have stood in front of an Art Deco theater once, or maybe in an old fairground, next to the carousel, the Wheel of Light. Stood in a junkyard when I saw it. The older one helped me bring it home in his pickup, and she took one look and said what in the world.

I said I would think of something. I thought of the Japanese.

"The Japanese," Mr. Dembo says.

They were working on a secret weapon near the end of the war. A death ray, not a secret anymore.

"Science fiction," Mr. Dembo says.

"History," I say. Killed a rabbit in a cage at a thousand yards, but it took five minutes and time was not on their side. I have plenty, and I work at close range.

I have another rabbit, another cage.

Mr. Dembo's attention wanders. He has heard some of this before. He glances around at the workbenches and shelves, at prototypes—the tire pump that fits in your pocket, the self-cleaning blanket, the perpetual motion machine—back to the corner where the washing machines sit in a circle. But the washing machines are covered and they are not why he is here.

Let's take a look inside, I say.

I open the door, show them how I've reinforced it, insulated it, how it's not a ticket booth anymore. It's the show. No helmet, no electrodes, no et cetera.

"Lightning in a bottle," the secretary says.

Something like that, I say. Complete disruption of the autonomic nervous system.

"You fry the brain?" Mr. Dembo says.

"Just turn it off." Instantaneous. Won't feel a thing.

"No seat? Where does the condemned sit?"

There is only a small table. I'll install a chair when a chair is called for. When there's someone to strap in.

I look at him. "You mean you thought . . ."

"Let's get on with it," Mr. Dembo says.

Pink eyes, white fur, trembling. The cage is made of wood. Built it myself—no metal goes in. I put it on the table and shut the door. Its nose twitches. Now I hear a melody, rhythm. It is coming from Mr. Dembo's pocket. He takes out his phone and his phone starts singing.

I'm not much on music. I like a radio that talks. But whatever misery lives in their land, it is not in their song.

It stops. Mr. Dembo starts talking. He holds up a finger.

His secretary asks for a glass of water.

I don't want to leave them alone but I am still their host. I tell him I'll be right back. Shut the door behind me, cross the breezeway in the dark and enter the house and go into the kitchen. Get some ice.

She calls from the living room. "Did you get my message?"

"My phone is off," I say.

"We got an email."

"Terrific. Can't wait to read it."

"They look like nice men," she says. "Are they nice? He didn't wear his medals."

"Probably a good thing," I say.

"Will I have to throw the breakers?"

"I don't think so." I run the faucet. "If it happens let me take care of it."

"Thank you," she says. Then she reminds me what night it is.

"How could I forget?" But I have to get back now, I say.

When I do they are standing in the back corner of the garage. They've swept aside the tarp and the old blankets and are looking at what they've uncovered with great curiosity. Mr. Dembo is holding the rabbit. His secretary is holding a phone.

He looks at me. "You are starting a laundromat?"

I give the secretary his water and pick up the tarp. "Just keeping busy," I say. "I like to fix things."

"Five, six of them," he counts. "From the looks of it you are doing more than fixing them."

The Maytags, a Whirlpool, three Kenmores. eBay. Portable, compact—the kind made for apartments, for those with limited space. I've made some modifications. I expect him next to ask why they're in a circle, but instead he asks why they are all connected.

"Just a drain hose," I say and cover them up again. I remind him of the reason they've come. The rabbit.

"Of course," but he lingers there. "Did I tell you I have a degree in chemistry?"

"Mr. Dembo," I say.

"If I could hazard a wild guess, I'd say . . . centrifuge?"

"Gentlemen," I say. "The wireless."

"Ah," he says. "The wireless. The Easter bunny, yes. But no. I'm afraid we will have to postpone the demonstration." An urgent phone call from his government. A situation has developed and they are being recalled to the capital at once. Of course he cannot go into further detail.

"You understand," he says and gives me his free hand. His secretary gives me an empty glass. I hope to continue where we left off in the near future, and Mr. Dembo says they have every intention. Of course he can't say exactly when.

"You know where to reach me," I say, the music still in my head, and what he mourns for in the music.

"Yes," he says and gives me back the rabbit.

I made rounds. The Alumni House, the Academy of Medicine, the dental school, the west quad. Ate my lunch in the School of Engineering. This was tolerated as long as you didn't attempt interaction with the students. Especially the girls. There is a lounge in the School of Engineering: sofas, vending machines, two microwaves, television. There is air hockey, *Grand Theft Auto*.

There is a TRIGA Mark II nuclear reactor.

Small, 250 kilowatt, not commercial. For experiments in physics and radiology. Back when I made my rounds, security was not what it is today—it was me. I had access. It came in little flat cans like shoe polish. I used my lunch box, my thermos, just a little at a time. I wasn't sure what I was going to do with it, then I knew what but not how. Still, they had more than they needed. It isn't stealing if they're going to throw it away.

She tore my ticket and I sat in the dark after work, my Igloo heavy on my lap, looking up. Novae and nebulae, the whirlpool of stars . . . I looked down, looked back up again, saw galaxies spinning in both places. Then the towers fell and they fired everybody like it was our fault. By then I had over a hundred pounds.

Talking to female students was grounds for dismissal.

It looks like instant coffee. It's better than the yellow stuff but still a long way away from making any music. There are steps. It has to be pure. You're going to need hydrofluoric acid (better store it in plastic milk jugs because it can eat through glass) and fluorine, which makes mustard gas look like bug spray. You have to change solid to liquid to gas, and then back to liquid again; you have to change tetra- to hexa-, and that's the easy part.

This is where Maytag comes in. Kenmore and Whirlpool. They're not just washing machines anymore—I've souped them up a little, patent pending. Spin cycle: One feeds into Two feeds into Three, and so on into Six, and then back into One where it starts all over again, a circle of greater and greater refinement and purity, of less and less of more . . .

I know I'm onto something. But it's going to take a while to get ten pounds of what I'm onto.

Dear Mom (and Fred?),

There is a line of guys behind me like you wouldn't believe, so Happy Easter from Red 2 Alpha. Well everything pretty much sameo. Not much happens around here till it happens, like before. This morning the mess hall was laid out, bunnies & colored eggs & a full feast of ham, turkey, and cake, etc. To be honest I forgot what day it was. To answer your Q, yes i heard. I'm sure she's better off, she could sure draw tho. Say hey to my younger half from R2A. And tell him yes, we have to burn it but all you smell is the diesel. What else? There was even a big screen tv playing music videos till someone changed the channel to religious. Thanks to Fred for keeping after my bike. Say it's not like when they're strapped to a table, no disrespect. All the Christians in our sector all week wished us Happy Easter. They kept giving us glasses of cold water. I wouldn't know what to say to her if you see her. I don't know what the Muslims wish us but I nevr turned one down. To answer your Q, I'm not sorry but I feel bad. Make sense? I didn't know he was a kid but he was driving right at us off the road. Maybe he was just testing our ROE like they do sometimes. What else. Sorry to hear about the grafitti. Hope at least he spelled it right (kidding.) I'll write him a real one after the push. There's a line of guys behind me waiting to use this. If he wants, give me his email and I'll send F a word or few. Or you can just forward this, you probably do anyway. Sorry to keep it so short. So Happy Easter and everything else. I'll write again, or see you when I see you (next month?)

Your Son

P.S. Tell Fred no wheelies! You should sell it if you have to. How's Krypto by the way? You wouldn't believe all the strays here.

I believe in the common good. I try to do my part. If you're at a party or a bar and in no condition to get behind the wheel, you can call me and I'll charge you a flat fee no matter where you call home. A service I would gladly provide free of charge if I didn't need the money. As it is: twelve dollars, no matter where. Within reason of course.

This time it's downtown. Tonight is a weeknight, just a few cars in the lot. The word EXECUTIVE is on the sign but the guy standing under it is not wearing a suit. He fills up most of the doorway.

"Eight dollars," he says. I tell him I'm driving and I give him my name. He tells me to go see the bartender.

The bar is across the room. There's a stage on the way, a little bigger than a pool table, its floor a grid of frosted glass that changes colors. A silver pole connects it to the ceiling but the stage is empty and the colors change slowly. A man sits at the edge with a drink, watching them change. He isn't wearing a suit either. There are only a few girls. They're sitting at the bar with the other executives, talking and laughing, doing another kind of dance.

I have been to these places before, and places where there are no women, and where there are no men. In the interest of public safety, it makes no difference to me. This one looks a little slow. The music makes it look empty.

"He's in the back," the bartender says and tilts his head like I should know what he means. "He'll be done in a minute."

"He's never done," one of the girls says. The seat next to her is empty.

I ask the bartender to tell him I'm here.

"He's almost done," he says, louder than he has to. "Care for a Coke? Juice? It's on me."

Sometimes I wait in the Buick, but they tend to hurry up if you come inside. I look in the back. It's an open floor plan but the darkness there makes it another space. I can make out a pale seated figure, then another, a shadow, standing. Then there's just one.

I ask for a ginger ale but stay on my feet. The girl who spoke gets up, comes over and sets up shop next to me.

"Take a load off," she says. "That's what the stools are for."

"I'm working," I say.

"Me too," she says. Then she says, "What are we working on?"

I think about it. "The greater good."

"Well I know I do my part," she says. "Let's drink to a better good. Mine's rum and Coke."

The bartender looks at me. I can't drink but I can spend money. The song fades out and now there are sounds from the place in the back.

The girl next to me looks young. I ask her how young and she makes a face.

"I have a father," she says. "What I need is a daddy."

A voice I haven't heard in a long time says, "It's no use, sweetheart, you're wearing me down to a nub . . . I'll take it from here."

It's twenty years older, that much thicker, but I don't have to hear it twice. I turn my back on the dancer and the bartender and look into the back room of time. I wait. She is saying something behind me, something they say about little guys. He comes into the light but not out of the dark. A girl leads him by the arm. He is wearing a pale suit that keeps changing color—used to dress in black. Twenty years, give or take, but time is not to blame; he hasn't been kind to himself. Still big but thinner, his skin another baggy suit, his face still red but jowly and gaunt at the same time.

His nose looks like something you'd pull out of the ground.

I misunderstood over the phone. Thought it was a figure of speech.

"Ride's here, Mr. D," the bartender says.

"It's not a cabbie, is it?" he says. "Guy like me's a cabbie's best friend. I got enough friends."

"You want to be my best friend, don't you?" the dancer says, and he says, "Then quit charging me," and someone else says something else and everyone laughs but me and him.

"Not a cab, sir," I say. "I'm in business for myself."

"Gypsy," he says.

"I'll get you there," I say. "Flat fee. Anywhere you say as long as it's home."

He waits. "Or what passes for it," he says and I can tell my voice didn't ring any bells. Maybe it's the state he's in, but I don't think he'd see me even if he could.

His white hair gone yellow, dark glasses looking straight ahead at nothing.

"You'll never get rich," he says, "but . . . works for me. Be right back. Got a little unfinished business to finish." He takes something out of his pocket and unfolds it, taps his way with it down the other end of the club where the restrooms are. Makes a joke about not needing a cane. The music starts again.

"If you want to wait in your car we'll bring him out," the bartender says.

I want to finish my ginger ale. The girl who was sitting next to me climbs onto the stage, starts showing the guy with no suit a better place: the one he came from. She lets the colors up inside her. Everything changing but his expression.

When they bring him out I tell him I need it up front. He's folded his money a certain way so he can tell the bills apart. At first he refuses the seatbelt. I tell him we're not going anywhere until, ask him if he needs help. He grumbles and gropes. When I hear a click I head for Ninth, make a left away from the lake. Ninth Street leads to every other road. He lives in a subdivision just two exits south of me.

Ahead of us nothing but taillights, those little red eyes. Like everyone's leaving and no one's coming back.

"I hear it's nice out there." I get on 90, west.

"Me too," he says. Then he uses a word you don't hear as much anymore, though I doubt it ever went away. More like it's in hiding, till it's time to come out again.

I have rules. They're taped to the back of the front seat—
for all the good that does him—but I let him break the one
about language. This is an occasion of some kind.

"I guess everybody's got to live somewhere," I say.

"Not by me they don't—and right next door," he says.
"Might not sound like it but I know one when I smell one. You
can smell em, you know."

I tell him my other four senses probably aren't as sharp as his.

"That's a lot of horseshit," he says. "You use what you have.
She says I'm crazy." His voice climbs an octave. "'They're just
like you and me, James.' Tells me to watch my language."

"Your wife?"

He makes a sound. "Sister. Her husband fixed up the basement for me. Tells her kids to leave me alone—guess I'm the
dirty uncle."

"How many?" Kids, I mean. Trying to get him off the subject of neighbors.

"Three, four of em, sounds like," he says. "Hey you're a
nosy sonofabitch, aren't you?"

I say I don't mean to pry. "They sound like nice people,"
I say.

"She's a cunt," he says. "I pay my way. No revenge like charity, know what I mean? Wasn't for disability I'd be . . ." He
doesn't seem to know where he'd be.

"Told me to watch my mouth," he says. "I told her I would
if I could."

The numbers change and we head south. What's left of the
skyline curving away behind us, the zoo asleep on the right.

"Rides nice," he says.

"Suspension," I say.

"Smooth as milk," he says. "Linc or Caddy?"

"You know your cars." I don't lie unless absolutely necessary, and then it isn't exactly lying anymore.

"If it ain't in the wheel, it ain't in the deal."

I tell him he sounds like a salesman.

"I sound like what I am," he says. "I'm a people person."

I say I had a feeling. "I always admired people who could pull that off."

"I pulled it off," he says. "New and used," he says. "Back in the day . . . not just cars either."

"What else?"

"Everything," he says. "You name it. Shit you wouldn't believe if I told you."

"Try me."

"When they say no is when the sale starts."

"You either have it or you don't."

"The hell do you know?"

"Just what they tell me," I say. But what else?

Electronics is what else. Sporting goods too, back in his day. Copiers, insurance, bonds, cemetery plots. "Cars, copiers . . . what else," he says.

Maybe he's too drunk to remember. Or too old. Or not too drunk to be careful.

He remembers stain remover.

"You sold stain remover."

"Didn't sell itself," he says. "Miracle solvent, door to door. Toughest gig there is, but I ain't proud—not by then I wasn't. A job's a job."

"Tell me about it," I say.

"I'm telling you," he says. "Knocked on doors to the end of the road. Eye contact's the thing. Make em believe you give a shit. I'd come in and truck mud on the carpet, ketchup on the sofa . . . you should've seen the looks. Shit worked too, you just couldn't overdo it. I'd even take a swig now and then to show them how harmless—non-toxic, right?" I hear liquid and look in the mirror, let him break another rule. A flask. He's taking another swig but it isn't stain remover. It doesn't get rid of anything.

"Don't believe what it says on the label," he says. "I woke up one morning and now look at me—still waiting for the sun to come up.

"Who needs a fucking miracle now?" he says.

I don't look at him. I suggest litigation.

"Can't sue em if you can't see em. Got me a dog and a stick though."

I ask him where the dog is.

He mumbles. "Stick doesn't bite."

I think of the inmates training service animals at the new facility; maybe they're turning out defective product. Maybe not. I don't say anything for a while. Then he says, "The hell are we listening to?"

"Talk radio." I turn it up. It's talking about the afterlife as a dimension whose existence can be proven scientifically.

"You believe this shit?" he says.

"I keep an open mind."

"Trust your nose," he says. "Got something against music?"

I think of Mr. Dembo's phone. Ask him if he has a preference.

"Anything but that foulmouth shit."

I find something we can both live with and leave it there. Read the signs, swing over into the right-hand lane. His address is in my head. I don't bother with GPS; the eye in the sky works both ways.

He wonders aloud if we've met somewhere before.

"What makes you ask?" I say.

"I guess you'd've said something, right?"

"You never know," I say.

"You sound like a little guy," he says.

"Not as big as some, I guess." If he tells me what they say about little guys, I'll drop him off in a field.

"No offense," he says, "we're just two guys talking," and I hear the flask again. "Want a taste?"

"I'm driving," I say. "You want to get home in one piece, don't you?"

"I'm already in pieces," he says, "and I ain't got a home. I got a sister. Makes her husband go outside to fart." Then something I can't quite make out, maybe something about putting him out of his misery, but he's talking into the flask like it's a dead mic. "You do this shit for a living?"

No living in livery, I like to say. "I take whatever comes my way. Guess you could say I'm sort of freelance."

"Freelance. Exit's coming up."

I don't tell him I have a background in engineering. I say I like to make things.

"Make things," he says, and he's right about the exit. A long curve with a yield sign at the end of it. When we straighten out he says, "What kinda things?"

Sometimes I say more than I should. Patents pending.

"I don't know what the fuck you're talking about but you sound like you do. Dumb it down a little—my phone's smarter than me."

I tell him about the nail clippers that discard your nails.

The American way, he says. Homegrown. Thomas Elvis Edison. Fuckin DIY.

"I used to know a guy . . . ," he says. "You sure I don't know you from somewhere?"

I tell him maybe it'll come to him. I tell him we're almost there and ask him the name of the street. He makes himself say it, and I see it on a big stone at a corner and turn. Night lights, tract homes, but they've gotten better at making them look different. One of them's different with dark windows and a sign the bank put out front.

"Nice," I say.

"So I hear," he says.

"Right next door," he says. "Smell em?"

I see an address on a mailbox and pull into the driveway. A light in the living room. "You're here." Notice I don't say home.

"Guess I gotta be somewhere," he says, but he doesn't move. He asks for my number. Next time he can call me himself; he has a cell phone that talks to him.

"Aren't there places around here?" I ask.

"Just the strip mall," he says, and he asks me if I get it.

I got it. He makes the sound that used to be a laugh. Slaps the top of the seat next to me, feels around, grabs my shoulder.

"They got laws against fun here," he says. "Hey, you *are* a little fucker, aren't you?"

He feels my face, my glasses. "And I thought I was blind."

I detach his hand like a seatbelt, ask him if I should honk the horn.

"Don't do me any favors," he says. "Just do me a favor: give me a hand to the door." Almost pleading.

I get out, go around to the other side, and grab the handle. He sticks a leg out. I take an arm: mush and bone. He takes it back angrily and grabs mine.

"We're supposed to pretend I'm in charge," he says.

I wait for a curtain to move, something, but there's nothing.

"You know the only good thing about being like this?" he says on the way.

I don't say anything.

"You can't see yourself," he says.

He tells me his name but he looks like someone else. He is not alone. He is holding a black briefcase, and he shakes my hand and smiles like it's me he's come to see. Usually I'm just the ride.

I drop the sign in a trash can.

He introduces the two young men with him. The yellow light flashes and luggage starts coming out of the wall. I make a move but he says, "Samir, Mustapha," and the two young men beat me to it. They come back with two big suitcases and a backpack and I take them to the moving sidewalk. He seems to be in no great hurry; we stand on the right while people pass on the left. Samir and Mustapha are serious and quiet, nice-looking young men, and I suspect they don't speak much English. We glide.

"It's never fast enough, is it?" he says. He is watching the people pass by.

367

Outside the sidewalk stands still and the afternoon is warm, the sun high. It's a long ways to Short-Term Parking but I'm not a cabbie and can't use the stands. I apologize.

"It's nothing," he says. "If all we wanted was convenience we would have rented a car." Then it occurs to me. I would comment on the resemblance but that would be familiar. I glance at the young men. I remember their names, but not which belongs to whom. One of them is either smiling or wincing in the glare.

They stow the luggage in the trunk. The man who looks like Omar Sharif sits up front with me. I crank the engine and ask where they're staying; he says they are staying with friends. "But first," he says, "I would ask you to do something for me."

He puts his briefcase on his lap and opens it. Removes a notebook and hands it to me. It's in Arabic but I know what it says. Someone has reprinted it, added covers, punched and bound it with a plastic comb. The cover is black vinyl embossed with gold letters, the cursive script, and it looks to have been read more than once. You would think it something sacred.

I'm not sure what to say.

"This is quite a surprise," I say. Then I say I'm honored.

"I came across it at the convention in Tehran," he says and hands me a pen. "I'm surprised you weren't there."

"I wasn't invited." A lot of people are listening to Rudolf these days.

"Rudolf puzzles me," he says. "A chemist who says you can't prove anything with chemistry. You have stood by your findings."

"Well I guess my traveling days are behind me," I say, but I'm listening to the silence in back. I wonder if it's a Mossad silence, the last thing I won't hear. I have rules but they don't mention garrotes. The .25 in a holster rig under my seat. A woman's weapon, some say, but ideal for close quarters.

I sign my name and for a second wish I hadn't. It feels like a contract. I give the man who looks like Omar Sharif his pen back.

He puts it inside his jacket and closes the briefcase. I wait. He didn't come halfway around the world for an autograph, but he takes his time letting me in on it.

"These friends of yours have an address?" I ask.

"You are in a hurry?" he says.

I tell him we have a few minutes. In Short-Term the first hour is free.

"A few minutes is all we need," he says. "I'll make it worth your while."

I turn up the air conditioning. Samir and Mustapha are no longer silent behind me. The man who looks like Omar Sharif says something brief and the conversation ends.

"You'll have to excuse them," he says. "They don't mean to be rude."

"No problem," I say. I only understood two words. The rest sounded like the language of the man who read the statement in the video. The one with the short blade.

Dairy Queen, they said.

"They are young," he says, "not men of experience. Like us."

Experience: do your time and pay attention. You'll see the wheel go round.

"They do not understand things as we do."

"I thought I understood some things," I say. "Now I'm not so sure."

"Certain things are a question of belief," he says. "Do you consider yourself a pragmatist?"

"I have a healthy respect for the facts."

"As one always should," he says. "You might say we have this in common."

"There's always something," I agree. I've never met a man I didn't try to like. "What did you say your line of work is, by the way?"

"I have something of a background in engineering," he says. "Princeton. But that was quite some time ago—another life, you might say. I've since diverted my energy to other activities. Perhaps we'll talk about that another time."

"That's up to you," I say. "You know, I've done a little engineering myself." Back in the day.

"So I understand," he says. "As a matter of fact, that's what I want to talk to you about."

"I'll try to keep up, but I'm afraid I didn't go to Princeton." I decide not to tell him I visited Harvard once.

"Maybe not, but you seem to have stumbled upon something men with lab coats and degrees have missed," he says. "I suppose there's such a thing as being too educated."

I don't stumble. I try one thing, then I try something else. I say, "I'm not sure what you're getting at."

"Of course you are," he says.

The sun starts to push through the windows. I ask him if Mr. Dembo sent him.

"I'm afraid I don't know this Dumbo," he says.

"Then I take it you're not in the market for a gallows."

"Where I come from the condemned are stoned."

"Maybe you should look into it," I say.

"Perhaps you don't understand this either."

"I'm not sure I care to."

"It's not what it might seem," he says patiently. "The stones must be of a certain size—not too small, but not so large as to cause immediate death. A man is buried to his waist. If he can escape before being killed, he is allowed to go free."

"I still don't get it."

"We leave room for God to express His will. The judgments of men are only guesswork."

"What if it's a woman?"

"A woman is buried to her neck," he says.

And I thought our God was a mystery. "Well," I say and start to tell him I am working on the most advanced, civilized form of capital punishment ever devised, but he interrupts me.

"I am only interested in your washing machines," he says.

I put my hands on the wheel. "Hour's about up," I say.

"I hope we're not making you nervous," he says.

"Not at all," I say, and the head on the Internet winks at me.

The man who looks like Omar Sharif says something else and Mustapha or Samir shoves something into the front from the back. A bill, not a blade.

"Keep . . . chains," one of them says, and parking is no longer an issue.

"How do you know about my work?" I say.

"First things first," he says. He takes something that isn't money out of his wallet and hands it across to me.

I didn't know fanatics had business cards. I look at it but don't take it. I wonder if they have a Facebook page too.

"I would like you to be reassured that we are legitimate representatives of our government," he says. "That we are not what you may think we are."

"Then what?"

I have the feeling he is going to tell me they have a saying where he comes from. Instead he says, "Are you aware that the extradition treaty between Germany and your country is being renegotiated? Perhaps your traveling days aren't over after all."

"Mustapha is a great fan of your Cookie Dough Blizzard," he says, "and has come a long way."

I look at the bill. I take the card. The man who looks like Omar Sharif gives me an address. I ask them to fasten their seatbelts and back out. We take the drive-thru.

At first he doesn't do much. Calls his friends but doesn't see them. Starts his bike and sits on it but doesn't ride it, and doesn't go farther than the yard if he leaves the house. He sits in front of the computer and takes a lot of showers. Sleeps. The younger one asks him a lot of questions, wants him to play video games. The answer is "Not now" or "Tomorrow," and when tomorrow comes the answer will be "Not now" again. Aunts and uncles and cousins visit. They stay for a while, then they leave. He oils his mitt. He goes out into the backyard and throws a stick, then walks to the other end of the yard and throws the stick back.

He's here for fifteen days. His tour is over but they've extended him another three months. Something they do. He still has a sense of humor, but he isn't trying to make anyone laugh. The guy next door strikes up a conversation, or tries to, then walks away shaking his head.

After a week or so we go out to dinner at the seafood restaurant across the street from City Hall. Just the four of us. They tell us there's a twenty-minute wait for a table, which means it will be forty. We mill in the foyer with everyone else, next to a big glass tank filled with lobsters. Their claws are rubber-banded. I guess we're waiting for each other. The younger one taps the glass, says, "Any last words?" and the older one reads his phone, out of uniform.

"Don't do that," their mother says.

"Does it hurt when they boil em?" the younger one asks his brother. Since he's been in a war, he must know everything.

"Does it hurt who?"

The younger one points to the tank.

"Ask Fred," the older one says. "That's his department."

"They say they scream when they go in the pot," she says helpfully. She's already holding a glass of white wine, like she carries them around in her purse.

That's just the steam escaping from their shells, I say. I say I don't eat them since the Belfast study. No one asks what that is and the younger one puts his face up to the glass. They seem to recoil like he's some ill-tempered minor deity.

He looks at his brother. "Bet we'd get a table right away if you had your camo on."

"If I had my M-4, they probably wouldn't charge us either," the older one says.

"The dress uniforms are nice," his mother says. "The green?"

"I'm not a Boy Scout," he says.

"The other guys wear em," his little brother says.

"I don't need anybody thanking me for anything."

"What's wrong with that?" she says. "Maybe they're just proud."

"Maybe they're just trying to get lucky."

"What's wrong with that?" the younger one says and his mother grabs his arm and loses a little wine. She puts her mouth to his ear and fills it.

They say they can live to be a hundred years old. Perhaps indefinitely, some say.

"Excuse me," a woman says behind us. A little nervous, a lot of makeup, reluctant spokesperson for some other family unit. She looks at the older one. "I'm sorry, but I couldn't help overhearing."

The older one looks at her without saying anything. He looks like someone who doesn't want to be thanked.

"Excuse me," she says, "but my nephew's in the Second Armored." Field artillery, she says. Gives him a name, locations. Hasn't heard in a while. She thought maybe.

"Ma'am," the older one says after a moment, "do you know how many guys are over there?"

"Well," she says.

"Well me neither, but I think you couldn't help overhearing the wrong conversation," he says. "I work at Blockbuster. Only action I've ever seen is in *Platoon*."

She looks confused. Then she says, "I'm sorry. I could have sworn."

"Not a problem," he says, and he says he's sorry too, and

she looks at him like she wants to say something else but can't think of anything, so she rejoins her family and someone calls my wife's maiden name.

The woman with a nephew looks like she's still trying to think of something.

A girl with an armful of menus takes us to a booth. The dining room always smells like clam chowder. The walls are made of planks and beams like the bulkhead of a hull, and there are portholes and lifesavers and the serving station is a forecastle. A waitress with copper-colored hair asks us if we'd like anything to drink. I stick with mine. She has another glass of wine and her younger son a Coke.

"Water with lemon, please," the older one says.

"It's on me, Red," the younger one says to the waitress.

"She has a name," their mother says. She looks at the older one. "Are you still following baseball?"

Out of the blue, like changing the subject when there isn't one.

"Who wants to hear about baseball?" the younger one says.

"Who doesn't," she says. She has her reasons.

"Don't worry, I won't tell him the good stuff," the older one says into his menu. He makes a face. "Everything has cheese in it."

"I want to hear about the desert," the younger one says. He wants to hear about armor-piercing rounds and camel spiders. The good stuff.

"The desert," the older one says. He takes out his phone. "Desert's hot."

"No kidding."

"A hundred twenty in July." He turns off his phone and puts it away. "And I'm still washing sand out of my butt."

The younger one seems pleased, it's a start. His mother excuses herself to the restroom like she's running for cover.

"What's better, a Bradley or a Hummer?" the younger one asks.

"A Harley Sportster Sport," the older one says.

"Ever ride an Apache?"

"Those things kill more of our guys than the enemy."

"Fifty or two-forty?"

"Nothing like a fifty," the older one says. "It'll turn you into a meat puzzle, a thousand pieces except nobody's ever gonna put you together . . . That work for you?"

"Outstanding."

"I didn't say it was never fun."

"Tell us about a mission," the younger one says but there is no us, only them.

He tells us about a mission.

Here she comes back from the latrine.

The younger one looks disappointed. He wants full battle rattle, not an episode of *Cops*.

"Sometimes we shoot the dog," the older one says. "Pistol-whip Grampa. You see that on *Cops*?"

She sits. "I miss anything?"

A mission, I say.

"Nothing you can't see on YouTube," the younger one says.

"It was better when it was still a war," the older one says.

"Well there's only one mission as far as I'm concerned," she says.

"Hooah," the older one says.

"What about the kid in Ramadi?" the younger one says.

"What kid?" the older one says.

"The kid in the truck."

She looks nervous and asks about baseball again, takes a sip.

"What kid in what truck?"

"The haji," the younger one says.

"Don't say that," his brother says.

"You guys do," the younger one says.

"Not all of us," the older one says, and without dropping his voice he says, "What if someone called you a nigger?"

"My God," his mother says.

The younger one corrects him: "Nigga."

"That's not even a word," she says. Then she says they're giving away tickets at the job. "Three per person. Are you still keeping up? I thought maybe the three of you . . ."

"I'm so there," the younger one says. "You couldn't get WrestleMania?" He doesn't like sports any more than I do.

The waitress comes with a basket of biscuits and takes our order. The older one has a question about the Admiral's Feast. She touches his shoulder. I stick with the sirloin and ask for more coffee and she takes our menus. They seat a young couple in the next booth. One of the occupants of the tank is served at the table across the aisle—no hundredth birthday for him.

EUGENE MARTEN

The younger one leans over and takes a look, takes off a hat he isn't wearing and solemnly covers his heart. "A kind and loving shellfish, a lobster's lobster . . ."

"You get your smart ass from your father," his mother says. Someone she doesn't talk about much. "And your nose."

"May he rest in pilaf."

She can't help it. He only makes her laugh when she doesn't want to—maybe he's good at something else besides belching to order. She looks at the basket, takes out her calculator. "The waitress sure is friendly."

"She's doing her job," the older one says.

"I thought she was gonna sit in your lap, soldier," the younger one says.

"Have a biscuit," his mother says and puts the basket on his plate.

"I tell you who's working at Walgreens now?" she says to the older one.

"You might have mentioned it in passing."

"They made her store team lead," his mother says. "She's taking computer campus, I forget for what. I told her you were coming home for a couple of weeks."

"Mentioned that in passing too, huh?"

"It might give you something to look forward."

"Only one thing she can give me right now," he says, "and it ain't a future."

"The clap?" the younger one says.

"What?" she says. "What did he say?"

"Don't humor him," the older one says, "that's my job."

"I thought it was Fred's job," the younger one says and puts a biscuit in his mouth.

Right now I'm more interested in the couple in the next booth. They haven't spoken to each other since they arrived. Their heads are down as if in prayer, but they are pushing buttons.

Someone mentions baseball again and I say I'll be happy to drive if they're up for it. A man comes and unfolds a stand next to the booth. The food is on a serving platter the size of the table. Mine is as bloody as they can serve it and still stay in business.

She asks the older one to lead us in grace, like he used to. She is talking to the boy who wrote home. We bow our heads and close our eyes.

"Heavenly Father," I hear. Then all I hear is restaurant, and one will get you ten that if you look up, the younger one is looking back.

And her eyes are still closed.

The dining room seems to get quieter, like they're joining us. So he reaches back in the dark and finds a few words.

From up here you can't always tell which team is which. Back row, upper deck, behind the visitors' dugout, as high as it is possible to get here without use of a helicopter. Seagulls. I know we are behind the visitors' dugout because I heard the older one tell his brother. The older one played in school, follows the game; he knows about RBIs and sacrifices, changeups, checked swings. I would ask him questions. I would ask him if a curveball really curves, but I'll let the younger one ask for me. The younger one speaks even less baseball than I do but seems just happy to be here.

They turn on the lights at the seventh-inning stretch, though it hasn't gotten dark yet. Though I didn't know stretch means stretch.

I didn't come here to watch TV but I watch the pitcher on the big screen, shaking his head. Sometimes he nods. Sometimes he rubs his nose. He bends, drops his arms, straightens, spits. Digs in the dirt with his foot. Eventually he'll get around to throwing the thing. I don't understand but I have a certain respect for ritual. I like watching the pitcher. I like the green. I like the guy in the bleachers who beats a big bass drum. I buy hot dogs and lemon ice and Pepsi products and even have a beer. The older one says thank you, and the younger one says it because the older one does. The beer is cold.

It is dark. Someone, one of us or one of them, sends the ball almost straight up into the night. The sound of the crowd says it's foul, but it's fair enough for me—I've never seen anything fly so high on only will and muscle. It rises, arcs, disappears in the glare of the lights, then the high quiet air above them. I wait but I don't see it again, don't know where it went.

I see only the white birds.

It smells like a basement, maybe a warehouse. They lead me by the arm.

Echoes. Cement floor. We turn, slow, stop. They tell me to lift my feet—stepping over some kind of threshold. The floor is softer now, a thin carpet; the air changes, a stillness, dryness.

They pat me down, advise me not to use any names. They advise me there is a chair behind and drop me into it. Upholstered seat, armrests. I picture something black. They leave my lunch box on my lap—they haven't taken anything from me yet.

He asks me if I'm comfortable. He sounds like he's sitting across from me, sounds like someone who looks like Omar Sharif. A legitimate representative of his government.

"Under the circumstances," I say. I say, "How long does this thing have to stay on?"

"While you're here, I'm afraid." He apologizes. "We need to build a certain kind of relationship. Next time it may not be necessary."

Next time.

"Can I get you something?" he says. "Some coffee?"

"Coffee," I say.

"Black?"

"Black," I say. No sugar, though I wasn't really asking.

I hear his first language again. I hear footsteps on the hardness, neither coming nor going, just falling. A rattle like the gate of a freight elevator. I wonder what the man in the video heard, then I think I hear a cat.

I have no plans for this information.

"If I may," he says and takes the weight off my lap. The other one is still there, every time I take a breath.

"How much?" he says, as if politely curious.

"Almost half," I say.

"Half for half, then."

Four pounds, eleven point three ounces. Give or take.

The latches click.

"Ah," he says.

"So small," he says.

"Yes," I say.

"But so heavy."

"I wouldn't touch it," I say, then remember he has some background.

"What's a little skin cancer between friends?" I hear more clicking then, but it is not the latches. Something clatters down on a surface in front of me. A hand takes mine and guides it to a smooth round edge. Soft but large, a man's hand.

It is a world without women. Look what we've done with it.

"The cup is not full," he says. They've thought of everything.

I raise it to my mouth—not as easy as it sounds. He closes the lunch box and speaks to someone else. I hear footfalls again but I think someone else is still there. My eyelids are sweating. The darkness fills.

He asks me how the coffee is.

"Never had anything like it," I say, but in truth I'm no connoisseur. Coffee is coffee, it's either weak or strong.

"I don't drink it, you know. I'm a tea man myself," he says. I picture one leg hooked over a knee. "Do you have any questions?"

"How long will I be here?"

"We can have the results in a matter of hours. As for the rest of it"—I don't picture anything—"the perfect arrangement would not require trust."

He never uses the word *money*.

"It's not a perfect world," I say.

"Perhaps that will change," he says. Till then they have a right to protect themselves. What's one more firecracker in a world that can kill itself two and a half times over.

I find the cup again, and this time I don't let it go. It's not a perfect world so I use the word he doesn't.

"When?" I say.

"A week, perhaps more." He sounds apologetic. "It's out of my hands, you know." Then he asks, in so many words, how I'm getting by.

"Why do you think I'm here."

"Well, I'm afraid we don't have the proverbial briefcase but . . . a small advance perhaps? A loan between friends?" Once the results are in, of course.

Like they keep a petty cash fund. I think about it, but the coffee is enough for now. I thank him anyway.

I finish the cup and we don't speak much, but he has a way of saying something without saying it. When it's time to leave I feel his hand take mine, like he's the friend I wish he wasn't.

He wears a uniform to the airport. He bought his own ticket— the Army won't cover his expenses before Baltimore. They don't pay much but he doesn't have much else to spend it on. Sometimes he sends money home.

The ticket agent checks his ID and says, "God bless you." She says, "We salute you," and thanks him on behalf of the nation. On behalf of the airline she charges him thirty dollars because his bag weighs over fifty pounds.

We stand in another line with him. He doesn't have to if he doesn't want to, but that's not why he's wearing green, he says. He doesn't say why. A family dressed for a tropical vacation—they've even tanned in advance—offers to let him cut the line and he politely declines. We get to the table where they check your carry-on in case you're planning to hijack the plane with a can of deodorant. They keep his Old Spice. This is as far as we can go. He lets her embrace him, then takes my hand when it lasts too long. Maybe that's why I'm there. The younger one isn't, wouldn't leave his room.

He doesn't believe in goodbyes but she does, so we stand at the vinyl rope. There is a sign and a security guard with a face like one. I need to use the restroom. She needs to watch him take his shoes off and empty his pockets and put things in gray plastic tubs. To watch him walk through the metal detector like he's getting his diploma. It makes a sound. He takes off his belt and walks back through and it makes another sound. He digs deep, finds a coin, but that doesn't help either. I think she's rooting for the machine. They take him aside with blue rubber gloves. He doesn't look back. I tell her I have to use the restroom and she answers without looking at me, like her eyes are all that's keeping him there. It's a long walk. Some things take longer than others. When I get back she asks me what took me and says she's starving.

Throws her calculator in the trash on the way out.

"How's a blind man tell a black man from a Jew?"
"You tell me."

"Jew's got a big nose, nigger's got a big"—wait for it—
"DeVille." Then he laughs in case I don't know I'm supposed to.

He's working on a stand-up routine. His tag line is "It all
smells the same to me." And sometimes "So what are *you*
looking at?"

He tells me I need to invent myself a sense of humor.

"So I'm told," I say and pull into the passing lane.

"I tell you they tried to give me one of those seeing-eye
dogs?"

"I don't think so."

"Said they were giving me a bitch to take me around the
block. I told em no thanks, I've already been married."

"You write your own stuff?" I say.

"So I tried it for a while," he says. "Turns out we're two
of a kind . . ." I look in the mirror. He's putting something in
his mouth so I can't make out the rest of it. I don't ask him to
repeat it.

"You're on fire," I say.

"Still smells the same to me," he says. He says it like a toast
but his flask is empty.

"Well hell," he says, and I let him talk me into stopping
for a pint. He's had plenty already but not enough to suit
either of us. There's a grocery store in the strip mall. I let him
stay in the car while I go inside. It's too late for Old Crow so
I get him what they used to call a fifth of something cheap, a
bunch of grapes on the label like brain cells ready to explode.
He's grateful but doesn't ask what he owes me. We'll settle
up later.

He picks up where he left off. "And what about you, sir?"

"What about me?"

"You getting any?" he says.

"This part of the act?"

"It's all part of the act."

I tell him I'm working on my second marriage.

"Well that don't answer the question," he says. "How old is she?"

Old enough, I tell him, and he says, "So you're in the same boat as me."

"How's that?"

"We both got to do it in the dark."

I take the exit out of the parking lot; he's too busy coughing to notice which way I turn. What he gets for laughing at his own material.

"What about you?" I say.

"Once," he says, "and that ain't no joke."

I turn down the radio (tonight it's Area 51). I ask him if he was in love.

"Love?" he says. "Hey who's the fucking comedian here?"

I turn it off. "They say we can't live without it."

"They," he says. "What the fuck." I hear the wine. I hear the word again. "A word people hear themselves say," he says. "Been in it and had to pay my way out of it. I know what happens to love." He takes another pill. "What goes up must come down.

"I tell you about the time I went skydiving?" he says.

"Go for it," I say.

"I'm working on it." Sometimes all he has are setups: got

into an argument with a deaf-mute the other day, how's a blind man spell relief? . . . I hear liquid and silence. Then I hear snoring.

He's quiet the rest of the way to my street. When we pull in he wakes up and doesn't make sense. Maybe he didn't wake up. It's late, past ten. I turn the key, switch off the lights, get out of the car. Fireflies in the yard. Unlock the garage, go back to the car; unlock, open, unlatch. Screw the cap back on the bottle. He moves.

"Where am I?"

"Almost there." I tell him to keep his voice down, though she took the younger one to West Virginia to visit his grandmother. Pull the fifth out of his lap, help him out of the car. His cane is in his pocket. He leans on me like a crutch and we make our way to the garage. The retired librarian retires at nine. The house on the other side is dark except for the night light over their front steps. I can hear a lawn sprinkler.

We get inside without toppling over. "Fucking dark in here," he says.

I lock the door, click on the light.

"More like it," he says. "I can smell lecktrissy you know." He says it's stuffy in there. I help him off with his dirty linen jacket and sit him down in a lawn chair. I take off mine.

"More better," he says. I tell him to relax, have another drink.

"I'll get to it," he mutters, then gets to it and then some. "Where'd you get this shit anyway, a hardware store? Not for the faint of liver."

I drag the tarp off the wireless. Put on blue rubber gloves.

"The hell are we?" he says. "This place ain't her place." He sniffs, head back. "Goddamn garage."

"Say something funny," I say and kneel down in front of him, take off his loafers.

"Where is everybody?" he says. Then he says, "I tell you the time I went skydiving?"

"I'm listening." I pull off his socks.

He uses his nose again. "You got a dog . . ."

"Used to," I say. "Shepherd-collie. He's not with us anymore."

"Rest in piss," he says and takes another drink.

Never felt a thing, far as I could tell. I hope he won't either. You do your best with what comes your way.

I unbutton, unzip.

"What the fuck," he says.

"I'm doing what you want."

"You're doing me," he says, "what you're doing."

"Lift your legs." I get his pants off and fold them like I'm doing his laundry.

A ring, a watch with no hands, dentures. I remember a gold chain, then remember someone pulled it off his neck at a bus stop. Said he could smell them too.

He doesn't care what I take as long as it isn't the bottle.

"Ready?" I'm standing over him. There isn't a lot of room.

"I was born ready," he says. "Ready for what?"

"You're going home."

"Home?" He says it like some kind of outrage, like love wasn't bad enough. "I was just getting comforble." He keeps dropping syllables, a good sign.

"You can't stay here," I say. "Need a hand?"

"I look like I need help?" He helps himself to the rest of the bottle. Drops it but it's made of plastic. Grabs me instead and pulls. I have to pull back just to keep from falling, and that's how we get him out of the chair.

"Your shirt," I say and pull the top button. He brushes me off and does it himself, lets it drop back into the chair. Stands there barefoot in his underwear and dark glasses and finds my arm.

"So where'd you park, sweetheart?"

"It ain't on wheels," I say and lead him toward the machine.

"Easy," he says. "This one of your"—he swallows something—"projecks?"

"Kind of a shortcut," I say. Zero to lights out in a microsecond. I put him on the scale. "You'll get there without moving an inch."

"Fuckin final frontier," he says.

"You could call it that."

"Alexander Graham Cracker," he says. "You beaming me up or down?"

"Watch your step." The booth is on a riser.

"'Where no man boldly . . .'" He sounds stuck. "How's it go again?"

"I wouldn't know."

He's in the booth, I'm half-out—there isn't room for two in there.

"You sure I don't know me from somewhere?" he says.

"Where would I know you from?"

"You tell me . . . I tell you I was in sales?"

"I have your card." I put my hand on his shoulder and sit him down.

"Easy," he says. Touches his chest. "We had this saying . . ."

I strap him in. Aircraft nylon. No electrodes, no gel, no helmet.

"Freakin John Glenn in here," he says. "Neil freakin . . . fuck."

"It's for your own safety," I say. "There's no sense of motion."

"There gonna be a countdown?"

"If you want one."

He starts at ten, makes it to seven and nods off. I close the shackles on his wrists. Maybe it's the sound that brings him back.

"'Today's the day, this is the place, you're the man,'" he says. "I like that black bitch that was in there, with that silver thing in her ear. I heard her and Capm Kirk . . ."

I kneel down, hope he doesn't kick me in the face. The ankle straps are leather.

". . . stick something in her ear," he says.

I stand.

"You think Alan B didn't get some?" he says. "I hear he peed his spacesuit." This is true. I take off his glasses. Lids mostly closed, a little cross-eyed.

"Hey," he says.

"Trust me," I say. There's metal in the hinges.

"I'm trusting you here. Where's my goddamn stick?"

"You won't need it where you're going."

"Where am I going?"

"The other shore," I say. "You'll see things you don't need eyes for."

I ask him if he's comfortable.

"Just gimme a happy ending," he says, calmer. "Go push some fucking buttons.

"I tell you I went skydiving once?" he says. I shut the door and step off the riser but I can still hear him; the booth is miked.

"It was great but the dog hated it," he shouts. Then he falls asleep again.

I turn on the fans, the motor, the electrostatic precipitator. I boot the hard drive. There is a green button on the side of the wireless and a red one. State of my art.

I power up. Somebody has to. The transformer hums for the greater good.

He lifts his head like he's wide awake.

"I tell you I was in sales?" he says.

I have a screen. I never said they weren't good for something.

"We had makes and models," he says. "We had names: Slo Moe, Az Iz, the Broom with the atomic pencil . . . Ice Man handled the blue-hairs. They were there, in the showroom. I was the liner and the closer. I put em together, tore heads off. Took em all to the box. We had a saying."

I tap his weight on the keys—it's not what I thought it would be. I let the computer do the thinking. It comes up with a number.

"Something smells funny, Orville," he says. "Think I mighta had a accident . . . I tell you I was in an accident? My whole life flashed before my ears." His mouth keeps moving but I don't hear anything. His face is red now, tight and shiny,

head shaking like no thank you. I move the dial, push my fucking buttons. You can feel the charge build, rising, singing . . .
It'll look like heart failure, it'll look like a stroke.

The windows fog. I switch on the defrost. Sweat runs down
his face and into his mouth. He spits it out: "Miss where's
your mom, you can't be lady of the house. If I could have just
five minutes of your . . . ten's even better it'll make the rest of
your coffee grease ketchup mustard vomit feces crayon ink
paint catpiss mud blood . . . lipstick. Works on carpetvinyl-
appliances, most painted surfaces and countertops . . . dirty
undies too. Comes in a bottle, spray or you can squeeze it out
of a tube." He makes a sound like mud bubbling in his throat:
"Squeezeitoutofatube . . ."

The computer counts up, not down: volts, amps, coulombs,
farads. I have capacitors big as garbage cans, high flux density,
a dump switch—some things you don't want to point and click.
Some things you want to pull the trigger.

If his eyes worked they'd be looking in mine. "You hear
something? Stinks something awful in here. Take a whiff citrus,
that's what makes it green. Childproof too. Tastesjustasgood
a swig before bedtime keeps me reg . . . You won't find this
shit on the shelf ma'am this ain't Procter Gamble little Jew
makes it in his bath . . . If I could see him I'd sue. Better yet an
eye for an eye. Ready for a demo? What's for supper? Better
yet spaghetti tell you what if I can't clean it I'll eat it off the
floor. Tell you what else is the manathehouse home? How
about me you make a stain of our own us two? Two birds with
one tablespoon and then just let it set . . . a minute . . . Clean

cloth and it's like nothing ever I'll never tell. Help yourself—what do you think I meant childproof?

"Ma'am?" he says.

"Ma'am?

"Ma'am?

"Ma'am."

It'll look like natural causes—for him that could be anything.

"Roger that, Houston," he says. "We there yet? Let me know if you find my teeth."

The numbers stop. I have a green light. No countdown, no fail-safe, just one more button. I ask him if he has any more last words.

"Don't do it to em, do it *for* em," he says. "Find out where it hurts. Gotta give before you can take. Jab jab jab, right hook. Give give give . . . Orville, I can't seem to move my . . . Blood on the carpet, ketchup on the couch. Helps if you can rhyme. I was no cherry picker either. Put em on the ceiling, then scrape em off and make a deal. I wouldn't shit you you're my best turd. We there yet? Jesus, one small step. How's it go? Went into a bar, bartender says, 'We don't allow dogs in here.' I tell him, 'But I'm blind,' and he says . . . says . . . he says . . .'" But he doesn't say what he says and I dump it.

A sound like a steel beam snapping, so loud it hurts you inside. The lights go out. Maybe the lights went out first. The hardware already cycling down, a sinking sound, a long drop. A smell like air burnt by lightning; plasma, charred components. The smell of failure. The punch line. I hear rain.

I say his name.

Obviously a major malfunction. Going to look very carefully into the situation.

I say his name again, louder.

"Don't move," I say, "if you can hear me."

Maybe it wasn't a failure. There's a flashlight around here somewhere. Going to look very carefully. Going to find it by feel.

Then I hear something: movement. A gasp.

I hold my breath. Listen.

"I'm right here," I say.

Now I hear more than rain.

Muffled. Stone-cold sober.

"Orville," I hear him say. "I can see!"

I believe that acquiring a work ethic and a sense of integrity in craft is the path to character development and inner discovery. We start with workshop safety, the proper care and handling of tools. I make him wear goggles. He wants to use the table saw; I want him to learn to do things without pushing buttons. He's all about the pushing of buttons.

She's at the end of her rope with him.

So the handsaw, the coping saw, the brace and bit. The framing square to square the corners. I rule it out for him and notch the first piece but let him do all the cutting. One-inch white pine. He keeps looking around the garage, into the back corners, and I tell him to keep his eyes on the blade. He finds a rhythm. Halfway through he's breathing hard and shows me his hand.

"That means you're doing it right," I say and toss him a

pair. He thanks me for the gloves; I tell him someday he may thank me for the blisters.

"Yeah, then I'll even brush off your headstone," he says, and I show him how to countersink the entrance hole so the rain doesn't get in. How to miter the back edge of the roof. We put it all together with galvanized screws, putty, two long roofing nails so the front panel pivots out.

"For cleaning," I say.

He makes a face. "That's her job. Let's build a model rocket."

One thing at a time, Mr. von Braun. I have him sand it smooth for painting. Twelve-grit. He turns it in his hands without speaking. He's not his brother but it's a passable job. He is himself.

"Is it big enough?" he says.

Big enough for bluebirds, I tell him. Bluebirds are all I know.

"What color should it be?"

I leave it up to him, "but nothing too bright or loud," I say. "Something that blends in—and don't paint the inside."

I tell him use a brush and not a spray can. Maybe I shouldn't have said that.

We mount it on a fence post with a couple of carriage screws, grease the top of the post to keep out predators. A week later one of them gets in anyway and blows it apart with an M-80. He swears he has no idea.

We drop him off at the Administrative Offices, across the lot from IKEA. The expedition coordinator is already there. So are the other truants, bipolars, online-gaming addicts, reactive attachments, oppositional defiants. At least none of them is in dog cages. (You hear things.) When everyone in the Challenge Group is accounted for, the expedition coordinator will drive them to base camp, to the Orientation/Introspection Phase.

"Have you signed the consent forms?" he asks. We have, online, but now there are hard copies on a clipboard. With the pen provided she consents again to backpacking, canoeing, caving, whitewater, rock climbing, a solo challenge, a minimum of six showers; to the Wisdom Phase, the Courage Phase, the Illumination Phase, which will involve a life-changing Rite of Passage. We're not sure what that will be but she consents to it.

"I don't see the Picking Up His Underwear Phase," she says and consents to the use of reasonable restraint.

We've qualified for financial aid.

Parents are not encouraged to stick around. He won't say goodbye and the expedition coordinator, a bearded sunburnt man who is the grandson of a lumberjack, has a degree in theology with a minor in psychology, tells us this is not unusual.

"See you in two months," we say. At the Parent Workshop Weekend.

"Eight weeks," the expedition coordinator says.

He gets to keep the sleeping bag.

A three-hour drive back. She isn't talking, so I try to think of something to say. I could remind her they have a ninety-seven-percent completion rate (they all do), that we're low on toilet paper, that she shouldn't worry about downsizing until it happens. I could tell her I have some money coming—they can't do anything with just half (and they gave me their word as legitimate representatives of their government). Consulting,

I could say, which isn't a lie; it's as much of the truth as you can see through a blindfold.

I go with the two-ply.

When we pull in I'm still trying to think of something else, but it's light enough to see it doesn't matter anymore. We carry the bags into the house and while she's putting things away I go back outside to shut the trunk and burn one. It's still light enough to see the tire marks. Faint, double tread. A truck. I don't light the cigarette. I go to the garage. Just a formality— I already know what I'm going to find, and what I'm not. Like the hole in the door where the lock cylinder isn't. The knob is still there but you can push the door open with your toe. I flip up the switch, and that is a formality too.

I light the cigarette. Look at the rusty squares in the floor where they used to be (there's iron in cement). All six of them— they even took the blankets. I wonder if the neighbors heard anything. Sometimes people just aren't nosy enough.

I go back out to the driveway and smoke and look across the street. Another empty house with a sign out front—people get in over their heads. I look at the tracks. She comes out and sees what I'm looking at.

"We didn't do that," she says.

"Somebody might have pulled in to turn around."

She looks. "Will it come out?"

"Pressure washer," I say.

"I don't think we have one of those."

I shake my head. "We'll have to rent one."

Why buy the milk when you can steal the cow? Something like that.

The guy next door pulls up, waves. He's in uniform—a tournament probably. He's got with him his wife, baby, the dog who replaced the cat. They are consumed by a flash of white light. There are squatters in the area—maybe they're selling them for scrap. Or just some kids. The younger one's gone but he has friends.

The white light fades.

"Maybe he's got one," she says.

"Maybe he does," I say. Going to take some serious PSI if it's in the sealer. Something gas-powered, professional grade.

You hate to ask, but it wouldn't hurt.

Evenings I pick her up from work, after the final program. I park outside and wait. It is not a dome but a big metal cylinder with a chamfered roof, slanted to point at Polaris. At night it glows—fiber optics, calibrated so as not to obscure the light of the real show. But it's not yet dark and I sit in the car while the last audience get in theirs, on their way home or maybe to dinner, or twilight drives to nowhere in particular. This is her last night.

She is always last to leave. Turns off the lights, makes sure the doors are locked. Usually she comes out through the museum, but tonight I watch the emergency exit on the far side of the facility. It's alarmed but she knows the code. I watch the door. When it opens she stands there and waves and I get out of the car, lock up, cross the grass, and enter the planetarium.

The door shuts behind us. We are alone in the theater.

The stage is right over our heads.

"Save me a seat," she says, "I'll be right there," but I always wait while she gets in the booth. She knows how to drive it, but this show pretty much runs itself. It's all coming down to one button anyway.

The lights dim. Five thousand stars come out and in their glow we find our way: middle row, aisle, though they say there are no bad seats. We sit and recline and look up, and James Earl Jones says, "Welcome to everything."

There is music.

There is Acrux. Aldebaran. Alpha Centauri. Planets, galaxies, pulsars, quasars. Welcome to the whirlpool, Hoag's Object, black holes, blue suns (courtesy of Sky-Skan DigitalSky 2).

It has been around a long time, James Earl Jones says. Fourteen billion years, they figure, give or take. Fourteen billion years is a long time, but it's not forever. What we see above us, says James Earl Jones, has not always been there, and one by one, the stars go out.

"Everything has to start somewhere," he says. "Even time and space."

The music fades, uninventing itself. The stars continue to disappear, and the darkness becomes so absolute we are just doubts in the virtual void. One hand looking for another.

There is something. In the middle of man-made nothing. Not a star but a point of imperfection, a trace not of light but of slightly denser dark. Not even a particle because particles do not yet exist.

Once upon a time, James Earl Jones says, there was no time. Then he waits to be born.

All this and less, everything we know and know we don't; you and me and the shoes in the trees and the guy in the bleachers with the big bass drum. Contained in a single point that isn't one, a region of impossibility, of zero volume and infinite fury. The little black egg. Before that, there is no story; the teller holds his tongue.

This is how this one starts. Waiting. One hand looking for the other. Before the beginning and after the last show.

We hear something. Not breathing. Wait for the next big bang.

END

ACKNOWLEDGEMENTS

The author wishes to thank his editor, Jordan Ginsberg, for his nonpareil work ethic and for doing what seemed impossible: giving this book another chance.

ABOUT THE AUTHOR

Eugene Marten was awarded an NEA Creative Writing Fellowship for *Layman's Report*. His work has been or will be translated into Spanish, French, Italian, and Russian. He lives in Albuquerque.